SPINWARD FRINGE
BROADCAST 12: INVASION

RANDOLPH LALONDE

BOOKS BY RANDOLPH LALONDE

THE CHAOS CORE SERIES

Trapped

Cool Pursuit

Savage Stars

THE SPINWARD FRINGE SERIES

Spinward Fringe Broadcast 0: Origins

Spinward Fringe Broadcast 1 and 2: Resurrection and Awakening

Spinward Fringe Broadcast 3: Triton

Spinward Fringe Broadcast 4: Frontline

Spinward Fringe Broadcast 5: Fracture

Spinward Fringe Broadcast 6: Fragments

The Expendable Few: A Spinward Fringe Novel

Spinward Fringe Broadcast 7: Framework

Spinward Fringe Broadcast 8: Renegades

Spinward Fringe Broadcast 9: Warpath

Spinward Fringe Broadcast 10: Freeground

Spinward Fringe Broadcast 10.5: Carnie's Tale

Spinward Fringe Broadcast 11: Revenge

Spinward Fringe Broadcast 12: Invasion

Spinward Fringe Broadcast 13: Warriors

Spinward Fringe Broadcast 14: Rebel

Spinward Fringe Broadcast 15: Pursuit

Spinward Fringe Broadcast 16: Hunters

Psycho Electric

FANTASY

Highshield

Brightwill

NEM: Awakening

NEM: Crimson Shores

HORROR

Dark Arts

For Audiobook versions of these books and more, please visit:

www.RandolphLalonde.com

Spinward Fringe Broadcast 12: Invasion © Copyright 2018, 2022
Randolph Lalonde

Spinward Fringe is a registered trademark of Randolph Lalonde

Revision 3

EBook ISBN: 978-1-988175-18-8

Print ISBN: 978-1-988175-20-1

BEFORE WE BEGIN...

The Spinward Fringe and Chaos Core series have collided! After receiving a message from a family member close to the Galactic Core, characters from the Spinward Fringe series departed between Spinward Fringe Broadcast 11: Revenge and Broadcast 12: Invasion so they could appear in Chaos Core Book 3: Savage Stars. It is highly recommended that you follow them on this journey, or read the entire Chaos Core series so far, which consists of only three brief novels, before continuing on to the adventure awaiting you in Spinward Fringe Broadcast 12: Invasion.

I'd like to thank everyone on the Patreon page for supporting the crossover. Thank you, neither series would be running this well or this quickly without the readers.

Let's get on with the show.

PROLOGUE

The Return of the Revenge

IT WASN'T the homecoming that Alice imagined for the Revenge. The War Forge was almost complete, with more interior space than all the military bases on Tamber combined four times over, and she had no problem believing it from the size of the spaces she saw within.

Most of the interior was dark grey with highlights in red in the sections she was allowed to visit on the day of the ship's return. The briefing and observation area was huge, with tiered seating that could accommodate a few thousand by her rough estimation. "This is encouraging, I like it," Iruuk said as he stayed close while they were looking for their seats. "My father says that humans didn't make big gathering places like this for a long time because they used technology to experience things simultaneously instead. This is better, being with people for real is better."

"You should send a message to the design team, I hear they don't get much positive feedback. Their inbox is full of requests and complaints about how all the furniture looks the same," Alice said, noticing the balcony overhead. They were in the first row near the end of the first tier, to her surprise.

"You're kidding! They did all this and people just complain about the armchairs? I mean, they could be bigger, I guess, but even I know that people who live here can put one in the recycler and get a better one in a day or so."

To Alice the furniture was a little large, but she liked having more room than she needed to curl up, so it was perfect. To someone like Iruuk, a growing Nafalli who was already at least a third again her height, she could see how everything might seem a little small. "Yup, make people feel safe enough, give them some spare time, and they'll use some of it to complain."

"Maybe that's the human way," Iruuk muttered. He was quiet for a moment as they searched for their seats, then added. "And, yeah, I guess that's the Nafalli way for some of us too. Our beds are never good enough, but then again, every bed has room for improvement." He looked around for another moment then nodded, an expression that was exaggerated by his long snout. "Yup, definitely sending the design team a nice note."

"They're pretty busy answering all those complaints, though, so you might not get a response for a year."

"I don't need one, they're doing good work," Iruuk said. "I

think we're being seated with the captains and their first mates."

"We're sitting here," Alice said, pointing to a pair of seats behind her as she looked down the long row. He was right, the admiralty and other commanders were settling in seats to the far right of the stage, while the captains were taking their places at the front of the seating level with the stage. Behind the stage was the vast black bulkhead, five storeys tall, it provided a solid backdrop. There were more captains than she could count at a glance, all in full uniform - jacket, military vacsuit, boots and gloves - black except for the stripes running down their sides. Most of them were gold, indicating that they were assigned to a bridge command crew, but several were red like hers. It was an indication that they were members of the Special Operations Combat Unit. A few of them had blue stripes, which was new. There were only three of them from what she could tell at a glance.

Alice sat down and looked to the right of the stage, where she could see Ayan in a uniform only she wore; a light blue vacsuit and coat that had a white stripe down the side with the insignia of Admiral. There was a discussion going on amongst the commanders there, and she was at the centre. It looked pleasant, they seemed happy to see each other. It was good to see many commanders who merged with Haven Fleet from Freeground Nation in good humour. There were even several people who were from the Tamber Militia, the last original military organization in the solar system. They were starting to merge with the Rangers, a few of them were immediately stolen into the ranks of Haven Fleet.

Still, amongst the mostly black uniforms, Alice's mother

stood out. Ayan was losing the fight to bury the fact that she was technically the queen and owner of the entire Haven System.

Regardless of the threat that the Order of Eden posed, civilization was returning to many parts of the galaxy and the best way for the Haven System to maintain its independence was to name one owner and a succession of inheritors. Alice still didn't know exactly how she felt as one of the people on that list. If Ayan then Jacob were killed, she'd inherit the entire solar system. That, along with several other recent decisions were made for her after she was put on mandatory shore leave.

The group of upper commanders took their seats and a hush fell over those gathered in the auditorium as her father, Jacob Valent strode onto the stage. He wasn't only in full uniform, but in full armour. The horizontal slats crossing his body were jet black, polished to a shine, and by the time he reached the stage the sounds of his boots on the metal deck was louder than everything else. He retracted his helmet into the collar of his suit, the pieces sliding together and down with a whisper of shifting slats.

Alice expected an occasion that was celebratory, meant to honour the crew of the Revenge, but his expression was sombre. "During a rescue attempt that could have become a disaster at any moment, the crew of the Revenge served bravely and did not hesitate to perform any task I put in front of them. Improvisation, dedication and service with honour are terms I use when describing the average crewmember aboard that ship."

Faces began to appear on the vast space behind him, all

equally visible as they cast their light on the audience. Their names and ranks were written on the lower half of their images. Captain Valent continued. "Three hundred one crewmembers made the ultimate sacrifice on the Revenge's first long-range mission. Not one of them knew the citizens of Freeground Alpha or the service people in Freeground Fleet. Their sacrifices were driven by duty and the knowledge that the Revenge and the Triton were the only ships ready and able to help. There was no one else coming. I'm happy we were wrong and acknowledge the debt we owe to our Nafalli allies. They are as ferocious and tenacious as they are reputed to be, but they are also honourable, intelligent, and kind."

"Ogun Sha!" came a response from a few dozen Nafalli in the auditorium.

"We honour them," Iruuk translated in a whisper. "They're talking about the crew the Revenge lost."

"Thank you," Jacob said. "Every one of the people listed behind me has their own story. Over the last few days I've reviewed their files so I know more than how their stories ended. These were remarkable people, the kind we can't afford to lose. Our mission in the Iron Head Nebula was a success, but they paid the ultimate price for it. I ask for a moment of silence before we continue."

Everyone in the auditorium stood and after a moment of quiet shuffling, lowered their heads. That included Alice, who didn't lower her head as much as some, keeping her eyes on her father instead. She watched him up there, his head lowered, his eyes closed, and could almost see the weight of the loss pressing down on him. Even still, he looked immovable, as though he was a permanent fixture in the galaxy that nothing could break. He raised his head and gestured to his right, where Minh-Chu Buu entered a moment later. "Thank you. Now, the Wing Commander of Samurai Squadron and my friend, Commander Minh-Chu Buu would like to say a few words before the Revenge arrives in visual range."

Minh-Chu crossed to the middle of the stage where he shook Jake's hand. He was in a newer black uniform with a silver stripe. His jacket was black with the Samurai Skull large on the back, it was a newer armour version that was the same as her SOCU model. "Thank you, Captain." He turned to the audience. "Thank you all for coming. I wish I could tell you a few stories about Freeground Fleet, about all the things those stories have in common with what's happening now, but I'm here to read a passage from the earliest version of the Regulations and Practices manual of Freeground Fleet, a passage that has been added to Haven Fleet's guide. Don't worry, it's not a regulation, it's a Charge." He looked to the wall of the fallen so the audience could still see his face. "I'd better get this right the first time, everyone for a million klicks in all directions is hearing this."

"More like five hundred million!" shouted a Freeground Rear Admiral Alice didn't recognize from the gallery to the side of the stage.

"No pressure," Minh-Chu said with a little bow.

That brought a trickle of laughter throughout the auditorium before they settled down again. Jake was off stage to the right, where he was standing at attention, looking up at the faces of the lost.

Minh-Chu began reciting the passage. "We have answered the call. The call to aid, to explore, and, to fight if necessary. I brave the hazard so my people may prosper in peace. May my cause and my service be noble." He cleared his throat as the images faded and the bulkhead became transparent. "Now, join me in celebrating the return of the Revenge and her crew." He snapped to attention and brought his hand up in a salute.

He was joined on stage by Jacob first, then the members of the admiralty and commanders who could make it to the ceremony. It was a diverse staff already, with humans towering over several Mergillians and Nafalli towering over everyone. The stage was full in short order, each of the commanders standing equal lengths apart, shoulder to shoulder in three rows as they saluted. On the right and left-hand side of the wall were live images of thousands of trainees, soldiers and officers standing at transparent sections of the War Forge's hull at attention. To the crew of the Revenge the gargantuan station's windows must have looked like they were filled with the silhouettes of thousands of people saluting.

Alice stood at attention and held her salute proudly as she watched the Revenge begin a slow fly-by. The nose of the ship was gone, patched lopsidedly, and the rest of the hull bore scars of heat and kinetic weaponry that were so deep in some places that the patch work was recessed several metres. It would be the last of its kind, a ship that was once a new Order of Eden design, then modified by Haven Fleet. They would no longer adapt or refit Order of Eden ships, they didn't have to anymore.

Despite that sombre thought, Alice was excited to see Ashley and the rest of the people she knew aboard that ship.

It would be good to have them home. She brought her thoughts back to the moment, with Iruuk standing straight, much taller than her at her left side, and a Captain she'd never met to her right, his arm held so stiffly that she swore it was shaking a little.

"Thank you for taking her and her crew the rest of the way home, Commander Vega," Captain Jacob Valent said.

"The Revenge has done her duty, returned home and will stand down," Admiral Rice said. "Thank you, and welcome home."

The ship finished its pass and to her surprise, the Triton began moving into view behind it. It was repaired and given an entirely new skin. The broad, stingray shape had a dark, black gloss that had opalescent highlights of blue and green. Alice had tried to see what they'd done to it in the refit but wasn't allowed to know more than the fact that it had taken three trips through the manufacturing lines of the War Forge and that it was on assignment in system. Its commander, crew, and all the details regarding the ship's capabilities were a secret to her and most of the fleet. The ship passed, its long tail taking the most time to clear the transparent armoured hull as they watched it. After a few more breaths, Alice heard Terry Ozark McPatrick's voice call out; "At ease."

The commanders sharing the stage with him left in orderly lines and he smiled at the audience. "That was the Triton, but not as you knew her. I'm happy to announce that the design for the Zhan Two class of close-combat carriers has passed. They'll be going into production soon. The Zhan Two Class is the most lethal rapid-response carrier ever built. The few of you who have the clearance to see the details know why already, but as this war goes on, the rest of you will find out. The experimentation on the Triton and the Revenge have made many of the advancements and the expansion of our fleet possible. The mission to save Free-ground Alpha, the return of the Triton, the Revenge and the discovery of our new Nafalli allies are worthy of a celebra-tion that should last weeks. I'm afraid we can only afford an hour, so make the most of the refreshments before you return to duty. Before I go, I'd like to acknowledge the work of Commander Minh-Chu Buu, Captain Jacob Valent and Admiral Ayan Anderson along with their senior staffs. These people avoid praise so well you'd think they were deathly allergic, but I know this mission would not have been successful without them. Thank you for your service." He saluted towards the seats filled with senior commanders, where Jacob and Minh-Chu had joined Ayan, then he left the stage.

Several squads of Academy trainees in white emerged from the left side of the stage pushing large floating trays of drinks and snacks into open space in front then, and people started milling around. "Oh, there's my dad, I have to see how he's doing on the station. I hear he's got a new assignment."

"You know where I'll be," Alice said, starting towards Jake and Ayan. Oz was talking to Minh-Chu, who looked nervous.

"Excited to see Ash?" Oz asked him.

"Yeah, but I had a rose for her and forgot it somewhere on the way here. I think it's still on the priority shuttle. Maybe Frost found it, he was having trouble getting cleared to wait with the families of the Revenge crew in the lounge, so he had to stay there to sort it out."

"I can't believe they didn't let you guys fly your own shuttle here."

"The squad doesn't technically have any ships right now. Our new interceptors won't be available until tomorrow, and the War Forge's security is so tight now that they're only using their own shuttles and pilots," Minh-Chu said. "Especially since Frost pulled that stunt last week."

"I thought you were in on that?" Oz asked.

"I say nothing, I know nothing," Minh-Chu replied. "Hey, Alice, how's shore leave?"

"Boring," she replied, keeping her volunteer service as a Ranger secret. Her and Iruuk were doing foot patrols on the outskirts of Haven Shore and standing ready for emergencies, but the watch commander, Lieutenant Gambon, was keeping the details of their volunteer work away from Haven Fleet. It was still boring, she gave a lot of people directions, helped track down children who wandered off, and did a lot of walking, but she felt like they were helping at least. "I can't wait to get back to work."

"Well, I'm sure Ashley will want some beach time once she's finally off the Revenge. I'll be flying a lot of patrol missions, so she could use company," Minh-Chu said.

"Tell her to call me," Alice said, nodding.

"Take it easy, look through the materials I sent you on the quad drive and some of the new gear for Special Operations," Oz said.

"I already did, I'll put my squad's order in soon," she said, remembering the huge list of gadgets and equipment on her wish list for her team and the Clever Dream. There was no way they'd give her all of it, but she'd definitely get more than she really wanted.

"I'll have Danvers send you more material to look through while you're tanning, then," Oz said. "But remember to rest your head, too."

"Yes, Commodore," Alice said. "I've got another week and a half to go, and I already feel ready to suit up, so I'm sure I'll be well rested by the end."

"Mind if I steal her away, Sir?" Jake asked Oz as he approached. He'd retracted his heavy armour into a long coat with plates across the shoulders and down the middle.

"She's all yours, Captain," Oz replied.

"It's strange that he's not an Admiral, isn't it?" Minh-Chu asked Oz and Ayan, who was just joining them.

"He has a promotion pending, but hasn't accepted it yet," she said, regarding Jake as she shook her head. "We're going to hold you down and put your new rank insignia on you if you don't accept that soon." It was a figure of speech. Any officer above Jake in the command chain could push his promotion through and change the insignia on his vacsuit whenever they liked. They held off out of respect.

"It's not the rank that makes me hesitate, it's the file work," Jake said as he stepped away with Alice.

"You should take it," Alice said. "They need experienced people to guide the new Captains coming up."

"I know, I'll take it, but I'm waiting for the Merciless to finish her shake-down cruise first. There's no way I'm doing anything that takes me away from the command chair of that ship. The impact I can have on the war from her deck will be huge."

"But you can do a lot more as a Commodore," Alice said. "Maybe as a Rear Admiral? Higher?"

"Keep it down," Jake chuckled in a whisper.

"They're trying to fast track you up the chain now that the British Alliance are out of the mix, not trying to tell Fleet how to run things."

"I know, that doesn't mean I agree with it," Jake said. Conversations with him over the past few evenings had brought them closer again, a lot had changed, but she only liked him more. One of the secrets he shared with her was about the admiralty, and how he thought that there were several officers who were fine, but promoted too quickly. It was something they both kept to themselves, since she agreed, because they knew the Fleet didn't have time to mature before a real threat came. She'd done enough to move the Fleet in the right direction, something he thanked her for more than once. "I'll get my place at the table when it's time, for now, I'll be happy with the flagship. You'll see what I'm talking about when you get a good look at the Merciless. Anyway, I know you're going back to Tamber soon, but I wanted you to be the second person in the fleet to get the new coat. I got the first, Commodore Post gave it to me as a sort of 'wish I had a chance to be your boss' gift, since I only served under her for a few days before I was offered a promotion. These are coming off the production line now." He handed her a thick roll that was heavy in her hands.

Her name appeared on it, then was replaced with the SOCU skull emblem before unfurling into a long coat like her father's. He helped her take her waist long jacket off, then put the long coat, which adjusted so it was ankle-length for her, on. Ayan approached with a smile and held her old jacket for her. It felt heavier, had thick armour slats across the shoulders then in a V going down the back and more down the arms, and she liked everything about it. There was something bulging in the interior pockets, and she looked, surprised when she realized what they were. "I can't put those on until I'm back on active duty. That is if those are what I think they are."

"The custom combat bracers you ordered," Ayan nodded. "I had someone make a few refinements then had them produced yesterday."

"They're based on the ones I made, but much better," Jake said. "Be careful with all the new gear, though. This jacket changes into a suit of armour so advanced that you qualify as a small starfighter if you take off in it."

"I'm going to have to get clearance to practice flying in it," Alice said, excited and relieved to find something else to do during her time off.

"Every captain will be given one of those jackets," Jake said. "They're hard to manufacture, but the best protection you can get."

"Thank you," Alice said, hugging Jake, who dwarfed her, but she enjoyed his comforting squeeze.

Then she embraced Ayan. "Don't worry, your leave will be over before you know it."

"I hope so," Alice said, stepping back and looking at the slick, black long coat. "What if I want my whole squad to have these? Well, the ones this would fit, anyway, the Nafalli already have heavier grade armour."

"Their jackets are getting upgraded along with the rest,

but only Captains and higher-ranking officers who want them get the long coats," Ayan replied.

"How's Laura now that she's moved into your quarters on the station?" Alice asked.

"She's sleeping better, growing fast, and she's happy," Ayan replied. "Having full-time help doesn't hurt, either."

The Lieutenant who was in charge of the shuttle that brought her aboard approached Minh-Chu and handed him his rose. "You left this on the shuttle, Sir."

"Thanks, has Frost made it over?" Minh-Chu asked.

"He came in on this trip and should be waiting in the port lounge now, Sir," the Lieutenant replied before he started towards Alice.

"There's my ride," Alice said with a sigh. "Now I really don't want to go. Are you sure I couldn't hang out on the Merciless?" she asked, looking to her father. To her mother, then; "Or shadow you? I'll help with Laura, learn about what you do."

"Your station clearance is suspended," Oz said as he stepped into the circle.

"I know, just appealing," Alice said.

"Hey, Alice! The shuttle's back," Iruuk called to her before receiving an aggressive hug from his father, who turned him around afterwards and pushed him playfully as though he needed some urging to leave. "Hey, I'm not a pup anymore," he muttered over his shoulder at him.

"It's time to go, Captain," the Lieutenant told Alice. "Your shuttle awaits."

"See you guys later," Alice said to everyone. The memory of being left behind as her father and most of the people she knew set off to save Freeground was clear in her mind as she fell in step behind the Lieutenant, Iruuk and a few other officers who weren't cleared to be on the station with the exception of the special event that they just witnessed followed. She knew it wasn't so bad, but she desperately wanted to get back to work.

ONE

Convalescence Day 5

TAKING patrol shifts for the Tamber Rangers, who were taking care of all the security and emergency situations on the moon, was a good fit for Alice and Iruuk. The rest of her crew were temporarily reassigned to Gabe, who borrowed the Clever Dream.

The Watch Commanders who took care of the boots-on-the-ground were happy to have her even if it meant that they didn't look too closely at the reasons behind her mandatory convalescent leave. She passed their stress check, so Lieutenant Weir had no problem giving her and Iruuk a section of Haven Shore to patrol on foot.

Iruuk was a natural. Always aware of his surroundings and he was great with people. Children liked him on sight, he was patient with the public and happy to be helpful whether someone's dog ran into the jungle and needed recovery, or someone wanted directions. Alice tried to be as easy-going as he was, but she secretly wanted an emergency to spice up her day. She felt like saying so out loud would jinx them both, but a little fire, someone - not a beloved pet - lost in the forest, or a criminal to pursue would have been nice.

"This was a good idea," Iruuk said after returning a Kawaii Kitten back to three grateful children. The fabricated kitten, who would never grow any larger, said; "Thank you!" in its high creaky cat voice as he was assaulted by petting hands.

With another mini-crisis resolved, Alice and Iruuk moved on, walking down the well-lit, paved path on the edge of the playground behind the Everin Building. "That's the third Kawaii Kitten we've saved from a tree in three shifts. Do you think it's part of their design?"

"It's smart, if it is. I mean, kids have to learn from someone's mistakes. It may as well be one of those, besides, the kittens always tell the kids to find an adult as soon as they realize they're stuck up there," Iruuk said.

They came to a large oval where enough tables and chairs for fifty were set up, and she looked across the people there, it was about half full. Not one of them was in a vacsuit and they didn't seem to have a care in the world as they sipped beverages in the early evening light. The communication bands they had were as varied as their former nationalities and most of the personal computers looked more like jewellery. Their assigned patrol route took them along the outer perimeter of the space, and she was still surprised at how many people smiled or gave them a little wave as they passed. They were obviously law enforcement, with a belt filled with tools, a large sidearm loaded with non-lethal rounds strapped to her thigh, and a rescue module on their backs. They stood out in armoured navy blue and white vacsuits, their colours were chosen based on the ones that had represented Tamber long before Ayan and Jacob arrived in the Haven System.

Their second day was spent outside Haven Government settlements, in Icara, a city that the Rangers had driven the major gangs out of. There were over a thousand Rangers there that day, most of whom were training for positions in the fleet and would be gone that week. Alice and Iruuk went through four packs of meal bars, giving them out to citizens there whenever they asked for one or when they ran into someone who looked hungry, or needed directions to one of the new re-homing centres. Those people regarded them with respect but they kept their distance and their silence for the most part. Few people said more than they had to.

"You're lost in thought," Iruuk said after they finished walking around the large oval space.

"This volunteer stuff isn't what I expected. Everything's under control here, there's no major crime, so we're kinda just community support. I know that's important, it's in my mother's design for Haven Shore, but I thought the Rangers would see two SOCU members and put us somewhere more dangerous. Like Icara, but even then, by the time we got there the mobs were broken. Most of the element that would take a shot at law enforcement were driven off world or already ran off to other cities. Even the Tamber Militia has signed up with the Rangers, and I thought they'd be a problem. I really thought we'd be helping people in more dangerous places. Maybe Celeste, where there are a whole bunch of gangs running around. Handing out meal bars and giving directions isn't what I'm trained for."

"You enjoyed that, though. You like taking care of people just as much as chasing bad guys."

"Yeah, Icara was filled with needy people, and I liked being there, helping out. One thing I noticed, and I don't really get it, is that most of the people who wanted to leave took our help and got out of there as soon as they could, but a lot of the citizens didn't want to go. It was a stagnant city without new opportunities for years. Gangsters squeezed them for the little they had. We were offering them tempo-rary re-homing where they wouldn't have to worry about where their next meal came from and could catch their breath before deciding where to go next - maybe one of our settle-ments, a city in better condition, or even back to Icara after we rebuilt the infrastructure - it was an opportunity to go to recover then start over from a place of strength. So many of them just... declined. They'd rather stay in buildings that were about to fall down because they were in such bad shape than take a rest somewhere else while we sent the bots in to make repairs."

"They might have been worried that they'd lose touch with family, or they wanted to watch over their little piece of the city. Maybe some of them had the same homes for genera-tions, that's important to a lot of people. I think it's why most sentients aren't space-farers. Before the Holocaust most people only left their home planet once or twice every ten years, and most of the time they went right back."

"I know, but if it were me, I would have scraped together

some platinum and gotten off Tamber, headed for some system where there's a big port opening up or expanding."

"There's a lot of opportunity around Tamber now, maybe not in that city yet, but with the Fleet pulling people out of jobs on the ground, there must be a place for everyone. If not now, soon. You wouldn't have to leave the planet to find something new, you know, in theory. Besides, you have so many people here," Iruuk said with a smile, playfully batting her shoulder.

"I guess I'm not used to that yet. I have a family now, and friends," Alice said, flashing him a crooked smile, "but for most of my life I remember moving on in the extreme, using a hyperdrive to put distance between me and trouble so I could start over again where no one knew me."

"Would you?" Iruuk asked, his eyes wide, tugging on the fur under his chin as he eagerly awaited her response. "I mean, if things got hard or sad for you here, would you leave?"

"Don't worry, Fur-Face," Alice said. "I'd rather suffer through hard times than be alone. I think it's just the boredom talking, maybe some wanderlust. When we reconnect with SOCU we could end up anywhere, but I know what I have at home. Every time I see Laura she's grown, changed a little more. It's like that kid has some kinda growth..."

A priority message came through on her and Iruuk's comms. "We're going to need your rescue training. There's a shuttle on its way now. There's a chemical fire in a re-processing plant in sector eighty-four."

"Fur-Face, I mean, Iruuk and I are ready," Alice replied. A blue and white emergency shuttle was already descending in front of them, filling the path ahead. It hovered a few centimetres above the ground as they leapt in.

"Strap in, we're going to push the dampers on this trip," the stubble-chinned pilot said as the shuttle rose abruptly. Iruuk strapped in and took fire suppression foamers from their packs and strapped one to their left arms, checked the seals on their suits then pulled up the incident feed. There were nine people still stuck in the old recycling building, and they would be coming through a breach on the west side of the structure on the second floor.

"We're going to use foam on our way in," she said.

"I've never done this before, not even in simulation," Iruuk said nervously. "I know how to use everything, how it works, technically, but..."

"Follow my lead and watch for changes in the situation. Talk your way through it, I'll guide you."

"You have training in this kind of situation?" Iruuk asked.

Alice nodded. "The Rangers put me through scenarios like this, I even had to crawl through a smoked-up course without a vacsuit or air filter. I felt like I was three feet tall while I was training with them, but I got through it."

"Why did you feel even shorter?"

"I was shorter," Alice said. "You've seen the images in my file."

"Oh yeah, you were so cute," Iruuk snickered.

"All right, seal up, we're ten seconds out and I have another pickup," the pilot said, starting to open the broad side doors.

Alice and Iruuk sealed their suits. "Ready, driver, thanks for the ride," Alice said.

"This is so exciting," Iruuk said, scanning the refinery's main structure. "I see who we're supposed to rescue, there's a spill between our entry point and him. It looks like he's pinned under something."

The shuttle dropped like a stone, and when it stopped almost as suddenly the dampers whined loudly, Alice could feel a few of the g-forces as her suit compensated. They leapt over the metre gap between them and a hole in the side of the building. They were far from Haven Shore, in a former province that was struggling as far as Alice knew. It was a city that was failing economically, and a large effort to invite people to new Haven Shore settlements was already beginning, but it was all new to the people there. "The man we're here to rescue might not know who we are, so let me do the talking," Alice said as she started spraying a jet of foam at blue-green chemical flames. They wouldn't burn through their armour, but she didn't know what kind of suit the worker would be wearing.

Iruuk kept foaming a path in front of them, smothering the flames and neutralizing the chemicals. "This is volunteer Alice Valent and Iruuk Murlen checking in with the Incident Commander. Are we in the right place, Captain? Iruuk marked our proposed rescue path and we're clearing our way to him now on the second floor."

"I see you on my tactical display," Captain Debon replied, his calm, baritone voice filling her ear. "That's the last rescue on the second floor. Get him out as fast as you can, structural scans are telling us the roof will collapse in less than three minutes."

"We're half way there already. We'll get out in time."

"Make it two and a half minutes, our scanners aren't what you're used to seeing in the Fleet."

"Acknowledged," Alice said.

"This is insane, no one should be here," Iruuk said as he sprayed foam in an arc in front of them. The black smoke filled their view, they had to find their way with sonic and wave scanners, which gave them a clear view of what was going on in black and white but only for a few metres at a time and she knew noise or a large collapse would render them completely blind while it was happening. Iruuk was over-treating the fire as well, making a path wide enough for five of him to get through shoulder-to-shoulder.

"That's why we're here," Alice said, taking the lead. "We have to move faster, follow behind me, attach a tether." She watched her footing and turned her structural scanner on, feeling a little embarrassed at not doing it sooner. The basic scanners built into her paired command and control wrist systems were far better than the Ranger service's standard issue, and she guided Iruuk around a patch of floor that was ready to give way. If she didn't remember to turn her structural scanners on, they would have fallen right through and never gotten to their rescue in time.

The foam spray she laid down made a clear path through the nearest spill and they rushed across the clear space between them and the man in a yellow suit trapped under a heavy beam laden with old suppression equipment. "Over here!" he cried, she could hear the pain in his voice.

"We're from the Haven Rangers, here to get you out," Alice said as she moved to his side and started looking at the problem. "I'm Alice, this is Iruuk, what's your name?"

"Bryce Sherman," he replied. "You guys are far from home." He said, struggling to get out from under the beam. His left leg could move, but the beam had crushed the other one. An old exo-frame strut on the thigh of his suit was keeping it from pinching it all the way through.

"Not for us," Alice said as she got ready to use the augmented muscle system in her suit on the beam to push it up.

"Wait!" Iruuk said. "Structural scan says that if you move the beam, this whole quarter of the roof will come down."

Alice's structural scanner didn't warn her about that hazard, but she backed off and looked at Bryce's leg. "There's no time for us to save your leg, we'll have to cut it off to free you."

"Cut the leg off," Bryce said, nodding. "If I don't make it, you have to get my kids. They're in a second storey apart-ment, Thirty-Five Adelaide Street, number Twenty-One."

"We'll take care of them, don't worry," Alice said, getting close to his leg and scanning. "It won't come to that, though, you'll see them soon."

"Hey, but if you don't have to cut my leg off, if there's another way, we can do that too," he said through a grimace.

"The building's gonna go soon, we've got to leave your original leg behind, but we can set you up with a new one. Oh, and you don't have to be awake for it," Alice said, finding the emergency medical access port on his suit and using it to inject a stasis dose.

"Just take care of my..." He was unconscious and on his way to full stasis before he could finish the statement.

"Kids," Alice finished for him, pulling a nano-blade from

her belt. "Get ready to pull him out and carry him," she told Iruuk. Before she could think about what she was doing, she followed the instructions on her screen on how to make a clean cut through his lower thigh and did it. The heat in the room was already starting to cauterize the wound as she followed through with a binding patch, re-sealing his primitive suit and protecting the stump.

"We're out," Alice said. "I'll re-foam as we go, follow my lead."

"Shuttle coming up to you," Captain Debon said. "Good work up there, but keep it moving."

"Thanks, we won't be long," Alice said, feeling a little claustrophobic as smoke closed around them completely. She paid attention to the scanners and foamed only as wide a path as they needed on their way out. "Edge of the building coming up in six metres, then there's a metre jump to the shuttle," she announced.

"Easy," Iruuk said, doing his best to conceal his fear. To anyone else he might seem calm, but Alice could tell he was staying focused on the task. If he stopped moving or didn't have someone to follow, he might have let anxiety take over.

It was strange and nerve wracking using secondary sensors to judge the jump from the edge of the break in the building's wall to the shuttle and jarring when they passed from the smoke-choked space into the clear air. All three of them made it and the same pilot looked and grinned at them, he said; "We're headed to Haven Shore Medical. The other medical centres are all busy."

"Why? Did something happen with the fleet?" Alice asked.

"Naw, it's always that way. Too few people on staff, folks on Tamber don't trust bots to treat them, but we have the beds, so those places are packed to the rafters. We'll have our rescue on a gurney in two minutes, hang on."

Alice and Iruuk put Bryce on a stretcher and strapped him in. Her scans said he could remain in stasis for days without any problems, but she wasn't about to tell the pilot to take his time.

"Thank you for the assist, Volunteers," Captain Doben said over their comms. "I'm glad some people from Fleet can see how important volunteer service is while we're short-handed. I'll make sure my report gets to your commanding officer."

"Thank you, Sir," Iruuk said.

Alice lowered her head, wondering how Oz, or rather, Commodore McPatrick, would feel about them playing smoke-eater when they were both supposed to be sitting around, relaxing.

"I have one more job for you two before I let you go," Doben said. "We found the file on Bryce, and we've tracked down his kids using the directions he gave us. We'll need someone to meet them once they touch down here and bring them to their father. It'll probably take the rest of your shift if you're interested."

"We could go get them for you," Alice volunteered.

"The Rangers already have patrols in Celeste. We just need someone to meet them in Haven Shore."

"It'll be our pleasure," Iruuk said.

"Tell us where and when," Alice agreed.

TWO

Little Citizens

LISTENING to the buzz and clamour of the street beneath her window, Shauna wrapped herself around her favourite pillow. The seat beside that window had been her bed and her day seat since they found the small apartment. Until recently she shared it with her brother, Amel, but he just got his own mattress so she had more room than she knew what to do with.

She kicked her small feet on the thin mattress, stretched then curled her toes before pulling her legs back up. Her brother was on the floor, playing ships and soldiers, the toy fighter pshew-shewing invisible bolts at the animated toy men who scrambled about, their little cries just loud enough to encourage him.

The noise was less irritating than her rumbling empty

stomach. As long as he was playing with the only automaton style toy set he had, he wasn't asking her where Dad was, and if he'd have dinner.

She puffed a lock of blonde hair out of her face and watched as five young men in the street below noticed a gentleman who carried a bag close to his chest. Shauna wished she could call down, tell him that he was about to be robbed. If she was older she might be able to do something, but at the age of seven she wouldn't be much help.

Like a pack, the grinning boys in matching jackets surrounded the gentleman with tall white hair. "No, don't," Shauna said under her breath as the older man fought to keep the silver case in his hands.

One of the boys, Jerrod with the fat arms, punched him while another drew a big gun. They got the case, and the man had no choice but to put his hands up, then back away. A shot exploded at his feet and he turned, stumbling into a run.

Amel stood and came to her side, looking for the action outside. "What happened?"

"No one got shot, just the Charons and their friends stealing again. Who's winning?" she asked, looking to the floor where her brother's dozen four-centimetre-tall soldiers huddled behind the cover of small rocks and old kitchen utensils.

"The Eden ship's got 'em pinned down, but Rangers are about to rally. They just need a plan."

"You know all the Eden ships are gone," she told him.

"I know," he said, slinking back down to the floor, his toy ship poised to resume its attack run on the soldiers. "When's Dad back?"

"He told us both when," she replied. "Sun down, when work's over. The sun's still high up."

"Think we can go outside?"

Shauna looked through the window and down. The street was busy, there was barely enough room for all the people as they jostled past each other. Predatory eyes stared from dark corners and doorways. She was happy to be on the second floor. "Not today," she told him, not looking in his direction so she could avoid his disappointment.

Taking care of her twin was easy, he was more well behaved since they were attacked in orbit, since their mother was killed. Their father said the Eden Virus was responsible, not one of the Eden ships, but to her brother it was all the same. He was nearly killed, and when they finished healing him, there was something wrong with his head. Something his father couldn't afford to fix, so he was simpler. She was the smart one.

The apartment their father found was tiny, just enough room for the three of them to sleep in, it was all they could afford. No one bothered them while they were there, and they had as much water as they wanted, but it was boring. Getting stuck in Celeste meant that their father had to work for food doing everything from manual labour to things that he wouldn't talk about.

With a sigh she rested her chin on her knee and watched the people below. A group of soldiers moved down the street. They wore black armour, walking in a double column. "Amel," she said. "Look, come up and look."

He retreated from his little war and crawled up on the window seat, looking through the open window so eagerly that she was momentarily afraid that he'd fall out onto the awning below. "Who are they?" he asked.

"I'm not sure, let's count them," she replied, pointing.

"One, two, three, four, um," he huffed frustration.

"Five," she pointed at the next one and he joined her in counting to fourteen.

"That's a lot," he said, staring down at the soldiers, mesmerized. "They're Rangers," he said in awe. "Dad told me about the Rangers."

Shauna knew well enough after listening to her brother tell her about them, ask her about them, and babble about them over and over again. Her father explained to both of them that there were still good people on Tamber, but they were on the other side of the moon. They helped people, but they were far away, so the three of them had to help themselves.

The soldiers stopped just up the street. "What are they doing?" Amel asked.

From the way he was fidgeting she could tell he was moments away from running down so he could get a closer look, but the street was dangerous. The people were dangerous. "Getting ready to leave. If you run down there, you'll miss it, so watch from up here, okay?"

"Okay," he replied. "Okay," he repeated with a sigh.

They didn't do anything, just stood there, she couldn't even tell if they were talking to anyone with their helmets on. She pulled her bead bag from where it was wedged in the corner of the window seat and took a half-woven bracelet out. Shauna was just starting to string a hematite bead when she heard a faint buzzing. As she looked up a small white and blue disc flew into the window and past them, stopping to hover in the middle of their small apartment. A bag hung from it, packed with something that looked too heavy for it to lift.

"Look!" her brother said as he started for it.

She caught him before he made it off the seat. "Wait! We don't know what it is yet."

He fell back against her. "But it could be from the Rangers."

"Let's see what it does, okay?"

The disc buzzed over to them and stopped to hover in front of their faces. "It's got little prop, prop..."

"Propellers," she finished for him.

It gently dropped the bag in her brother's lap. The thin cloth fell open to reveal a green-yellow apple and a few dark-skinned plums along with a pair of wrapped rectangular bars. "What's that?" her brother asked, pointing at the large apple.

"It's a Tamber sour apple, you like those, remember?"

He picked it up, not indicating whether or not he remembered before sinking his teeth in. His groan of pleasure was proof enough that he had his reminder. She knew what the plums looked like, but never had one, so she tried it. The sweet juice burst from the fruit, and she couldn't help but giggle at herself.

The holographic image of a young man appeared, projected by the small white disc that brought the bounty. "Hello, I'm Officer Fisher with the Haven Shore Immigration. Our Rangers were called to Celeste when there was an industrial accident a few hours ago. Bryce, your father is safe and recovering after treatment. He was one of the workers we rescued. Again, I need you to know that he's okay. We were able to save him. He told us about both of you. Are you safe?"

"We're okay," her brother replied. "Is Dad okay?"

"He's all right, you're Amel, right?"

"Yeah," he said, chomping half a mouthful of apple.

"And you're Shauna," the young man's holographic head said, turning to her. "Rangers, our people, are on their way so we can give you a ride to be with your father. All the worker's families are being brought here. We're going to start with the youngest people in your neighbourhood first, and that means you. Is that all right?"

"Dad's not coming home?" Amel asked.

Sometimes Shauna couldn't understand how her brother's mind worked. After everything the Officer said, that was his conclusion. She was more than a little stunned, but she replied for them both. "We're going to see Dad. The Rangers are going to come for us and bring us to him."

"That's right, Shauna, a shuttle will pick you up. Your father said the roof is stable enough, so it'll land there."

"We can't leave the apartment for long, someone will break in," Shauna said. "But okay."

"Shauna," her father's voice said. The perspective of whatever was recording things on the other side turned so her father's face appeared. "Get the box from under my bed, the locked one, and your bag so you're ready. We're moving to Haven Shore."

"Dad! You're okay?" Amel asked.

"I'm fine. Do you think you can follow your sister onto the shuttle?"

"I'm going on a shuttle?"

"You and your sister. I know you don't like flying, but follow her, okay?"

"Okay," he said, resigned.

"Now go gather your soldiers," her father said.

Leaving half his apple uneaten, Amel rushed to the floor and started recovering his toy soldiers.

"Shauna," her father said at a lower volume. "They say they have medicine here that can help him. They're going to take care of us, and we won't be going back to Celeste. Most of your friends in the neighbourhood are coming too, everyone who had someone working in that plant. What do you think of that, sweetie?"

"Are you really okay? Is it really safe there?"

"I'm fine, they took good care of us, and it's completely safe. Can you get the box I told you about and make sure your brother and you are ready when they knock on the door?"

"Yeah, um," Shauna hesitated, having a hard time believing that she and her brother were about to leave Celeste forever. "Yeah, Dad."

"See you soon," her father said.

She rushed across the apartment, it was a short run, and slid under her father's bed hands first. The metal box he talked about was where she expected it to be. All the family keepsakes – mostly things belonging to her mother – were in there. Unsure of what else to do, she returned to the window and picked up her bag. She was wearing her favourite clothes, and her brother was wearing the only outfit he hadn't outgrown. Shauna had a thought then and hopped from the bed onto the counter. Above the shelves they had a can of Poulto, chicken preserved in jelly. The stuff was awful, but it was the emergency food, just in case her father didn't make it home until morning. She put it in her bag and filled a water bottle just in case the journey would take a long time.

The buzzing white disc was gone, and at a glance she could see more white discs than she could count drifting through nearby windows. Her brother joined her, breathless with his soldiers in a bag in one hand, taking her hand in the other. "Dad's coming?"

"We're going to him on a shuttle," Shauna replied patiently. He sometimes had trouble remembering things he just heard.

"When?"

A knock at the door made her smile. "Now." As a last thought she stuffed her bead and string kit then the plums into her bag. "C'mon."

THREE

Propaganda

THE BRICK PATH under Dron's feet was perfect, a nice medium brown winding between thick patches of wildflowers and natural grazing lawn. It wasn't the kind of sod that Regent Galactic subsidiaries sold, the kind that would grow anywhere for a year at a time, but the type of lawn a real gardener could appreciate. It was cultivated from the forest then grown on the city grounds. The park area he was in was called Queen's Overlook. The completed portions stirred admiration and jealousy in the Overlord as he strolled by children playing on the green and purple leafy grass. There was an instructor, no, a teacher showing a small group of very young children a small vegetable garden that was set up on a little tiered hill. Under her instruction little hands tried planting even smaller seeds.

"How is education handled in Haven Shore?" Dron asked Ayan, glancing at her briefly. She was in a long, white and blue two panelled dress that was split up the sides to mid-thigh, a simple garment, but it looked comfortable and its design made her look a little taller. Her red ringlets were loose, falling around her shoulders in a fashion that looked random and wild to him. He preferred short hair and didn't trust people who spent extra time taking care of longer locks. It reeked of vanity to him.

"The Haven Government requires that children enter a flexible curriculum that takes their learning styles into account. We focus on reading, communication skills, math and critical thinking. There are a number of electives, but it's still limited because we don't have enough qualified teachers right now. We're low on manpower everywhere."

"It would be easier if you used androids," Dron offered.

"Most of the people who come to Tamber don't trust them, even if their artificial intelligences only have emotional emulation, not the real thing. I can't say I blame them."

"The virus has had a long-term effect," Dron nodded. "So all the resources it took to make this could have been spent elsewhere. You're short on manpower but someone built this massive garden."

"Early on we found that people who were waiting for placement wanted something to do, so the Council created a number of projects that were relatively easy to plan and coordinate. A lot of people waiting to be assigned to a real job or looking for something to do during their time off spend some time working here. Most of the hard fixtures are installed by robots late at night, when most people are sleeping, but the grass, flowers, even the hobby vegetable gardens were put here by our citizens. It helps give them a sense of ownership."

"How does any of this matter in the end? It's a beautiful place, but my intelligence says you have two colony movers and some older ships on the surface, ready to evacuate these people. Is it all just busy work?"

"I'm afraid I don't have the data I need to answer that question," Ayan replied as they came to one of the overlooks.

Dron leaned on the railing and looked at the blue-green freshwater ocean. From the cliff he could see the shallows where white, brown, and black sands were interrupted by growth here and there. He looked further out, to the deeper blue that stretched to the horizon. Above there was a strange shadow effect where the stars could be seen a little through the artificial blue sky. "You can go," Dron said with a sigh.

"Call my name if you would like me to answer any more questions," Ayan's hologram said before fading away.

Lucius Wheeler walked towards the railing leisurely. "So, what do you think?"

"I admit it's impressive," the Overlord said. "This simulation, the holographic companions, and the amount of information you can access would be enough to entice anyone who has had a rough go of things. You said Ayan is the favourite companion for 'A Walk Through the Garden?'"

"By far," Wheeler said. "Why? What do you think of her?"

"Not to sound shallow, but I find her chubby, plain and vain. That old British accent she puts on makes it all worse."

Wheeler laughed and nodded. "That's the worst part, it's not fake. She's a modified human with memories that were implanted from the original Ayan, so she never had a chance to be anything but a spoiled Brit."

"It's amusing, but not that amusing," Dron said, sobering Wheeler quickly. "She is a Queen, after all, and if her demeanour is anything like I've seen in the news footage, she projects an image that is almost wilful, and as much as I like to insult this holographic representation of her, I'd be an idiot if I didn't recognize her intelligence."

"Yeah, that's the truth," Wheeler said. "I was on my way to a citizenship before you took over and recalled me, though." He pointed to his head as if to remind Dron that it was his message that forced him to leave Tamber and return to Order of Eden space. "It took me a while to figure out how to get your framework tech through their scanners, but it worked."

"It took a lot to get you back behind our lines," Dron said. "The fact that you have your own operatives behind enemy lines is just another reason why you should be part of my command structure. I only wish we didn't have to probe your memories to find out about them."

"Yeah, I'll make sure you never have to do that again, boss," Wheeler said, leaning on the railing. He looked more like one of the enemy, with a handgun strapped to his thigh, another, smaller stunner up his sleeve and a thick jacket over his dark green uniform. "So, now that you've seen a bit of their propaganda, what do you think?"

"The galaxy is in turmoil, raiders everywhere, gangs standing in for governments, organized crime taking control of that slowly, with pockets of robots who either resisted the antivirus or never got it randomly distributed across worlds that are in ruin. Even Order of Eden territory isn't completely under control yet, and word is getting out. In the face of that Tamber and the Haven System look like Camelot. They even have a royal family that's so charming I could retch. A Queen who is known for her intelligence shows an emotional side by adopting an infant refugee. Her consort and daughter are warriors in her army. The whole family serves, actually, and to top it off, the Queen is reluctant, letting a democracy control the system. A democracy that includes a dutiful father. It's a very modern royal family, and if I didn't expect that half of it was staged somehow, or that there wasn't some kind of hidden corruption, I'd just leave them alone. But they make allegations about the Order being responsible for forced population control," Dron said.

"The Holocaust Virus proves that," Wheeler added.

"Then they present evidence that we're responsible for the controlled settlement of Edxi."

"Brood worlds that are filled with human inhabitants, sometimes even other races like the Mergillians," Wheeler interjected with a sigh.

"And they oversimplify our system of government and peace-making, countering our personal profit and debt citizenship system as well as our military structure with their open democratic society. Without a real measurement of how you are performing, like our credit system, how can you feel connected to the government and industry?"

"So, you're saying the fact that eighty four percent of the Order Worlds' population is in debt is a good thing? That it's just a measurement of how a person is doing in society."

"It works," Dron said, pounding the railing. "You work hard, pay all those people and companies you owe until you're out of debt and then you can take full control of your destiny. Most people start lending once they reach an early stage of wealth, so we know it works."

"So they can control people who owe them," Wheeler laughed. "I'm on an Order Command Ship, so I see it all the time. As soon as people are off-duty, a whole other command structure takes control. The wealthy boss their debtors around like they're on leashes, and they play along like pets so they can work that debt off faster. I know it's hard for you to grasp, but if I were deep in debt, I would take Haven's deal in a heartbeat."

"What is Haven's deal?" Dron asked, exasperated. "I don't understand why people don't join up, stay for as long as they need to earn some luxury credit, then cash out and leave with the platinum and all the technology they can carry."

"They value happiness and well-being over platinum or credit. If I didn't see it working from just over their border for myself, talk to a whole bunch of citizens, I don't think I'd get it either, but the people who live in Haven settlements are loyal, they take personal pride in being a part of that rosy machine, argue over politics like it's life or death sometimes, sure, but that's because they know they can make a difference in how their little corner of Camelot is run."

"It sounds like you'd rather be fighting for them," Dron said. Wheeler's argument sounded hollow and borderline seditious to him. It was plain that Ayan and her family had a good sham going, where first impressions of a good meal upon arrival, the promise of luxury credits in a market they controlled, and cheap housing tricked people into serving them.

"Oh, don't get me wrong. I don't fit in their world, their government, I'm the kind of guy they close their gates to, so I want to break this socialist love-fest up as bad as you do. I had a plan to interfere with things from the top down, remember? You got into my head, saw all those details, and I don't hear you telling me it was a bad plan, either."

"So, even if all these simulated propaganda programs are real, you'd still help me take the Haven System?"

"I don't exactly have a choice, you've got me by the bones, but yeah, I would if you didn't. I might do things differently, but now that I've got a nice flagship and a crew that knows what they're doing, I'll do my part even though every computer in the fleet needs fine-tuning."

The new operating system that was distributed to fix the damage Captain Valent had done was enough to keep his ships mobile, but most of the fleet still wasn't fully combat ready. It was frustrating, watching programmers try to patch things system by system, even though he knew most of them had to learn a whole new programming language. "Don't remind me."

"When will everything work again? What's the new date?"

"You know the date."

"Oh, right, in two more days. Every morning I see a delay notice that adds another day, so maybe your programmers should say 'eternity plus two days,'" Wheeler sneered. "Part of my plan's ready to go. I just have to send a little message."

"The Edxi are ready to begin their assault," Dron said. "Perhaps they're right. Perhaps I should just send them in and let them take the system as a brood world. They have the drones to do it."

"You've tossed most of my plan out, just let me finish this last piece. It took months to put together, and it might not pay off the way it could have if I could follow through right to the end, but it'll mess with them, it'll be worth it."

"Why play with their heads when the wisest course is to arrange for them to be wiped out completely?" Dron let the question hang in the air, Wheeler didn't bother answering, turning towards the ocean and leaning on the railing instead. "Fine. I'll let you have your fun, but it won't change anything." He turned around and looked at the garden as the sun began to set, its rosy light colouring the scene. The opalescent Everin building, standing tall and broad made of segments piled together much like an Issyrian underwater settlement started to glisten. "Is it really like this in Haven Shore?" The designer in him wanted to see it for himself if it was.

"Well, last I heard the garden wasn't finished, but the rest of it is pretty much like this, yeah. They have a special shield over the island chain that controls weather and day cycles. If their timetable holds, they'll extend the shield around the entire moon using satellites."

"How long?"

Wheeler suppressed a grin, reducing it to a thin-lipped smile. "Two days. Knowing what I do about Ayan and their military, they'll hit their deadline, too."

"It still sounds like you'd rather be on their side," Dron said.

"Hey, I'd rather be on my side, flying far away from here. Maybe I could go to the core, I hear there are some great opportunities in the chaos there, interesting people as long as you stay away from the British."

"I've heard from the core recently, I wouldn't recommend it," Dron said, watching as the lights along the path and the main concourse beyond the garden started to turn on. "Too bad I won't get a chance to see this in person," he sighed, looking up at the statue of Ayan, who was gazing back towards the garden with a kindly expression on her chubby face. "Hurry up with your head games, I'll delay things a little while."

"You won't regret this."

"You're bad for me, Wheeler, I normally don't get behind petty cheap shots," Dron said.

"If you knew about my whole plan, you'd see how it all adds up." Wheeler's image faded as he disconnected from the simulation.

"I do, and I'm still not impressed," he said to the empty space where Wheeler's image was. Dron took one more look at the garden and shook his head. "It must be faith that makes them feel safe. I wonder how they'll do without it. End simulation," he said, and the world around him disappeared, giving way to his stiff bed and darkened quarters.

With a thought he opened the special interface, a system of oval windows that would connect him to the Edxi mothership closest to the Haven System. The message he had for the swarm the Order was trying to control was a simple one. The system would be theirs to take soon.

FOUR

Why We Serve

THERE WERE SO many children in the shuttle, but it still seemed half empty. Amel fidgeted in his seat, looking at the soldiers dressed in black who had carefully, but swiftly strapped them in. He glanced down towards the door leading to the cockpit as it swished and clicked closed. There were big windows across from them, and he looked to those nervously. There was nothing to see but blue sky, and the slight rumbling of the craft drew Amel's attention to the rear.

A guard knelt down for a moment, retracting his helmet to reveal a surprisingly young face. "It's okay, we're taking you to Haven Shore, you'll be safe there," he said.

Amel squeezed Shauna's hand, and he whispered; "Dad?"

"No, I'm not your dad," replied the soldier, looking a little perplexed.

"We're going to see Dad," Shauna answered, but it didn't do anything to allay her brother's rising anxiety. "Are we going to get there soon?" she asked the soldier.

"Well, soon enough, we have to go around a few things where there's trouble, nothing to worry about, but we..."

Shauna could see the explanation was doing her brother no good; his eyes were beginning to dart around faster. She dug into their bags, only opening them enough to get one of his soldiers. "See, it's Marty," she told him as she tried to put it in his hand.

"That's Roger," he replied, barely looking at it. It wasn't enough, Amel was still too nervous, and whatever reassurance he needed, she hadn't found for him yet.

She glanced at the solider, who was still saying something about where they were going, or how they were getting there, and thought of asking for help, but he was too busy explaining whatever he thought was so important. It was then that she noticed that, between Amel's glances around the craft, he kept looking back through the window across from them. "You want to see outside?" she asked.

He looked at her, so afraid that she knew he'd be inconsolable any moment. Once he was in full panic, he would spend the rest of the ride screaming and crying. Most likely longer, and nothing made her feel worse, more like a failure. "Let's look outside," she said, unclipping his restraint belt, then her own.

"Hey, you can't do that," said the guard, who had finally stopped prattling on. Shauna and Amel got up on their knees, turned towards the backs of their seats and leaned against the padding to peer through the window.

Amel gasped as he took in the view of a green expanse of land and the blue ocean beyond. Most of the children did the same thing, and the shuttle was filled with the chatter of them as they took in the sights.

"It's not safe," the guard complained. "You have to sit back down and get buckled in."

"Ah, leave 'em," said another guard. "It's perfectly safe. Those belts are more there to control passengers than anything. This shuttle runs so smooth you can barely tell we're flying."

Shauna tried handing her brother his action figure again and he accepted Roger absent minded, putting its plastic face against the transparent bulkhead beside his. "Look, Roger, birds."

Shauna looked down to the tops of the trees and saw a flight of uncountable colourful birds glide across the thick jungle. To her relief, she could see signs of her brother's anxiety melting away as it was replaced with awe and wonder. He hopped a little as a pair of sharp-winged fighters swept into view, they were so close that Shauna could see a Rangers emblem on the side. "They're from the Rangers, look."

Amel waved, grinning excitedly. He and their father watched the news reports about the rangers taming Tamber all the time, they weren't like the knights in the stories she enjoyed, but she liked hearing that they were trying to make the moon safer for everyone. He started waving again, and the nearest fighter wobbled its wings briefly, making him and another younger girl a few seats down squeal with delight.

The fighters banked away a moment later, and the shuttle turned after them heading directly over the ocean. For a moment there was nothing but blue waves and blue sky, then Shauna gasped at the sight of silver shapes in the water, jumping out and diving down swiftly.

"Freshwater dolphins," said the previously nervous guard. "There's life almost everywhere on Tamber, you'll see."

The shuttle picked up speed, leaving the creatures behind. Small clusters of beach and green covered the islands that passed beneath them as they crossed a body of water larger than anything Shauna had ever dreamt of. Her brother was busy trying to take it all in, looking from one thing to the next as quickly as the islands appeared and disappeared from sight.

The shuttle began to slow down, and in the distance, they could see the outlines of tall buildings and a large land mass. "Those are agricultural towers, they grow most of our food now. We've got three working, and you can see where we're building four more there."

"That's where the fruit you had came from, kids," said the other guard, leaning towards the transparent sections of the hull and tapping the metal. "Lots to go around."

Shauna didn't realize how large they were until they got much closer, they were taller than any buildings she'd ever seen, and through the transparent sections on the sides she could see rows of short, leafy trees and shrub like plants on the different levels.

"Haven Shore, almost home," the younger guard said.

In the middle of the lower section of the island there was a mountain surrounded by thick jungle. Atop the mountain she saw a mound of a building with bulbous, rounded sections that shifted in colour as they slowly circled. It looked like the inside of a seashell her mother had. When she shined a light on it, a rainbow of colours would reflect. "Mother of pearl," she whispered as she remembered what it was called. She almost didn't notice that there were two more being built along the top of the mountain behind it until the lower floors were nearly out of sight.

The shuttle set down gently next to the second tallest building. She looked up as far as she could, and even though it looked like it was still being built when they were looking down on it, she couldn't see the top from where they were. It looked new, but as busy as any finished building. She took her brother's hand. "We're going to see Dad," she told him. They slid off their seats and were gently but firmly put back into them before they took two steps. "Now you really do have to stay in your seats until we know where you're going."

Amel wouldn't hear it, and he regarded their guardian with an expression of angry determination as she turned away to maintain control of the rest of the children. Her little brother was about to do *something*.

The rear door lowered and Amel sprinted towards it so quickly that Shauna didn't have a chance to react. She ran after him, to the displeasure of the guards, and nearly ploughed into his back when he stopped suddenly, looking up and dropping his action figure.

She looked up and saw a furry giant smiling down at them. He had blonde fur with dark brown stripes. "I'm

Iruuk," he said, kneeling down, down, until his big, friendly looking muzzle was almost at their eye level. Amel's mouth hung open in shock as he stared silently at the mountain of a creature. Iruuk picked the boy's action figure up and put it in his hand.

To Shauna's surprise, Amel began to grin as he grabbed Iruuk's hand with both of his. She noticed another person then, standing beside Iruuk in a white and dark blue uniform. Unlike most soldiers and guards Shauna met that afternoon, she had three emblems on her chest. She didn't like the skulls in the centre of each, but she realized that it must mean that the young red-haired woman was important.

She looked at Shauna with a smile and knelt down to her level, it didn't take her much effort, the young woman was much, much shorter than her furry companion. "I'm Alice," she said. "We're here to take you to your father."

"Whoa!" Amel exclaimed excitedly as Iruuk picked him up and sat him on his shoulder. His surprise was replaced by a big grin.

"He's okay," Alice said. "Iruuk has so many brothers and sisters, I can't keep count."

"You're important here, aren't you?" Shauna said, taking Alice's hand and following her and Iruuk to a tall doorway.

Alice seemed surprised at the question but realized that Shauna was looking at the emblems on her chest and smiled at her. "I'm just experienced," she said. "This one means that I serve Haven Fleet, the people who defend Tamber," she pointed at the top emblem. "This means I'm a member of Special Operations," she said as she pointed at the middle one. She tapped the lowest emblem on her chest then. "This tells everyone that I'm a trained Ranger. Iruuk and I are volunteering here while we're taking a break, we're probably going to be sent into space to protect this place. I'm a Captain with my own ship."

"Wow, you're going to protect us from the 'bots?" Shauna asked in a whisper.

"We'll protect this whole world from anything that wants to hurt it."

They stepped inside the building with a few of the other children and their minders, guards who were in blue and white or black, all of them had Haven Fleet emblems on their chest, a few of them also had Ranger markings. A transit car arrived, speeding into the tube in front of them and stopping abruptly. The people inside didn't seem to be jostled at all. They piled out, many of them offering smiles as they passed by. Everyone was wearing uniforms, they were form fitted for the most part, but what struck Shauna most was how new everything looked and how clean everyone was. They entered the transit car, a ten-meter long vessel that hovered in the middle of a tube without touching the edges. It was made completely of transparent steel that had a slight blue tint.

A glance at her brother told her that he was entranced by Iruuk, who had brought the boy down from his shoulder to cradle him in one arm. The creature made faces at him, crossing his eyes, then letting his tongue hang lazily out of the side of his mouth. Amel held his action figure up threateningly, and it activated, drawing its tiny rifle and pointing it at the nafalli's nose. Iruuk held his free hand up and feigned fear, delighting Amel.

Shauna didn't feel the car begin to move as it suddenly

accelerated down the tube then shot up several levels. "What's going to happen to us?"

"The people in Haven Shore will take care of you while your brother heals and while all three of you rest for a while. You're in our family now, and we take care of our own. You'll have a safe place to live, good neighbours, you'll use the education centre with your brother, and your father will help us by working while you're there, learning all kinds of things."

The car entered a place that looked like it was under water, and they were surrounded by colourful fish and a landscape filled with plant life drifting in gentle currents. "This is one of our source tanks," Alice explained. "It helps provide everyone in the building with food and it waters the garden tanks in everyone's apartments. We learned how to do this from a ship that was made on Earth."

"My mom used to tell us about Earth," Shauna said. That seemed to quiet Alice, and her smile diminished a little. Adults didn't know what to say when she and her brother mentioned their mother, they often stopped talking to them altogether, which was better than the pats on the back or comforting hugs. She didn't want Alice to quiet down, though. As the transit car moved upward and out of the flooded section, she asked, "Do you like it here?"

"I love coming back here when I'm not in space," Alice replied. "I gave up my house so a family like yours can have it, though. I'm going to be too far away to enjoy it anyway."

"Will my dad have to be a soldier?"

"Your father is a very smart man. Did you know that he used to work on the machines that kept your air clean when you were living on the space station?"

"I kinda remember something about that," Shauna replied, it seemed like it was a long time ago.

"He's going to help us keep the air and water clean on ships, in these buildings, and he's going to help us build things. We don't need him to fight at all, and he'll be close to home all the time, close to you and your brother. It's going to be a safe job for him."

The transit car came to a quick stop, and Alice walked her by the hand down a clean looking hallway, white and light blue, where a few medical robots with several retracted arms and scanners roamed around with men and women in red and blue uniforms. This was a hospital, she'd seen enough of them in holo-movies to know what one looked like, and the smell was what struck her the most. It was character-less, absent any odour, it was like the place was too clean.

"Your father is in recovery, he lost a leg in the accident but they're going to give him another one today so you won't be able to tell the difference," Alice said.

"We're going to see him now?" Shauna asked, unsure.

"Right now," Alice said, leading her through a doorway.

Her father was there, alert, a few tubes were running from a machine with different liquids in it to the bed, disappearing under the sheets. His lower half was covered by a stiff barrier, and he smiled broadly at them.

Amel squirmed suddenly, nearly breaking free of Iruuk's arm and falling, but the Nafalli put him down on his father's bed instead. "He can stay there, just keep it above the privacy barrier," the doctor said in a pleasant tone.

"Hey, buddy," Bryce said, returning his son's enthusiastic embrace. His free hand reached for Shauna but she looked up at Alice instead. "This is a safe place, we're in a good place now, right?" The question didn't seem like enough, as though it left out all kinds of details and didn't ask after so many things she wanted to know, the most important of which was; 'are we going to be safe now?'

"It is, you'll see," Alice said, kneeling down. "It was good meeting you, Shauna, you're a brave girl, but you don't have to be anymore."

Shauna gave her a sudden hug.

"You'd better go, your Dad's really excited to see you," Alice said, squeezing her a little before letting her go.

Shauna ran towards her father. He caught her with his free arm and helped her up onto the bed, where she joined her brother. "That's why we serve," she heard Iruuk say from behind them.

"Sure is, Fur-Face," Alice replied.

FIVE

Final Details

IRUUK SHOWED the nervousness that Alice shared with him in the questions he asked while they were waiting on the War Forge. A classified shuttle picked them up that morning and within minutes they were delivered to a hangar aboard the massive station. The shuttle was blacked out, blocking the scanners built into their uniforms and keeping the War Forge's location a secret, but Alice knew the short transit time meant that it was close, probably in Tamber's outer orbit. That meant there was something serious going on, probably the deployment of a lot of hardware, like the orbital defence satellites that most people wouldn't know anything about until they were in place and turned on.

Iruuk wasn't too talkative until they were waiting in a broad hallway, surrounded by dark deck plates, sitting down against the bulkhead where there were twenty seats lined up. It was a waiting space for one or more briefing rooms, she guessed. It was difficult to tell since they were in one of the high security sections of the stations where doors were hidden until you were supposed to enter.

"This is about our unauthorized volunteer work, right?" Iruuk asked. "I knew it would get us into trouble." A few moments later he said; "Fleet knows everything though, so if we weren't supposed to do it, we wouldn't have gotten an assignment."

"I'm your commanding officer, so I would have been told that we were in the wrong," Alice said. "I don't think it's that, but if it was, I'm good with whatever punishment they have for us. I slept better than I have in, well, a long time last night."

"Me too, told my father about the rescue and those kids. He told me he was proud of me twice. If I couldn't be in the military, I'd be a Ranger. Maybe a rescue worker if I couldn't do that."

"We're not getting punished for volunteer work, though," Alice said, "Probably not seriously, anyway. What would it say in our file? 'They were supposed to be on vacation, but decided to volunteer as Rangers and Peacekeeper Patrol while they were under staffed instead?' No, a big punishment would set the wrong example."

"Then it's the invasion, and they're reactivating us and putting us somewhere useful. They're just keeping it quiet so Tamber citizens don't panic."

"Maybe, but I think it's more likely that we're going to be told where our boundaries are from here on out. Our instructions were to relax, get some recreation time in. I think they're going to tell us to stay put somewhere. Probably means more family time for you, and more concourse time for me."

Iruuk looked surprised and stood. "Why don't you think I'd spend time with you in the Main Concourse? I like restaurants, and meeting people, and the other places they have there. I'm finally old enough to enjoy everything they can offer, too."

"Sorry, I just thought you'd spend your free off-time with your little brothers and sisters. That's where you disappeared to in the past until I found something interesting to do."

"You only call me when you have one of your ideas, like volunteering for foot patrol," Iruuk said. "Or want to track something down for a report. I'm not complaining, you just don't call when you just want to hang out. Like tanning on the beach. I only heard you were there after you came back."

"I didn't know you'd be into the hot sand and barely dressed humans. Besides, it was more of a 'reading on the beach' kinda exercise. I wasn't exactly playing Zero Ball or anything."

"Then why go to the beach?" Iruuk asked. "You could have read and watched briefing holos at home. Well, before you gave your apartment away."

"Some humans like sunning, getting some colour on their skin when the atmosphere's right. It's relaxing, especially after a swim."

"I like swimming and laying in the sun too," Iruuk said. "If we did more of that, maybe we wouldn't be in trouble."

"You're not in trouble," Oz said as he came through a

hidden door. The section of bulkhead remained open, and he beckoned them inside. "We're in here, come on in."

Alice and Iruuk followed his lead. Before they passed through the entrance they couldn't see more than a couple metres inside, but as they crossed the threshold, a hangar was revealed with the Clever Dream as its main occupant. The lower rear section was open. Several workers led robots in an effort to make some kind of modifications. They moved with urgency, and Alice wondered why the dimension drives that were installed on her ship were on the deck behind it, detached and being rapidly disassembled by several small skitter bots. "What's up, Commodore?"

"You have the fleet's thanks, and a fair payment of luxury credits for loaning them the Clever Dream again. I can't tell you what the ship was used for, but it didn't take any damage, and its mission was a success," he replied. "In the week you've been on leave the fleet has started installing a standardized system for creating and travelling through trans-dimensional wormholes. Only a few ships, the Clever Dream being one, will have a singular backup, open dimension drive system that can be reprogrammed. Everything else in our fleet will have the standard model."

"Oh, the Quad Drive, I started reading about the design," Iruuk said. "It's called the Quad Drive because it has navigation, a dimension drive, a fusion power source, and all the regulation, power storage and cooling systems required in one safe package. You just put one or more of them on a ship and plug them in. Power them up and they'll run on their own until they're uninstalled. You can add more power for better transit times, of course, but it makes everything safer and easier."

"I read about it, there's already chatter about these on the 'net," Alice said, recalling posts from companies and captains in the region that wanted one. If they were as efficient and quick as she guessed they were, every ship with a quad drive would be a target for theft. A pair of large bay doors opened behind the Clever Dream and several treaded robots pushed a cargo sled with a black armoured box towards the rear of her ship. It was only a metre and a half high and three across. "That's it, that's a quad drive," she said, as much a question as it was a statement.

"The Clever Dream is getting four, and like I said, it will keep one of its older dimension drives. She'll be one of the fastest ships in history," Oz said.

The urge to get aboard and start exploring struck Alice like a hard pang. She kept it hidden but was frustrated as Oz laughed lightly. "I would have liked to be asked first," she said, trying to change the topic.

"I'm barely an empath at this point, but even I can sense that you want to use this, you would have asked for six or seven drives if we made this an offer instead of an order. I've never had a need to explore, to get out there as strong as yours, and there are few things I love more than being on the bridge of a starship," Oz said. "I'd like to tell you that these drives are being installed so you can go visit the unexplored parts of the galaxy, or even represent fleet by visiting known settlements. The truth is that the Clever Dream is getting her one-hundred-forty-millimetre cannons installed along with the quad drives because the mission of the Special Operations Combat Unit has changed. I've recruited more people into the unit, and several corvette class ships have been assigned, all designed much like the Clever Dream with the latest technology aboard, so they can serve as flexible, quick response squads. So, no one will be borrowing the Clever Dream from this point on, even though it's considered the flagship of the SOCU fleet."

"Gabe finally got his own ship," Alice sighed with relief.

"Along with the other seven commanders in SOCU," Oz said, watching Iruuk as he was mesmerized by the robots lifting and loading the quad drives onto the Clever Dream through the open aft section. "Before I let Iruuk go watch them install those drives, I'm obliged to tell you that Fleet is proud of your volunteer service. The playback of your rescue in the factory fire has done fleet some good in terms of our reputation. It shows that even though we're drawing a lot of manpower from Tamber's services, Fleet wants to give back."

"I signed us up because we were bored, and that rescue happened because I have Ranger training," Alice said. "I'm glad it's good for Fleet's optics, though."

"I know, and I'm restricting you from all duty for three days, that includes all branches of ground service," Commodore McPatrick said. His tone was firm, official. "There will be a favourable note added to both your service records, but you know that wasn't why I sent you home. You're on mandatory leave so you can clear your head."

"My head was perfectly clear in that fire. It had to be," Alice retorted.

"And so you could relax. Both your stress levels were too high, and they're settling down, but some leisure time is necessary. Three days of doing nothing but reading manuals, watching a couple briefings, and enjoying what Haven Shore has to offer, then I'll have work for you. All right?"

"Yes, Sir," Alice said without ire. Iruuk did the same.

"Good," Oz said. Theodore came in from a door behind them, in uniform with a heavy pistol strapped to his thigh and a full utility belt on. There was no flaw in his guise as a human, even his gait seemed easier. Anyone who wasn't an expert on androids would see nothing more than a handsome, dark-haired gentleman soldier. Oz nodded at him, then turned to Iruuk. "You should go catch up on the modifications to the Clever Dream."

Iruuk gave Theo a brief hug, then nodded. "Good idea," before dropping to all fours and rushing across the hangar at speed before effortlessly standing back up then loping into the ship.

"Everything go all right?" Alice asked Theodore. "How's my crew?"

"In perfect health. I can't tell you anything about the mission, I'm afraid, but Knud was the first to call it a 'milk run,' and he wasn't the last," Theodore replied. "It's good to be back. Lewis says 'hello.'"

Alice looked at the revolver style sidearm Theo was carrying and was relieved to see that it was loaded with non-lethal rounds. "I can't wait to get aboard."

"Sorry to delay the reunion," Oz said. "But Theo and I have to talk to you for a few minutes first," Oz said, directing her to a set of stairs that led to an observation booth with seats. When they closed the door behind them Alice sat down in the front row. Oz sat down across from her on a stool, and

Theodore leaned against the window, the Clever Dream in the background. "This morning a notice went out to all the commanders in the fleet. The topic of people with empathic abilities in the fleet and amongst our Lorander allies has been re-classified at level seven. That's Captains, higher ranks, and specific special operatives only. You and Iruuk didn't get it because your access to that level was restricted while you were on leave. Everyone who knows about us, fewer than a hundred people, have been spoken to about the secrecy that will surround our abilities. They will face a severe punishment if they reveal what they know to anyone, and since Nafalli have a few of their own empaths, they are going along with the changes."

"Why the secrecy?" Alice asked, aware that Iruuk seemed distant for the first couple days of their mandatory vacation. He seemed to get over it, but then, they hadn't talked about what he saw her go through while fighting the Geists since, either. Known empaths amongst the Lorander representatives that visited were sometimes treated with trepidation, too, but she wanted to hear Fleet's reasons for secrecy. It couldn't have simply been to make everyone feel more comfortable.

"One of the reasons why your advancement to Captain isn't chalked up to nepotism by the Admiralty is because of your past," Theodore said. "The last update in your file clearly states that you have recovered the memories of your travels, and from what the Fleet has been able to compile based on travel records and the Clever Dream's logs, you have seen ninety-one space stations, forty-two land-based ports, and an undeterminable number of cities. Your resting stress level is normally very low for someone who has met so many races, some of whom see humans as a viable food source and is aware of the strife humanity often faces abroad. Anyone who reads your file can see that you are calm under pressure and have a great deal of experience to draw on. Now that you've shown that you are an empath able to reach out telepathically, command is excited. While you were on Tamber relaxing, I've had to explain why training those abilities past your current passive empathic state would be foolish. I've been happy to be an advocate for you while Commodore McPatrick has championed the secrecy that will hide your abilities."

Alice put the frustration at not being a part of an argument about her future aside as well as she could and asked the most important question on her mind. "So, what was the decision? Am I going to be trained to spy on people's thoughts?"

"No," Oz said curtly. "You can train your empathic abilities as much as you like, and we've seen that you've gotten very good at closing those off while we watch from a distance, so you can just keep doing that too. The decision was made; Fleet would love to see you develop your empathic abilities by allowing yourself to sense how other people are feeling. They think it would be a great edge for you, and for your team, but they're leaving it all up to you."

"So it was a lot of conversation that came to the same conclusion we did a week ago. I don't turn my brain to jelly by picking fights with Geists and other telepaths, but I can leave my channels open if I want so I can pick up emo-waves from other people," Alice said with a sigh, leaning back in her seat.

"Emo-waves? Is that a new technical term for emotions I

haven't heard before?" Theo asked Oz, who shook his head, smirking a little. "Oh, never mind then."

"You're right, though," Oz said. "Our win here is that our status as empaths is need to know only, unless we want to exercise our right to disclose."

"Right, the same citizen right that androids have," Theodore said. "I can tell anyone I want that I'm an android, and you can tell anyone you want you're an empath, but whoever is told doesn't have the right to share that information."

"It's a good right to have, but I won't be sharing. I'm actually happy I can keep all the crap other people are feeling out of my head. The last thing I need are a bunch of people around who are paranoid about me finding out about how they really feel," Alice said. "But what do you want me to do, boss?" she asked Oz.

"Fleet has been recording your stress levels and Lorander has had several of their people bump into you on the ground to see how you're doing mentally. Nothing intrusive, they've just gotten a few people close enough for a few minutes so they can see how you're recovering."

"I noticed a few telepaths brushing up against the barrier in my brain," Alice said. "If they didn't move on so quickly, I would have made it an issue."

"They said you were really aware, most of them couldn't get within line-of-sight with you before you noticed them. It's a good sign. Now that our status is classified, and we've seen your quick recovery, everyone is going to leave you alone with regards to your mental care. I still think you need to de-stress and team build a bit, but I think you should practice your empathic abilities. Let your senses open a few times a day, get used to catching a few of those emo-waves," Oz said, obviously amused by the new term she made up. "Remember, no reaching out, you will definitely do damage if you push that, but practice your empathic abilities at least until you can tell who the emotions you're sensing are coming from. I'm almost at the point where I can do it without concentrating, and I only practice four or five times a day."

The advantage she had wasn't lost on Alice. If she could practice enough so a busy space wasn't mentally overwhelming, so she could instantly tell who was feeling what, then she could take the guess work out of numerous dangerous situations. "It fits," she said. "SOCU's work happens off ship, or at least it's supposed to. Will Quan or some other telepath be helping me out?"

"Not unless you want them to," Oz said. "Lorander is pulling all the people with extra mental abilities back. They disapprove of the secrecy and how we might use our abilities. To them, I'm their prime example of an untrustworthy empath. I use my abilities during negotiations while keeping it a secret as best as I can. When they look at you they see someone who had their abilities unlocked by force and immediately used them maliciously. They believe we'll face persecution and prejudice with the way we're going."

"I'm definitely going to use this to get the upper hand," Alice said. "Maybe Lorander thinks that's sneaky and underhanded, but I don't care. If me and my people are in a dangerous situation, I'm going to use every dirty trick I have."

"So, you'll practice using your empathic abilities?" Theodore asked.

"Yeah," Alice sighed. "I can't leave that advantage alone."

"Well, you'll have a reason to start using it right away," Oz said. "Of the people you and Gabe lost recently, we were able to bring one back. Yawen. She'll be joining you for the rest of your leave along with the rest of your crew. The Clever Dream will be ready in two hours, and you will move into it with them after it undergoes a thorough check. You and your crew are to stay together over the next three days, since the whole solar system is on heightened alert. Once those three days are up, you'll be assisting with system patrols unless we need you for other missions. Use the next three days to practice your abilities, relax, have some fun with your crew, get to know each other, and make the Clever Dream your home. The Fleet is putting a hold on upgrades for current generation ships, so the Clever Dream will be as-is for years unless you make modifications yourself."

"Good. The upgrades are nice, but I love that ship," Alice said. "I'd rather have things my way."

"Well, she's all yours for as long as you like. Fleet would love to buy her, even without Lewis, but I'm happy to see it back in your hands with all the upgrades we've been able to build in."

"When do I see Yawen?" Alice asked.

"She just finished her mental integrity scan and she's healthy," Theodore said. "No one has told her that she was brought back as part of the Resurrection Program, but I'm sure she knows. It would be good if you were the next face she saw."

"So, now," Alice said, standing up.

"Now," Theodore agreed.

"Why wasn't anyone else brought back?" Alice asked.

"Lack of resources, and they've found a problem with the program. Most of the people who they simulate final resurrections for have a very bad mental reaction. They can't handle the reality of their own deaths. Yawen and eight of your father's crew have been brought back successfully. The Resurrection Program is scoring a less than three percent success rate Fleet wide. That's classified level five," Oz said.

Alice let herself sense him and felt his relief. It was surprising, not pure, mixed with a disappointment, but he really was relieved. "Why are you relieved about this?"

Theo regarded him with mild surprise as Oz turned towards the Clever Dream and watched as several robots began putting the rear hull segments back into place. They were heavy load lifters; the aft section was thick and heavy. "There was this growing notion in lower ranks that they were disposable because we could grow them a new body and implant a brain scan onto them if the originals get killed. Some felt unimportant, others were starting to use this program as an excuse to be reckless, thinking that they'd just get remade and put back into service. It's stupidity. Once someone dies, they're dead, their journey is over. It doesn't matter to that person if a copy is made to continue on, they've already come to an end. If we don't get this problem solved, it'll be a blow to the fleet, but once news of these problems gets out our people will feel their importance again."

"What are the chances that this'll get solved?" Alice asked.

"It's not likely that they'll overcome it with our current technology," Theodore said.

"All right, but Yawen turned out right?" Alice asked.

"Perfectly in simulation, and she's reacting the same way now that she's on her feet in a new body. She is aware of how her original died. You'll have to catch her up on the rest. We're hoping that your empathy will help," Oz said. "So, your official orders are to go pick her up in the Resurrection Centre, return to the Clever Dream where your crew will be waiting, then to go have fun for three days within the boundaries of Haven Shore. That is, unless an alert goes out and you're all called on, then you're back on full duty. Stay close to your ship."

"Mission accepted," Alice said, saluting.

Oz returned the salute and smiled at her. "Enjoy your time off, I think it'll be the last for a while."

SIX

Patrol

THE URIEL TWO FIGHTERS let the gravity of the craggy third moon to the planet Carole draw them down into a slow arc. Their scanners were on their highest setting, taking data in from the rocky surface, using the craggy features below as a giant reflector to enhance the information they were taking in about the space around them.

The results scrolled across one part of Carnie's display as his tactical maps populated with more and more detail. Their thrusters and most of their other systems were off, the momentum they had would carry them past the moon and the planet much further below in minutes. Carnie looked up through his canopy and watched the stony surface of the moon sweep past. The distant light of the sun made exposed crystals shine, sending colour across the plains and painting valleys in a kaleidoscopic riot of hues. "Man, if fleet knew that extra scan and patrol duties were anything but a punishment, I think they would have put me on extra watches instead. Hey, do we know the story behind this planet's name?" Carnie said as he kept one eye on his trajectory and the other on the display of nature.

"The moon we're buzzing, or the planet?" Minh-Chu asked.

"Well, this moon is called Remnant Eighty-Four, so, yeah, I'm taking about Carole, the planet."

"No one knows the story behind that one's name, no," Minh-Chu replied. "They think the moon was dragged here because it was rich in water at one point. Too bad they never finished terraforming Carole, someone probably loved someone with that name a lot to name a goldilocks zone world after her, though. I like to think it was a father naming it for his daughter, though if I had the chance to name a planet after someone, it would be Ashley, but I hear there's already one a few light years away."

"A planet named Ashley?"

"Yup, I've been meaning to look it up. Wish we knew the real story about Carole, though."

"Yeah, the original terraforming engineers didn't leave a lot of records behind when they died out." Noah Lucas, known as Carnie to most people, loved old history, and the Haven System promised a lot without giving up many of its secrets. Carole came into view then, a large planet only one percent more massive than Earth, and he looked at its white clouds, the harsh, bright green and dark brown land masses, and light blue oceans. "It's like all of humanity has this ticking clock running. If we don't finish big projects like terraforming or building, or even recording history, something like a disease comes and wipes most of us out. Places like the Haven System go unfinished. We even fall back in our tech."

"I don't think that'll happen this time," Minh-Chu said. "Maybe enough of us survived to keep our advancement going and the stories alive. Why so interested in the big picture today?"

"Just making conversation, I guess," Carnie replied.

"You've been trying to get a look at that report on you again, haven't you?"

Carnie re-checked his trajectory and made his computer double check his calculations, just to make sure they'd sling-shot around the planet and escape its gravitational pull and was satisfied with the results. "Yeah. I can't believe they won't let me see what she wrote about those logs I recorded."

"You could meet up with Alice and ask her," Minh-Chu said. "I bet she'd tell you all about her report, it might actually be fun."

Carnie's status monitor told him what he already knew; his heart rate jumped at the mention of meeting Alice. He knew Minh-Chu could see that on his end too. "The timing hasn't been right, besides, fleet took the file over after she finished. I sat down with a Lieutenant for two hours to answer questions and fill in blanks so he could make some kinda supplementary report for her main report. Fleet is thorough, I'll give them that."

"We're just looking ahead, trying to learn about our surroundings, and you're the expert on that planet, so..."

"Yeah, I get it. Still, the report is about me, and the file has additional holographic data, so there might be a narration avatar."

"Of Alice," Minh-Chu added. Carnie could hear him grinning.

"You're clear to see it, Commander. You could show it to me."

"There's no information there pertaining to an upcoming mission, so it would be irresponsible."

"Wouldn't you enjoy hearing your story retold by someone? I mean, she studied all the stuff I recorded and made it into a presentation or something so people could hear her retell it in a couple hours."

"That's vanity, young man," Minh-Chu replied, pretending to scold him. "It's unhealthy to indulge in that for too long."

"There's just no convincing you," Carnie sighed. "Especially since you and Ash are conspiring to get Alice and me at the same table."

"Is it a conspiracy if everyone knows about it?"

Carnie watched as one of the polar towers far below became visible. There was one terraforming tower at the north and south poles of the planet, and they'd been dormant for at least a century according to previous scan data. Their sweep would provide much more information on the old technology, and he hoped they were ready to reactivate so they could finish terraforming Carole. There was something amazing about the idea that he could visit a world a few times during the process of terraforming, watch it become a vibrant, hospitable place. "You have a point. It's not going to work though," Carnie said.

From what he knew and the little he saw of her, he liked Alice. More than liked, she was a beautiful woman who was so independent and interesting that it was a little intimidating.

"What? You're saying you don't like her?" Minh-Chu asked, his voice heavy with disbelief.

"She seems great, but we're never meant to meet up. Chance is against us. I'm on extended patrol duty, assigned to the Merciless, and she's on extended leave, not allowed to get away from Haven Shore."

"Oh, so you've been following her Crewcast profile," Minh-Chu said.

"I'm part of her circle because Theo is on her crew," he said. "Anyway; I have leave coming up, but it's two days and I don't exactly have a ton of luxury credits since my punishment came with a suspension of pay."

"I can loan you whatever," Minh-Chu said. "Just keep it quiet, because I don't want the whole wing using me as their bank."

"Okay, sure. So I could go down to Haven Shore and hang out, but there's one thing overshadowing all that other stuff. She's practically royalty,"

"Don't let that stop you," Minh-Chu chuckled. "If you call her princess, she'll probably break your nose."

"Fine, but she's a Captain in Special Operations, has all this experience in the galaxy - so I have heard - and her father is Captain Valent. One of the scariest bad asses I've ever heard of. You know; former bounty hunter, survived a live rebuild of his whole body, came out even better on the other side, and commander of the flagship, which happens to be called The Merciless. Oh, and her mother, an Admiral and Queen,"

"Again, don't call Ayan Queen or you might get a shoulder so cold that you'd have to step out of the nearest airlock to warm up," Minh-Chu warned.

"Fine, but she's an Admiral and one of the hardest working people in the fleet. I mean, she seems nice, but what would dinner with that family look like if I were the first guy to date their daughter?"

"You're forgetting Alice's grandmother: Admiral Rice is one of the best tacticians Freeground has ever known, and her grandfather, the Defence Minister. Yeah, that would be an interesting dinner party," Minh-Chu said. "I need to be there if it ever happens."

"You get it though, right? That's crazy intimidating, I'm this nobody guy. Even my callsign marks me as this fringe wanderer, Carnie."

"She's probably one of the only people who can appreciate how much that callsign means to you," Minh-Chu said more seriously.

There was a lot of meaning behind it. He was given the name because of the stories he used to tell about his life with the people who adopted him after his biological parents abandoned him. It was a tribute to the travelling carnival family he lost, as far has he was concerned. "Yeah, but you get what I'm saying, though, right? Who am I to even sit at the same table as someone like Alice."

"You're thinking too far ahead. For all you know, you and her sit down and once the nervousness shakes off, you're just friends. Maybe she's as excited to meet you?

Have you thanked her for getting Theo back up and running?"

"No, I recorded a message, just never sent it. I sleep, eat, work out, study, and fly patrols."

"You owe her that much, Theo is amazing, and a good friend to you. If it wasn't for her, I don't know if he'd be around right now."

"He'd still be in a storage locker. I'd still be saving up and trying to find someone to clear his infection then recondition him," Carnie said. "Yeah, I already owe her. Maybe when I get back..." a bloom of energy appeared on his tactical scanner. "You see that? A wormhole emergence about eighty-seven million klicks behind the dark side of Carole."

"I see it," Minh-Chu said. "Streaming sensor data to the Merciless."

More information began coming through, and he read it aloud even though he knew Minh-Chu could see the same data while he performed a quick check of his systems. "It's a Pegasus Transport Company Starliner, number seven-four-nine."

"Confirmed," Minh-Chu said. "Ninety-one life signs aboard, reading in stasis, but..."

"Is that stasis?" Carnie asked, looking at the readings his sensors were getting from the passengers as the starliner emerged from the wormhole. "It's more like they're in a deep sleep," he said.

"Automated flight systems are in charge over there," Minh-Chu said. "We can say for sure no one's awake, anyway."

"Ronin, Carnie," Agameg Price said over the communicator. "Approach and perform a focused scan with caution. We see your scans and can confirm: the people aboard that craft are not in a type of stasis that we've seen before. They are in a deep sleep, probably drug induced, and immobilized in their seats by some kind of organic compound. Your scanners are failing to penetrate the cargo section in the lower half of that craft, so there could be anything in there. Perform a single pass, then get clear. We're trying to open communications and connect with their helm from here."

"Will do, Commander," Minh-Chu said, taking the lead in his fighter. It was still the same Uriel Fighter body, but all the technology inside was upgraded, and it felt amazing to fly, especially since it tracked neural commands.

Carnie activated all his systems and kept up with his Wing Commander as he changed course to intercept with the standard commercial starliner. The tactical readout on it showed several patched holes in the main fuselage. One of the engines at the rear had been removed and replaced with one from another, similar ship. He could hear Liara's voice repeating on their Navnet channel; "This is the Haven Fleet Merciless to Pegasus Transport Company Starliner, number seven-four-nine. We are sending patrol craft to intercept you. Please acknowledge so we can link with your helm and direct you to the nearest port."

The message repeated in the background of his audio feed, but he could tell from the data his scanners took in that no one on that ship was waking up. "This doesn't feel right," he said as much to himself as to Minh-Chu.

"My gut agrees," he replied as they drew closer to the star-liner. "There's no antimatter aboard, but the damage is definitely from combat. We're at ten thousand klicks, starting my focused scan."

Carnie did the same and watched as his computer started building a history of the ship based on the type of damage it sustained, the repairs made, the amount of fuel it had left, it's trajectory and a few other finer factors that he didn't take time to think about as he watched his tactical displays. "No one's waking up," he muttered. "Maybe these guys over jumped? Put themselves to sleep because their interstellar travel time would be longer than their life support could keep them going if they were up and walking around?"

"That's as good a guess as any," Minh-Chu said. "Merciless, this is Ronin. It might be time to call a rescue team in on this. I'm not picking up any contaminants, antimatter or wea..."

"Ronin, Carnie," Agameg addressed from the Merciless Operations centre. "We've analysed your scan data. The damage on that ship was made by Edxi weaponry. Monitor the ship from a safe distance. Destroy it if it tries to enter Carole's atmosphere."

"Are you on your way?" Minh-Chu asked as he led Carnie into an arc that would keep them over five thousand kilometres away on a parallel course.

"One moment, Ronin," came the response.

"You know, I was hoping I'd never have to hear about those bugs again," Carnie said as his fighter settled in a couple kilometres behind Minh-Chu's. His scanners alerted him to something new. "I see a new heat source inside the starliner's cargo section."

"Weapons' fire from within," Minh-Chu said. "That's a Trojan horse."

The sides of the lower half of the starliner burst open and Carnie's scanners picked up thirty-three ships. "New contacts, Merciless. Thirty-three ships, armed, my tactical computer has no idea what they are other than some kind of Edxi based tech."

"We have been fired upon," Minh-Chu said as bright, long projectiles were shot in their general direction. "Aggressive retreat," he said.

Carnie turned all his rotary thruster pods to fire backwards and brought them up to full power while he returned fire at the nearest Edxi ship. He wasn't getting away fast enough, and there were too many of them. "We could use a hand here," he said, locking on to the nearest ship and rapid-firing explosive rounds at it. The ship came apart with a surprisingly bright explosion and his antimatter alarm beeped for less than a second. "These fighters are running on antimatter," he said as he lined up the second ship and opened fire. It jinked quickly, firing back, hitting Carnie's fighter on the nose with one of several rounds.

His shields read a twenty-eight percent loss from the single hit, and he redoubled his efforts, using his neural link to select five ships for missile locks while he fired at the nearest. Ronin was up to three kills, and his missile system was selecting four targets.

Carnie did some quick math in his head and decided that overkill was the way to go, rapid-firing three missiles at each of his targets instead of just one. His mini-turret began firing pulses as another enemy fighter came in range, and he transferred as much energy as he could to recharging his forward shields. "This swarm is about to overtake us," he said as two of his targets were struck by missiles. One exploded in a cloud of shrapnel, the other was sent spinning towards the planet below.

"The Merciless will be here in a sec," Ronin said.

"Negative," said Captain Jacob Valent's voice over their communicators. "We are under attack. We will send support as soon as we can."

Another direct hit knocked Carnie off course, and he adjusted, watching his shields start recovering from forty-seven percent. On a whim, he looked to his social communication icon, then made the gesture that would send his recorded message to Alice - a wink - and returned his full attention back to the crisis at hand. One of his salvos struck an enemy fighter, and it came apart with two quick flashes as he focused on targeting the next batch. Fifteen missiles managed to take out two fighters, knock one out of engagement range, and miss two entirely. "I'll have to do better than this if I want to make that dinner date," he grumbled as he fired at another fighter with his main guns.

He could hear Ronin start laughing on the other end then abruptly stop. "Two more wormhole emergence points. Focus and keep your shields charged, Carnie."

SEVEN

A Complex Resurrection

THERE WAS an additional wait time added to Yawen's release as Alice started to make her way to the Biological Research Department aboard the War Forge. She decided to finish the journey there on foot instead of taking the rapid transit system. For long minutes, her footsteps and the sound of her breath were the only sounds in the halls. The lighting was low, set to minimum safe levels and it would probably go out shortly after she passed. Dark grey decks, black and blue bulkheads began to blend together and she started to feel the reality of how short-handed fleet was compared to the facilities they completed.

The raw math of it didn't make sense to her. More Nafalli were arriving in system all the time, many of them were aboard older warships, heeding the call of tribes that sent news out any way they could that there could be a new home for everyone in the Haven System. Their numbers were about to swell to two million, and she knew first-hand how quickly they could train aboard Haven's warships.

There were Mergillians who were coming from some of their oldest cities in the neighbouring star system. Their Issyrian allies showed them what the Order of Eden did when they decided to take territory. Intelligent aquatic people were always the first to be suppressed then eliminated. They had ships with thousands of people living on them, all warrior volunteers, and Alice wondered if they were anything like Ute Shulikeet, the new pilot aboard her ship. She was the best navigator and pilot she'd ever seen but she didn't have a chip on her shoulder. In fact, the little Mergillian had a brilliant explorer's spirit, and was a pleasure to have aboard.

The young woman's strategic skills were worth recognizing too, to the point that Alice trusted her to make split-second decisions on her own. That brought her thoughts back to her time at the Academy. Her head felt clearer then, with fewer memories to cloud things and less experience to draw on. She filled her hours and her mind with the knowledge the Fleet wanted her to take on. Remembering that dedication, the drive to be a high achiever brought back how she felt in general then. She felt younger, so new and unburdened even though she was trying so hard to be the best officer candidate she could be. The need to accomplish great things changed since then, but it didn't fade completely.

That girl might not have survived long in the war without the experience that was returned to Alice. It wasn't time for bright optimism or blind obedience. The fleet needed every crew to count as five times their number, and that meant every captain had to be that much better. They had to think ahead further, adjust to changing situations faster, and that took intelligence and experience. She was happy to have her memories back, but as she remembered her time working her way through the Academy curriculum, especially the time spent with Yawen in their shared quarters, she didn't want to let go of that youthful, brightly ambitious feeling. Maybe they could lean into that while they tried to enjoy their last three days of leave.

Her comm unit made her aware that there was an incoming call and she answered it using the nerve path that sent her the notification from her left bracer to her brain. "What's up, Fur-Face?" she asked the semi-transparent image of Iruuk as it appeared in front of her. She kept walking down the hallway, it was empty like the two lengths she'd walked previously.

"They finished installing the rapid-fire magnetically assisted hundred forty-millimetre cannon turret on the Clever Dream. I didn't know we were getting one!"

She grinned back at him, his excitement was contagious. "I requested it before the Clever Dream came back, but I didn't think they licked the problems with the turret version. How much space does that take?"

"We're only losing a couple square meters on the lower deck, I think it'll be worth it. The Clever Dream is pushing into the next power class with the new quad drives and that triple turret, Lewis is very happy. He doesn't quite under-stand why I'm so excited, though. He thinks I'm just the science officer aboard."

"That's your main role," Alice nodded.

"Well, yeah, but I was hoping I could go on more missions," he said. Knud and Jessen, two of the tallest humans Alice knew, appeared in the hologram behind him, sneaking up with big grins.

"You will. This squad is still new, so be patient. I'll need you as much as anyone else on our missions off-ship, you'll see." Alice decided to play along and keep Iruuk's attention so Knud and Jessen could get close enough to surprise him from behind. It was good seeing that they were back from their mission with Gabe. "Has anyone from the team come to the Clever Dream yet?"

"Woone, Faloo, Krooke, and Noro just got back. They're stowing their gear. They asked how much time we were getting off and were pretty happy when I told them we were off for three days. Gabe is taking his new ship down to the south most beach on Haven Shore, and he's invited us so they're assuming..." Knud and Jessen jumped him from behind, surprising him with an affectionate bit of scratching and grappling once he was tackled down to the deck. Callum doubled over with laughter, watching Iruuk's reaction turn from startled to joyful as he embraced Knud and Jessen under each arm, trying to pin them.

Another message came in. She was surprised to learn it was from Noah Lucas. "Hey, guys, good to see you back. I'll see you after I pick up Yawen, then we'll link up with Gabe and his people." She switched over to Carnie's message.

He was in his bunk, his bomber jacket folded under his head, in his vacsuit uniform. His head and shoulders loomed large. "I found out you kinda wrote the book on me a little while ago, and I didn't really know what to think about that, so I guess that's why it took me a while to record... Gah, that sounds..." he dragged his hand down over his face in aggravation. "...All right, this is take nine or ten for this message, so I'm just gonna push through this time. Yeah, so there's this huge report you made about me from all the stuff I recorded from my crash on Iora. I talked to Minh, since I couldn't get into the report and he looked at it, told me you did great work and I came up looking pretty good. He thinks Iora could be a strategic hot point because of all the information I got while I was there, and some higher-ups know who I am because you put the work in, so I guess that's where I start saying 'thank you.' I sat down with Theodore before I moved to the Merciless, and he told me you and a Nafalli named Iruuk got him out of storage, cleaned the virus out and got him fixed. Maybe you know how important that guy is to me, maybe you don't, so let me tell you that I can't thank you enough for getting him on his feet and setting him up with a job he's proud of. I know he likes you, and it goes past him being grateful for everything you did for him, so, uh, you must be pretty amazing..." Noah trailed off for a moment, and Alice watched him look to his left. Most of the youthful round edges he had from his recording as an older teenager were gone, replaced with more chiselled features. He'd become more well-muscled as well, with the shoulders of someone who used suit resistance training - slim but toned.

"Message home?" asked a high, female voice in the background.

"Classified," Noah said with a teasing smirk.

"Oh, I'll see you in the Crew Den," she replied.

"Not tonight, sorry. Swim, then a few hours in my rack, then I'm back out on patrol."

"Oh, see you tomorrow, then," the female voice replied with a hint of disappointment.

Noah waited for her to leave then looked back into the recorder, giving Alice the feeling that he was looking right at her. He smiled a little before continuing. "Life in the racks; you're never really alone, but Sticky's good people, most of the wing is easy to live with, so I'm pretty lucky," he said quietly. "Right, I guess this message has gone on long, but I appreciate everything you've done for Theo. At first, I was pissed that you went through my storage locker, but the inventory shows that you weren't exactly pilfering, everything you and fleet didn't need is still there, and I know what you did for my best buddy, so it's all good. Thank you again, Captain, I'll probably meet you next time I get the chance because Theo seems dead set on making that happen, so if there's anything an Ensign like me can do for you, say the word."

His image faded out and Alice caught herself grinning. "Save to personal storage," she told her comm system. The thought of meeting Noah in person made her equally eager and nervous. She tried not to think about him too much so she could avoid becoming infatuated, but she checked on his location and status daily through Crewcast, resisting the urge to use her rank to find out a lot more about what he was up to. Seeing how he looked only three days before, when the message was recorded, and recognizing how much he'd changed since he was that skinny guy who escaped Iora added fuel to the torch she was carrying for him.

She liked him as he was but seeing the difference some

time and life with the Fleet made for him, how well it transformed him only made her like him more. "Nine or ten takes?" she asked under her breath. Maybe he was as nervous about meeting as she was? Ashley had already tried to get them in the same place at the same time, making sure that Alice knew there would be a party in the main food concourse in Haven Shore after the return of the Revenge. Ashley wasn't satisfied until Alice promised to be there, but the event was cancelled hours before it was about to kick off because a large portion of the crew were ordered to transfer to the Merciless instead. Mama Buu wasn't the only one disappointed by that change of plans.

Alice took a turn down another broad corridor and realized that she was in the Biological Research Department. Their halls were coloured white and blue, and there was a guarded checkpoint a few metres in. It was controlled remotely by a guard who was probably watching all the entrances. "Captain, we've been expecting you," a voice said as the thick security doors parted. "Follow the flashing green line on the deck."

"Is Sergeant Yawen Blake cleared to join her crew?" Alice asked as she started walking down the hall. A door to her right was opening.

"Oh, she's been clear but we had to lock the ward down for search. Completely unrelated."

"Did you find..." Alice was interrupted as a tall, grim faced man ran from the open door to her right, then past her, barely making it through the security doors.

"Stop him!" two nurses shouted as they rushed into the hall.

Alice turned and manually opened the doors, running after the tall man in a black and gold command uniform. She caught sight of him right away, already over twenty metres ahead of her and turning down a hall to his right. She was just ahead of the taller nurses as she pushed herself to run as fast as she could. "What's going on?" she asked.

"High suicide risk, he can't leave this section!" One of the nurses said as he struggled to keep up.

"He got his security privileges somehow, while we weren't looking!" said another that was close behind.

They came to the next corner in time to see the officer closing the inner airlock door behind himself. He was half out of his uniform. "Rear Admiral Gillen, you don't want to do this!"

Alice's hand was punching her override code into the controls as she arrived, colliding with the door. One of the nurses was already calling a rescue ship, while the other was trying to talk to him as he attempted to stiffen the Rear Admiral's suit so he would be trapped in it. "You shouldn't have brought me back," Gillen said mournfully. "Not to this, not with what I remember."

"Just take a minute, Rear Admiral," Alice said through the transparent metal door. Time seemed to halt as he looked her in the eye.

He wasn't afraid, the frenzy seemed to drain out of him, but he looked deeply sad. "Young Captain Valent," he breathed, the speaker in the controls picking his voice up and carrying it through.

"Security can't get the door open, he did something to the controls," one of the nurses told the other.

"You want to make a difference?" the Rear Admiral asked, pushing his suit the rest of the way off and moving to the outer door controls. "Tell your mother, your father to gather everyone who will listen and run. This is a fool's Haven." He punched a sequence into the outer door controls, shaking his head.

"Just take a breath, I want to hear what you have to say. What did you see?" Alice asked. "Don't do anything you can't take back!"

"Ask about Baila," he said, looking over his shoulder. "Goodbye." Rear Admiral Gillen slapped the emergency purge icon on the controls and the outer airlock doors opened suddenly, sending him and all the air inside the airlock into space in a rush.

The emergency ship was nowhere in sight, and the nurses were silent for a long moment before one said; "One in fifteen."

"Shut up, Rico," the other whispered harshly.

"One in fifteen, what?" Alice asked, turning towards them.

The pair were silent, worried.

"Speak up!" Alice barked as harshly. There were more people coming, for all the good they'd do. The seconds ticked by, and she wished she had her rifle. She could have blasted through the airlock doors and gone after him. The sidearm wouldn't do the job at all, not on the War Forge's armour.

"The Resurrection Program is failing. We've tried to bring forty-five good candidates back so far and only three have made it through all the testing. That's not the first suicide."

"That's classified," a doctor that didn't come up on Alice's comm unit said as he came around the corner. "You're getting reassigned, Rico. That's if you keep your mouth shut from now on. Go check in at security and surrender your kit."

"Yes, Doctor," Rico said after a moment's shock.

The tall, dark haired Doctor looked at Alice, his scowl not lifting. "Come with me, Captain. Yawen's looking forward to seeing you."

"Is it true? Three in forty-five have been successful?" Alice asked.

"Normally I wouldn't say a damned thing, but I know who your parents are, who your grandfather is." He replied quietly, leading her back the way they came. "That's not quite as grisly as it sounds. We've gone all the way through the simulated resurrection of hundreds of people, brought only a small portion of those, so tragedies like this aren't as common as they could have been. The Rear Admiral was borderline, we knew it, but Fleet wanted his experience, so they pushed his reproduction through. Everything was going fine, he even made it through the suicide risk check, got his privileges. He's been with us for four days and we thought he was suffering a little depression."

"It takes more than a little depression to push someone to that point," Alice said. "He planned that in advance."

"I know, he's not the only suicide we've had, either. What Nurse Danven was saying, about the average of one in fifteen is right. Everyone we tried to bring back with Yawen's group failed to pass pre-waking testing. That's a series of simulations we run on the brain of each completed resurrection before they wake up for the first time, and all but one of them were resistant to coming back. Acute clone shock caused multiple organ failures, or psychological problems like prosopagnosia - the inability for them to recognize their own and other familiar faces - and deep depressions have made finished resurrections unviable. Yawen came through with flying colours, and we don't know why."

"So, you're going to study her," Alice said, remembering how the technology that gave her a final rebirth was researched.

"We did. We have everything we need from her, the next phase is to put her into the wild, to be herself and see what happens. I predict that she'll do well, but there will be some change. She's already embraced a seize the day mentality that's come with its own kind of amazing drive. It's like the process brought her back with a new kind of vitality. We'll watch from a distance, but there's no trace of the problems the other candidates had, so we're optimistic."

"You're hoping to duplicate whatever you found in her," Alice said.

"Impossible. Well, that wouldn't be completely impossible, but the Resurrection Program isn't about duplicating one soldier. It's about giving our people another chance and maintaining a professional fleet. We hope the simulations we run based on her and the other two that came through as successfully here lead to a breakthrough so we can develop a new process."

They passed through the security checkpoint and Alice allowed the Doctor to lead her down the hallway, where the green line still flashed for her. "What happens to the people you can't wake up?"

"They are put into deep stasis. We hope to make adjustments and bring them back successfully at a later date."

"Moving the program forward at any cost," Alice said.

"I think you've misunderstood my role here, Captain," the Doctor said quietly as they came to a blue door. They stopped and faced each other. His scowl faded, and he spoke to her earnestly in hushed tones. "I've been put in charge so I can shut down all primary operations for the Resurrection Program. We're not producing anything more until we can show greater success. The other two successful candidates are already back in place in the fleet, doing well. Yawen will be the last, most likely for months, maybe years. Everything's been moved to the Biological Research section of the station because that's all it is now. This week I'm a curator, taking care of my predecessor's failures, making sure they're all safely in storage. Next week we start researching using simulations only."

"I'm sorry, I didn't realize you were leading the damage control team here, good luck," Alice said, shaking his hand. "Tell me if you need a scan or something, I've been through a few resurrections."

"We have what we need," he replied. "A lot of this research was based on you." He looked to the blue door and smiled a little. "Take care of Yawen, we're all proud of her. We all like her here."

"I will," Alice said, watching the Doctor walk down the hall for a moment before turning towards the door and opening it.

Yawen was in her black uniform, the red stripe indicating that she was a member of the Special Operations Combat

Unit was prominent running down her sides. She shut the holographic news report about Haven Shore and the Triumvirate meeting with Nafalli leadership as soon as she saw Alice. Her blonde hair was tightly curled, cut jaw length but still wild-looking, and the sudden joy that overtook her was so visible that it was contagious.

With a squeal and a huge grin, she ran-leapt across her temporary quarters and collided with Alice, kissing her then embracing her tightly. "Now I'm really back. Now that you're here it feels real," she said.

Alice realized that she'd been avoiding thinking about Yawen until she got word that it was time to pick her up. She knew the Yawen she was roommates with, had come to enjoy and trust was dead. Her sacrifice was real, even though everyone acted like she was just away for a while because they knew the Resurrection Program was remaking her, but Alice was painfully aware that the first Yawen was truly gone. The grief she felt for that was never more real than in that moment.

At the same time, she was overjoyed to have her back. It wasn't like Yawen had returned, Alice knew better. It was like she was getting another chance to be with, and to appreciate her friend. A friend that reminded her of a more optimistic time, when she was so focused on ambition that she almost missed her chance to get to know Yawen the first time around. That was, almost. Alice squeezed Yawen to her and buried her face in her friend's curls, hiding her tears. "It's all real, and I'm so glad you're here."

EIGHT

Cave Fighting

THINKING IN ALL DIRECTIONS. That was the term used in the new fighter pilot training offered by the Academy. It referred to an advanced style of flying, where the pilot's three-dimensional awareness was solid, their awareness was heightened, and they were so familiar with their systems and displays that they could take incredible amounts of information in rapidly. That wasn't all, though. The pilot's reaction times would peak as they moved their ship around obstacles while leading it into the best evasive course, adapting and controlling their rig using neural and physical controls without hesitation. Adding the last step in the exercise is what undid most pilots. Firing back while maintaining all those other activities was usually enough to tax their concentration enough so failure was common.

The moon, Remnant Eighty-Four, in orbit around Carole, had become the refuge for Noah Lucas and Minh-Chu. It could be their salvation, the cover gave their shields time to recharge and provided the conditions they needed to turn things around on their attackers. It was also the cause for them getting split up, something that could be their undoing as much as finding no cover at all.

The nose of Noah's fighter was pointed at the nine fighters that followed him into a cavern system that he and his navigational computer agreed was extensive and large enough to give him the cover he needed. The thrusters swivelled and pulsed as he tightly controlled his ship's direction and speed, ducking behind walls of stone, turning down tunnels as his fighter flew backwards.

Backwards. To him that word had come to mean nothing. It was common amongst space-faring fighter pilots who had spent as much time as he did in the cockpit - real time and simulation - words like up, down, forward, backwards, didn't matter anymore. Through the neural interface he could see what was coming up behind his fighter as clearly as he could see what was in front of it, and after countless hours of practice, he could adapt to flying his ship in any direction, so direction was strictly relative. Minh-Chu devised the new training style. Some said that it was inspired after he saw Hot Chow fly an entire combat encounter backwards and become an ace in only a few minutes. The man had the best three-dimensional thinking in the fleet, and Minh-Chu had all his pilots start training in the same advanced simulations the Fleet Academy was using, only they weren't allowed to fly nose first. It was hilarious at first, then a challenge to surmount, and finally a point of pride when the entire Samurai Wing managed to complete the whole set of courses backwards, then flying dorsal side first, making the training regimen the Academy was offering look too basic once the scores were submitted.

Noah was so annoyed at the whole exercise at first that he had to get away from the simulations for a couple days before calming down and trying again. As he rapidly made his way through the cavern system, picking his moments to fire at the enemy fighters who pursued him carefully, he was glad he stuck with it. His fighter felt like an extension of his body. He didn't know what happened to Minh-Chu, only that he ducked into a canyon, luring several of the larger enemy fighters down with him once he broke their line of sight. That was followed by an explosion that brought down millions of tons of stone on top of the enemy, but Noah didn't have time to stick around and see what happened to his Wing Commander.

It was unusual to intentionally separate from your wing-man, but Minh-Chu knew he had a chance at taking out several of the heavy fighters that were causing huge trouble for them. The larger Edxi attackers were firing some kind of heavy plasma round that were short range, but two of them in succession could take out their shields. They also had greater acceleration and some kind of grabber arms underneath. When all but one of them broke off to pursue Minh-Chu, he told Carnie to head down another tunnel while he drew them off.

That's what led Noah to the caves, and as soon as he entered the dark, extensive system, it was as if Noah Lucas, the young man with friends, concerns about the Haven System, a desire to return to the main entertainment concourse in Haven Shore, and memories of friends, loved ones was gone. He was completely replaced by Carnie. A pilot who had already earned his Ace Star and was on his way to an Ace Cluster. Carnie could put all those personal details aside and be one with his fighter, concentrate sharply, react quickly, and get his enemy into his crosshairs long enough to rip their hulls apart with his guns.

He emerged from one part of the cave system into a large cavern, locked his missile system onto two of the V shaped enemy fighters, lined his guns up with another and let loose at close range. The encounter was less than three seconds long, but in that time he saw the navigational warning that told him that the cavern would collapse behind him if he made the shot, fired a missile at each of the fighters he locked on to, and retreated down another cave entrance while his guns drew a broken white line of fire between him and the last large fighter following him. The rest were smaller, more agile but weaker ships.

He managed to hit the heavy fighter several times, breaking its shields down and sending three rounds through the port side fuselage. An alert appeared on his scanner that read; BIO MATTER ANALYSIS REQUESTED. "Don't have time for biology, sorry," he muttered as he guided his ship into a narrower tunnel. The cavern collapsed behind him as his missiles went off. He knew they hit their targets, and those smaller fighters didn't survive direct missile hits, but he hoped that the collapsing cavern trapped or destroyed more. Seven fighters against one was better than nine, but he hoped he could get that number down to five, or maybe two.

As he made his way through the cavern system, his shields reporting a graze as he squeezed through a choke point, his tactical scanner showed the heavy fighter with two light fighters ahead and three behind. "Dammit," he breathed. He'd been flying through the cave system for several minutes and knew that there were more fighters in low orbit around the moon, he couldn't surface. The enemy fighters in the caves with him were speeding up, they'd catch him if he didn't go faster. He could see where it would happen, too: there was a straight length of cavern coming up. If he wanted to stay out of their direct line of fire, he'd have to accelerate so hard that making the turn at the end would be impossible, he would smash into the rocky face and lose control, possibly destroy his ship if his shields were too damaged.

He thought quickly, running options through his mind, and shuddered as he got an idea that might work, or it could get him killed. "All right, you want to get close? Here we go." He made the jagged turns that took him into the long, straight length of cave then dropped one of his four micro-missile pods while he shunted all available power to shields. His thrusters would only have the power that was already in the pods, a few seconds of thrust at full, but he hoped he didn't need more as he reduced power and let his ship drift back-wards, his nose pointed at the armed missile pods. There were eighteen small missiles left in there, enough for five or six difficult firefights with Order of Eden fighters.

He watched the enemy fighters move through the cave system towards him on his tactical display. They were quick, agile, and he spotted something unusual. One of them extended four thin appendages from the underside of the rear half of the fuselage, climbing along a rock wall at a run before retracting the legs, or arms, or whatever they were then thrusting into the open.

Carnie refused to let it distract him, focusing on the arming and detonation keys in his neural interface while his left hand rested on the throttle, his right hand and feet on the controls. "Come on in," he said to himself as he watched the enemy fighters start rounding the corner. They were almost through, at the far end of the long straight length of cave.

The heavy fighter stopped, moved to one side of the cavern to let the smaller fighters pass, then turned around and started accelerating back the way it came. Carnie was frustrated. That was the one he wanted to blast the most. The lighter fighters surged through the far end of the tunnel, firing a wave of rounds that started taxing Carnie's shields right away. They were needle-like rounds with kinetic explosives loaded inside, and they could fire dozens in seconds.

They ignored the missile pod, and Carnie detonated it, blasting the walls of the cavern, the enemy fighters, and he thrust towards the opposite end as quickly as he dared, making the turn towards the moon surface just in time. His shields grazed the cavern wall, but he didn't lose control of his fighter. He was headed towards the shallower caves, where he might be able to scan the skies above the moon surface to see if he could come out. Letting the heavy fighter go stung, but there was no easy way back to it. It would be in the labyrinth of caves below, trying to find a new way out between a few collapses that Carnie caused while he was trying to shake and kill the other fighters.

"...got that one, now it's your turn to take out the one on me," Carnie heard through his communicator. It was Flex, one of the fighter pilots in Samurai Squadron.

"I've got you covered, stay evasive for just one more second," Sticky said.

"Carnie here, how is it going up there?" he asked, watching his tactical scanner populate. A glance at the new data on his tactical display showed him that there were fourteen small Edxi fighters in a full-on dogfight with Ronin, Sticky, and Flex, and his allies were in good shape.

"Was all that seismic noise you, Carnie?" Flex asked, chuckling.

"Guilty as charged. Coming up to help you clean up," he said, finding a short path of caves that would take him out to the surface.

"We could use a hand, I'm not gonna lie," Sticky said as the tactical scanner reported that she took one enemy fighter out with guns and another with a missile lock. "I make it look easy, but the numbers are not good."

"Ah, you've got this," Carnie said as he started accelerating towards the next cavern that would take him closer to the surface. An alert sounded in his helmet, flashed on his tactical display, and one wall of the gallery shaped cave ahead burst open. Carnie focused his guns on it, dumb-fired a pair of missiles and tried to thrust past.

The missiles went off against larger chunks of rock, sending red hot gravel in all directions. His gunfire briefly raked the front of the heavy fighter, and his momentum took him past the enemy. "Holy shit! It tunnelled!" he shouted as his fighter collided with a dense chunk of stone. His shields and one port side thruster took most of the damage, but he was in a bad position. No shields, lessened manoeuvrability, close quarters, and the heavy fighter was slipping in behind him, right into the kill position.

Carnie burned his thrusters hard, pushing towards the cave ahead while he tried to correct course. He barely made it, one edge of the narrowing cave screeching against his dorsal hull plating. The heavy fighter was only metres behind him. He could feel rounds impacting on the nose of his fighter as he exchanged cannon fire with it. The enemy didn't have shields.

It had a face made of metal and organic armour. A grimacing insect with glowing blue-green and red eyes, a dozen of them or more that stared at him as rounds spit forth from either side of its head. The explosive rounds that struck it blasted pieces of armour from its main body, a few failed to damage the thing's face. "This fighter's alive," Carnie said.

There was another gallery coming up, and Carnie saw that his forward shields were down, the emitters damaged, so he flipped his fighter around so the rear, partially charged shields were facing his attacker. It raked Carnie's fighter with a barrage of small rounds, and there wasn't anything he could do about it in such close quarters. He manually targeted a thin part of the large cavern opening ahead and launched a string of missiles, punching a hole through to the surface. "I'm going to squash this thing like a bug. Get the rescue team ready."

Watching the exit approach quickly, his rear shields begin

to fail, and doing calculations in his head, he armed all the missiles in his remaining pods, set an automated ejection sequence, turned the shielding and dampening systems on his pilot suit up all the way, finished programming a sequence of commands into his ship, then executed them.

His fighter flipped so the canopy faced the upcoming large cavern and the opening in the top, then ejected him. His seat thruster blasted at full intensity. He watched his tactical screen as the heavy Edxi fighter collided with the rear of his ship as it stopped at the mouth of the cavern. The missile pods detonated, and Carnie saw a wave of stone coming up towards him thanks to the powerful blast.

NINE

Wasps

THE BRIDGE of the Merciless was one of Commodore Jacob Valent's favourite places, bar none. In schematics it was efficient, a broad oval that served as a well-protected hub for all commands aboard. In images it was classically designed with black panels and rounded edges that reflected like chrome, the seats and stations spaced out just right so everyone could work in comfort while they stood during standard operation or sat during alerts.

The technology used in its design utilized lighting, air circulation and sound buffering fields to make sure everyone could perform at their peak. Interfaces were intelligent, learning from the operators and adjusting to the needs of the moment using non-invasive neural tracking along with traditional inputs and holographic displays.

Lessons learned in design from Lorander, Earth, Issyrian, countless corporations, other races and Ayan's team were incorporated into the entire ship, balancing efficiency with the creation of enjoyable spaces. The oval bridge used subdued lighting overall, adjusting illumination for each station depending on the demands of the user. Jake's space, the circular platform where his command seat was placed, was dimmed the most so he could concentrate on looking at his crew and what they were doing. The holographic display around him faded whenever he looked past it at someone like Finn who was manning the Engineering station, or Kadri, who was running the Scanning and Sciences section of his ship. Every department had their own leader and a console on the bridge around the captain or his first in command. The rest of their staff were at stations behind them, where they were close enough to communicate quickly and clearly with their Commander or Chief, but sound baffled enough so the Captain wasn't overwhelmed by standard chatter.

Jake looked to his command interface, a ring of holographic status windows around him, and was glad to see a report from Flight, which was run by Lieutenant Commander Looph - a Nafalli with almost silver fur - that Sticky had been able to retrieve Carnie. His suit put him into stasis after detecting a medical emergency. "I'm going to direct Sticky to deliver Carnie to Haven Shore Medical," she said.

"Good call, I have a feeling that ship is going to engage us at too close a range for us to safely let them into a retrieval bay," Jake said, turning his attention to the fighters that were responsible for keeping targets at a distance from the Merciless. They were slowly losing ground. A group of five fighters led by Fury were doing their best to fend off a swarm of the smaller, less deadly enemy fighters. "Any chance we can get a vulnerability analysis on these bugs, Lieutenant Commander?" Jake asked Kadri, who was directing her team of four science specialists through their analysis of scan data. She'd told them a lot so far. The fighters they were seeing were coming through short wormholes that originated just outside the edge of the solar systems' asteroid belt.

"The front of those ships are less vulnerable than the rear, where they have short antennae, a small sensor panel and their main thrusters," she replied. "Our database doesn't have anything like this, so we're figuring out a new ship and species type here."

"Do your best," Jake said, looking at the fighter for a moment. It looked like some kind of four-legged, four-armed insect that fit into a complex spaceship carapace. Its head was behind a fully transparent metal shield. The pilot seemed to plug into the ship in several places biologically and technologically. Some inlets and outlets seemed obvious, while others were less so. The reaction times of the small fighters was as good as some of his best pilots.

"We're trying to get a good shot at these fighters, but they're staying close to that freighter and if they give us a chance to hit them from this distance, they're right next to one of our fighters, so we don't get much of a chance," Lieutenant Commander Huun said. He was a short, squat burrower Nafalli who had dark brown fur and reminded Jake of cartoon bears that he faintly remembered from Jonas' childhood.

"Just keep trying to get your shot. Is the antimatter aboard the Cloud Break still stable?" Jake asked. The scan they had of it was alarming. There was a balanced core inside the ship that should remain safe for a century, but their scans saw that there were several insect creatures wrapped around it. The casing had been scratched at until the shielding was less than a millimetre thick. There were two hundred and thirty-three life signs aboard. All of them were human, and all of them looked like they were in a deep sleep. Their scans turned up the identities of several who were from Baila, a massive civilized world with a system of terraformed moons and large stations that was less than five light years away. He knew of it. The last he heard was that it was a ruin, an empty wasteland that had been ravaged by machines after the holocaust virus. Artificial intelligences outnumbered humans and other intelligent races by a ratio of nine to one, they never had a chance. If these bugs with Edxi DNA were finding survivors there and bringing them along for their attacks, then Jake had to save them and find out if his fears were true. He didn't give his supposition on why the humans were brought along more than a moment's thought or share it with his crew. They were handling enough as it was.

"Report from Navigation," Commander Agameg Price said. "Two more ships coming in. Both are freighters from the same company as the Cloud Break. Used for local service before they were damaged. It's the same as its predecessor: roughly repaired, two hundred thirty-three humanoids aboard. They are on an interception course."

Jake looked at the Scan and Sciences results on the two ships. Just like the first one, the hull was covered by enemy fighters that clung to it like the insects they were. One had several of the larger, more dangerous vessels. "Kadri, turn our secondary scanner bank all the way up." Antimatter alarms went off, marking the new arrivals. There were creatures wrapped around the ship's core, ready to breach containment and cause a massive explosion at any second. "We need to keep a safe distance. Go evasive."

"The Excalibur is reporting in," Lieutenant Commander Liara Erron said. "They have cleared their sector and are offering assistance."

"Tell them to check in with Fleet and thank Captain Worton. Our situation is about to be resolved," Jake said.

"Aye, aye," Liara replied.

Jake checked their shield status and, at a glance, he could see that they had barely been scratched. One of the fighters holding off the enemy, piloted by Slider, slipped behind the Cloud Break and came back into line of sight with low shield power and damage to its sensor suite. There were still enough fighters there to do damage if they focused their attention on the Merciless, and they were hiding their firepower. "All fighters, return to the Merciless immediately."

"You heard him," Fury said. "Hard burn back, cover Slider. We're going to do this in box formation, hold for five seconds then break so the Merciless' big guns can get a shot at whoever's unlucky enough to chase us." He ordered.

Ashley's course adjustments kept the new freighters far enough away so an antimatter explosion wouldn't do any damage to the Merciless. It was good flying, but he saw a problem. "Ashley reports that the manoeuvres the enemy are making look like they are trying to push us out of position faster than before, enlarging a space so they can jump other ships in," Agameg relayed from his position in the second command seat. He was right behind the Sciences and Helm stations. "I concur."

"Keep your distance, but fly under them," Jake said. "Liara, alert Haven Defence." He watched as the fighters held their box formation on one of his holographic displays then split. The enemy fighters that were following them were blasted with high velocity anti-fighter rounds from the gunnery deck of the Merciless. The nine Edxi ships were reduced down to three in bursts of metals, viscera and components. The remaining ships split off and returned to the cover they brought with them, the Cloud Break. "Tell your people; good shooting today," Jake told Huun as he saw that none of the rounds that missed the enemy fighters hit the freighter behind them. The enemy fighters on the newest freighters leapt off the hulls, starting an acceleration run towards the Merciless. "We get all the scans we need, Kadri?" Jake asked.

"Yes, Sir," she replied. "Your Sciences department is happy."

"Good. Tactical; take those freighters out with our main batteries. Aim for the antimatter cores," Jake ordered.

Huun stood straighter than normal as he marked his targets and passed the order. There was a slight shake as a barrage of ninety heavy intelligent shells were fired from the largest auto-cannons aboard and less than a second later there was a super-hot bloom of light where two of the enemy's repurposed freighters were. Everyone on the bridge knew there was no other choice. The enemy were holding four hundred and sixty-six people prisoner on those ships for reasons unknown, but they also had enough antimatter to seriously damage, possibly destroy the Merciless. Jake didn't let himself flinch. It wasn't his fault. The enemy put him in that position. He looked to the tactical display and saw that the small portion of Samurai Squadron that was left behind to put some distance between the Merciless was almost a safe distance from the Cloud Break. The freighter was turning, firing its engines and starting to accelerate towards them. The fighters opened up with weapons from where the few remaining enemies clung to the hull of that ship, and as if to show that they knew who the leader of the five-fighter group was, they all shot for Fury. The seven small fighters attached to the hull of the Cloud Break wouldn't do much damage on their own, but together they launched a focused line of quill like rounds that exploded on impact that numbered in the hundreds.

He jinked, dodging most of the assault. "Cover Fury! His shields are down!"

"Do not fire back at that freighter, you'll pierce the hull and could set the core off," Fury said as he fought to spin his fighter so his forward shields took the next wave of hits while flying evasively.

Slider moved into the path of some of the enemy rounds, draining most of her shields as she crossed behind him, but there was another wave right behind it. It was aimed expertly, catching Fury just as he was pulsing his thrusters in that direction. His shields went down, canopy armour was compromised, then his suit failed an instant before he was killed. Jake watched as his wingmen and women crossed the safe distance line. "Take that freighter out," he ordered, highlighting the Cloud Break on his tactical display. "Flight, get ready for retrieval."

"Aye," Looph replied. "Our Emergency Response ship is ready to launch."

The Cloud Break exploded in a white ball of fire the moment the first rounds from the Merciless hit it, its last anti-matter reaction destroying everything for several kilometres. "Target destroyed, the engagement board is clear," Huun said quietly. "That was the only way."

"It was," Jake said. "Kadri, Liara; get a package ready for Fleet Intelligence. I want to know what the brightest minds in the fleet think about what we're seeing. Looph, link up with ships in neighbouring sectors and find out how many losses their fighter wings have taken."

"What am I trying to discover, Sir?" Looph asked, her silvery muzzle turning towards him.

"It feels like we're being tested. If those smaller fighters started focusing their fire on one of our Uriels at a time, we would have come out a lot worse." Jake said, checking on Minh-Chu's group. They had finished clearing their sector and were signalling for relief. The Merciless' Flight Control officers were passing the signal on to Fleet, and Jake wondered how soon another ship and fighter wing would show up to relieve them. "I feel like the enemy is investigating, not invading."

"They just lost over a hundred fighters," Huun said.

"To a colony that can make what we're seeing, I'm guessing that was nothing. If they have larger ships, they've made sure that we're not seeing them." He scanned the database to see if any other ships scanned anything other than the fighters they encountered and saw that he was right. "Instead of using their own capital ships, they're using salvage from the biggest ruin within ten light years. If you think like we do, they lost over two thousand fighters today, but if you think like an insect running a large colony, say with a few million drones, then it's a small cost."

"They were transmitting the whole time," Liara said. "It's indecipherable, but it's a language."

"Then there's something out there receiving, something close to the edge of the solar system, maybe hiding in the asteroid outer belt. Alert Fleet. There's something we haven't seen, and it's learning a lot about us," Jake said.

TEN

Thus, We Change

ALICE AND YAWEN were diverted as they walked towards the Clever Dream. The crew was reassembled and waiting, the status from most of the members simply stated that they were settling into their new quarters. In her spare time Alice changed the quarters assignments so every crewmember would be as close as possible to their combat stations. The turret access points were pull-down and drop hatches that were installed between the bunk rooms. The new Nafalli crewmembers were assigned there so they could go from their bunk to their turrets in seconds.

While they moved through the station, Alice ordered a new crew module to be installed in the Clever Dream, reducing the cargo capacity of the ship but giving her people more room to relax. She ordered a set of small armoured cargo pods that could hold extra cargo to be installed on the exterior of the ship. They would collapse so they were flat until they were needed.

Yawen watched every part of the process, nodding her approval. "So, the new corvettes really are patterned after the Clever Dream?" she asked, looking at the list Alice was ordering modifications from. "Pretty much exactly this time?"

"Oh, yeah, but the Clever Dream changed a lot too. I'm glad the ships match up so well, because there are all these surplus modules sitting in storage with an army of skitters ready to install them. I don't know why we're being told to take the long way back to the launch bay, but if it's as long a walk as I think it is, most of this stuff will be in the ship by the time we get there."

An image of all the Nafalli in a pile in the middle of the hangar beside the Clever Dream's ramp appeared on her comm unit, and Alice projected it as a hologram so Yawen could see. There was a thick human arm sticking up from the middle of it, Jessen and Callum laughing in the background. The caption read; *Pile up on Knud!*

"I think I like the new crewmembers already," Yawen giggled.

Alice looked up from the hologram and saw a pair of main doors with a thin gold line around the frame. "We're in the High Command section of the station," she said.

"That's inward from the hangar bays, right?" Yawen asked, looking around.

"Right, this place is so huge that you can get turned around without even realizing it." A holographic pointer appeared in front of them as the door opened, and they passed through into a conference room made more for comfort than anything. It was a new concept. There was no table. Instead there was a circle of plush seating in a dimly lit space. The fixture in the middle was a projection unit that anyone in the room could use with a refreshment dispenser built into the base.

"Everything you experience in this room is classified level eleven," a passive voice told them.

"Okay, this is definitely not what I expected on my first day," Yawen said. "I thought we were on our way to the Clever Dream, then a beach somewhere."

"That was the plan," Alice said. "I don't know what's going on either. I'm cleared to level seven normally, this is really weird."

"Well, I'm going to see if these fancy dispensers can make a good mocha." Yawen stepped into the middle of the seating circle and ordered a hot mocha on a holographic interface that greeted her. Alice ordered a savoury cold vanilla cream drink, thinking about what might bring them to the conference room made for eleven high ranking officers. She knew there were many layers of armour and defence systems between her and the stars made to protect the section they were in, but she felt like she was underground, as if all those layers could trap them as easily as they could guarantee their safety.

"What's on your mind?" Yawen asked, sitting down on a double seat.

Alice looked at her before she took a seat beside her and saw how thin and small Yawen looked. She was always built that way, even in great shape like she was just then, Yawen only occupied a third of the seat made for two, maybe less. Something about her expectant look and her diminutive size made Alice want to protect her even more, but she knew that was the wrong instinct. If everything the Resurrection Program promised came true in Yawen, then she was perfectly capable of taking care of herself.

Taking a seat on the opposite end of the sofa, Alice took a sip of her drink and was surprised at how good it was. The milky blend wasn't chalky or chunky at all, and it was nice and cold. "I was just remembering how people treated me when I changed. The last time is the clearest."

"What was that like for you?"

"The last time, the one that's clearest in my mind, was a lot like the first even though there was nothing wrong with me. The first time I changed, going from artificial intelligence to human, I couldn't walk, talk, I could barely do anything. Trying to eat on my own was a disaster for a while. Never mind how some people laughed at me instead of helping, the most irritating thing was how many times I bit my tongue, or my cheek while I was so hungry. I even bit my own finger once. Sometimes I was happy when someone like Bernice helped, getting hungry and not being able to feed yourself is so frustrating, but other times I didn't want help and people wouldn't take no for an answer. I was really capable the last time I changed, so I didn't have any of the motor skills problems, but you'd think I did because there were people who wanted to offer help or sympathy every-where. The first few days after the change were so bad for that, then I learned to ignore them and some people thought that was rude. Then I started prepping for the Academy and I think that proved that I didn't need any special treatment."

"The only time I worried about you was when you kinda wore yourself out a few times," Yawen said.

"Yeah, I pushed myself pretty hard," Alice said.

"I guess I don't have to ask why all this is coming up now. I must be a grand reminder of those rebirths."

"Not in a bad way. I guess I'm sort of looking at my experience and trying to avoid annoying you with stupid questions," Alice chuckled.

Yawen looked around the room. "I guess this quiet space is probably where Fleet wants me and you to talk whatever problems I have out with one of the only people who can understand what I'm going through. I'd be irked if it didn't come with one of the best mocha snack drinks I've ever had." She took a drink of the hot beverage and looked back to Alice. "I've got some questions, some I've been wondering about since I first heard that you made a few transitions."

"Shoot," Alice said, happy she didn't have to start.

"When you went through the change the last time, from framework to full-on human, was that like dying, or are you all the same?"

Alice thought for a moment before answering. "I went to sleep, the system rebuilt me, but it was like being remade piece by piece, so I guess it was more like a transplant. My whole body was never dead."

"Okay, what about the time before? I don't know much about it."

"I died on the Triton," Alice said. "I remember being unable to do anything while my father was visiting and something old seemed to click in. Like a piece of me from the artificial intelligence days took over and packed up what was left of my memories, who I was before transmitting itself and all that somewhere else. I barely remember anything before coming back in a framework body. I definitely died that time, I don't feel like the Alice who had an artificial eye and all that confidence much anymore."

"Okay, so that's probably a lot like how I feel. I know a Yawen died, I saw the footage, had the report read-through, and a councillor made sure I wasn't about to go off the edge. I feel different now, like I completely understand how short life can be, how important it is to do what you need to while you're here, and that I'm not the same Yawen. It's like you said; I don't feel like her."

"What's different? Just off the top of your head?" Alice asked.

Yawen answered without giving herself time to ponder. "I need to prove myself." Her Irish accent was sharp, but her words were spoken quietly. "I feel like I need to pay more attention to the people who really matter, too. There were all these people I served with who didn't send me a single message after we got to the Haven System and I tried to keep in touch but I don't think most of them mattered now that I see it from this side of things. Then there were people like you and Regan and a few others who would check on me while we were in training. Like Ute, who kept in touch even while she was assigned elsewhere. That kindly frog sent me two messages a day every day after we had one good talk after exercises in the Academy."

"I know, Ute will answer her comm no matter how late or

inconvenient it is, even if it is to say that she's busy flying," Alice said.

"You never let me down, either," Yawen said, taking Alice's hand. "You worked yourself to the bone in the Academy, but every day you'd check in on me, your roomie, and you were always there to help if I needed it. Before I thought I should have taken you up on that more, but now I'm glad I didn't. If I placed higher, I wouldn't be a part of your squad, and that's where I want to be. Especially now that I feel like I'm starting over instead of continuing on like the Resurrection people want."

"They wanted you to feel like you were continuing where you left off?" Alice asked.

"They never told me directly, but aye, I could see that straight away," Yawen nodded.

"I've never felt like that. A new life always felt like a new opportunity. I always picked up what I could from my old life and tried to move on." Alice could see Yawen was listening closely, staring at her expectantly and went on. "When I made it from artificial intelligence to human, it was a fresh start, and I was directionless. That was the most difficult. Then I died, became an artificial intelligence again, and when I came back I wanted so badly to get back to Jake. I remember clinging to the idea of becoming a soldier, of needing to do something helpful but I kept on reverting back to this little teenager. Then I got the cure and, yeah, I wanted to be in this fight, but the Academy felt like the reboot I needed. It was so different, a great way to train my brain, to challenge myself. Now I have my memories back and I find I relate to the Academy newbie who wanted to be an over-achiever more than any version of myself. I want to experience so many things for the first time, some of them I know I've done before, but I realize that everything still feels new."

"That puts us in the same place," Yawen said, but it was just as much a statement as a question.

"I think so," Alice said. "I've got all this experience, but I still feel like everything is still new most of the time. I mean, when I got the memories back, there was kind of a clash in my head, but it's like a few therapeutic habits and time took care of most of that or is taking care of that..." Alice shook her head. "It's an ongoing thing."

Yawen nodded and embraced Alice. "I could sit here with you for days and days."

Alice squeezed her back and realized that she was feeling something from Yawen. The young woman loved her like a sister, there was something less platonic as well, but it was old, like a faint memory. For all the information she'd seen on empaths and telepathy, Alice didn't expect to sense her friends' affection so deeply, and she reciprocated powerfully. Her and Yawen had a bond, and Alice had turned away from the grief of losing her as much as she could but having her back made her happier than she could have ever expected. She kissed Yawen on the cheek and they parted slowly, concentrating on shuttering her empathic gift even though she wanted to keep feeling Yawen's admiration and affection. *There,* she thought. *There's my pitfall with this new trick. It's not the potential to open my mind right up and get burned out, or all the noise I hear when I let my guard down in a crowd by mistake, but how good it feels to sense someone else's love. Wow, that felt good, I could have lived in that moment forever.*

"Are you all right?" Yawen asked.

Alice realized that there were tears on her cheeks then and wiped them away. "I'm just glad to be sitting here with you."

"It's good to be missed," Yawen said, wiping a tear from her eye. "Thank you for this, I needed to talk to someone who wasn't hoping to hear all the things they wished someone they resurrected would say."

"They really gave you the sense that they were ticking boxes while you were being treated after you came back?"

"Yes, but it was more like an interview. The therapist - can't remember her name - was good, but everyone else seemed to have hopes for specific results. By the end I was just looking forward to getting picked up and forgetting that I was born yesterday, so to speak, as quickly as possible. When they said you were picking me up, I..."

The holographic system filled the air between the seats with a large command centre. Many of the faces were blurred, but the gold trimmed uniforms and presence of Ayan, Oz, and several highly ranked personnel around them made it clear that they were being shown something important. A gentleman with the rank of Admiral marked on his uniform looked at her directly. "We haven't properly met; I'm Admiral Lamonthe, head of Fleet Intelligence." Colonel Violet Black, the head of the Haven Fleet Academy, stepped in beside him as he went on. "Looking through the reports on your experiences with the Edxi and the Clever Dream's old logs, we see that there might be some information missing. Are you sure what you described was accurate and complete with regards to those encounters? Were there any other Edxi or insect type beings you encountered that you forgot to describe or didn't think were relevant?"

Alice didn't have to think about her answer as she got to her feet and stood at attention with Yawen. "No, Admiral, I didn't leave anything out. The evidence collected was as complete as it could be and those logs were never tampered with or edited."

"Are you positive? There will be no repercussions if you forgot to include details. We only want to make sure we have your accurate accounts of each Edxi encounter," Violet Black added.

"I have nothing to add, Colonel," Alice said, watching Oz shake his head in the background before speaking with Ayan quietly. "Is there something you need to know? With respect, a direct question would help," Alice offered.

"So, you are holding something back?" Colonel Black asked.

"No, Colonel, I am not," Alice said clearly.

Ayan tapped a sequence into the control table between her and the other commanders and the image of a fighter appeared. The metal was grey-brown, and it looked like a thin creature with natural insectoid armour was straddling the middle of the jagged, V shaped vessel. Two of its long, jagged looking arms and legs were folded up close to the bottom of the craft, and the glint of metal along with its natural armour made it unclear as to whether or not they were part of the creature or the fighter itself. The face of the thing was visible through the transparent metal armour at the head of the fighter. Sharp mandibles, small red and black eyes were visible between overlapping armour plates that reminded her of the Beast. The top of the fighter was thickly armoured with openings for several smaller weapons, and two large, covered ports for some kind of broader weapon. The pair of thrusters at the rear and numerous small manoeuvring rocket ports looked almost like they didn't belong there, they looked less organic than anything else on the ship. "This is one of the heavy fighters that the fleet ran into today," Ayan said. "We think it's a cybernetic insect type pilot that's plugged directly into the fighter. It either evolved or was engineered to survive in space without a compressed cockpit. Is any part of it familiar?"

"The legs," Alice said. "The plates around the face look a lot like the ones that the Beast had. I think his were organic, they looked attached. If I could see the torso, I would be able to tell you more, but..."

Ayan adjusted the image so she could see a cut-away version. "Here's a different detail."

The creature's torso was connected in several places by organic looking plugs, including two thick linkages that led to the large firing ports on the front of the fighter. The upper half of the being looked thick, broad, covered in protective natural armour that had a brown but pearlescent sheen. The lower half was still armoured, but with finer pieces and it was more flexible looking. She could see where the four legs connected clearly, and two were linked into the ship for control while the others were outside. "Okay, there's some kind of exo-skeleton I can see in some places, the Edxi I saw grew ones that extended outside their skin. I think that's what some of their carapace armour grew from."

"Did they indicate that they were warriors? Or that there

was another type of Edxi that filled that role?" Admiral Lamonthe asked.

"I didn't talk to Zarrix long enough to get more information than I gave you. He didn't describe anything like this, Admiral," she replied.

"All right, thank you, Captain. Enjoy your time off. We're going to have a lot of work for you and your squad once you get back, so make the most of it."

"Yes, Admiral, thank you," Alice said.

The image began to fade away, then Oz stepped into the foreground, tapping a control that was too low for Alice or Yawen to see and winking at her before he returned to Ayan's side. Admiral Jessica Rice stepped to her other side as Colonel Black and a Vice Admiral who had his face blurred was at the other end of the table. A mute symbol appeared along the bottom of the transmission that made it clear that Alice and Yawen weren't being recorded or broadcasted into the room. "Did Commodore McPatrick just leave the recorders on so we could see what's going on?" Yawen asked.

"I think so," Alice said, watching Oz. He and Ayan were exchanging glances, then Admiral Rice was doing the same with Ayan. It was good to see them getting along, from what Alice had seen, Jessica Rice was the closest thing Ayan had to a mother, but there was something else going on that she didn't think was connected to that.

Admiral Lamonthe looked up from the display between them, glancing to Oz, Ayan, Jessica and two more blurred Vice Admirals that were coming into recording range to stand behind them. He cocked his head, looking to Admiral Rice, who nodded, then he stepped away, wiping his black gloved hands in the air as if washing them before leaving the frame entirely. "There is something big about to happen," Yawen breathed. "Something our head of Intelligence can't or won't be a part of. Where does a Colonel stand in our ranks again? I should know, but Violet Black is the only one."

"It's the same as Rear Admiral, which is below Vice Admiral and above Commodore," Alice replied, watching as two more Commodores stepped into frame behind Ayan. Violet Black and her blurred companion were across the table from the group that had quietly assembled around her. "They gave her that rank in Freeground Fleet Academy tradition, the headmaster or mistress was always called Colonel."

"Oh," Yawen said, nodding, watching as Violet Black looked up from the intelligent round table and realized that there were seven high ranking officers across the table from her. "This looks bad for her."

"Colonel Black, you are relieved," Ayan said, her voice, British accent and tone clear and cutting. "We'll decide on your place in the fleet later today, but you are no longer responsible for the Haven Fleet Academy or recruitment. You will be escorted to your quarters now."

"What? I only wanted to ensure that Haven Fleet had the best service people," she retorted as a pair of guards in full armour stepped up behind her. "I will always put the best interest of this fleet ahead of everything else and develop best practices for myself and the people under me."

"We'll take that into consideration when we place you, thank you," Ayan said.

"Oh my God, I've never imagined your mother could be so cold," Yawen said under her breath.

"I think this is what it looks like when she's angry," Alice said, watching closely. "No, furious." *Afraid, maybe?* Alice thought to herself.

"Colonel Black has worked herself ragged trying to properly train everyone her people thought adequate to join the fleet," protested the Vice Admiral at the Headmistress' side. "This is the sort of thing that is put before a panel and decided after reviewing the record. This ambush is unlawful."

"I don't need a panel," Ayan said with rare intensity. "But there are seven officers here. I could have acted as a Queen, Vice Admiral. Do you understand?"

He seemed very still for a moment then bowed before leaving with a quiet; "I understand. By your leave, I'll return to my command, Admiral."

"I don't understand," Yawen said.

"If she officially takes the position of Queen, no one can outrank her and she can override any decision however she likes. Being Queen isn't like the old-timey type of Queen, it's just a title they give people who own a planet or solar system with a population. According to the Galactic Courts, owners have the final say in everything." Ayan took a breath, looking down at the illuminated table in front of her. A partially holographic image of the solar system was there, and she seemed to use the sight to strengthen her resolve. Alice guessed what was about to happen and gasped as Ayan's gaze rose from the map and she looked at the people gathered around in the command room. She wished the hologram would show more of the people there as her mother steeled herself for what she was about to say next. Several Nafalli and Mergillians stepped into frame along with what must have been half the admiralty.

"I ask all of you to bear witness as I assume full responsibility and control of the Rega Gain System, now known as the Haven System. I've resisted the titles of Queen and outright ownership except for in the documentation that would allow us to develop as an independent democracy, but in this state of emergency, I must take direct control of the military and oversee the civilian government. The removal of Colonel Black from Haven Fleet Academy is only the first step to righting this sinking ship."

"I liked Colonel Black," Yawen muttered. "Bit stuck up, though."

"She was holding recruitment back years and didn't let most non-humans enter the Academy. There was a serious bias there."

"Oh, then down with the Headmistress. I hope her next command is an orbital tug."

"That was a quick flip," Alice snickered.

"I think I'm fickler now," Yawen shrugged.

"I'll be taking Carl Anderson's place as Minister of Defence until this crisis is over and a new election can be held for the position," Ayan continued. "My first act as Defence Minister will be to invite the allies who are standing ready to help us to complete a fast-track training program that the new Headmaster of Haven Fleet Academy, Commodore Terry Ozark McPatrick, will implement and oversee starting today. He will not be called Colonel during his service with the Academy, that practice is now over so the Academy is tied into our Fleet operations more closely. Trainees will have experience on ships in service much sooner and more fast track programs are starting this week. I humbly invite people of all kinds to join us and acknowledge the military qualifications results submitted by Mergillian, Nafalli and all other people who are loyal to our cause. There are over a hundred five thousand of you ready to serve who were denied entry into the Academy even though all of you passed the qualification tests for service. I need every one of you. I invite every one of you, and I'm afraid we'll need more."

Many of the Nafalli bowed low, clapping their hands over their heads, while Mergillians stood as tall as they could, broadly smiling and applauding. When it calmed, Ayan's expression was more serious than ever. "I look beyond a victorious result in this war to a prosperous time when I may step down. Democracy will return, and our military will leave the borders of this solar system to explore, make firm ties with new people, and assist those in need. The future will be inclusive, not only led by humans. Before that, we have to survive and defeat enemies that have no sympathy or respect for us. All hands to battle stations. The hesitant voices have been silenced. This is war."

The hologram flickered out, leaving Alice in stunned silence for a moment, then Yawen leapt screaming; "Yes!"

Alice flinched, nearly falling back into her seat and laughing. "Time to get back to the Clever Dream."

"But wait, if that was highly classified, how will everyone know that anything's changed?" Yawen asked as she followed Alice out into the corridor.

Their command and control units buzzed, and the answer became apparent. A Fleet wide message informing everyone about the change in command was already coming through, and Alice saw that Commodore Jacob Valent had been put in command of SOCU. The Clever Dream was to be fit for duty along with its entire crew and report to the Merciless after two days of preparation. "I just got our new orders," Alice said, excited and unsure at the same time.

"There's an edited version of your Mum's speech going out to everyone on the network," Yawen said. "They cut some of the sensitive stuff, and put her on a stage, but it's mostly the same."

"I think Oz and maybe my Mother wanted me to see how it all really happened. We'd better get ready for some serious fighting," Alice said as a section of wall slid aside to reveal a high-speed transit car. "Well, it's about time I found a better way to get around the station."

"Why? You couldn't find them before?" Yawen asked as they got in and sat down.

"Everything in the secure parts of the station is hidden behind panels and walls except for security checkpoints and unused leisure areas. You could hide a tribe of Nafalli here and you wouldn't know for years."

"Maybe they thought walking would do you some good?" Yawen asked.

"I'd rather get down to the Clever Dream in forty seconds," Alice said as the doors slid closed, the wall beyond sealed, and the ten-person oval capsule surged down the transit tube.

ELEVEN

Fathers

THE DEAL WAS FINAL. He was elevated to the rank of
Commodore with no fanfare. He'd keep his current command
and assume command of the Special Operations Combat
Unit, most of which would run from his ship. He knew his
crew was ready, and the opportunity was exciting. As for
other requests, he didn't have many, and the Fleet agreed to
each one. He needed a special second in command for
SOCU, and that would be Alaka Murlen, a Nafalli he always
respected.

Jake was on his feet, looking at the entire history of
Alaka's time with them in hologram form. Reports and video
playback spanned the width of his quarters, a space he
thought was just right for him. There was a bed large enough
for he and Ayan that was as comfortable and as portable as

the ones on the Triton. A sliding wall could separate the sleeping and personal area from the rest of the room if he wanted privacy, but he left the thin, rolling divider retracted. Below was a pair of sofas and arm chairs arranged in a semi-circle that could tilt up so people could watch a large holo-gram display or rise a little so nine people could eat at a fold-away table. There was a separate bathroom as well. It was small, with a double sized grooming stall with a vibro shower and several water jets. The only thing missing was a bath, but it was one of only fifteen private bathrooms aboard the ship, and it was the nicest, so he felt pampered. The quarters were lavish, certainly, but they also took the place of a ready room since one door led directly to the bridge. A pull-out desk and worktable with storage gave him a place to work privately, and the table and leisure systems built into the space made a Captain's Mess unnecessary while taking the role of confer-ence room as well. The quarters were lavish, but their adapt-ability eliminated the need for four other compartments in the ship. Jake liked the elegant efficiency of it and didn't mind that he had an ensign who took care of them for him. He made sure that it was set up properly for whatever was coming up on his schedule, that everything was stocked, and that his space was clean.

Jake was just as happy with Alaka's file the second time through. The first time he looked at it thoroughly was before he chose him as his second in command for SOCU. It was going to be an active unit, a complicated group of squads that would require attention and the ability to adapt from their commanding officers.

Alaka's record since he joined the fleet was remarkable.

He was part of the small team that developed the advanced physical training exercises for Haven Fleet Academy, but that was the least of his activities there. When he wasn't spending time with his tribe of children or doting on his wife, he was working his way through qualifications. His position at the Academy gave him the best access to training and he made his way through technical, tactical and practical combat qualification tests while he worked his way through all the officer training material he could cram into his spare time. He tested from the bottom of the command chain all the way up to Lieutenant Commander, and Jake requested that Alaka be promoted the moment he finished the qualifier for Commander so he could have a rank that reflected his dedication and skill. Jake would have liked to have him made a Captain, but he believed that there had been enough people skipping past ranks in the Fleet and wanted to see Alaka get there on his own.

The other thing that made Jake excited to work with the Nafalli was how he looked in on his wife and children every day while he was away. Even Iruuk, his eldest, who wasn't always in reach. A soft beep on his arm told him that Alaka was only a minute away. Jake closed the man's file, bringing the holographic tactical view of the Haven Solar System up instead.

It had been one full day since Ayan announced that she was taking over as Defence Minister, and with the removal of Violet Black from the recruitment process, Oz was making long, progressive strides in bringing a horde of non-humans who were ready for service aboard.

Jake could see the changes in the defence map for the

Haven System most. There were three new carriers on patrol near Tamber, in a distant orbit around Kambis. Each already had an active fighter wing that was filling gaps in the patrols. The crews aboard those carriers were all from military organizations, and they had been preparing to serve on Haven ships for weeks, waiting for the chance to climb aboard. Jake predicted that they would move further out into the system within days as the crews checked out. Their loyalty wasn't in question, every one of them submitted for a deep scan and only those without affiliation or an over-abundance of sympathy for the Order of Eden were allowed in. It was a highly invasive measure, but Jake agreed with Fleet Command: if someone didn't approve of the screening measure, they didn't belong in the military.

The larger change was visible further out, closer to the other planets and in the outer solar system. There were old mining, science and defence stations from forces and companies that started working in the solar system but eventually left for various reasons. They were being repurposed by teams who knew the older technology and quickly re-armed with portable sensor and weapon modules. Jake touched one of the holographic images showing an old mining station and looked at the rough design. It was industrial, boxy, but sturdy with thick metal armour. There were fifteen Mergillians and three humans from the Fleet who were busy installing portable reactors, repairing the railgun batteries and setting up portable missile pods. The life support systems were already back online and they were waiting for a portable shield and cloaking system to be delivered. It was already being built by the Solar Forge and would be there in an hour.

Once it was installed, the old station would be a cloaked listening post with some serious firepower.

A soft, low pitched bell sound announced Alaka's arrival and the double door opened when Jake gestured at it. "Welcome aboard, sorry I couldn't meet you, but I'm waiting for a few classified calls to come through."

Alaka crossed the room and gripped Jake's hand. "Thank you, I'm happy you chose me for this position, I will make you proud." The giant Nafalli was more impressive up close, Jake forgot how tall he was. The tree tribesmen often had lighter, longer fur than their burrower relations, and Alaka was one of the most impressive climbers that he'd ever seen. Until his arrival on Tamber, the long-limbed warrior hunted for a living, and according to his son, Iruuk, he was gifted.

"I'm honoured you accepted," Jake said, gesturing towards the largest arm chair in the room while he sat in the one opposite.

He sat down and looked at the arms of the seat as if he was surprised he fit. "May I speak freely, Commodore?"

"You may as well start now, we're going to be working together a lot," Jake replied.

"I'm wondering if my assignment is connected to the friendship your daughter has with my son. She has been a great influence on him, challenging his intelligence in the Academy, then giving him responsibilities in his new position. She's even shown him new ways to put his hunter's gift to use in public service. I see that he's ready to be independent, maybe thanks to their work together. I don't need to watch over him."

"I'm sure you want to anyway," Jake said. "But no, that's

not why I chose you. In fact, your son being in SOCU was a strike against putting you in this position. I have to be sure that you can make command decisions impartially, even if it means putting your son in danger."

Alaka thought for a moment before answering. "I know he wants to be of service and will sacrifice himself if necessary. I'll always try to honour that. I can't say for sure what I would do in the moment, though. I hope I'd do the right thing every time, but I can't be certain until I'm in the situation. I understand the need for impartiality but haven't proven that I can be yet. Have you?"

Jake was stunned at having the question turned back on him. It was done so politely, even changed into a more important query, and he realized that he hadn't proven that he could send his own daughter into certain danger, not as she was. "I guess we both might have to prove that before this is all over. How is the rest of your family doing?"

"They've never been closer. When I go home now, many of them are nested, all surrounding their mother. She has all but two of her children around her, helping with the newcomers. I've never dreamt of having such a large, happy family. Several of the youngest are starting to show hunting instincts, filling up on milk then slipping out of the pouch even though their eyes are barely open. Their naming days are coming faster than we expected. Their eyes will be open, and they'll be too big for the pouch before we know it. Like Iruuk, he could ride on my shoulder a little over a year ago, and then he had his growth spurt and if it keeps going, he might be a fair challenge for me in... what do you call it? Luno... er, wrestling."

"I'd like to see that," Jake said, imagining what it must be like to have a family so large that your children are measured in double digits. "Iruuk is an impressive officer, eager to go see the universe for himself. SOCU is lucky to have him."

Alaka's manner became more serious, he stroked the fur hanging from his long muzzle. "What is my place here? I am honoured you chose me, but what will I do for you and SOCU?"

"I'm giving you and Remmy Sands a team. His team will be like any other SOCU except they're going to be in the heavy suits."

"Ediiro," Alaka said, nodding. "Walking Tanks."

"Right, they're the first tech the War Forge teams have adapted from Nafalli designs. Your team will be the last to leave this ship. It'll study the Merciless, know all the details of the other teams and have access to every equipment type that our unit has. That includes a full set of Ediiro, or HAS armour."

"HAS?"

"Heavy Armour Suits," Jake explained. "You and your team will help me manage SOCU and provide the most effec- tive rescue option for the other SOCU teams. The idea that always bothered me about SOCU was how we were drawing the best people we had into teams that were taking the most difficult missions and they were expected to do it without backup. Sure, we could send another team after one that needed help, but the whole idea behind SOCU is that they are active, every team is used as often as possible. I want you to train your team to go after a stranded or captured SOCU squad and to defend this ship if it's boarded or if it needs the help of a special squad."

"That sounds challenging," Alaka said, looking a little excited. "Who are the members of my team?"

"I've chosen two people who I think represent the humans well, you can choose whoever you want from the Fleet's recruiting pool. I'd like to see a lot of Nafalli and Mergillians, to be honest. All the Issyrians who signed up yesterday are already spoken for. I was only able to get one for the Merciless."

"How many were there?"

"Two hundred seventeen. They came to Tamber initially because of the freshwater ocean. Most of them are science officers, something the fleet needs badly."

"What does the one that you recruited do?" Alaka asked.

"He cleans my quarters," Jake said. "He's an Ensign taking courses while he's serving. He should finish his damage control qualification for the command section of the ship in a couple of days, and he wants to train on the starship operations track after that."

"Oh, well, at least Agameg won't be alone."

"Commander Price has been a little hard on him, actually. He won't call him by his name. Instead, he calls him a Tlotu."

Alaka looked at the translation on his right command and control gauntlet, and his jaw dropped for a moment before he said the word in English. "He calls him a Dung Guppy?"

"Yeah, it's a form of negative encouragement. The nickname is something Ottun has to earn his way past. Agameg described it as a sort of professional, figurative egg sac. I asked

Ensign Ottun if he thought it was irregular and he asked me not to interfere, he says the challenge is an honour."

"There is going to be a lot of that; learning from other cultures," Alaka said, looking to the fighting staff mounted on Jake's wall.

"I'm looking forward to it. It's one of the best things about being an explorer. We expand our minds when we learn about other cultures instead of judging them."

"My people, the Nafalli who chose to travel the galaxy, have always seen it the same way."

The door leading to the hallway opened and Ottun entered the room. His vacsuit uniform was sealed, but his helmet wasn't filled with fluid as it was when he first came aboard. It was a good sign, one that meant that he was steadily becoming used to a dry environment. "A Haven Fleet Security Corvette has docked with the bridge section. They dropped the Queen off and departed to a safe distance to cloak and await her instructions. She is here to see you." His yellow-blue eyes were open wide, taking up half of his face, and his fine cilia were standing up on the rest of his head, making him look like he had a dark blue beard and head of hair. It all added up to one thing: he was nervous.

Jake stood and tried to look around him. "Is she waiting in the hall?"

"I thought you'd like a minute warning, to prepare?" Ottun asked, a squeak in his voice.

Jake played along, looking to Alaka who was surprised but more amused. "Do I look ready?"

He nodded, chuckling. The gesture was exaggerated by his long snout. "I think so, Commodore."

"Send her in," Jake said to Ottun. "You're off duty for the night, so that'll be all."

"Yes, Commodore, thank you, Sir," he said, turning around, coming nose to nose with Ayan, jumping a little, then stepping to the side as he bowed low.

"It's all right, I'm not supposed to be here, so you can pretend I'm just a visitor like anyone else," Ayan told him as he retreated down the hallway, bowing repeatedly.

"I don't think that's his style," Jake said, meeting Ayan at the door.

"Not used to that," she said, rising on her toes and giving him a brief but warm kiss.

"I have company," Jake told her, turning so she could see Alaka, who was watching them with quiet amusement. He imagined the Nafalli was enjoying a brief look at the softer side of his new commander and the Queen of the solar system. When he realized he was caught watching, he rose to his feet in a rush, bowing briefly, an act that didn't diminish his towering height much.

"Oh, it's good to see you," Ayan said, crossing the room and accepting a hug from Alaka that made all but her calves and boots disappear. "How are the pups?"

"Happy, well fed, and getting a little restless already," Alaka said, releasing her and holding her at arm's length for a moment. "How's Laura?"

"Sleeping more soundly all the time, growing fast," Ayan replied. "It's my first time being more than a minute away from her, so I'm nervous. She has everything she needs, and she's in the hands of my mother and the nanny, but I still want to check on her every ten seconds."

"That's natural. I still check on my oldest every day, my youngest ones whenever I can. I peek in at my wife so often that she's tired of me." He looked to Jake and nodded. "I think I'll give you two some time, this doesn't seem like an official visit."

"Thanks, Alaka. Take that door," Jake said, nodding to the door leading directly to the bridge. "Say hi to everyone there while we're out of the patrol rotation. They're about to go off shift."

Alaka checked his uniform and straightened one of his command and control bracers, nodded at Jake, Ayan, then walked through the door.

"He seems really nervous," Ayan said, making her way back to Jake, who put an arm around her.

"It's the third highest performing bridge crew in the fleet, and Commander Price is in the Captain's seat. I'd find it intimidating too. I didn't know you and Alaka knew each other so well."

"I used to visit Iloona and her brood when I was spending more time in the Everin Building. She let me lay beside her and help feed whichever pup was left out when she ran out of nipples."

"She couldn't feed all her pups at once?" Jake asked.

"No, so I got to know the runt pretty well. Her litter was abnormally big because she was eating so well and feeling pretty safe while she served as the medical officer aboard the Triton." She looked to the sofa almost longingly and Jake took the hint.

They sat down together, he enjoyed feeling her at his side

with her head on his shoulder. "I hope we can get through this quick so litter sizes can rise again," Jake said.

"Is that a hint? I don't want to have a litter," Ayan snickered. "Just one's a handful, and she's nowhere near walking or talking yet. It'd be nice if she had a friend to grow up with though." Ayan closed her eyes and wriggled in closer to him.

He remembered idle conversation between Jonas and the first Ayan about children, but the topic never came up between them. The thought of her pregnant, having a child with her made him smile. "We haven't had this conversation yet."

"I thought it might be too soon, and I've been a little distracted," Ayan said, looking a little tired as her blue eyes searched his face.

This was a sensitive topic for her, and he was suddenly aware that things could go horribly awry. "We're not doing things in order this time, remember?" he said, drawing her a little closer. "I'd love to add to our family with you, but we'll do it when you want. I'm going to be on this ship for a few years, and the Merciless doesn't have day care..."

Ayan smiled and kissed him lightly before settling down, her head on his chest. "The details don't matter, not right now. I'm just happy this didn't turn into a fight. I couldn't handle that right now."

"Everything okay?"

"I thought I prepared for this, but one full day as Defence Minister and Queen has me questioning everything, and it's completely wiped me out."

"I think you're the right person for the job, things are running better so far," Jake said, getting no response back. He gently stroked her face for a while, and when he stopped, she put his fingers back to her cheek so he could continue. "What can I do?"

"Hide me tonight," she said, already half asleep. "Everyone knows their job now, what they're supposed to be doing. They don't need me until tomorrow, but they won't stop double-checking."

"One night of uninterrupted rest," he said, kissing her forehead. He was glad she came to him to find refuge. It was good to see her, sure, but he didn't imagine that she'd show her vulnerable side to anyone else.

"Thank you, I'm sorry I'm so boring," she muttered. "I'm a boring girlfriend."

It was her nearly asleep voice, and he secretly enjoyed listening to her mumble when she was on her way to slumber. He'd never seen her so tired, though. "When was the last time you slept?"

"The night before replacing Violet with Oz," she said, waking a little.

That was almost two days before, by his guess. "All right. We'll eat, then get you to bed."

"Oh, Jake, you scoundrel," Ayan said with a tired but suggestive smirk.

"I don't think either of us have the energy," Jake said with a chuckle. "From the looks of things, we'll be lucky if we're not found face-down sleeping in our dim sum."

Ayan roused a little. "Dim sum? I'm awake."

TWELVE

High Speed Anticipation

THE LATE MORNING air was warming up, the only thing in the blue sky was the blazing sun, turned to yellow hues by the conditioned atmosphere. Alice felt closer to it as the sky luge sled coasted along the near zero friction force field track. The safety collar told her that she was a hundred twelve metres above Tamber's ocean, and she was moving at twenty-eight kilometres per hour and speeding up.

The emergency collar around her neck was the only thing protecting her, and she was happy she opted for the Active Two-Piece swimsuit design instead of the string-and-bow choice Ashley suggested in a message a few days before because she thought it was cute. "So, I just steer by shifting my weight and flexing my calves?" she asked as she looked from her toes up to the three agricultural towers in the distance. Their plastic-concrete shells of green, blue and yellow caught the sunlight and looked awfully solid.

"Just like you practiced on the ground. You're a natural, don't worry," the science officer of the Sky Stalker, Dakota, said through the scratchy comm channel in the collar.

The feeling of the air moving over her as she picked up speed, watching the blurry blue translucent track ahead as it tilted down more severely, felt amazing. It was as if she was flying, but there was no sound other than her own breath and the whistling wind. Trying to calm her breathing, she let the brake, which she'd been riding just a little even though she was on a mild decline, go entirely.

The speed indicator hologram in front of her eye went up to thirty-five in a couple seconds and kept going up. "First bank, coming up. It looks far away, but you're about to dip, so get ready."

The shimmering track dipped so quickly that she felt like she left her stomach behind. She approached the bank in the track rapidly, and nearly lost control as she saw that it turned down sharply as soon as it straightened. The thought of curving ninety degrees at nearly fifty kilometres an hour then gaining more speed was intimidating, but she braked, leaned, and steered through the turn. There was no time to do anything other than see that her speed was down to twenty kilometres an hour at the end of the turn, she'd braked hard, then it was at twenty-one and climbing fast as the next curl in the track took her and the sled into a downward turn that had her screaming and laughing.

All the sides were enclosed in a force field tube, there wasn't much she could do to control her descent, and the brake disengaged automatically, sending down a section of the track that made her feel like she was riding down a curly straw. One section had her moving so quickly that she was upside down at one point, laughing uncontrollably.

She gasped as the sled settled into the middle of the track again and bled off speed as it was sent up a sharp incline. "You're back in full control. Next part takes you on a tour between the agricultural towers, then you'll be headed back to the beach on the challenge part of the track."

"Challenge part?" Alice asked, her tone more urgent than even she expected as the sled moved down a stretch between the green and blue agricultural towers. There was a gentle looking turn at the end.

"The challenge portion is made to see if you learned how to really control the sled, like a pro. You might fly off, but don't worry, that's what your emergency collar is for. You'll drop into the water and have a little swim back to shore."

"Let me guess, most people get wet," Alice said as she glanced to the blue tower, watching an Issyrian wave at her from a window as they looked up from the hydroponic garden in the agricultural tower.

"Four out of six so far, but I'm still gathering data. You are lucky number seven," Dakota said. "Turn!"

Alice was so busy thinking about the end of the track that she almost forgot to lean in and steer through the high corner. She was still thirty-five metres up, and it was a gentle if quickening corner. By the time she came to the short straight, she was already going forty-four kilometres an hour. The next corner came up, and she was able to negotiate the long curve that took her around three sides of the green agricultural building. She shot through a short straight afterwards, excitement rising as the sled picked up more speed.

A tap on the brake brought her speed back down to forty-two kilometres per hour from sixty, then she watched it start climbing as the next long, declining turn pushed her speed back up to seventy by the time she guided the sled around the yellow agricultural building. Several people watched from the windows only metres away, she didn't get a good look, only saw the shadows of shoulders and heads of people who must have been curious about the swimsuit clad streak flying past their window.

The thought brought a fit of giggles on, and Alice struggled to focus as the route of the upcoming turns came up on the holographic heads-up display projected from the emergency collar. The straight leading to them would end a kilometre away from the beach, and she prepared for the first turn, which was a closed loop that would take her in a wide circle.

A Uriel fighter seemed to drop in beside her from nowhere. It followed the curve of the course closely, and she barely managed to tap the brake the instant before she entered the closed loop ahead. Even though she was splitting her attention between the track and the new, black Uriel fighter, she enjoyed the pull of gravity as she was taken around the ring, which surprised her by ending half way.

The sled nearly flew off the banked part of the track before she braked a little more, leaning and steering harder. It let her out into a short straight that took only a couple heartbeats to cross before she braked again, barely made it through a turn to the left that put her parallel to the beach, where she could see the Clever Dream and its twin, the Sky Stalker floating on the shore, their black hulls glossy in the sun. The Uriel fighter followed her all the way, finally rolling so she could see through the cockpit window, where Carnie was waving and smiling at her.

Alice smiled as a collision of thoughts and sensations assaulted her. *I have to meet him in person, in this bathing suit? He's going to mess me up so bad, I'm definitely going for a swim! What is he doing here? Isn't the whole Samurai Squadron on patrol? Oh, my God, my stomach is under attack by a flight of butterflies. Seriously? In my bathing suit?*

Her sled almost caught the edge of the next turn, she barely made the corner in time. The quick, winding section of half-tube tested her reflexes and coordination: left, right, a short trip up then a longer one down that took her closer to the gentle blue waves.

The next part looked complicated, a quick right then left through a highly banked curve and she barely made it. The banked turn bled off most of her speed, reducing her back down to twenty-eight kilometres per hour.

There were five turns left, and if she made the next one it would take her down through an underwater force field tube that would give her a surge of speed before sending her back up. Carnie was watching, and she was determined to finish the track. With an involuntary giggle she made it and was sent almost straight down into it. The force field held the water out, and she released the brake, taking on as much speed as she could. To her surprise, the fighter followed, splashing into the water and keeping up effortlessly. Carnie looked down the nose of his fighter and pretended to freak out for a moment.

She peered down the tube, taking in the view between her feet and watched the patch of ocean at the bottom grow nearer, its deep fresh water coral blue, green and red. The rainbow of aquatic life down there didn't seem to care about what was going on, but she could feel her heart beat a tattoo against her chest as she picked up speed. When the tube turned up, gravity crushing the air out of her, Alice's laughter returned after her first breath.

The thrill was overwhelming as the speed she'd gathered took her up steeply. She could see the blue sky through the hole the field made through the water grow larger, larger, larger until she broke the surface. Carnie was right beside her as though he was locked to the course in his fighter, the grin on his face as they approached the surface was enough to get her giggling, even harder, then she realized she should have been getting ready to brake.

There was a turn, a minor one that took her left, then there would be a more significant one to the right that would take her down a long curve. Alice realized as she tried to lean into the turn that she was moving way too fast and was flung free of the track completely. With a squeal of momentary terror, she cartwheeled up through the air, free of everything, including the sled. It must have looked like she was trying to imitate a starfish, splayed out as her arms and legs looked for purchase. Then she saw Carnie, staring at her with amused shock as he rose to a similar height. At the apex of her flight, he twitched at the controls, getting his fighter away, probably so there was no chance of her colliding with him, but for an instant she thought; *why doesn't he put that thing under me so I can get a ride back to the shore?* She was nine metres up, gaining a little altitude in nothing but a swimsuit and a slim emergency collar. The water was below her, to her right. The beach, her crew, and Gabe's people were in front of her, watching as she was shocked to silence. The emergency collar showed that she made it as high as fourteen metres above the water before she began to descend, the waves moving by quickly. It activated a protective shield, showing her the strength of the field it generated around her, and Alice laughed. It was much stronger than she'd need.

The low friction field was enough to keep her from getting knocked out or so much as bruised when she struck the water. She started swimming back up and it deactivated as her head broke the surface. The water was chilly, but she enjoyed the ocean's embrace and the swim back to shore.

She, like so many other spacers, learned to swim in simulations. Just like the Sky Luge track, swimming for real was somehow different, it was more tiring. Alice enjoyed swimming for real more though, it was relaxing, the opposite of Sky Luge, which, even though it was a slow, leisure track, was enough to get her adrenaline pumping.

Her emergency collar crackled with the sounds of Theodore's voice garbling, cracking up and going silent. It was out of power, but Alice guessed what he was trying to tell her. Noah Lucas had landed on the beach. Her foot touched the sand, and she could feel her nervousness rising anew. She adjusted the shimmery powder blue halter and bottom of her bikini, trying to calm down as she took her first steps towards the shore. *I'm going to kick his ass.* The thought made her laugh. It was difficult to stay angry at him. There was no harm in what he was doing, though she was sure he'd be in trouble if she reported him for showboating in a heavy fighter. *I'm going to pretend to be seriously pissed at him.* That left a smile on her face, did nothing to quiet her nerves, but it at least gave her some idea of how the upcoming greeting would go. *Then... who knows?* Alice thought to herself. With a twist and a pull, the emergency collar came off, she'd keep it as a souvenir after it was recharged.

Alice stopped walking for a moment, enjoying the cool water and taking a few seconds to think. If she was wearing her vacsuit, she could expand it for more coverage, but that was another reason for taking a little R&R in nature: to get some distance from all the technology and support that reminded them of their service. "Everything okay?" Dakota said as she splashed towards her.

"I'm fine," Alice called back before ducking underwater. She emerged, taking a couple of steps, whipping her curls back. "That was a blast." She told Dakota. The Science officer was nervous, eager to hear her reaction.

"I've never seen anyone get so much height on an amateur track before, when you starfished it was hilarious. Carnie feels pretty bad, though. He just got released from medical after major reconstruction and was excited to drop in."

The ploy of pretending that she was angry at him fizzled. "I didn't see anything about that," Alice said.

"He said it was a classified thing," Dakota said with a shrug. "The course was good though? You had fun even after Carnie started messing with you?"

"It's a great course," Alice said. "I think I liked it so much because I felt anything but safe when I was thrown," Alice replied, her heart leaping in her chest as Theodore pointed in her direction and started walking Noah Lucas towards her. He straightened his bomber jacket and started walking towards the water's edge. Yawen noticed what was about to happen and started towards Alice. She was only a few metres behind Noah and Theo.

"Wow, he looks good in uniform," Dakota said, following Alice's gaze.

It was true, and he looked much more masculine than she expected, even though she watched a recent message from him. A message she forgot to reply to. She meant to but had no idea what to say. There were things she wasn't allowed to talk about, like her lengthy, detailed report about the journal he recorded during his time on Iora. By the time she finished, she felt like she knew him. Not only that, but she had grown fond of Noah and thought about him often, checked in on him through Crewcast. That drew his attention, or at least something did, because she knew he checked on her almost daily.

It made sense, Theodore was a dear friend to both of them, but she wondered if there wasn't something more on his end. Dakota suspected that too, Alice could feel her intrigue as the tall science officer looked from where Alice was emerging from the water, her back straight, a shy smile on her face, to Noah, who was making his way over the sand between his starfighter and the shore with Theodore at her side.

Oh, no, my senses are wide open, I'm coming down from an adrenaline rush and I'm more nervous than I can remember ever being. Alice realized. Theodore was oblivious. She hoped she looked like the girls in swimsuit calendars that were popular in some berths as she ascended from the waves. Theo rushed to her, meeting Alice as she was knee-deep with a grin. "This is Noah, you know him. They just released him from hospital, cleared for flight, but he has two days off for recovery while the Merciless is close."

"They say it's mental leave, for stress," Noah said, but she could feel that he was playing things cool. He'd had a bad time in medical, the thought of the place made him want to run, to take shelter in better things. "So I can de-stress. I checked on Theo and he called me down here. Sorry about the flyby. Dakota said it was a newbie track, I didn't expect you to come out of that tube like a cannonball," He stepped to the water's edge, his hand extended.

As Alice took one more step towards him and extended her hand, his anxiety washed over her like a wave. He was intimidated, and actually a little afraid. That was surprising, and her own nervousness quieted a little, but she felt something else that made her blush furiously and brought a smile to her face. He had deep admiration for her, and there was a warm amorous feeling that was a little urgent on top of it. She shook her head and struggled to close her empathic abilities off, and when she looked back he stared at her with a little quizzical smile. "Sorry, water in my ear," she said, noticing that he was trying to focus on her face, and she could feel the struggle he was fighting to keep from taking the whole sight of her in. It was a fun feeling, being so adored - even if just physically for the moment - that he had to struggle to keep his eyes from drifting down.

She made sure that her swimsuit was in place, just in case there was more to his struggle than she guessed, saw that it was then looked back at him. There, in those eyes, in that face framed by shoulder length dirty-blonde hair, she recognized the Noah that she'd come to know and wished to meet. That, and knowing that he already had expectations that rivalled her own, made her feel bold. "It's good to finally meet you," she said, moving past his hand and leaning against him, embracing him. There it was again, a feeling so good that she wanted to stay empathically connected to it, to him, for days. His arms wrapped around her and the combination of relief and happiness from him was intoxicating, even though there was a little excitement that was far from innocent, but that only made it better.

"Oh," Theodore said in quiet surprise.

"Now that's how you say 'hello,'" Yawen added, Alice could hear her smiling.

THIRTEEN

The Surface Details

ADMIRAL TAFFORD KNEW what was important. His wife, two sons and sister were on Lore, the most desirable paradise class planet in the sector. His own people checked on them, confirmed and watched over them. Every favour he had, credit he could accumulate and deal he could make went into providing their lasting safety. None of them bought their place on Lore. That was the Overlord's doing. His family was moved there and Tafford would soon follow.

On the surface that seemed like a great idea, living in a well-guarded paradise with his family, but he would be removed from power, removed from current knowledge of how the galaxy was changing. It was an important time, and he had a chance to determine how the new era, what some called the Basic Era, when emotional, independent artificial intelligences capable of unlimited learning were rare again, would begin. As he waited in a secondary hangar aboard his base ship, the Untouchable, he watched the new barrier shield shimmer. It was an upgrade from the Core Worlds, able to keep the air in but let cleared solid objects through without allowing the pressure to change. It was still eerie looking straight out into space, but he knew the technology was sound.

An Arcyn Starskipper slipped through the field and landed smoothly. As it touched down, the small crew access at the front of the ship lowered and Admiral Lucius Wheeler stepped out. His long coat was cut for style, with a high collar and dark colours, but Tafford knew it was part of his armour. He carried a heavy sidearm as though he expected trouble but didn't seem to have any guards with him. When the ship settled, a woman with black hair came down the narrow ramp. She wasn't in a uniform, but a fitted suit with a partial skirt behind. She seemed very familiar, and Tafford would look her up later.

"Hey, Albert," Wheeler said, his smile broad, ignoring the silent line of officers standing at attention behind Admiral Tafford as he offered his hand.

Albert Tafford shook it, there was something limp about Wheeler's grip, as though he was more interested in getting the gesture over with than making any kind of statement with the handshake. That wasn't the way it was done. "Admiral Wheeler. I thought we'd talk before you took command of my battle group."

"Oh, that's not why I'm here," Wheeler said. "I had you come down to the hangar so you could see me arrive in this thing," he gestured over his shoulder at the pristine hull of the Star Bender. "It's an Arcyn Starskipper, Version Three, one of the last ones off the line. We found her in perfect condition and I gave it to Duchess Dermen as a little 'hello' gift. Isn't it amazing?"

"It's a classic ship. The same model as the Clever Dream, if I'm not mistaken?" Admiral Tafford asked, relieved that Wheeler wasn't sent to replace him. "I was sure you were here to replace me."

"Like a dog with a bone," Wheeler turned to him and nodded. His companion stepped in beside him, closer than she would have if they were only acquaintances. "Yeah, I'll explain that so you can stop trying to figure out why you're not throwing a retirement party today. Dron and I talked for a while, and we agreed that I wasn't ready to sit in the middle of an Overlord Class base ship, directing millions of people into a complicated invasion. You're still the right guy for the job, and you're doing just fine getting the Edxi to soften the Haven System up before you go in. I don't know how you talk to those stubborn bugs, but it's working out, so why change anything? I told Dron; 'Look, the guy seems happy in command, and his family's all set up in the middle of Order territory, safe and sound, so let him do his work. I'm sure he doesn't hold anything against you for showing him his place, it's the military, it happens.' Dron said he'd leave it up to me, he has bigger fish to fry now that he's got the biggest governments in two sectors hanging on his every word. I can stick with my smaller, easier to manage little battle group, or take yours if I don't think you're working out where you are. I mean, it's an easy decision for me. If things look good here, I don't have to take on more responsibility. If they don't, then I get to ship you off to Lore to be with your family. Damn, if only every decision was so easy." He turned his head and was kissed by his impatient companion. The salacious display went on too long, so Tafford gently cleared his throat. Wheeler extracted himself, his full-lipped, lovely woman smiling at his side. "I have to send the Duchess here away tonight on this mint ship. Now, that was a difficult decision."

"I'm sure. So, you've decided to leave me in place?"

"Definitely and indefinitely," Wheeler said. "I've seen the warrior swarm that's about to head to the Haven System. I don't know what you said to convince the Edxi to put so many of their resources into one attack, but I'm impressed. That, and how quick you're getting your fleet back on its feet after the Mary Virus hit it is pretty amazing. I couldn't have done better."

Admiral Tafford looked over his shoulder and nodded at his command team. "You are dismissed." They fell out of formation. Most of them would return to the duty shifts he had to pull them from. He returned his full attention to Wheeler. "I appreciate the praise. Communicating with Edxi isn't so difficult. Remembering that they put honour first, family second - a concept that includes a sort of dynastic power for them - and food third at all times is key. Once you understand that, you can reason with them. There is something odd that I'd like to share, however."

"Oh?" Wheeler asked, intrigued. He was doing his best to ignore the Duchess, who was nibbling at his ear.

"I'm afraid I can't speak of it in current company," Tafford whispered, hoping that he wouldn't offend the royal in their midst.

Wheeler looked at the Duchess. "Would you mind leaving the Admiral and I for a while? Make sure you have everything you need for your trip? Especially the dress."

"I still don't understand why giving her that dress is so important. I have jewellery that would be more appropriate. Pieces that you just bought for me and I haven't worn yet," the Duchess said.

"Add a piece of jewellery if you like, but you have to present her with the full-sized dress-box, sealed."

"It has to be that dress?"

"Sealed just the way I gave it to you, so, yes, that dress in that dress box. Don't worry, she might think it's a little too daring in front of you, but the Queen will love it privately. If you want your family to have a relationship with her, then this is the way to go."

"I'll trust you," she said, her lisp combining with her accent, making it impossible for Tafford to guess where she came from. She nipped his earlobe, nodded at Tafford then walked back to her ship.

Wheeler waited for the ramp to close before muttering; "I'm going to miss her. Now I see what Minh-Chu always liked about that brunette model."

"I thought I recognized her," Admiral Tafford whispered, trying to keep the surprise of the scandal from showing. "How does she look so much like Ashley Lamport? How was it unnoticed?"

"She's from the coreward edge of the sector, a doll that was bought a generation ago to fill a gap in the Dermen family. They called her Tammy and took her in as their daughter. The whole Ashley line was one of those secret doll rollouts, only available to the super-wealthy, the nets were scrubbed regularly of any evidence that there was more than one of them, but with the artificial intelligences that used to do that down, it's only going to get easier to find them, like I did. Man, was I surprised. I was able to find the Duchess because there was a search on shortly after she ran away before the big virus hit. Tammy was in stasis, one of our patrols picked up the wreck she was drifting in, and she was in storage. I checked with her owners, sorry, her family to see if they wanted her back and found out that they have three young daughters now, they weren't interested in having her back home, but liked the idea of her earning credit for the family with the Order of Eden, so I got her out of the freezer. She thinks I rescued her and that she's being given an opportunity to make inroads with Queen Ayan Anderson just in case they manage to negotiate peace with the Order."

"We have no intention of negotiating," Admiral Tafford said in a hush. It was a convoluted scheme from what he was hearing so far. There were too many moving parts. He had no idea what Wheeler could be planning, but he doubted it would turn out the way he expected.

"I know, but I have to get a package to Ayan, and shaking Jake's crew up by surprising them with a copy of their famous pilot, who will probably fly to pieces when she realizes that she's a doll, and that the only other copy she's seen is an oversexed socialite, is just too good to resist. I am going to miss her, though. She's all kinds of fun, especially since she thinks I'm her hero."

"Does the Duchess know she's a doll?"

"No, I've kept all images of Ashley Lamport far away. This gag has an expiry date, but if I can get the Duchess in front of people in the Haven System, it's going to be hilarious," Wheeler chuckled to himself. "Especially since the Duchess thinks she's on an important mission of peace. Her family was very cooperative, setting her up with all the paperwork and even taking some time to say hello through a couple recordings, all full of relief that she's been found. This will blow their minds, give them all kinds of drama to deal with."

"What about this dress? Is there a plot to kill Ayan Anderson I should know about?"

"It's too early to reveal details, but it's part of a long term plan. I've tried to get in with someone Ayan trusts before to put this plan into motion, but it didn't work out. I was so close when Dron yanked me back from Tamber, I didn't think I'd get a better shot. This time I think we're golden. All the pieces fell into place. I'm keeping everything I don't need to tell you and the rest of the fleet out of the files, I don't want anything getting in the way just in case Ayan and her people survive the invasion. This plan will shake them up, crack their leadership pretty good. Kill Ayan now, and you have an angelic martyr. Force her to break down, to retreat from the public, and you demoralize everyone. I'm surprised I can get around Dron pulling me off Tamber at all, so many pieces of this plan are just gone."

Tafford decided to venture a guess at what Wheeler might be doing. "You're starting a propaganda war with a smear campaign."

"Holy crap, I can't believe you get this," Wheeler replied

enthusiastically. "Like I said, I'm not giving more details, but that's exactly what I'm doing. The Order is intercepting more ships headed for Haven every week, all of them filled with idiots who are eager to sign up based on Ayan and Jakes and whoever else's rising public image. We trash that, and we can really isolate them. If this invasion doesn't stick, but my campaign works, then we won't even have to blockade the Haven System, which would take hundreds, maybe thousands of ships. Trust me, when I'm done they'll be distracted, discredited, and demoralized."

"I'm happy you're on our side again, Lucius," said Admiral Tafford.

"Oh, good, we're on first names now," Wheeler said, his happiness genuine as far as anyone could tell. "Now, what was it that you wanted to tell me?"

Admiral Tafford turned his surveillance scrambler on, no one would be able to overhear or record them. "I've met one of the biological leaders of the Edxi people."

"Wait, what do you mean, 'biological leader,' what does that mean?" Wheeler asked.

"They're merged beings, hybrids that are hundreds of years old. The Beast was the closest thing we've had to them in this galaxy, even though he was completely different. These beings take genetic traits from species they encounter to improve and strengthen themselves. I was surprised to see that the one I spoke to was mostly human shaped, but it has a mask that looked grown, and an under layer of bone as hard as armour. She explained a little about what she is, why she is so important. They were once very similar to humans, but her people began to bond with new beings from three different galaxies. Most of them stopped after blending with humans, but her group didn't. When they encountered the Edxi, they were a more basic tribal insect type of creature. There was a war on, so the leader I spoke to, Larsis, created a disease that spread across the population of one Edxi world, giving them increased intelligence and a genetic bond with her. Larsis was one of several hundred leaders who did the same, taking on hives, whole planets worth of Edxi and they won their war. There was one problem with their new servants: they needed to expand. It's the biological imperative for all Edxi, to feed and grow their tribes. Every Edxi under Larsis and the few who showed how the people of the Milky Way abused them through experimentation when Zarrix found evidence that they are biologically bonded with her. They can't challenge her, have to obey her commands."

"Someone's feeding you lines, Albert. There's no way there's some mysterious humanoid queen controlling this invasion," Wheeler dismissed.

"Have you ever seen anyone speak to an Edxi? I mean about strategy, or something broader than revenge, expanding their broods or hunger? No, that's reserved for the most trusted commanders. People with empathic or telepathic abilities especially. This is why. This is the secret they're hiding. A handful of leaders who control everything."

"Okay, your file doesn't say anything about you being a telepath, so why is she calling you up?"

"They want the Haven System more than any they've seen in this galaxy. They don't want any radiological damage done to Tamber or the nine planets they can terraform in short order for new hive worlds. If they get it they can breed warrior tribes into tens of billions within a decade while they use Haven as a base to take six more solar systems. Cefa, Gemri..."

"I know which solar systems, the Cluster. I thought the Order wanted it for the same reason."

"Dron has made a deal with her and the Edxi rulers. They get The Cluster, and the Milky Way gets thirty-five years of peace. They're discussing what comes next after that, but Larsis doesn't trust him. She trusted Hampon, respected his drive to cling to life and admired him for trying to develop new strategies despite his success or failure. His success with the Holocaust Virus as a reaction to her broods moving into the galaxy got her attention. It was ruthless, calculating to try to thin the population so much that the Edxi wouldn't bother with the Milky Way, would see the honour debt owed to them paid in full, but they didn't leave because of Larsis. It was impressive enough for her to reveal herself and open a dialog. Hampon was always willing to share his plans with her, but his younger brother, Dron, isn't so open. She sees the power base he's created and how quickly it's growing, and understands that it could be a threat. He knows this galaxy better than her, has dominant battlegroups in three sectors and took his place as Overlord before bringing the old guard in this sector to heel. That's enough for her to start looking for allies elsewhere."

"This info could blow up the whole command staff from the top. Why are you telling me? You know I'd abandon this Order the moment I thought it was losing the upper hand and could get a clean getaway."

"I need someone like you," Admiral Tafford said, pushing

on to the core of his gamble. "Allies, trades, the ability to play the system and climb the ladder got me where I am. Their importance falls in that order. You're only as good..."

"...as the friends you have and the crew on your ship," Wheeler finished with a smirk. "Classic spacer saying, I get you, go on."

"Right, so I'm somewhere in the middle between these juggernauts, and it's time for me to have a new kind of friend. If my commission continues for long enough here, I can sort like-minded people onto the most important ships. We can arrange things so there is a trustworthy group within the Order who will follow me no matter which plan I decide to put into action. My family are safe for now, surrounded by my people, so I can get them off Lore the moment they get the word, but Dron is watching me."

"He's watching me too, but he's given me enough rope to hang myself. You need me in your pocket as an external actor. Someone who knows what you do with more freedom so I can act in your best interest on a moment's notice."

"Exactly."

"What's in it for me?"

"The best Knights in the fleet."

"You'll transfer the Razer Knights?" Wheeler asked, excited.

"All yours. Put them to work and impress the Overlord."

"Man, okay, that's one thing my carrier group was light on; examples, leadership. Half of 'em haven't seen real combat, but these guys will get them in shape. I almost feel like I'm getting the better end of this deal. Want anything else?

Wanna be rich? Want a moon? I know of a nice tropical place. Clear out some crazy 'bots and it's all yours."

"I'll rebuild my wealth in a month from this rank, and I'd rather stay mobile. Just come to my side the moment I need your help, Lucius, and that'll be good enough."

"My kind of deal," Wheeler said, shaking his hand. "And I'll even keep the info about the Master Bug to myself."

"That would be best. If she hears you talking about her we're both dead."

"I've heard that before. Last time I died, I broke a thousand hearts. Killing me will always come at a price no one wants to pay."

FOURTEEN

Taking Sunshine

WOONE CHASED Krooke as only Nafalli burrowers could. Alice, Gabe and Iruuk watched with amazed amusement as Krooke erupted up from under the sand, shaking grains off his fur. "Where'd you go?" he asked, looking in all directions, his nose twitching.

Woone popped up closer to the shoreline, coughing. "Too much water in the sand that way!" she announced.

"I knew I lost you!" Krooke shouted, diving into the loose, dry sand, disappearing deep under the surface.

"How do they keep from suffocating? The sand must close in around them as they move," Gabe asked.

"I bet that's what would happen if they stop moving for too long," Yawen offered as she and Noah joined them. "The flyboy's fighter is docked to the Clever Dream. I have him set up in a guest bunk." She was in a bikini that was more like three patches, too daring for Alice, but it looked good on her, and it looked like Noah reduced his uniform down to trunks that were recoloured green and blue.

Woone ran up the beach, away from the waterline, her short legs moving so fast it was almost comical, then she dove into the dry sand, disappearing beneath the surface in seconds. "You're right," Iruuk said. "Burrowers are always making room for themselves ahead. They don't turn around often. It makes them good navigators, they always know which way is up and north. Well, almost always. No one's perfect. The legends say they were also the first to start exploring the oceans in wooden ships. The real age of exploration didn't really begin until the tree dwellers joined in, though."

"Keep telling yourself that, stretch," Faloo said, joining them and looking up at Iruuk.

"Water's wet," Iruuk said as he squeezed a spongy ball over Faloo's head, dripping a small bucket's worth of cold water onto her carefully groomed fur. "Oops, I didn't know there was so much in there, sorry!"

"Oooh!" she growled, tripping him and grabbing his foot. "I'll show you water!" she said dragging him by his ankle to the water's edge.

He struggled for a moment, trying to yank free, then clawing at the sand. "Wow! You're strong!" Iruuk laughed.

Giggles pierced the air as she fought to pull him into the waves with her. He started finding his feet and a war of splashes began between Faloo and Iruuk.

"Hey! Fur-Face! My ball!" Gabe shouted.

Iruuk tossed the water-logged ball back to him, still splashing Faloo back with his other hand. Gabe almost failed to catch it and sighed with relief when he had it firmly in hand. "Wow, that almost got messy."

"It's just water," Yawen said.

"Catch," Gabe said, whipping the soft ball at her. It struck her squarely in the shoulder, half covering her with yellow and green colours. The crews in folding chairs arranged in a semi-circle facing their ships laughed and gasped. "It's a Splatter Ball. If you catch it you get a little wet, but if it hits you after you don't, you get painted."

"Popular where you come from?" Yawen asked, picking the ball up and looking at the dripping yellow and green paint.

"Yeah, we get in a circle to start the game, then start throwing. Losers run the ball back to the water and get to throw back," Gabe explained as he started backing away from Yawen.

"Oh, sounds simple." Yawen burst into a run towards the shore to re-soak the ball, then looked at Gabe, brandishing the dripping toy.

"Game on!" Gabe laughed, breaking into a run.

Half the crewmembers in the folding chairs got to their feet and Alice almost didn't notice that Yawen targeted her before she whipped the ball in her direction. Alice caught it more by reflex than skill, cold water splashed her, but it didn't turn to paint. "What do I do?"

"Pick a target!" Gabe shouted from a distance.

Alice spotted Knud in the corner of her eye, sunning on the sand in a bathing suit that was more of a modesty pocket with string. Jessen noticed and rolled away. "Get him!"

Alice threw the soft ball hard, and cold red and purple paint erupted from it as it struck his side. He stood up with the ball in his hand, his eyes searching for whoever threw it.

"It was Yawen!" Alice pointed at her as she emerged mostly paint free from the shore and laughed as Knud charged after her. Yawen ran towards the crowd of crewmembers. Another ball made an appearance, something Alice only realized as it struck her in the forehead, covering her with green and white.

"You had that coming! Callum said, putting distance between himself and Alice."

Noah grabbed the ball from the sand and rushed to the water. "I've gotta get in on this!"

"No!" Alice shouted, running after him. "My throw!" she laughed.

THE GAME MOVED UP and down the beach, eventually forming into a crowd of multi-coloured crewmembers trying to catch each other whenever they weren't paying attention to the three throwers. The three soft Splatter Balls were re-soaked and thrown more times than anyone could count, and most of the shots landed, especially when Theodore joined and was hit from all sides at once. Jessen, Noah and Iruuk learned their lessons quickly, however, since Theodore was faster than all but the tall Nafalli, and could throw with more precision and speed than anyone. They all found themselves thoroughly splattered.

. . .

WHEN MOST OF them were exhausted and covered in every colour the toys could produce, Noah approached Alice with a small bag in his hand. "Can I drag you away for a while?" he asked.

His nervousness was clear to her, there was no need to find his mood empathically, and she was glad to feel normal again. Maybe someone from Lorander would see that as closed off, but she felt calmer when her mind wasn't open to the feelings of the people around her. "Sure, let's walk."

Neither of them bothered washing off. Most of the crewmembers were still covered in colours as they took tall bottles of chilled fruit drinks from refrigeration chests. Yawen looked up from where she was making a spiral on her belly in the paint and winked at Alice as she started walking off with Noah.

Alice shook her head and started away from the gathering, snickering under her breath at their motley colours. It would all rinse off easily enough, she'd dunked in the water twice to get rid of paint before getting her final coat from Knud and Iruuk as she caught a Splatter Ball tossed by Gabe. She decided there had to be one in her vacation kit, a bag she wanted to put together for rare days like the one her crew were having.

When they were far enough from the crew to be out of earshot, Noah offered her the small, loose weave bag. "I ran into a little girl named Shauna at the hospital who tracked me down through Crewcast. She said you and Iruuk saved her father, and she made something for you."

"Did you find out why she was in the hospital?" Alice asked.

"She said her brother, Amel, was getting his head fixed. Her father said that he suffered traumatic brain damage when they were getting away from some mad 'bots, and Haven Medical was repairing the damage."

Alice opened the bag and found two bracelets. Hers was made from opalescent blue, white and green beads held together by soft black string. Iruuk's was longer but only had a couple extra beads, but she also added a metal wolf head to the end of the piece. "These are amazing, she's really young to be this good. I'm going to have to visit her," Alice said. "Help me put it on."

Noah tied the bracelet around Alice's wrist above her command and control bracer. "She said your roommate kept on telling her that you weren't home and weren't taking deliveries."

"Roomie," Alice shook her head. "That stupid AI probably still thinks I live there. I gave my house up a while ago, the Clever Dream and a hangar are more than I need. I think Roomie was one of the things that made letting that place go easier, she could barely make a cup of coffee."

"You got your hands on coffee beans?" Noah asked, surprised.

"No, she'd be mystified if I told her to make real coffee. I mean the synthetic stuff," Alice snickered. "Thank you, Noah."

"No problem," he replied, rechecking the knot holding the bracelet on before letting go.

They continued down the beach quietly for a few

moments, and Alice was tempted to reach out, find out what he was feeling, but said the first thing that came to mind instead. "I know you." She regretted it immediately.

Noah regarded her with an expression that seemed caught between confusion and surprise.

"I mean, I'm not supposed to tell you this, I could get into real trouble, but I listened to and watched everything you recorded on Iora. I've been following you on Crewcast ever since. The only thing I haven't seen are all the reports from the Iron Head Nebula." It came out in a rush, one that stopped abruptly when she took a long drink from her vanilla peach beverage. The relaxing effect of the inebriant took the edge off the moment, and she stopped drinking, surprised at its potency.

"You got into my storage, too," he said after a moment. "So?"

"Uh..." Alice looked at him, he didn't seem angry, not even shocked or confused anymore, he just looked down the shore-line as they walked it.

"I mean, what did you think? When I recorded all that stuff, I thought I'd be dead when someone found it, so I really didn't hold back. Now I'm around, and you saw it all, so I could run away screaming, maybe try to dig like the burrow-ers, or I could just ask; 'what do you think?' and hope for the best."

Alice chuckled nervously. The thought that he never thought he'd be around to have his logs reviewed never occurred to her. There were memories from a time when she knew how to talk to people, to be convincing, even alluring but they didn't help her. On the spot, she didn't know what to say, how could she sum up the week or so she spent going through his experiences, listening to his voice. When all the recordings were reviewed, the holograms watched, that's what she missed most - listening to him talk to her - but she forced herself to let it all rest instead of giving her comm unit, or Roomie Noah's voice, though it was tempting.

While he waited for her answer, glancing at her with growing uncertainty, she was tempted to run back to the social safety of the group too, but nodded to herself and stepped in front of him instead so she could be face to face as she walked backwards. "You're here, and it does my head in because I'm used to listening to you talk to me, I mean some listener you recorded all that for in the future. I don't know what to expect from the live version," she smirked at him, enjoying how he regarded her with a surprised half-smile. If Theodore was monitoring her heart rate, he might be alarmed, and that was after she'd had a good pull on her relaxer beverage. "What do I think of hours and hours of you? Watching you go through everything you did on Iora unvarnished? I..." *I missed you when it was over,* she thought, blushing. "I want to know more," Alice said instead. "But it wouldn't be fair to start asking you questions the first time we meet up, not since I have such an unfair advantage, so if there's anything you want to know about me, I'm an open book, but it stays between us, no sharing."

Noah laughed, sweeping his paint spattered hair out of his face. "I'm not crazy enough to share your secrets."

"Why's that?" Alice asked, pretty sure she knew the answer already.

"Let's see, your father is a well-known badass."

"Generous and a loyal friend if you get on his good side," Alice said.

"Your mother is officially our Queen now," he said.

"A caring, smart woman who would always rather be nice and considerate before anything else, you don't have to worry about her... much," Alice corrected.

"Much," Noah laughed ruefully for a moment. "You know a lot of people running the fleet from there, including my Wing Commander, my boss." He sighed, looked her up and down, smiled a little before focusing on her eyes. "Then there's you. I mean, I only know what you put on your Crew-cast profile, but you set records after dropping the framework stuff, set a high bar in the Academy, and even if half the rumours are true, you've seen almost as much of the galaxy as I have, survived more trouble than I would have if I was on Iora for a decade, and you can still be fun, beautiful." He smiled as though getting those compliments out, especially the last one, was a victory for him. "Even in a dozen colours of paint."

"You were expecting Captain Buzz Kill?" Alice replied, happy that he found her fun. It had been a long time since she'd unwound and enjoyed herself like that.

Noah laughed. "I don't know what I expected. Maybe a nod or a handshake before you went about important business, that's kinda how I get treated with most higher ranking people. You're a Captain, and a famous one, so..." he shrugged.

"You tempered your expectations," Alice said. "This is not a business suit," she added, glancing down. "And rank is not an issue on this beach. Not my rule, it's Gabe's but I'm going by it. So, ask me anything."

Noah tapped his command and control unit a few times then looked back at her. "Oh, I'm not setting it to record, I'm enabling privacy mode. A buddy in engineering set me up with the best blocker out there."

Alice held up the slender, transparent blue command and control unit she slipped on after her ride on the sky luge track. It looked completely ornamental, a bracelet, but it had all the communication and computing functions most people would need. "Modified for privacy. This thing records but doesn't share unless I want it to or someone knows the override, and only two people in the fleet will know it if something happens to me."

"Glad we have our privacy sorted," he smiled. "Even after meeting you in person, you seem so together, like you have your whole life figured out."

Alice laughed and fell in step beside him. "Oh, wow, you have so much to learn about me. My head's just starting to come together, I'm a mess."

"You don't look like a mess to me," he said, causing a resurge in her blushing, which she hoped he couldn't see well under the paint. He glanced at her and chuckled. "Well, maybe you're a mess right now, but a short swim would fix that."

"Good idea," Alice said, draining the rest of her bottle in a long pull, crumpling it up so the glass reverted to harmless sand, then running into the water.

He stuck his mostly full bottle in the sand and rushed in after her. The paint dissolved completely by the time she swam out far enough to tread water. She turned and was surprised to see that he'd caught up. "Okay, Open Book," he said, finding a little bravery in the moments it took him to swim to her. "What's it like being a Fleet Darling?"

"Ouch," Alice laughed, splashing him. "It sucks! Everyone's watching, it feels like most of them are just waiting for me to screw up. I'd trade places with you in a second."

"Me? I'm just a pilot. Yeah, I feel like a pretty big deal when I'm out there, like part of a team with important work to do, but you have this awesome ship and a crew. You must see some pretty amazing places."

"Not since the Fleet formed. It's mostly been rescue and emergency work so far. You miss travelling around?"

"Yeah, but I love flying, so if I had to choose, I don't think I'd change anything," Noah said. "What about you? What would you change?"

"Nothing. I think I've changed enough for now. Sometimes it feels like I was a completely different person a few months ago, then I remember that teenage girl and realize she's still here a little." The relaxation effect of her drink was making her muscles feel warm and her mind calmer. It was a welcome change, but not overwhelming. "Gimmie another question."

It was clear, right there in his changing expression: A question came to him, then he decided it was either the wrong question or a bad idea.

"What was that?" Alice asked with an upraised eyebrow.

"If you could be anywhere..."

"That's not what you were really going to ask, was it?" She punctuated it with a splash.

He regarded her more seriously. "You just seem more comfortable watching people, not being in the middle. Like the Splatter Ball game. The moment you had a ball you couldn't get rid of it fast enough, then you avoided getting the ball back so someone else was the centre of attention. Every time I ask you a question, I feel like I'm putting you on the spot, even though you ask me to. You're amazing, why do you want to stick to the background?"

Alice knew what he was talking about immediately. She was more social before she met Jacob Valent, only stand offish because she was afraid knowing her too well might get them into trouble while Meunez was chasing her, but she was having trouble finding the ease and confidence she once had with people. Her hesitation prompted him.

"Maybe I'm just seeing you at work? Like you're a captain whenever your crew is around?"

"No, that's not it," Alice said, starting to swim back to shore.

"I'm sorry, it didn't feel like a good question," Noah said as they walked out of the water a few moments later.

Alice stopped, he nearly collided with her. "I'm just..." she didn't know how to finish her thought aloud.

"Hey, it's okay," Noah said, touching her shoulder. His hand felt warm on her cooled skin.

Maybe it was the light effect of her drink, or a need to tell him, but something drove her to look up into his eyes and just speak. "When I started listening to your logs I didn't feel really connected to anything. I had a friend or two I liked, but I was a clean slate, studying hard, chasing my goals at the Academy. Then I listened to you talk to me for a whole week, saw you do a lot of growing up. Then I got to the end and..."

Noah didn't look surprised. Instead he looked maybe a little pleased? Amused? What was that little smile stretching his lips and narrowing his eyes. She reached for her empathic gift and failed to get a read on him. *When I don't want it I can't shut it off, then I want to read him and I can't concentrate enough to open up. I want to cheat, for once, I need to know how bad I scare him off.* She thought, barking a short laugh at the thought. "You got to the end?" Noah asked quietly.

"Then you stopped talking to me," she finished. "And I missed you."

It didn't take an empath to see that he was pleasantly surprised. "I could start recording logs again. Send you daily reports on my days aboard the Merciless." He was teasing.

"I'm being serious!" she laughed, in disbelief that he was actually teasing her about a huge revelation that she expected would send him running for his starfighter.

"So am I!" he said, grinning. "'Day twenty-one. Patrol was boring. I definitely shouldn't eat the apple-cinnamon mix before flying again. I am amazed I made it back to the ship before using my suit's plumbing. One of my roommates has a squeaky drawer they keep opening once or twice a night. Tonight, I'm going to set my command and control unit to record, so I can catch the bugger and force him to service that thing so he doesn't wake me up again. I keep dreaming of squeaky kawaii dragons chasing me,'" he said in a narrator's voice.

"No, I miss you," Alice said, rejecting the falseness of it, then realizing what she said and blushing. "The way you recorded before, like you were talking to a friend." It seemed important to explain.

He took her hand gingerly and looked into her eyes. It felt like her mind and all the thoughts within paused. "Hey, just..." he started to say softly, then an alert turned her command and control unit red.

"We have to get back to the ship," she said.

"Yeah, one sec," he gripped her hand a little.

His light blue eyes met hers the moment she turned back towards him. "Quick," she said.

"I just want time to catch up, okay?"

Some of that confidence she remembered returned just long enough for her to squeeze his hand back and smile at him. "I'm your open book." Excited, elated, she turned away from him and started running up the beach.

Carnie passed her momentarily, but he had to slow down to retrieve his bottle from the sand. With him close behind, a more serious mood began to settle on her. She had to be a Captain again by the time she got to her crew.

FIFTEEN

Captain Stephanie Vega, Fleet Intelligence

WATCHING Agameg command the Merciless with great calm and grace was reassuring to Jake. He knew what kind of commander the Issyrian had become: calculating, intelligent, very present moment-to-moment and he was a lover of efficiency. It was too early to admit it, but Jake learned from him often. There was definitely something to be said for watching a commander do their job, especially when their style was different.

Jake was in his quarters, watching the bridge holographically, it surrounded him, made him forget he wasn't there. All the preparation work for the meeting that would start in ten minutes, hopefully less, was done. Agameg and Captain Moore, the new Nafalli third shift Captain, were spending more and more time in the chair. Captain Neel Moore was sitting at one of the reserve stations at the rear of the bridge, watching the ship's status overall while he chatted idly with Finn.

They were flying a course that took them around the middle of the Haven solar system as they prepared for a patrol route that would keep them out there until it was time to break from the fleet. Jake was the only one that knew that they were going to be doing so other than the upper ranks of Intelligence.

Kadri, Liara, Agameg and Finn were good people, *his* people, and they were accommodating, welcoming the new navigator - Gubba the Mergillian - as well as the new Nafalli captain with two others - Looph with her silver fur, and Huun, a brown burrower - without reservation. They were already working together, even though Huun was a little shy about his new responsibilities at first. He was standing in for Frost on the bridge, the lead Starship Tactical officer, and had better strategic style, but he didn't have the understanding of the weaponry that Frost would have, so he accepted a great deal of assistance from Finn and his engineering team, which fit perfectly with the way the crew were to work on the ship. The engineering and damage control teams took care of every system aboard, there was no longer a separate team for weaponry and shielding. That suited Finn fine, since he seemed addicted to reviewing the new tech, learning every piece by destroying and rebuilding them in simulations over and over again. Every time he solved a new problem, he put it out to his teams as a challenge, and some of them were getting a little tired of being tested, it kept his people learning, and it made some of them stand out.

Newly minted Captain Stephanie Vega entered the bridge. She was in a black vacsuit with a long coat and sidearm. The gold stripe down her sides marked her as command staff, and the tiny half-skull on her collar marked her as a member of Fleet Intelligence. Everyone turned. It was her first time on the ship, and her old friends were happy to see her. "Welcome to the Merciless, Captain Vega," Agameg said, turning the command chair to face her. "And congratulations on your pregnancy." In an instant his head ballooned into an overlarge, cartoon-ish, pink and white, exaggerated baby head. It was so sudden that Stephanie actually jumped backwards. "Gah!"

Jacob recoiled like most of the bridge crew, giant blue baby-eyes on a bulbous, pinkish large baby-head made for an unsettling sight. "It's so hard to look at, but I can't look away," Kadri said.

Huun looked up, saw Agameg, gagged, then locked his station, tapping the subordinate behind him so she would take over tactical as he rushed to the small bridge bathroom, and the crew could hear him project his lunch until the door slid closed behind him.

"What? I made sure this was as accurate an imitation as I could manage on short notice and added size and bulbosity for comedic impact." He looked around for a moment, noting how the bridge crew recoiled, some of them snickering in the dwindling sudden shock of it, then turned back to Stephanie. "It worked on Finn."

Finn was the only one who was laughing, he was nearly doubled over, but Jake suspected that he'd seen Agameg shape change more often, and was used to the Issyrian's sense of humour.

"That's a misfire, Sir," Looph said from the Flight Control console, snickering and holding her nose.

Agameg sighed, a gesture that was only exaggerated as his head deflated back to normal and regained its former shape. "Congratulations, nonetheless. I'm sorry if I frightened you."

"I was just startled," Stephanie said, patting Finn on the back as he wiped tears from his eyes. "Thank you, Agameg."

Huun walked back to his station, his head low. "I apologize for my reaction, Commander Price."

"I'm sorry my humour provoked such a strong response," Agameg said as Stephanie stepped up to the command seat, stopping to stand beside him.

"It's all right. You reminded me of something that was much worse, it wasn't really your fault."

"Oh? What did I remind you of?"

"I'd rather not say, Sir," Huun replied, the brown fur on his back and neck standing up for a moment.

"Oh, now you have to share," Stephanie said, looking something over on her command and control unit.

"My father and I found a wood worm nest in the den once. They dry soil and eat wood, can destroy entire homes if you don't catch them. I was still a pup, and he didn't warn me about what would happen when he poured pure salt on the nest. They inflated like your head did and popped in my face, hundreds of them, expanding and exploding, making this high screaming sound." He shuddered and covered his nose.

"I understand," Agameg said.

Captain Moore was watching the exchange, shaking his

head and grinning, his long maw twitching as he tried to supress his amusement. He took a deep breath then let it out in a long, calming exhale as he turned to face his station. "The Clever Dream is in Bay Three," he announced.

"Thank you, Captain," Lieutenant Commander Looph said from where she was monitoring the Flight Operations station. "The Sky Stalker is next in the pattern. We are moving Carnie's new fighter from the Clever Dream's outer mooring point to a service bay for inspection."

"Thank you," Agameg said, turning his command seat forward.

A chime at the door sounded, and Jake gestured for it to open by pointing at it and curling his fingers. "Deactivate holographic monitoring." The hologram of the bridge disappeared, revealing his quarters. He was standing at the end of the table closest to the door.

Remmy Sands entered, his new uniform bearing the red stripe on its sides and his new rank insignia. Jake had him fast-tracked to Captain. His new long coat looked too new, and he came in offering his hand. "Thank you for this opportunity, Commodore," he said as Jake took it and shook it firmly. "My squad just finished checking in, everyone's accounted for and ready to go."

"You chose Sergeant Dotty Bedel as your second on the ground, I'm impressed. I looked at her record and was surprised to see she hadn't moved up faster, you found someone who has been overlooked."

"I can't take credit. She's a good friend, I've been lucky to serve with her. She should have her own SOCU team, if you ask me, but not too soon. I'm going to need her help." Remmy took his long coat off and put it on the back of one of the chairs in the middle of the table.

He still looked young to Jake, but not too young to have a team of his own. Remmy's tactical prowess and surprising ability to bring a team together was well known, but this was his first real command. "I gave you the assignment because I think it's the best place for you. I've seen what you can do, I've never been disappointed, so I'm sure you'll prove me right."

"No pressure." Remmy nodded and made sure the arms of his uniform were straight, tugging his cuffs. It wasn't necessary with their suits, but most of the people who were trained by Freeground couldn't drop the habit of minding their uniforms. It wasn't a flaw, in Jake's opinion.

Stephanie entered the room. "Nice ship, cute trick you, Ayan and the fleet pulled on everyone."

"Oh, you noticed?" Remmy said. Then he remembered that he was talking to a Captain. "Sorry," he snapped to attention and saluted.

"At ease," Stephanie said, returning the salute. "Still not used to the promotion? We're the same rank, Remmy."

"Right," Remmy said. "Better to salute than forget, anyway."

"True, good rule of thumb," Stephanie nodded. "Jake got me used to an informal ship, it's led to a few bad habits. Like I was saying; your people made sure there were a few corvettes ready to go on the Merciless. It's like they knew you'd be running SOCU before you did."

"The things you find out when you work for Intelligence," Jake said. "How's the new job?"

"I see a lot more people every day," Stephanie said. "I can't wait to get aboard Freeground Station, though. Everything's up in the air as I learn the ropes. I'm getting put down on Tamber in the meantime, though. The military bases don't have enough people running the show, so it looks like I'm going to be filling in here and there."

"Oh, so no staff yet?"

"Not yet, still passing quals and doing runner work, but I'm seeing how the wheels turn behind the scenes. Delivering data and making sure your Special Operations people are ready is a nice break though."

"Good. What do you think of Noah Lucas on this mission?" Jake asked.

"He's an expert, qualified on everything he needs, but I wonder if he has the mental fortitude to handle it," Stephanie said, sitting down at the far end of the table.

"Carnie's going on mission with SOCU? Which team?" Remmy asked.

"Clever Dream," Stephanie said. "You know him, don't you?"

"I do. He's gone from kid in a cockpit to ace quick, and he's seen some things. I think he'll be fine, no matter where you send him."

"I think he's good for this," Jake said. "As good as any fish out of water, but I saw the report on him. Anyone who went through what he has can handle this."

"Oh, man, how is my clearance not high enough for the details?" Remmy muttered with a soft snicker.

"Oh, it is," Stephanie said. "We're just sparing you the details so you hear them with everyone else."

Alice, Iruuk, Gabe and Noah entered the room. Gabe

and Iruuk had multi-coloured painted faces. "What happened to you two?"

"Game of Splatter Ball right before we got the alert. We suited up and came right away, ready for a fight," Gabe said.

"Sorry, we're in a hurry, but there's no fight. Not yet," Jake said. "Splatter Ball? I'll look it up."

"You know, you could have used your suit's auto-clean to get rid of that," Stephanie said with a cocked eyebrow.

"Didn't want to fill the output pocket unless I had to," Gabe said. "The paint you see from the neck up is only the tip of a very messy iceberg. I'd be happy to show you."

"That's all right," Stephanie chuckled, raising a warding hand. "Okay, we're all here, and we don't have much time." Turning to Jake she asked; "Mind if I run the briefing, Commodore?"

"Please, go ahead," he replied, sitting down.

A hologram of a fleet of ships that looked like they were a collection of brown and black girders trailing behind a central hub with a vicious point at the front appeared above the table in a hologram with data readouts surrounding it. "This is classified level seven. Iruuk and Noah are being given special allowances so they can sit in at this briefing. Have a seat, please."

Everyone took a seat, Alice at Jake's left hand. She looked at him, a little surprised as though she just realized where she was sitting. He winked at her and was satisfied that she smiled back at him a little before turning to Stephanie.

"Commodore Valent will fill you in on more details and assign you to your missions, but I'm here to fill you in on the broader strokes. Here's what you need to know about what's going on. The clock is ticking. The fleet of insect type ships you see are charging jump drives. The fourth and fifth ships in the Special Combat Operations Unit have spotted them from a distance. After collecting data for several hours, we've determined that it'll take forty-nine hours for them to finish charging all their jump drives and regenerating the biological materials they use to load into their weapons. The British Alliance has taken the lead in organizing a direct attack on them. I can't tell you when exactly, but they'll be attacking well before that time has elapsed. SOCU's involvement in this action is limited to monitoring the enemy fleet. None of you will be involved unless this fleet somehow survives the British Alliance attack and makes the mistake of jumping to this system. Questions before I move on?"

"How many bugs are in there?" Gabe asked.

"We estimate that there are over thirty-eight thousand space and atmospheric fighters and two-hundred-ten-thousand warriors, give or take a dozen. Every few hours a new ship arrives, balancing their charge by drawing from the rest of the fleet, then charging up their jump drives at the same pace as the rest. Their dimension drive technology is very primitive, requiring much more power than ours, but we predict that they'll move quickly once they're in trans-dimensional space."

"Are they Edxi?" Alice asked.

"We're still working on that answer, but as far as we can tell from DNA and other facts we have about the Edxi and their culture, we believe they are a subspecies that are largely used for war. No one in this galaxy has actually seen the Edxi go to war, not really. We're thinking this is what it looks like.

They use less intelligent, insect species with cybernetic enhancements to act as their first wave when they suspect their target will be a challenge. The Prime Edxi may be in control from a distance so they stay out of danger. Finding a Prime Edxi and capturing it alive is a priority for Intelligence."

"If we're not bug watching, what are we going to be doing?" Gabe asked.

Minh-Chu entered the room then, moving swiftly and sitting at Jake's right hand. "Sorry I'm late, good to see you, please go on."

"You don't have to be here, but you're welcome to listen in, Ronin," Stephanie said. She turned to Gabe then. "There are a number of short-term objectives that SOCU can knock out while we wait for the Order of Eden and the Edxi to pounce. Since you won't make the difference in an all-out in-system war, Intelligence wants you going after objectives that will change things for the better in the short and long term for the entire Fleet, maybe for the entire solar system."

"Every ship will count when we face Three-Oh-Three Day," Remmy said.

Hearing that term from him was a surprise. There was a highly classified command briefing given partially by Ayan where she and a Mergillian Admiral calculated how long it would take for the solar system to fall to invasion by a real coordinated assault by the Order of Eden. It came to three hours and three minutes. Somehow that information got out and it was spreading.

"There are ways we can use SOCU to not only increase that number but make it a memory. The Cefa System is one of the most important hot spots for the Order right now. Thanks to the rescue of Wanda Teller by Captain Valent and the Clever Dream crew, we were able to discover several resistance strongholds where thousands of fighters are hiding out from the Order of Eden in that area. One SOCU team will find the hiding spots, alert the people that there is a pickup coming, then a small combat group will jump in and evacuate them."

"Captain Vernor," Jake said. "That's yours. I have a few suggestions on how to create a distraction if you have to while the rebels are being picked up," Jake said. "Will Teller be along for the ride?"

"Absolutely. She can't wait to see her people rescued. She is a consultant only, there to make sure people believe you're on the right side, but not to join in on any combat action. Not only has she failed her first suit qualifier, she is too important to put in the line of fire if we don't have to," Stephanie said.

"All right, looking forward to going to new places, meeting new people," Gabe said.

"Someone else will have the lucky task of making a slow trip to Baila. It is in the Rosen System, a highly civilized area that we thought was torn to bits during the Holocaust. The emotional artificial intelligences that were vulnerable to the virus outnumbered humans three to one there. This is a scouting mission. The only requirement that Intelligence has of a SOCU team is for them to come out of faster than light travel well outside the system, cloak, and gather data. Get as close to Baila and its moons as you can without revealing yourselves, then leave without being detected. There are particulars that Commodore Valent will fill you in on."

Alice looked to Jake expectantly, she couldn't have sent him a clearer message if she kicked him under the table. He knew there was one more mission coming though, and it was for her. "Remmy, this one's yours. A good shakedown for the Raven."

"Acknowledged, doing some dangerous scouting," Remmy said. He was good at hiding disappointment. His team were ready for a heavy fight, but Jake knew this was the mission for him. The reports from Baila were daunting. The only ship that passed through that system saw five brood ships in orbit around the planet before they attempted to make a hasty retreat. The commander of that mission, Rear Admiral Gillen, managed to send a transmission pod with a mind imprint through a wormhole back to the Haven System, and his clone didn't want to share what he saw past those details.

Jake knew that Alice encountered him, and was sure she'd be eager to investigate, but it wasn't going to be her job. What came next was made for her.

"Here's the one Admiral Lamonthe will be watching the most. Actually, most of the Admiralty wants to see success here. First, some background. Quantum Communications are a pipe dream that a few scientists and tinkerers have been able to get going, but not reliably. You can go through the science on your own, but let's just say that everyone has been so desperate to make instant communication across light years a reality, that they've been willing to try everything, including the pursuit of unreliable technologies like unstable quantum entanglement communications. The drawback to that tech is that it can work for centuries, or seconds before external factors turn your expensive communicator into a pile of spare parts. It's a miracle anyone got quantum communication to work for any length of time. Echo Corporation claimed that they had the technology, and some of it is still in use because, somehow, it works. We know the Order has stolen several nodes and they use them to communicate on their own network."

"We're going to steal their nodes?" Noah asked quietly.

"Please wait until the end," Stephanie said.

"Sorry, sorry," he said, leaning forward attentively.

"All right, so Echo Corp tricked the galaxy into thinking that they got it working and stable. Thanks to data down-loaded by Noah while he was on Iora, and Alice highlighting it in her report for Fleet to see, Fleet Sciences has caught a glimpse of how Echo Corp did it. For encryption they used advanced quantum entanglement technology, but we found out that they're using their own type of dimension drive tech-nology along with some kind of compression system to actu-ally send the communication. It's over my head, but we need one of their nodes. We know where it is on Iora, again, thanks to the data we found on Noah's pet, Lurk, now someone has to go get it. It doesn't matter if the node is functioning or broken, what we can learn from it could teach us how to make our own. Our most recent intelligence tells us that the planet has been turned into a brood world, so it might not be easy."

"Can you just open with the mission I'll be getting next time, Captain?" Alice asked.

"Right, everyone knows you're going on this one," Stephanie said. "You two are the experts on Iora. Carnie was there for the better part of a year, and you wrote the book on him, that experience, and have been tracking his career ever since. The Admiral wants him on your team for this mission."

"Who am I to argue with the Admiral?" Minh-Chu said.

"Pardon, excuse me," Noah said, putting his hand up.

"Yes, Carnie," Stephanie acknowledged, amused.

"Sorry, question: but if you got all that data from Lurk, and Fleet Sciences knows how to build a dimension drive, why do we have to go get you a broken node?"

"Fleet Sciences knows how all these things will work in principle, but there's something wrong with their prototype. It reduces the amount of time a transmission takes, and the technology they have works with current Quad Drives, but it's far from instantaneous. There's something - a setting, or a device inside - that they need to figure out the missing piece. They're trying to recover more data from Lurk, but they're having difficulty."

"Faster communications could win the war," Jake said. "So, getting this tech going sooner rather than later might be one of the most important things we do."

"Wait, so if the tech as Sciences knows it can work with the quantum drive already, then when they figure this out it might require a quick software update?" Iruuk asked.

"Like I said, I haven't fully figured it out myself, but from what they were saying it's possible," Stephanie answered.

"When do we leave?" Alice asked.

"As soon as Commodore Valent is finished telling you how he'll fit into your plans," Stephanie said. "I'm finished here, and I have a shuttle to catch." Flashing a little smile at everyone, she made her way out of the room, telling them all; "Good hunting," before the door closed behind her.

"The Merciless will be in stealth mode, holding position on the edge of the solar system, waiting to jump in to assist any of the SOCU teams or engage Haven System invaders. That could change depending on when the first wave comes and what our place in the defence is. I know Captain Vega said I'd have more details to go through with you, but I've sent everything you need to know about all your missions to your command units since none of us have time to waste. You have half an hour to get underway. Good hunting." As everyone rose, Jake tapped Alice on the shoulder. "Mind staying back for a minute?" he asked her.

"Make sure the ship is ready and do another check on our Quad Drives, just to be sure," she told Iruuk. "Oh and tell Theo that he's in charge of making sure Noah's got everything he needs."

"Yes, Captain," Iruuk said, looking excited.

Once they'd all gone, Alice gave her father a big squeeze of a hug. "I was so happy to see you got SOCU."

"Me too," Jake said, squeezing her back a little. She felt small, too small in his arms.

"What was with Steph running that briefing through?"

"She needs the practice more than I do. She's on her way to fill in where she's needed on Tamber's military bases, then she's hoping they follow through on getting her an Intelligence post on Freeground Alpha. She'll be sitting in on and running more briefings than you or I could stand. What do you think about going to Iora?"

"Iora," Alice sighed, pacing along the length of the table, pushing her fingers into her dark red hair so it was drawn up then letting it go. "It's exciting. I feel like I already know what it looks like, I spent a week reviewing footage and journals."

"Noah's journals," Jake said.

As though she had been hit with some kind of freezing stunner, all of his daughter's motion stopped for long seconds before she turned towards him. "Wait, was there some kind of matchmaking involved with me writing the report on Noah?"

"There was a little bit of intelligent sorting, I think, but only to see if you could be objective while writing a detailed but strategically sound report. They didn't match your personalities, just set the cadets up with lower or higher importance assignments based on how well you were expected to do."

"So, Fleet didn't put his data in front of me because they thought I'd fall for him or anything?"

"Fall for him?" Jake asked with a growing grin as Minh-Chu returned.

"Fall for who? What'd I miss?" Minh-Chu asked.

"I did not mean that," Alice said, holding up a black gloved finger. "You know what I mean, like giving me a challenge to make sure I could review a lot of information about one person without making it... personal."

"Oh, Carnie? Yeah, he's a great guy, kind of a rogue, though. Real hit with the ladies, but word's starting to go around that he's actually harmless, a big softie. At least, that's the scuttlebutt ever since he turned Sticky down late one night in the bunks."

"Sticky? Why do they call her Sticky?" A little confused and concerned, Alice looked a little ambushed.

"First briefing, before half the pilots had call signs, she

kept complaining that her seat was sticky, so there you have it," Minh-Chu said. "He turned her down like a gentleman, if you believe the talk."

"Oh, that's good. I mean, bad callsign, but I'm glad he turned her away... nicely." Alice looked relieved.

"I shouldn't share scuttlebutt, but what can I say? Ash's got me into some bad habits, she can't get enough of the Merciless crew soap opera." Minh-Chu sat down in an armchair with a sigh.

"Oh, yeah, gossip is useless, I don't think I've ever learned anything useful from it."

Transparent was never a word that Jake would use to describe his daughter before, but her relief at whatever she learned was plain enough to make him wonder about Noah Lucas and her. "Well, best to keep things professional while you're on mission anyway," Jake said.

"Exactly," Alice agreed. "So, was there anything else?"

"Just wanted a minute with my daughter, and to tell you 'good hunting,'" Jake replied. "Oh, and you don't get bonus points for objectives you invent on the ground."

"Don't worry, I'll do this by the book," Alice said, giving him another brief hug. "Unless something comes up."

Minh-Chu stood and accepted a quick hug from her too, picking her up a little. "You're almost as tall as I am," he said as she moved on towards the door.

"You're almost as short as I am," she shot back as the door slid aside.

Minh-Chu gasped in exaggerated offense then called after her; "Good hunting!"

The door closed, and Minh-Chu sat back down. "She really seems like she's found her place."

Jake discarded the opportunity for casual conversation, opting for something more pointed instead. "So, Minh. Tell me about Carnie."

SIXTEEN

All Aboard

THE MOMENT ALICE arrived in the bay where the deck crew were getting the Clever Dream ready for its mission, she noticed a growing collection of modules beside the ship. The Fleet were busy removing the extra crew accommodations section that she'd just had put in, replacing them with a set of combat support systems. Noah didn't think it was a great time to mention how amazing he thought it was that they could break huge modifications up into smaller modules, installing and removing them on a moments' notice.

"If I need extra capacitors and the high-speed loader for mines, then the mission has gone completely off the rails and I've disobeyed orders. If I need more life support, and extra crew support, then everything is going great," Alice told the Deck Chief firmly.

"Plan for the worst," the Deck Chief replied, tapping a paper-thin tablet with a holographic manifest hovering above it. She was taller than Alice by a head and trying not to show that she found Alice intimidating, but failing. She was averting her eyes, and nearly shouted her response as she tried to hide behind her device. "Hope for the best."

"That's fine if you're talking about a normal mission, a normal ship, but this is SOCU, this is my ship," Alice said, moving the Deck Chief's pad to the side with one finger. "If we get into serious trouble, we're not supposed to stick around and fight it out. We need to get the hell out of there as quickly as we can. I don't need a heavy fabricator and enhanced weapon systems for that. I need cloaking, nice big engines, and quad drives. Oh, look, I have all that. What I don't have is something to address directive two." Alice brought a hologram up on her left command and control unit and enlarged it so even Noah could read it from several metres away. It read: RESCUE ENEMIES OF THE ORDER WHENEVER POSSI-BLE. "See that? I used to have room for seventy-seven aboard, now I'm back down to twenty-eight or forty-two in an emergency."

"Thirty-nine," the Deck Chief replied.

Alice cleared her throat and regarded the tall, blonde woman coldly. "The next words out of your mouth will be; 'Yes Ma'am,' because I'm only going to tell you one more time. You will replace the pieces of the extended crew module you removed and check them properly. It will take fifteen minutes."

"Yes, Ma'am," the Deck Chief said, offering a salute.

Alice responded with a surprisingly stiff, proper salute of her own. "Thank you, Chief. Dismissed."

"I'm so happy you're along for this mission," Theodore said as he descended from the smaller crew steps at the front of the ship. It was strange to see him in uniform, a red stripe down his side, bomber jacket and boots that could turn into heavy armour, and a large looking sidearm on his hip. It was an Elasta Big Shell gun, and from experience he knew that you could load any of over a dozen types of lethal and non-lethal rounds in it. It was an intimidating weapon, but Noah was pretty sure Theodore had it set up with suppression and stun rounds. "I just got instructions to make sure you're set up in your own quarters, so I'll set you up. Normally that would be the duty of Faloo, the Nafalli have designated her as the 'Den Mother' on this ship, but Alice passed the order to me."

"Must be pretty different serving with a mixed group of people, right?" Noah asked, still watching Alice and the robots that moved around her.

"I would say it's interesting. Perhaps challenging at times, but their cultural differences haven't emerged that much yet. I believe most of the Nafalli and Ute, our Mergillian pilot, are focused on fitting in with fleet. I expect to see more of their cultures as they relax into their roles. I am surprised at the lack of shedding, however. Though Lewis complains about the odd deposit of fur, I expected much more."

Alice was checking details amongst the long-limbed, track footed robots that were busy moving the modules they'd removed from her ship back into the main ramp leading into the lower deck. Skitters moved around rapidly, making preparations and doing finer work, their little tool and leg limbs tapping the deck as they moved their small dome bodies from task to task. Two thick-bodied Nafalli that Noah was pretty sure were Woone and Noro along with Iruuk, who looked an awful lot like his father, only not as filled-out came out to join her. "I told them; 'The Captain just ordered these modules to be installed, she doesn't want them removed,' but they wouldn't listen."

"It's all right, Fur-Face," Alice said. "Let's scan their work while they put it all back together, make sure they don't miss anything."

"She is a very good Captain," Theodore said. "Used to working alone, I think, but she's getting used to having a ship with a full crew. It's remarkable. Do you want to see where you'll be staying? Your mission bag and a few replacement items have been delivered."

"Lead the way," Noah said.

The Clever Dream was similar to the other light corvettes he'd seen, but there was much more character. The sheen the interior of the newer corvette he'd seen had, thanks to the intelligent plating throughout, been converted to warm and dark matte colours and blacks. He wanted to see the cockpit, but instead he was brought directly to his new quarters. His rucksack was on the bed, which was against the bulkhead. He had his own sink, desk and hygiene system that used an energetic barrier to keep water and other matter in. He watched as Theodore demonstrated how everything but his bed could fold up, convert into more beds until there were four in the room, and be reconfigured in moments. He made it look easy, but some of it seemed more like a three dimensional puzzle than convenience features. The storage under and behind the bunk was ample, more than what he was used to in the quarters he would be sharing with Hal, and he was amazed as Theodore revealed a pop-up toilet in the retractable hygiene cubby. "Upon the insistence of the Captain, the Clever Dream was upgraded to have a private commode installed in every hygiene cubicle. The Nafalli use the full-sized bathrooms, since they use a different style of toilet, so they don't have them in their quarters, but I expect human crew morale will rise as they learn to appreciate having a more convenient facility of their own. Apparently, sharing a bathroom with Nafalli is not a good experience for smaller bipeds."

"I can imagine," Noah said. He pulled his new sidearm and belt from the black box Fleet left on his bed and secured them.

"You seem distracted," Theodore said, concerned.

Noah made sure the door was closed and sighed. "Yeah, that's a good way to put it." Telling him to remain on Tamber after he was cleared by medical was by design, he was sure. "Command told you I was cleared by medical, right? That's why you invited me to the Clever Dream while they were on leave?"

"I invited you to my location because I wanted to see you. I was able to do that because Fleet made me aware of your location, and the timing was perfect," Theodore said.

"I think they know what to expect from you, Theo," said Noah, nodding more to himself. Fleet knew that he would follow an invitation to hang out with the Clever Dream crew, especially if it came from Theodore. They knew Theodore would invite him the moment he knew that Noah was in range.

"Of course they do. They know what to expect from you, too. Aside from moments where your performance exceeds satisfactory levels, rising to exceptional, that is the way military organizations work. We pass qualifiers that measure our competence, demonstrate that we can follow orders, and then we meet expectations by following them. That, along with a detailed psychological profile makes the whole system work."

"Yeah, I don't think I'm used to it yet, at least not outside of a cockpit." He looked at the inspection tag and the serial number on his weapon then dropped it into his gun box before closing it and stowing it in the drawer beneath his bunk, then started unpacking the rest. "I mean, I was on mandatory leave, and it seems like they used you to make sure I linked up with the Clever Dream, even got to meet Captain Valent."

"I'm sure they did," Theodore said. "Didn't you want to meet her?"

"Yeah. I didn't picture it happening on a beach, I mean, maybe at a club or..." he sighed and shook his head as he pulled two rolled spare vacsuits from the bag and put them in his drawer.

"Oh, I think I understand. I recall how your pupils would dilate when you observed her state of relative undress at least on a few occasions. Your heart rate was rather high for some time as well, and there was some..."

"Whoa," Noah laughed. "That's some detailed observation. Don't go around sharing that with the crew, okay?"

"Oh, I suppose exposing your attraction to her would be socially awkward, though it would definitely provide a 'make or break moment' that could accelerate the progress of your relationship with her."

"'Make or break moment?'" asked Noah. Conditions had changed. The stakes had risen, and he was increasingly aware of that. He would be on the same ship as Alice for at least a day, possibly more, and there was every chance that the Clever Dream would return to the Merciless, where he was stationed long-term. If things didn't go well, Alice would be difficult to avoid.

"Oh, it's a theory proposed and studied well. It is said that when two people know more about each other romantically much earlier than is normal, they are often forced into deciding whether or not the relationship will continue to develop. This can accelerate the formation of bonds between two people or force an early end to a courtship that was most likely doomed to fail from the outset. Not in all cases, but in the majority."

"Okay, let's not do that," Noah said, shaking his head emphatically. That was all he needed, Theodore putting him and Alice on the fast track to... what? Awkward encounters in the hallway? Dating aboard a warship? Them sneaking into each other's bunks in the middle of the night on her father's carrier? "You see how that could make other things complicated, right? Professional relationships, you know, how she's technically my commanding officer right now?"

"I see," Theodore said, cocking an eyebrow. "Even fleet knows the psychology of it, though. Professionals can have a full relationship aboard..."

"Can I find my own way through this with Alice? I mean, you're right, I like her, and more than dilated pupils at the sight of her in a swim suit and increased heartrates can show. I think she's actually pretty cool, and I want to get to know her, but we are way off from any kind of fraternization that we'd have to disclose to the fleet, and I think I want it that way for now. I mean, this doesn't feel like something that would be a little bunk-bumping and light conversation in the morning when we're pretending it didn't happen. I can see something better here, but not while she's in command over my head. I want to respect that, so whatever flirting or what-ever is on hold, I've gotta respect that she's in charge. It would help if you didn't do anything that shook that up."

"So, the chain of command being what it is, keeping you apart romantically for a while is a good thing. It will provide you both with a social excuse to slow things down and discover more about each other's personalities."

"Exactly. So, no sharing data about what kind of responses I had to her when we met, all right?"

"All right. You know, I would have assumed that you were interested in a longer courtship if you hadn't met her on the beach. When I saw your reaction, and hers when you shifted your vacsuit into a swimsuit - it was definitive - my assump-tion changed, however. It really seemed like you both wanted to 'get to the good part' or 'honeymoon phase' of your relation-ship sooner rather than later."

"She had a reaction? A good reaction?" Noah asked, drop-ping his brain bud box into his drawer and standing up.

"Completely positive, like I said it was..."

"Wait!" Noah said. "I shouldn't know this. Listen, I have to concentrate on doing whatever she orders me to do, and it won't take long for us to get to Iora in this ship. I need to clear my head by the time we're there. I know watching Alice and me must be entertaining, but I don't want to know anymore relationship or physiological reading stuff, all right?"

"All right," Theodore said, smiling a little.

"What? What's that little grin about?" he asked.

"The ship's back in shape, and we're five minutes away from departure," Alice announced over the ship-wide.

Theodore deactivated his whimsical smile. "You just told me not to talk about relationship stuff."

"Okay, just that little smile you had." Noah enjoyed challenging his absolutes and smoothing out Theodore's communication skills. He was happy to see that they were still far from perfect even though he'd come a long way.

"Oh, I was amused that, no matter what happens in this situation between you and Alice, every provocation and change provide a result to observe. You're both quite expressive in this situation, it's highly interesting."

"Noah, would you like to take the co-pilot's seat?" Ute asked through his command and control unit.

"Be right there," he replied.

"You're not completely unpacked," Theodore observed.

Noah hurriedly pushed his rucksack into the large drawer under his bunk, pushed the clothing and other articles within flat then forced the bed down onto it until it clicked into place. "All unpacked."

Theodore looked at the bunk, back to Noah, then shrugged and started leading the way to the cockpit. "You never were the neatest companion."

"As neat as I have to be. My bunk is always made, and I know where everything I need is."

"I remember the backseat of our hover vehicle being riddled with food packages and other refuse."

"I thought it was the apocalypse," Noah said, passing Jessen in the hallway. She nodded at him and smiled as she overheard his comment. "No one needs to be tidy in the apocalypse."

"I could dispute that point at length," Theodore countered. "But we're at the busy end of the term; 'hurry up and wait,' so I'll save that discussion for another time."

"You tell 'em Theo," Jessen called after him with a chuckle.

The thick hatch to the bridge slid aside. It was an efficient cockpit that had room for seven modestly sized humans, some sitting on pull-out stools. Ute and Faloo were already talking, Ute finishing the pre-flight checklist while Faloo watched the systems and communications panels behind her. "...takes all the elegance and craft out of this kind of travel."

"But it's so much safer, and it cuts the training required to use dimension drives down so much that even wormholes are more complicated to plot," Faloo replied. She turned to Noah, smiling brightly. "Did you get settled in okay? Do you need an extra blanket, or maybe a few meal bars just in case you get hungry at night?"

"Everything's great, thank you," Noah replied. "I'm sitting here?" he asked, pulling on the co-pilot's seat. It moved out a little.

"Yes, the heavy lifting is already finished," Ute said, gesturing to the completed checklist. "You only need to confirm that there are no problems with our departure instructions and answer to Navnet if something comes up," Ute said.

"What were you two talking about?" Noah asked as he sat down and started looking at the navigational data. They were already cleared and would have to check in if they didn't leave in the next two minutes.

"Oh, the quad drive system," Ute said. "It's all good and fine that they put navigation, power, a D-drive and other elements in a highly efficient box, but I miss the raw science of plotting a course through uncharted dimensional space. There was an invigorating challenge to going through a highly energetic dimension, it was like an art."

"I used to read about navigators on Earth's early sea ships. Before it was a science, a lot of navigators felt that way. It wasn't something everyone could do," Noah said.

"Many major discoveries were made by mistake as a result," Theodore added from the communications station.

"I think Theodore has a point again," Faloo snickered.

"Check linkage twenty-nine, please?" Alice's voice asked from the Nafalli's station.

"Perfect placement and contact," Faloo replied.

"Good, that's the last one. We're good to go," Alice announced with relief. "Next time someone tries to make mods to my ship, lock it down and call me up, Lewis. That's an order."

"Aye-aye, Ma'am. I'll be glad to. Oh, and I stole a few skitters and am reprogramming them so they work with the ones we already have. It's only fair," he replied.

"We're going to have to discuss your definition of fair again," Alice replied. "Let's get going."

"Informing Flight that we are finally leaving," Theodore said. "We are still clear."

Ute grasped the controls, her bare, three-fingered, one thumbed hands glossy and green. "I have the controls," she said as she began to guide the ship up, out of the bay then towards space. "Like I was saying; there's no elegance to quad drives, unless you're an engineer or some kind of efficiency worshipper."

"What does it do differently? I only started studying the qualifier for it," Noah asked.

"That'll be an easy qual," Ute said with a snicker. "It does all the calculations for the pilot, performs several safety checks on its own, manages the power required and even provides a list of modes so you can tell it how urgent your journey is. Oh, and it checks with other nearby drives if there are any in range, something that I'm sure they'll improve on. The worst thing is that it barely shifts the ship dimensionally. We're in-between dimensions, so the rules are just different enough, and a lot of force is being exerted to pop us back into our home space. Even if the drive dies, which is almost impossible, a ship would pop back into normal space at a safe velocity, you know, relatively."

"That's why dimension drives are faster now? Because we're not actually shifting out all the way?" Noah asked.

"Well, yeah, but that's just the science of averages," Ute scoffed. "If you plot along a path of high energy, looping through a neighbouring energetic dimension, it could be much, much faster, but no, the quad drive won't allow that. With the quad drive doing all the thinking for us, we don't even need to know which dimension we're skimming into.

There are so many safeguards in place that the worst thing that can happen is getting stranded in our own space if something goes horribly wrong."

It sounded pretty good to Noah, but Ute was obviously still sore about having the technology simplified. "Sounds like anyone could use it now."

"Yeah, it's kinda sad. Now the best method of faster than light travel might become common and un-special," she sighed. The ship cleared the bay of the Merciless and she pointed at his navigational map. "Here, plot our course and run the quad drive."

"I'm not qualified," Noah said.

"Bah, do it anyway," she said, pointing to the holographic representation of Iora, a red dot inside a circle.

"Supervise me." He selected the Quad Drive interface, pointed to their origin point, selected a space ahead that they were clear to use for departure, then highlighted a space near Iora, where they could emerge outside of known Order of Eden patrols.

"Everything looks correct," Lewis said. "I'm just going to move our arrival point a little further out to be sure. Call me a paranoid android."

"I would not, since you are neither paranoid or an android," Theodore said stiffly.

"Just because I don't look like a human..." Lewis started to reply.

"They do this sometimes," Alice said as she came in through the hatchway. "Pick fights that last for hours even though one side is clearly wrong. It's like they're flexing processors at each other. It's not the time, guys."

"Hey, I'm plotting my first dimension jump," Noah said with exaggerated excitement as the holographic display showed him that his course had been tested three times and was ready to activate. "Man, that is fast."

"Heavy duty computing power in those quad drives," Faloo nodded.

"Yeah, I'd be surprised if the Shadow Star isn't busy trying to steal one from Fleet already. The British Alliance aren't much better, either."

"We're not sharing this tech?" Noah asked.

"No way, this is something Fleet wants full ownership of, and I can't blame them. If we make it through this invasion, it could be our best advantage." Alice shook her head. "God, I've watched so many briefings this week that I'm starting to sound like one. We clear to get out of here?"

"Aye, Captain," Noah replied.

"Hit it," she said as she sat down at the tactical station behind Noah and turned her seat so she could watch the main display that was wrapped around their consoles as if they were cockpit windows.

"It's all you, Carnie," Ute said, smiling one of those outrageously broad Mergillian smiles at him.

He activated the quad drive and watched as the space ahead of the ship split and the Clever Dream leapt inside with sudden, powerful acceleration.

SEVENTEEN

Departures and Arrivals

IT TOOK Laura only a few moments to slip off to sleep after being fed and burped. Every moment Ayan spent with her daughter was precious, and she tried to spend as much of that time purely focused on the infant, holding her worries and fears out of her thoughts. Being able to take care of the child herself most of the time was a rare privilege, and one Ayan suspected she'd have to give up soon.

The invasion was coming, and she knew her daughter wouldn't be safe anywhere in the Haven System. Not even the War Forge could protect her if the worst were to happen. "I'll take good care of her," Daisy said. She was a rare find, the same model as Theodore with decades of child care experience. The android also moved and sounded so convincingly human that Ayan often forgot she wasn't. She wondered if

Theodore would eventually be just as human like. "The security team the fleet put together will keep us well hidden and safe until the situation has been resolved."

"I've never been so afraid in my life," Ayan said, leaning down into the crib and gently planting a kiss on the infant's forehead. Her skin was soft, and the curl of hair was silken. "Not for myself," she clarified, brushing a tear off her own cheek. It wasn't the first.

"If it makes you feel better, I can have the technician who is accompanying us make a few changes so I look and sound like you. He can even activate a mimicry system that will accurately imitate all your biological elements. Your breathing pattern, heartbeat, even your fragrance. I would be proud to assume a role as a parental double."

Ayan thought for a moment. There had been so many decisions to make during every waking hour. Most of them she was able to delegate to the correct departments, especially in military matters, but there were some that only the Defence Minister could make, and they all had far reaching consequences. "You should do what you think is best. I'm her mother, but you're the real expert."

"Then I will become your double for stability's sake. The fewer mothers she knows at an early age, the healthier she'll be."

"You're needed, Admiral," Lieutenant Leon Baca, her assistant said quietly as he half stepped through the door. He left just as quickly.

There was a diplomatic matter to take care of, of all things. She was functionally the Defence Minister, but the royal brat that just landed at Fort Roman was demanding to speak to the Queen before anyone else. There were two gifts as well, and one of them was taking up half her dinner table. It was time to get that over with so the right people could get to work on negotiations with the royal newcomer.

With a light touch, Ayan brushed the soft strands of hair back from Laura's forehead. "I'm going to miss you, and I'll make sure we're not parted for long."

"Good luck, Ayan," Daisy said.

"You two won't be here when I get back?" Ayan asked. She knew the answer, but she had to ask anyway.

"The Preserver is boarding now. I'm afraid you're right," Daisy said.

Ayan kissed her on the forehead again, whispering; "I love you." She straightened her uniform coat then, looking at her android. "Thank you, Daisy."

"It's my pleasure."

Without looking back, she walked to the door, reminding herself that all the senior officers who wanted to move their children out of the system were going through the same thing. The War Forge would be a place absent young, and while it wasn't fair that the upper ranks of the military got to move their children out of the system to a hidden location while the civilians didn't get the opportunity to do the same, it wasn't her fault. The civilian Haven Government were busy debating whether or not some of them would be evacuated. It was a hotly debated issue that the council made complex, and while Ayan was tempted to resolve it by edict, she swore she would allow Haven to have its democracy as much as was possible.

Leon met her on the other side of the door, waiting for it

to close behind her before looking up from his holographic feed. There was sympathy in his expression, but his job was to keep her on track, so he had to press on. "Are you ready? I don't expect the conversation to be long, especially since she's representing a single system monarchy that only actively rules three planets there."

"Their territory is contested?" Ayan asked, checking her holographic display as well. The feed included a little window that showed her Alice's status. She'd been gone for three hours already, when it seemed like she'd just left. The section beside that showed her the known status of the Merciless. It had cloaked and was patrolling the Haven System in an undisclosed pattern. She could have looked deeper, found out what that pattern was, but she didn't need to know.

"Yes, there are three parties in her home system with claims to parts of the ruling Monarchy's kingdom. This information is old, though, from before the H-Virus."

"Oh, so she might really have negotiating power," Ayan said.

"Not as much as we'd like. There's another factor that suggests she might be an expendable errand woman." He brought up an image of her - a black haired woman in a long blue dress - and Ayan was amazed at how much she looked like Ashley Lamport, Jake's lead pilot.

"Is she a lost twin?" Ayan asked, hoping that her assumption was wrong, that Ashley wasn't about to find out that she was the product of a slave factory.

"A doll. One of the rare ones, very expensive. Fleet has plenty of scans of Ashley Lamport, and we couldn't tell she was grown in a facility until we compared them to the scan we took of this Duchess when she arrived. Intelligence has a pair of investigators down there already, and as far as we can tell there's no indication that she knows she's one of maybe three dozen, probably fewer of this model."

"So, Ashley and this Duchess are in for a shock," said Ayan. The idea of discovering that there were several women who looked and sounded exactly the same as she did made her shudder, and she couldn't be sure why. "I'm not going to be the one to tell either one."

"I think that's good, you shouldn't be the one. It's my opinion that you shouldn't get wrapped up in this situation when you have so much going on already. Pardon me if that seems a little cold," Leon said.

"You're pardoned," Ayan said. "I agree. This is a mess. I hope Ashley gets through okay, because she will find out eventually, but you're right. I have too much to worry about already."

"If it makes you feel better, the Intelligence file on Ashley says she's highly resilient, and she's surrounded by friends, so I think she'll be fine. Shaken, who wouldn't be, but I wouldn't actually be surprised if it's something she suspected, considering her background."

Ayan remembered that Jake bought her out of slavery before putting her to work on his ship as a member of his crew like any other. She hoped that Leon was right, and suspected that he might be. "All right, let's have this meeting with the Doll Duchess." Ayan regretted the nickname the moment she heard herself say it. "Let's make sure no one calls her that," she said. "Or any other derogatory if we can help it."

"I was just thinking the same," Leon nodded as he walked

her to the table where he placed the metre and a half long dress box with the smaller case on top of it. "These have been scanned, there's nothing dangerous inside."

"Good, but what will I find?" Ayan picked up the smaller box, definitely a jeweller's case, probably a necklace.

"I suggest you open them while you're speaking with the Duchess."

'You know, don't you?" she asked Leon.

"You'd have to order me to tell you. I think opening them early is against my best advice," he replied, putting his nose up in the air. He had a little theatricality to him that she liked, and hoped she'd get the opportunity to introduce him to Oz soon. She was sure he'd like Leon's sense of humour even more.

"All right," Ayan said, turning towards the empty half of the room. It was the perfect space for a large holographic projection, dark and plain. The thin bed and other furniture for the room was folded into the closet. "Open communications."

A moment later, Duchess Tammy Dermen appeared in front of a window in one of the upper storeys of Fort Roman's newest buildings. The officer apartment had a thick aquarium wall to her right that was waiting to be populated, and the window overlooked the terraforming effort the Nafalli were taking across the Dower Wastes. Brown, green and blue mud was becoming black soil as a large conditioner vehicle dug the soil up in the front and laid it down at the rear, the toxins in the dirt treated. It was one of two bases Haven Fleet were allowed to have on that continent at the moment. "Queen Ayan Anderson, I'm honoured that you have accepted my request for contact. My only regret is that we cannot meet in person." Her lisp was familiar, but she had an accent that seemed like a combination of Irish and new British that was hard to understand for the first few seconds. It was still like watching Ashley speak to her, though, the pair were identical at first, though the Duchess did seem a little more official.

"You've come at a dangerous time," Ayan replied. "I'm serving as the Defence Minister until this emergency passes and a proper election can be held. It's an honour to meet you. Unfortunately, I'll have to introduce you to Minister Pamela Grey, the Minister of Public Welfare, who is listening in with our External Affairs Team. They're taking care of negotiations with foreign governments when the military isn't involved, at least for now. They have my proxy as Queen as well."

"I didn't come to speak with a proxy, but to make an impression on you. My people believe you should open a parley with the Order of Eden as we did. I'm here to tell you that it's not too late for negotiations to take place. That should be your highest priority, for your own sake and for that of your people."

"The Order of Eden has made every indication that they intend to take this solar system, but I'll send them a message. I doubt it'll change anything, but I'll do it just in case it can save some lives," Ayan said. The entire idea that they would offer an opportunity to negotiate with the Order, when they were using many different methods to enslave people across the galaxy, made her stomach turn, but she took the role of Queen, so it was her duty to investigate the possibility of a truce. "The idea of negotiating with the Order of Eden isn't popular with my people, as you'll discover if you spend time here."

"What does it matter if lives are saved?" the Duchess asked. "My people are willing to open trade talks with yours, so we can prepare for the day when you and the Order are at peace. In a gesture of goodwill, I've brought you two gifts that were made by my people."

"I see that," Ayan said, hoping that she was hiding her doubt from the Duchess. The promised trade talks would probably never come to pass. There was little to no chance that the Haven System would ever be at peace with the Order unless they came and defeated the whole system, taking it for themselves. It wouldn't matter if that came to pass. She moved to the table and picked up the jeweller's box.

"Oh, please open the larger box first. I'd rather keep the other for last," the Duchess said, smiling expectantly.

"All right, my pleasure. I'm afraid all I can offer you are good accommodations during your stay. The Haven System isn't known for building or crafting anything rare yet." Ayan slid a button cover at the bottom of the box then activated it. The lid opened in the middle, the halves of the lid slid to the sides to reveal a fine white dress carefully pinned inside. The sheen was almost pearlescent, and the cut was revealing but elegant. Fine ruffles trimmed the bust and an opening that was made to point down low, and there was a high collar of the same design that would frame her head in a stiffened oval of cloth. "It's beautiful," she breathed, wondering where she would ever wear it.

"I selected it myself. We produce silk from spiders only

found in caves deep in the world I was raised in. The dress was made by hand, very fine, but made to fit to form."

"Thank you very much. I hope you don't mind if I leave it in the box for now."

"I thought the box was overlarge, since it would have been much easier to bring it here in a stiffened bag, but if you have the space for it, please leave it until you find the right occasion for it. I studied images of you for hours before selecting that one in particular, so I'm sure you'll be delighted once you've tried it on."

"I'm sure I will," Ayan said.

"Now, please, open the other box," the Duchess said, clapping lightly and grinning. "I chose what's inside to go with the dress and what I've seen of you."

Ayan did so, and found a simple necklace adorned with glittering green stones. One silver chain hung down from the middle, showing a thin, broad cut green stone larger than the others. "This is lovely."

"It's pure platinum with our finest manufactured green diamonds. We've mastered the manufacture of any kind of diamond that you could need or want. They feature in the finest jewellery across the galaxy. The platinum was mined in the Dermen System, so you have a piece of my home in your hands."

"Thank you," said Ayan, wondering if she should ask the next question on her mind and deciding that it was worth her time. "I'll remember this meeting whenever I wear this. I'm wondering, though. Will you be going home soon? You're welcome to stay, but this isn't a safe place."

"My father's last communique instructed me to stay here

until I had a final deal to bring back to the Dermen System. I am here to weather this storm with you, your Highness."

Ayan was surprised and concerned. To outsiders, the peril the Haven System was in was dire, enough to stop ship-ments of heavy metals and raw foods going into the system. Even their Xetima fuel sales was down to nearly nil since the threat of invasion was clear. "I will make sure you're comfort-able, but I can't guarantee that you'll be any safer than the average Haven citizen. Oh, and please call me Ayan, or Minister if you need to use a title."

"I will. Don't worry about me," said the Duchess. "I'm here to do my duty, and you'll find I'm quite brave."

"Very well. I have other matters to attend to but thank you very much for the gifts. You'll be speaking with the Minister of Public Welfare next, and she'll be able to begin negotia-tions. I think you'll enjoy speaking with Pamela, she's more well-travelled than I am, so she's one of the most interesting people in government."

"Thank you, Defence Minister," the Duchess said as her image faded.

Ayan clicked the jewellery box closed and pressed the button on the large dress box so it began to re-seal. "All this looks too expensive for me to keep," she said more to herself than to Leon, who stepped in from the doorway.

"You're going to keep them, though. You should at least wear the necklace sometime."

"I don't think it would go well with my uniform," Ayan told him with a crooked smile.

"I mean at one of those social events you keep getting invited to. When this is all over, you'll have to address your social calendar, maybe take the opportunity to be seen with your dashing Commodore boyfriend." Leon retorted with a cocked eyebrow.

Ayan shook her head and let her thoughts return to something much closer to her heart. "Are Daisy and Laura still here?"

"The Preserver is almost under way, so she couldn't wait," Leon said.

Ayan took a moment to wrap her head around the idea that her daughter would be light years away by the end of the day, then nodded to herself and straightened her uniform jacket, making sure that the bottom crossed seven centimetres below her belt, then looked at her assistant. "What's next?"

"The new Nafalli Rear Admirals that begin their service tomorrow morning. You wanted to be there when they were officially assigned their commission. It should be a fairly light appointment."

"I could use a piece of cake," Ayan said, aware that these gatherings were mostly social occasions, but she wanted to be there to show support for the Nafalli who would be joining. Their entrance into official service would pave the way for thousands more to join within days.

"Before we go, I was wondering something," Leon said.

"I promised I'd answer any question when you were brought on, so please, fire away."

"Why talk to the Duchess at all? Intelligence suspects that she's a spy at worst, and no one is sure that she actually has the power to negotiate for her people."

"There's going to be a news report with her and one of our top ministers speaking sometime in the next day. That'll trickle out across the local systems and show everyone that we're open to making new alliances. The Nafalli were found by sheer luck, and the Mergillian are here because they feel they'll be the next system the Order takes over after us. They have the pilots, but their ships don't stand up in combat, so they need us. The British Alliance are trustworthy, but they keep their own counsel, so we don't know how they'll respond to any given situation. We need self-sufficient allies who have more to bring to the table, and who realize that this is going to be a long war. I talked to this Duchess so the local star systems will know that we're willing to talk to anyone."

"I hope it works," Leon said. "God, I hope it works."

"Oh, don't forget to send a basic query message to the Order of Eden's nearest known ship. Tell them we're willing to negotiate if the conditions are favourable."

"Why?" Leon asked, almost looking offended. "Sorry, that came out wrong. I will."

"Just doing my duty," Ayan said, amused at his initial response. "I doubt they'll offer anything reasonable, and if they do, I'm sure it'll be a trap."

"I hope you don't mind me asking, Ma'am; what then?"

"We'll find a way to turn either one into an opportunity," Ayan replied.

"What about Ashley Lamport? Maybe you should..."

"Warn her?" Alice asked. "I'll send Jake a message about it while we're in the transit car. He or Minh should be the one to tell her about the Duchess," Ayan said, hoping Ashley would take it well. She didn't know the pilot well, but Ash was always kind to her, and she made Minh-Chu very happy. That was enough to make her dear to Ayan.

EIGHTEEN

Iora Arrival

THE HURRIED HOURS OF SIMULATIONS, questioning and studying for the upcoming mission on Iora were exciting, but by the time Noah Lucas learned everything he needed to know his head felt full. Yawen and Noro, one a slim woman who couldn't have been more than a few years older than him, and a thick-bodied friendly Nafalli, walked him through what he needed. The simulated training on the KK2, modified Knight Killer rifles, came first. They were different animals, with variable loads and more settings than he thought one rifle should have, but it didn't take him long to learn how to handle the weapon properly.

He liked the guided hand rockets much more. They were small grenades with a tiny thruster system and a variable load, his favourite were the gel rounds, which he became extremely proficient with within minutes of simulated target practice. He could toss those at a run without activating the guidance, landing them beside moving targets without much thought. His natural ability with the things had Noro laughing so hard that he rolled onto his back and grabbed his feet for a few moments. "It's like he's got radar brain!" he howled as he watched the simulation in the main crew gathering area at the rear of the Clever Dream.

There were several other instructional simulations, like operating a quad drive navigational system, hooking one up, setting the self-destruct, and basic repair. He also got a run through of piloting the Clever Dream and was happy to discover that most of the systems were fairly easy to use. The controls were made to be as responsive as a starfighter. There were several sub-systems he didn't explore since he didn't have time, like the tug, extended weaponry and shield modules, but they weren't installed, so there was no rush.

He spent half an hour in an advanced tactical training simulation as well. It was long enough for him to see that his instincts weren't all wrong, but he wasn't up to the same level as anyone else on the ship. That would take a lot more practice than he had time for. A large portion of his time was spent on special damage control training for the Clever Dream, which was amazing and daunting. The new intelligent plating could regenerate, but there were systems that required special attention, and he was glad he knew which ones they were. He almost started wandering into training that he didn't need as a pilot, but Yawen drew his attention back to more pertinent material before he started exploring.

She gave him a few tips on how to move with the Special

Operations Unit on the ground, and where he should be depending on what was happening. It was obvious to him that he was being protected, not offered as much opportunity to shoot back as the rest of the team, but he understood. He passed the basic infantry qualifier shortly after joining Haven Fleet, but they were well ahead of him.

Flying the Clever Dream using emergency controls was where he needed a lot more training. The exercise was made to simulate what it was like to crash-land the ship after it had been struck with a series of electromagnetic pulses that took out all but the emergency control systems, which were mostly manual. His biggest problem was that he expected to do better. After his first two attempts, which were both failures, he started to get the feel for how the heavy ship handled using extendable glider wings, backup thrusters and gyros. It was not easy to fly without all the computing and main thruster power the vessel normally used. The wings seemed to take too long to extend, the backup thrusters only had so much fuel, and the controls were touchy, so any miscalculation could send the ship spinning. It took five simulated crashes for him to learn to activate the emergency systems in a way that didn't take too much time, but once he did, Noah finally landed the ship without killing everyone aboard. He only had time for two more tries, and he managed to set the ship down once without destroying it. The other attempt was a complete failure. "I commend you for attempting this without studying the manual on it," Ute said as she observed.

"There's a manual?" Noah asked, pulling the brain bud off his forehead.

"Of course. You can find it by searching; Emergency

Systems Flight Procedure for The Clever Class Corvette, Version Two Point One. Don't use any earlier versions though, because they don't account for a few important particulars."

"Oh," Noah said, wondering why the manual wasn't in the file list for the ship but keeping the question to himself. "I'll take a look." Alice was sitting beside Yawen on the section of sofa nearest to the door. Theodore was sitting behind them, on the tier above. "So, how did I do, overall?"

"Pretty good," Alice said. "Lewis gives you a passing grade on flying, he's been watching all your sims."

"I'd like to remind you that this ship has a grapple system permanently installed, so skipping the tug tutorial was a mistake," Lewis said from the audio emitters hidden in the ceiling. "You should go through it next time you have the chance."

"I will, thank you, Lewis," Noah said. "There's a lot of material I should go through, I know. How about everything else? Am I going on mission with you guys?"

"Well," Yawen said, sucking air in through her teeth. "Yes, but you're not exactly going to be front-line. If things start going wrong down there, you'll have to cloak and return to the ship. While you're on the ground with us, you won't fire unless you're given a direct order. That aim of yours with grenades and the sharpshooter settings on our KK2's will come in handy, though. You're in the top three percent on the rifle, and top two with the grenades, so, I hope we won't need to use you, but if we get into major trouble, you'll be good to have around."

"How are the rest of you guys ranked, in terms of combat.

I'm not asking because I'm sore about being a package you're bringing along, I'm just curious," Noah asked carefully. Knud and Jessen emerged from the quarters they shared and took a seat, Knud nodding at Alice. "She passed Infantry Qual Nine."

"Nine?" Noah asked, surprised. The Advanced Infantry Qualifier he was working on was marked as level three.

"I'm hoping to get through ten and eleven once we get back home, so I can catch up with Yawen," Alice said.

"So, why even take me with you? I can consult from the ship," Noah said.

"All the infantry qualifiers after three are there to sharpen your skills and get a read on how well you deal with a fight in harsh environments, situations where you're at a huge disadvantage from the start or have to deal with variables that almost never come up. After Qual Seven, it's more like super soldier training. You're doing things that should never come up, disasters that no one in infantry has ever faced. They're what we like to call 'Worth the Failure,' or 'WTF' simulations. Even though most people will never master them, they're worth doing because you learn something new every time. They're also brutally frustrating."

"Like the cracking planet in ten," Yawen nodded. "The whole simulation takes place while the planet you're on is cracking apart. You have to get a delicate circuit board before leaving that's guarded by a crazy quick race with these lizard hounds that can see right through cloaking. I can't tell you how many times I broke that board before getting back to my ship."

"I've only seen the board twice," Knud said. "Haven't gotten it yet."

"My point is," Jessen interrupted, pulling her shoulder length purple hair into a ponytail. "After finishing the basic infantry qualifiers, one and two, you've shown that you can move with a team and follow orders in a hurry while under fire."

"Besides, we found out you already raided a bunker a lot like the one we're after," Alice said, bringing up an image from Noah's logs.

It was a squat, three storey building with thick walls and armoured transparent metal windows. He recognized it immediately. "Yeah, sure, but the one I found wasn't locked down. I think there were a half-dozen packets of junk food and a couple workable flimsy displays." A memory struck him then. "Wait, there was a section of the building I couldn't get into, but I moved on."

"Right, we're guessing you got into the office section but the research and development area was sealed," Alice said.

"That makes sense. I could probably get you back there quick, but you have scanners for that."

"Not on this mission," Theodore said. "Any active scanning will be picked up by satellites that the Order of Eden have left in orbit. They are watching for signals from advanced technology, that is why all your weapons will have to be set to sub-sonic and you will have to use dumb fire rounds."

"Ah, right. Those Order dicks don't like anyone having nice toys," said Noah.

"So, you'll be our guide, and since you have so much experience with the way things were built on Iora after visiting more places than either of us could count, you might be surprised at how handy you'll be," Alice said.

"I'm better in a starfighter, but yeah, I'll help any way I can," Noah told her. He liked seeing her in uniform in person, and watching how everyone looked to her, respected her. It was impressive. The insecurities that he saw while she was on the beach were gone.

"Emergence in one minute," Ute said from the bridge.

"Everyone get armoured up, we're not going in slow," Alice said.

KNUD RAN Noah through his systems check once they were in the debarkation cabin below, and Noah grinned at how much being in that suit of 'Ground Pounder Armour,' as he called it, reminded him of a small starfighter. It was like the discontinued Ramiel in how it fit to you, the Heads' Up Display felt like it was in your head, not just seen, and he felt like he was wearing a second, very tough, skin. He'd trained on compatible armour before, but he could feel the extra weight and power all around him. He'd see about keeping it when the mission was over.

Alice descended the ramp in the long coat version of the same armour. The lighter material in the lower half swayed with her steps, she seemed to loom larger, and the confidence in her gait made her seem almost commanding. As she activated her heavy armour, reforming her boots and heavy long coat, he noticed that she lost none of her sure-footed grace. He was seeing her in her element, perhaps for the first time. "Tune in to the CDF feed if you want to see what's happening out there."

He didn't ask what that meant, only looked it up with a few eye movements and found the Clever Dream Fore sensor feed, then opened it in a large window on his HUD. They'd arrived on the edge of the Iora System and cloaked.

The ship was decelerating towards the planet he called home for what seemed a long time. The tactical map picked up a large fleet of Order of Eden ships, and they kept their distance, passing by with hundreds of millions of kilometres between them. They were running fighter patrols, but those small ships were all staying within ten thousand kilometres of their carriers, as though it would be more important for them to be able to return to the ship than to secure a large area. It made things easy for the Clever Dream, until he saw another obstacle ahead. There was a line of Order of Eden destroyers twenty-five across in front of two massive Edxi brood ships in orbit around Iora.

A new moon had been added to the sky there, and after a few minutes of approaching, the scanners were able to determine that it wasn't solid. No, not solid at all, but a collection of nightmares. Thousands of wrecks had been drawn together around a heavy asteroid so they would be attracted to its gravity and stay in place. The broken hulls were drawn together to form that corpse moon, a graveyard of vessels that had been destroyed during the onset of the Holocaust Virus in that solar system. He was sure the Daring Dickenson was among them but didn't perform a search of the scan results. He wanted to remember that ship in particular as it was when his adoptive family was alive.

Everyone who was going out on the ground mission were ready, suited up and silent. Jessen handed him his rifle, tapping on his visor. "You're going to do great, just follow Captain Valent's orders."

"Aye," he replied, looking at the list of active squad members on his HUD. Alice, Knud, Jessen, Iruuk, Noro, Faloo and he were on that list. The rest were staying aboard the Clever Dream, most of them forming a reserve team that would armour up the moment the first team was on the ground. Then they'd man the guns and other stations aboard and would be available to back up Alice's team if they needed it.

The Clever Dream flew around the perimeter that the Order of Eden Destroyers had set up around the brood ships. He could feel most of the crew holding their breath as they passed through a section of space that was probably highly monitored, hoping that their stealth systems would hold up. His eye was drawn to the brood ships. They were bulbous, brown-black, three-kilometre-wide vessels with silvered domes that looked as much like strange skin as metal pockmarking the hull. "The planet must be crawling by now," he said under his breath.

"I'm afraid preliminary passive scanning verifies that assessment, Noah," Theodore said through the communications system. It sounded like he was right in his ear. "Early estimates indicate that there are over six hundred thirty thousand Edxi hatchlings on the main continent. The Order of Eden is in the process of building a fortified military base on the second largest continent. It's an unusual phenomenon we haven't seen before. Our intelligence tells us that the Edxi take whole planets, not sharing with the Order."

"Hatchlings, that can't be so bad," Noro said, adjusting the swivel on the cannon mounted to his hip.

"They have serrated forelimbs and mandibles that can cut through most metals. They're exceptionally sharp because they're so young; age and use has not dulled them. Hatchlings are also quicker than adults with keen, fresh senses. They also have much larger appetites, so they spend over seventy percent of their days hunting," Theodore said. "But they are smaller and their carapaces are thinner, softer. So, there's that."

"I should really stop thinking out loud," Noro groaned.

The Clever Dream aimed for the atmosphere and changed its energy shielding to ease its entry, and with little turbulence or friction, they moved through without rattling a single hull plate. Carnie knew the new shielding could perform a nearly unnoticeable atmospheric entry but hadn't seen it done outside of simulation. It seemed almost wrong, like some kind of physics violation, but it was exciting. "Everything okay, Carnie? You're pretty quiet." Yawen asked on a private channel.

"Fine, just geeking out over all the cool things this ship can do," he said.

"You really have to train on the new corvettes, they're all pretty much the same. I think you'll sign up to fly one of these instead of that little fighter once you're done."

"Leave my fighter behind? Thanks, but that's not likely. Any last words of advice before I head out with the troops?"

"Keep your head down, on a swivel, and listen to the Captain. She knows what she's doing," Yawen replied without hesitation. The channel closed.

With surprising celerity, the Clever Dream descended towards Zorbo Isle, where a cluster of towering buildings stood out on one side, and a thick forest filled the other. "Good hunting, Alpha Team," Theodore said. "We'll move on to the secondary objective and start gathering data. There will be a burst transmission at the predetermined time."

"Stay out of trouble," Alice said.

The buildings, the matte, grey tone of the streets Noah was seeing and the sound of Theodore's voice all started to bring back that feeling, the sensation he had while he was moving across the landscape of Iora that he was barely aware of until he left. It was part dread combined with a sort of electric anxiousness and the knowledge that at any time his luck could turn in any direction. The people he met and left behind ran through his head, their expressions accusing, and he wondered where they were, if they were alive and if there was any chance the Captain of the Clever Dream would take the risk to save them. More than anything, he was realizing for the first time that he was really back, under different conditions, sure, but as the reality of it sank in, he realized he'd rather be anywhere else.

The ramp began to lower as they came within a hundred metres of the hard-paved ground and he watched as their rapid descent brought them down to street level, a knot tightening in his stomach.

With Captain Valent in the lead, they rushed out and Carnie's heart started to pound. He couldn't believe he was back. Even though he'd never been to that island before, the style of construction, even the shade of blue in the sky was so familiar.

NINETEEN

Zorbo Isle

PASSIVE SCANNERS BEGAN GATHERING data the moment Alice and her team set boots on the ground. The Clever Dream was busy elsewhere already, scanning settlements and hiding places that were noted in Noah's recordings. When they were finished its pass there it would move on and gather data on the large military centre the Order of Eden were building. From orbit Lewis spotted five distinct military bases and two other sites that didn't have clear purposes.

The new Directives for the fleet made the secondary and tertiary objectives of every mission where there was time to address them clear: The first directive was to defend the Haven System. For the moment, that was suspended for the Clever Dream and the crew.

The second was to rescue enemies of the Order of Eden whenever possible. The third was to collect intelligence whenever allowed by the primary mission. The list of what intelligence the Fleet wanted was long, but Alice summarized it into categories for herself. They reminded her of the mission of the First Light, Jonas Valent's first command. That ship was after alliances and technology.

Her team were after alliances, sure, but the Third Directive had the entire fleet collecting intelligence on their enemies, allies - both current and potential - new technology, the changes in the galaxy on every level, and anything that could be noted as anomalous. The last part was intriguing to Alice, but all this intelligence was to be collected while they were achieving their mission objectives and the other two directives, there wouldn't be time for actual anomaly hunting, even though the appeal of that was growing on her.

Her team crossed a broad avenue made for foot traffic, its interlocking, slate-grey brick had shoots of green grass pushing between them. Cloaked, they came to rest closer to the walls of the tall buildings. "No sign that anything has detected us," Iruuk said. "This world is beautiful," he added. "It's about as perfectly terraformed as any can be, completely stable with an abundance of nutrient rich soil."

"Iora has whole sections of continents covered in farmland. The forest behind us was probably put there for natural wood harvesting. This place was super-rich before the whole killer virus thing," Noah said. "Really nice, too."

Alice checked her Heads' Up Display, something she was getting so used to that she didn't think about the information there or regard anything specifically, the biometric readings

on her team, Clever Dream status feed, tactical map, equipment and armour status, communications feed and sciences
window were getting so familiar to her that she kept up on it
all effortlessly while she watched the world around her.

"Feels almost wrong to keep my helmet up," Noro said.
"The air is reading as perfectly breathable. Even healthier
than Tamber."

"We don't know what we'll be running into yet. There's
movement in a few of the buildings nearby, but whatever
we're picking up is sticking so close to the walls that I can't get
a clear reading," said Alice. The results told her something
she was sure she didn't have to say aloud. Humans didn't
crawl on walls like that, a Mergillian might stick to one for a
rest, but they didn't like to climb for long, preferring to leap
instead. "Passive scanners aren't doing it at this range."

"I'll turn the gain up on mine, make some fine adjustments," Iruuk volunteered. He was the most gifted in the
sciences and second most gifted in pure mathematics, second
only to Ute. He routinely outscored her on pure theory
assignments during their short time in the Academy.
Someone might guess that she kept him around as a valued
friend first, but where her team was concerned, he was one of
the most valuable members.

"Go ahead, but leave your auto-compensation on, just in
case we get jumped," Alice said. "I don't want you sensor-
blind if something big goes off."

"Aye," Iruuk replied.

"What's our approach?" Knud asked in his quiet but
intense way. He was itching to get on with the mission, to see
what was around the next corner.

"The entrance to the research and management complex is two point eight blocks away. I don't see anything moving within a block radius. Iruuk?"

"I see a little movement in the lower levels, wait, now there's nothing," he waited a moment. "It looked like something crawling on the walls, like you saw."

"What I saw was about a block out," Alice told him. "You're picking up movement closer to us?"

"Just for a few seconds. Looking over the readings, there were five objects about one metre long causing vibrations on the ceiling of the second floor of the building across the street from us, and two ahead. The type of activity makes it look like they were crawling."

"Crawling upside down?" Jessen asked.

"Yes, four were definitely upside down, the rest were inconclusive. It's very subtle movement. I can't get much of a shape, but the weight is at least forty-two kilograms."

"That's about right for a hunting age Edxi," Faloo said. "From the little information Fleet has on them."

"Keep your eye on it," Alice ordered. "We're going to rush to the research centre. If Iruuk picks up more movement, we'll re-assess."

"Are you saying these things might be able to see through our cloaking systems?" Noro asked. "Our 'seven layers of technology, perfect invisibility' cloaking systems?"

"We don't know yet," Alice replied. "All right, let's go." She rushed down the avenue, the team moved at her pace, holding formation. Being the shortest didn't stop her from moving her team along at a fast run, rifles and cannons at the ready.

"No increase in movement signs," Iruuk said. "I want to get a read from higher up."

"Go ahead, don't go too far," Alice replied. "And come back if you see anything unusual."

"Aye," he grunted as he leapt up three storeys above and grappled to the side of the building. He flung himself across to the building on the other side of the avenue, sticking to the wall. "Cloaking systems are working, impact dampening systems are keeping me hidden. Not picking up... wait..."

"Hold," Alice said, and her whole team stopped a little less than a block from the entrance to the research centre. "What is it?"

"Cleaning it up and sending the readings to your tactical display now, getting a closer look," Iruuk said as he dropped to the avenue, ran on all fours at incredible speed while he looked every which way, then leapt up and stuck to the corner of the research centre.

Alice saw what his passive scanners detected. There was movement. Three human figures who were hunched over. It looked like they were eating from a pile of something she couldn't make out, but it was on the ground, like a mound of meat. "That's not normal," she said under her breath. Another analysis on the readings verified that they were human, but her computer highlighted a malformation around their necks. "Come back, we're going in as a group."

"They're in the basement level." Iruuk dropped from his spot on the wall and rushed back to the group. "There's some-thing alive, clinging like a pup around the front of their necks, leaning on their upper chests, but there are tendrils wrapped around their necks too, pushed up into the base of their skulls.

"You think it's a parasite?"

Iruuk sent a cleaned-up scan to her and she saw what he was talking about. There were missing details, but the insect like things were clinging to the human's chest in the front, tendrils penetrating the base of the skull, long graspers holding to their shoulders. "This is not on record," Alice said as she finished running a check on the shape of the thing against the fleet database. She sent the readings to the rest of her team. "Anyone else see something like this anywhere?"

"No," came Carnie's answer right away. "What are the humans eating?"

"I didn't get inside to see, I only got the scans and cleaned them up. It's all sound, vibrations and air movement," Iruuk explained.

"In other words; 'Don't ask me, man, I just work here,'" Noah said, causing a few snickers. "These guys are right near the entrance to the secure basement, though. There's a vault door down there, I'm pretty sure."

"Sure, or pretty sure?" Jessen asked.

There was silence for a moment, then Noah answered; "Sure. I raided a building just like this one and I couldn't get into the basement because of the big doors down there. Just wasn't worth the cutting time."

"Okay," Alice said. "We don't know that these things started moving because of us, so we're continuing our approach slowly. I want to get a better look at those infested targets, but if they attack, waste them. Our main objective is the lab." She took a moment to make sure all her people had their weapons set to use dumb rounds and to fire at sub-sonic speeds. That combination would give them the best chance at hiding their technology and their actions from the satellites above, especially when they got indoors.

Alice's tactical scanners were eerily still as she led her group to the building entrance. There were fortifications there made from chunks of concrete piled like roughly shaped stone, chain, wire, logs and other salvage. Someone was trying to keep invaders from entering that building, but the barricade was broken inward.

"Saw and chop marks on the wood and metal plates here," Iruuk said. "Hunting bugs definitely broke this down."

"We're going inside," Alice said as the three humans Iruuk picked up earlier appeared on her scanners. They were close enough for her to get a read without turning her systems' sensitivity up too high. "Three unknowns."

"I see them," Jessen verified.

"We going the right way? Is this the shortest route to the vault doors?" Alice asked Noah.

"No, this is going to take you to the elevators, we want the stairs," he replied.

"Signal!" Iruuk cringed. "I'm turning my system gain down. Anyway, the signal is definitely man-made, using the Echo Corporation secure band."

"Play it," Alice said, watching her communications feed pick up a signal from the Echo Corporation as they continued progressing through the main floor of the building. Noah was marking directions on everyone's tactical maps, taking them through hallways with scratches and dents on the walls, the floors, even the ceilings in some places. They were well into the building, half way to the staircase leading down before they saw the hollowed-out corpse of a young Edxi. The carapace had been cut open from the bottom, and all but one of its long legs were missing. "What happened to this?" Alice asked, knowing that Iruuk and Jessen would investigate.

They stopped a minute, the sound of a male voice playing in Alice's ear. "...ships in range. If there's anyone on this network with armed ships, we need help. My colleagues and I are trapped in an Echo Corporation facility on Iora, the exact location is in the header of this transmission. We will share our knowledge with you if you can send help. The Order moved thousands of people onto the island, then the Edxi dropped eggs into the forest. We tried to go in before they hatched but were attacked by some kind of parasite bug who turned our people against us, so we had to retreat. That was weeks ago, now the Edxi young are out, and they're taking over the city as they kill and eat more humans. We've barricaded a few defensible buildings, but they're falling one by one. Please, help, and we'll share our technology with you, build you a zero-latency communications device of your own." That was the end of the message, it started over. "To anyone with a non-Order of Eden Echo device, and all ships in range..." Alice turned it off. She hoped whoever sent that was still alive somehow but couldn't reply. Any transmission would give their location away, even low powered ones thanks to the satellites overhead. The vault door had been breached, she didn't think there was much chance that she'd meet whoever recorded the plea.

"Okay, our bug here was gutted. It looks like it was for meat, but it was quick," Jessen said. "Reminds me of the sea crabs I used to eat on my home world, only this thing would feed a family of five for a couple days. If I could get a good scan, I bet I'd be able to tell you it was filled with good protein."

"Nice to see humans could eat the bugs back," Knud said. "Only fair."

"Move on," Alice said, leading the way. They passed a main hallway and she caught a glimpse of the main elevator bank at the end. The doors were welded shut, but the predator bugs tore through the metal, making a round entrance for themselves.

"These people just kept running out of luck," Noah said under his breath.

"Bet you're glad you missed it," said Iruuk.

"Hell, yeah. The stairs are just ahead, then there's a straight hallway that leads to the secure section of the facility, and I'll be all out of advice."

The stairwell was once clogged with furniture, metal shelving and there was even a gate that had been put into place to block the progress of an invader from what Alice could tell. Everything down there was burned black or melted. The corpses of several bugs, most of them intact but well done, were strewn around. "This fire burned hot," Iruuk said. "Serious accelerant was used."

Alice watched each insect corpse carefully as she picked her way through the wreckage of the barricade. The fire had made it ineffective, but she guessed whoever set the fire did so after it looked like the bugs were getting through. The insects she saw looked leaner, their carapaces were longer and their six limbs all had serrations. They were similar to what she'd seen before but there were enough differences to make her wonder if they were an entirely different species.

The worst thing about the insects were their faces. Two rows of eyes between their upper mandibles and the top of their chitin heads stared at her, burned out in the fire, they were hollow. When their side and upper mandibles folded in with their lower ones, it created the illusion of a broad smile that seemed madly eager. The third one she saw revealed that they had two fine arms that folded under their upper appendages that ended in hands with three claw like fingers and two thumbs. That was very familiar, not in the number of digits, but in how the fingers seemed bony, more for clawing and less for fine work. "Humans, just ahead," Alice reminded everyone as they finished picking their way through the barrier.

"I'm surprised the Order hasn't come down and picked this place clean already," Noah said.

"The local transmission we're hearing is very weak," Iruuk explained. "It barely makes it past the vault door. I'm amplifying it several hundred times so..."

The three human figures near the end of the hallway all turned at the same time and started running towards them. "Stand ready," she said as four more humans shambled to their feet behind the trio that were rushing them from nearly thirty metres away, right in front of the vault door. Her rifle's light activated, revealing strange, bulbous mounds near the end of the hall, two of which were broken open and leaking. That's what they were eating, and she couldn't tell if it was a plant or a creature, it bled like the latter, but stood out from the bottom of the wall like plant life.

The red and brown matter dripped down the chin of the lead human. An insect clung to his chest and neck, tendrils wrapped around his throat reaching under his skin in several places. His hands were curled like claws, and he screamed as he got closer overwhelmed by animalistic aggression. It wasn't a medical diagnosis, but a feeling that there was nothing human left in the gaunt madman that rushed her. Even still she slung her rifle, was satisfied to hear it click into place on the back of her armour and she started running towards it. "I'll take this one down, shoot the rest."

"Aye," Knud and Jessen said from their position right behind her.

"What?" Noah asked in surprise.

It made Alice grin, surprising him like that, and she was sure he wasn't the only one shocked that she would tackle the frenzied human, but Noah was the only one who actually said anything. The one behind the lead attacker's head exploded as Jessen blasted him with two rounds.

The lead assailant leapt at Alice, and it nearly knocked her over, even with the resistance her armour had to such assaults. She flipped him over her, turned and put her boot down on the middle of his back, pinning him as she ducked low. Knud took the next human out with two bursts of his rifle, then they started on the four humans who were charging from where they'd risen closest to the vault. The cacophony of their screams, and the screech of their parasites as they were shot were shockingly loud.

As Alice fired a capture bag onto her catch and made sure it enveloped him properly, sealing then injecting him with stasis medication, she watched as her tactical readout lit up. "Now tracking thirty-one targets in the floors above. Some read human, others are those parasites, the rest are either inconclusive or Edxi young!" She checked the vault ahead and was surprised to see that there was no movement within. It was either some kind of trap, or the vault was abandoned.

"I'm seeing the same thing," Iruuk said. "They're coming down, the stairwell will be full in a minute."

Alice sprinted towards the vault, watching her passive scanners closely for traps. The source of the signal told her exactly where the Echo Corporation device was. The lab was surprisingly small, and she saw why there was nothing inside. There were drag marks in blood that painted a brutal picture. The Edxi young killed or subdued the humans within after the final barricades broke. A hall by the vault door led to the elevators, and there were bones mixed in with the shattered, makeshift defences. More drag marks within showed that the final barrier, steel rods and plates, just inside the vault door was broken inward, and there was a gory trail leading outward. The Edxi found their prey here, may have even killed most of them in the vault, but they didn't eat them in the sterile looking space.

The device was just inside, wired up to the doorframe of the lab nearest to the entrance so it acted like an antenna. Faloo was right behind her with an armoured bag, and Alice hurriedly disconnected it from the lab's power, then pushed the thick, heavy, round device into the container. The recorder that was playing the message back for it was still running, so she turned it off and pocketed it.

"We have to go! They're in the stairwell!" Iruuk shouted. He'd taken her capture and affixed the body bag to the back of his armour.

"Take up position, we're going to rush as a team," Alice

ordered. "Keep shields off until I say so. As soon as we turn them on, we'll be like beacons to those satellites." Alice and Faloo rushed to re-join the team. The Clever Dream wouldn't return for another nine minutes and thirty-three seconds unless she sent them a message, she hoped she wouldn't have to do that. Her tactical sensor showed the first of the Edxi coming down the stairwell, they were parasites. She unslung her rifle and took position in the middle of her people with Faloo and Noah.

Boots crushed debris from the battered walls, broken insect chitin and other evidence that was best left for auto-mated sensors to track. They rushed to the stairwell, Knud, Jessen and Noro opening fire on the parasites as they arrived on the landing, scurrying towards them. "What's Iora really like? Run into any of this the first time around?" Noro asked as he blasted one as it leapt through the air towards him.

"I left before the bug party," Noah replied, his rifle at the ready.

"The stairwell is not viable," Iruuk announced.

Alice saw it as he spoke. There was a traffic jam at the top of the stairwell slowing large Edxi from coming down, but the space would be choked with them soon. "Back towards the elevators," she said, turning around.

Iruuk led the rush in the opposite direction as Knud and Jessen covered their retreat, blasting several parasite infested humans to pieces. Alice took her place beside Iruuk and saw the first live Edxi young as they turned the corner. Its mandibles were open wide, forelegs raised high with the points of its serrated limbs pointing down to attempt to pierce her chest, those dark red and black eyes were solid colours from edge to edge. All six of them twitched and turned as they tracked her, somehow calm while every other part of its body moved with savage purpose.

The first burst of solid rounds didn't pierce its carapace armour, sparking against the shoulder and chest plates. She held the trigger down for a longer burst, sending a barrage of rounds into its head and watched it fall down twitching, its lower four limbs scrambling to drag its upper half away in retreat. The briefing on Edxi biology suggested that there were two and sometimes three brains but seeing how one could react while the other was dead was unnerving.

Her attention was on the next two, as she and Iruuk pressed on. The elevators were the realm of the Edxi young, it seemed. A wave of them rushed, shoulder to shoulder, at her team as they progressed up the hallway. The rapid thumping sound of their rifle rounds and the high, hollow sounding screams of the Edxi filled the air. It was such a racket that Alice expected the whole city to wake up, and she suspected that most of the citizens were hungry insects.

Half way to the elevator shaft her clip ran out. She dropped the empty, had a fresh one in her hand. An Edxi predator charged at her faster than the others, and Iruuk caught it just as the forelimb scratched the shoulder of her armour. Red and white matter spattered across the walls, broken chunks of chitin filling the air as the creature went down screaming.

Alice's clip failed to slide all the way into her rifle after two tries, and she looked at the magazine only to find that a piece of chitin had gotten into the top. "Faloo," she said as she fell back and the Nafalli took her place in the lead. Her rifle was up and firing as soon as she had a shot, ripping through another charging Edxi.

Alice looked at the broader picture on her tactical window as she cleared the blockage from her magazine then slipped the magazine into place easily. Her call to head to the elevator was the right one. The shaft was almost empty already, and the stairwell was fully clogged with Edxi who were fighting each other to get through the burned obstacles left behind by the previous failed defence.

Loud, angry screeches ahead caught her attention, and she looked up in time to see a pair of darker coloured Edxi, their natural armour was thicker, weathered, they were larger, and they charged at incredible speed. Alice was unable to get a shot from the middle of the group. Iruuk opened fire at them with his rifle on full automatic, his sidearm blasting at the same time in his off-hand. His rifle was accurate, the sidearm less so, but when it hit it left burning circles on their armour that spit white and yellow sparks.

Faloo's rounds were all hits, and she fired calmly, putting the one on her side of the hall down as its mouth and eyes were pecked to shreds by her gunfire. Its partner on the other side of the hall went down as well, but there was a third that used those two as cover so it could get close. At first it poised to strike Iruuk, then it turned and grabbed Faloo with its primary mandibles, fine arms, and forelimbs. In an instant it rolled, gripped the wall with its back legs for leverage then hurled the Nafalli behind it to a group of Edxi who immediately began to bash at her armour. They worked frantically to pierce the flexible metal that protected her, and she fought back quietly at first, firing at the only Edxi she could get a shot on, sending one of its limbs flying.

Alice and Iruuk blasted the Edxi that flung her to its brood mates, and with Noah joining in, it was dead in seconds. He joined their firing line as they pushed towards Faloo quickly. Two of the Edxi trying to pierce her armour turned towards them, shielding themselves with their forelimbs as they charged.

The Clever Dream would be back in four minutes, forty-nine seconds, and Alice was willing to sacrifice their secrecy for the Nafalli. "Faloo, turn your shields on and all the way up!"

"No! The Order will spot us!" she shouted back. Her claws were out, the armour she wore covered them, but also converted into razor sharp, hardened metal so she could fight back. One Edxi was gutted by her strong swipes, but the others were undaunted and poked hard at her armour in the same places over and over again. One broke through and the sound of her high-pitched scream prompted Alice to find a new level of urgency that she didn't know she had.

The pair of Edxi that tried to hold them back finally went down. "Rush! Go hand to hand, Iruuk!" she said, bursting forward at a run. An Edxi turned to her, she had a clear shot, and she dropped into a kneeling position so fast she slid for a moment as she took aim. Her barrage caught it fully in the face, enough to send it reeling for a moment.

It twitched in retreat as rounds from Noah's rifle caught the base of its forelimb, sending a burst right through a chink in its armour. It turned, screeching, about to charge, and their combined fire rendered it sightless before sending explosive slugs down its throat. Iruuk was there, then, the fingers of his armour adapted into long claws.

He was the predator as he dodged an Edxi who sliced at him with both forelimbs then grabbed onto one of the plates on its back. He jabbed his clawed hand underneath. It screamed as he pushed into its soft flesh, grabbed hold of something inside and yanked. The two remaining Edxi turned on him, and he used the flailing, panicking victim he had in hand to ward them off.

That gave Alice and Noah a clear line of sight on the last of Faloo's attackers. One went down right away, Noah's first burst catching it in a weak point at the base of its neck, hers blasting it in the side of the head. The second turned on them and charged so the thickest parts of its natural armour protected it. Noah and Alice nearly emptied their clips taking it down, trying to land shots on its face, which it was hiding behind thick forelimbs. It was still twitching when they ran around it. Faloo's medical system already put her into emergency stasis. She had severe piercing wounds through her side into her chest and lower torso, but to Alice's relief, she was intact from the shoulders up.

The last Edxi between them and the elevator shaft died with a piercing shriek as Iruuk yanked hard, drawing a flood of white and dark red gore from under the armour protecting its back. He shook the blood off his clawed hand, picked up his rifle, replaced the clip with practiced speed, then leapt up the elevator shaft. It was only a floor and a half up, and Alice wouldn't have been surprised in the least if he made the leap without help from his armour, even with a full-grown human in a bag on his back.

"Noro, take her up!" Knud said as he and Jessen fired at an Edxi that was coming around the corner behind the group. They had less than a minute before the hallway was filled, and there were more on their way to the elevator shaft above.

Noro turned and hefted Faloo onto his shoulder, where her armour bound to his. "I've got you, here we go," he said as he stepped into the shaft and jumped up to the first floor. Iruuk was already firing at Edxi and what looked like humans as they rushed him.

"You're next," Alice told Noah.

He rushed into the elevator shaft without hesitation, then jumped to the hole in the door above almost overshooting it. Alice made sure Knud and Jessen were ready to go, saw that there were more Edxi than her tactical window showed and started firing with them. There were four coming, two on the ceiling, two on the floor, and they were rushing as if eager, as if they sensed that they had her team surrounded. There were more Edxi behind those, the slow rounds they fired were barely enough to take out the group of four in the lead. They were replaced an instant later, they didn't have time to take their fingers off their triggers.

A glance at the status of Noah, Noro and Iruuk above told her that they were about to face a wave of at least fifty more enemies. The street was alive with them, and from the shape most of them looked Edxi, there weren't many infested humans in that pack.

It was time to turn everything they had on, the Clever Dream would be there in one minute and nineteen seconds. The Order wouldn't be able to respond before they got away. "All right! Turn..." the thud of a pressure grenade sounded, and her tactical window showed the main group of Edxi split as the blast sent them in all directions. Before they could recover, Ute, Callum and Theodore were right in the middle of them. To her surprise, Theodore was carrying a pair of rifles, and every shot struck its target.

"Up the shaft, now!" Alice ordered, it was their chance. Knud finished putting an Edxi down, sending pieces of its armour flying back into the faces of the other attackers several meters behind, then turned and joined Jessen, who was already running into the shaft.

Alice dropped two concussion grenades set for ten seconds then followed them up. They went off as she passed through the torn elevator door.

"Hurry, there's a wave of hundreds coming from the woods," Theodore relayed to her through a laser link.

"Go, go!" Alice shouted as she made sure they didn't leave anything important behind. She grabbed the Echo transmitter box from where it was still affixed to Faloo's back and rushed through the opening that Theodore, Ute and Callum created.

Everyone who was able fired at the encroaching Edxi as they ran. They had no choice, several were caught in mid-air, their bodies twitching as they landed between the members of her squad.

Two leapt at Knud, and he blocked the first with his rifle, both the forelimbs sliced into the metal deeply enough to ruin the weapon. He backhanded it just far enough away for Noah to rake its underbelly with rounds until it stopped trying to right itself. The other was caught by Iruuk, who roared as he gripped it by a chitin plate protecting the base of its neck, then blasted the back of its head until it screeched its last.

The Clever Dream was still fully cloaked, they were the only ones who could see it as a shadow on their HUDs. Callum and Ute covered their retreat as he stood just tall enough to easily fire over her head while she was short enough to keep firing without kneeling. He had one hand on her back as they retreated together.

Theodore was the fiercest of them, however, as he fired like a turret, a rifle in each hand blasting with deadly accuracy. He reloaded so rapidly that Alice missed it the first time, and he seemed absolutely unmoved judging from the look on his face. His was an expression of perfect passivity.

He was the last up the ramp, one Edxi, half shredded by Theodore's relentless barrage, managed a final leap. It pierced the android's side, and to Alice's surprise, Theodore dropped his rifles on the ramp, grabbed the forelimb and yanked it free before kicking the Edxi in the face hard enough to burst its last remaining eye.

The ramp started closing, and before everyone's eyes, Theodore's android hand punched through the lower half of the Edxi's belly. It screamed as he pushed, then stopped abruptly. "This ought to be a prime sample for Fleet Sciences." He withdrew his hand, then turned to the Clever Dream crew. "We can leave, Lewis," he said.

"Theo, man, I didn't think you could shoot lethal rounds," Noah said, his shock and amazement plain.

"My programming recognizes Edxi as a threat to civilized life as my programmers knew it. It seems I'm quite adept at killing them."

"Glad you're on our side," Alice said. "We have a patient for you."

TWENTY

An Hour with The Queen

SEEING Public Welfare Minister Pamela Grey in a blue diplomatic uniform, with the final Haven System flag of a double circle against a yellow sun, Kambis and Tamber on a dark field, on the right side of her chest and the green star of her position on the left, was a little strange. There was high tech armour built into a slightly thick vacsuit and jacket along with a shield system and many other components. You couldn't tell by looking at her outfit, and that was the point. "You were right to speak with the Duchess using a Hologram instead of coming down in person," her holographic representation said.

Ayan's assistant, Leon, and two admirals were behind her, sitting down out of the capture range of the holographic recorder. The small conference room was one of Ayan's favourites on the War Forge, close to home, secure, and designed for secrecy. The walls were blacked out, the lights were low, and to anyone watching her end of the hologram they wouldn't be able to tell where she was. "So, she isn't what she seems?" Ayan asked, trying to prod the Minister along so she'd get to the point.

"Well, she is a Duchess. Regent Galactic taxation records we stole show the transaction between Numo Life, a human analogue producer who resold a few types of popular Dolls, and her royal family. It took some digging, but we found out that the Duchess entered the royal fold as a toddler and grew up faster than a normal human. Their entire kingdom is in the Iron Head Nebula, so not much news reached outside of their solar system. The Duchess is not aware that she was purchased, she thinks she was born into the family. She really thinks she has the power to make an offer here, but our attempts to transmit to her home system aren't going to reach them for a year."

The Order of Eden had locked them out of all hyper transmitter nodes with new passcodes that the fleet hadn't cracked yet. Getting any transmissions out using secondary re-transmitters would take much more effort. Ayan could tell there was something else, that the Minister was continuing her annoying habit of saving the most dire news for last. "So, she's somewhat legitimate and has no idea that she was adopted. What else did you find out?"

"After speaking with her for a couple hours, she let something slip. She was in stasis for some time, and that saved her from the Holocaust Virus. Lucius Wheeler was the one who tracked her pod down and freed her. She thinks he is her hero. She also called him an Admiral, but she doesn't know his exact location. That's around the time I started hearing an Intelligence Operative whisper to me through my secure comm. When I asked her about her role, as was requested by my new eavesdropper, she said Wheeler told her that she would be the instrument of peace between the Order and the Haven System, and when her mission was finished she would be able to return to her family. I asked for more details, but other than the terms she offered before, she didn't have anything of note. I asked her if she'd submit to a deep memory scan so we can build trust with her, and she agreed. I really didn't think she would when Intelligence told me to request her participation. She's fine with it as long as its painless."

It was, but Ayan knew that it wasn't a comfortable feeling either. It felt like there was someone else with a cold, detached purpose rapidly recollecting your most prominent memories and digging a few forgotten things up. There were things Ayan remembered that she knew she was never meant to recall, but none of them were traumatizing, just curious, like recalling a time when she was floating, wrapped in warmth, and there was ancient classical music playing. She wondered what a person who was more mass-produced would find dredged up by the deep scan, and hoped the memories would be as harmless as her own. "Anything else?"

"Intelligence is taking it from here and we've assigned a support companion to her, a therapist, so that's all I can do. I'm not going to clear her to leave the base or join our population until we know her alliances for sure. Oh, one more thing before I let you go. Admiral Rice has approached me about becoming the top administrator in the civilian Legal Standards and Practices Board once the invasion is over. She said she'd be retiring from the military after the emergency. I'd like to know if you had any thoughts on her taking the position."

It was the first Ayan was hearing about it. "It's a surprise to me. What I want to know is whether you want her for the position."

"She's over-qualified, to be honest, and her record makes her the best candidate. Her morals are in line with the legal system we're developing and she hasn't had a breach of regulation since she joined Freeground Fleet. If this is how she wants to retire, then I want her in the top spot, overseeing all legal practices."

"When we emerge from this emergency we'll be fairly top heavy in terms of leadership. Considering her long service in the military, and the need for someone like her on your end, Fleet will have to let her go, but it might not happen right away. It depends on what kind of mess the Invasion makes."

"Good, thank you," the Minister replied. "Is there anything else I can do for you while you have me?"

"How are spirits on the ground? How are people feeling?" Ayan asked.

"Nervous, but the shield around Tamber is reassuring. They're putting a statue of you up in the new garden tomorrow. They're postponing the ceremony celebrating it, and you, but they are desperate to have the monument up. Considering how unpopular you were only weeks ago, this is a big swing. Most people love their queen, especially after they saw that recording of you sorting things out up there. I'm glad they're coming around quickly."

"So am I," Ayan said, dreading the thought of having to

stand beside a giant white statue of herself while people speak about her, and looking forward to having to give a speech even less. It was the first time she was relieved that they were in a state of emergency. It was an excellent reason to put that day off. "Thank you for taking the time to investigate the Duchess."

"My pleasure. Best of luck up there," the Public Welfare Minister said before her communication stream ended.

"Intelligence is going over the Duchess' ship from end to end, taking it apart," Admiral Lamonthe said.

"Take the gifts she brought me as well," Ayan said.

"The dress and the necklace? They were molecular scanned before you got them, they're safe," Leon said.

"If there's a chance that Wheeler had anything to do with that stuff, I want it scanned again," Ayan said, supressing the urge to tell her assistant that it wasn't a good time for him to voice his opinion about it.

"And if they come up as harmless wardrobe items?" Admiral Lamonthe asked.

"Then dump them into the nearest recycler, boxes and all."

"Aye, Minister," Lamonthe said. "What about this Duchess? My feeling is that she's an unknowing peon. Her family has naturally born heirs now, and the information we could find on the Stellarnet shows a succession without her in it at all. She's not even noted as a Duchess anymore. Everything with an image or description of her has been scrubbed. What do you want us to do with her if deep scans verify that she's harmless?"

"Offer her a place as a citizen," Ayan said. "We'll have to

do some fancy footwork once she's out of our secure lock-down, especially considering her relation to Ashley Lamport, but if she doesn't have a real alliance that's counter to Haven after she finds out the truth about how she's been used, and if she's not welcome in her home system, we should take her in if she wants to stay."

"And if she doesn't want to stay?" Lamonthe asked, running a hand through his silver hair.

"Then she can go, but she doesn't get anything from us other than standard provisions. Make sure that she knows that if she leaves, she won't be welcome back."

"That makes sense," Leon said. "If she was tricked by the Order to come here, that's fine, but if she goes back to them then tries to enter our space again, that tells a different story, right?"

"Right," Admiral Doolth said, stroking the fur under her chin. "Or she joins a criminal organization like Shadow Star. She doesn't seem like the sort, but you never know."

Ayan acknowledged the Nafalli's thought with a friendly nod before asking Admiral Lamonthe, the leader of Fleet Intelligence, about a topic that was nagging at her more as time went on. "How are things going with your people's infiltration of Shadow Star?"

"Badly," Lamonthe said, shaking his head. "We have a couple people in their lowest ranks, but at this rate it'll take months, maybe a year or two for them to work their way up so they can stand next to the leaders. One thing's for sure: Patrizia Salustri funded its foundation and set up the organization. Once the invasion is over, we'll have to use part of the fleet to stop their growth. On the brighter side, they're so well hidden that we only know of one small base in the system, and they hate the Order as much as we do. Every couple of days they lose a few low-ranking members to one of our recruitment centres. Their numbers aren't growing now, but I expect they will once we get through this emergency. There's one more thing, though. Our best intelligence is starting to make it clear that a lot of the people joining are doing so instead of coming to a Haven Intake Centre. There's a growing perception that the Haven Government exerts extreme control over its citizens. I can see where that comes from, in a way. The military performs loyalty scans upon entry, and there's a rumour that we do that to all citizens."

"Never outside of an investigation into a serious crime and that's only if consent is given," Leon replied.

"I know," Lamonthe said. "But the perception is spreading. The weapon restrictions, communal space programs and a few other details about everyday life, which most citizens support, are all being twisted perception-wise, probably by Salustri herself. Once the emergency is over, we'll have some work ahead of us to correct perceptions. We may even have to support a few ideas that could clash a little, like having a few cities or large stations where the rules are more relaxed, a place for people with a lot of doubt to visit without being afraid that big brother is watching everything they do."

"It's a good idea," Ayan agreed. "As long as it isn't in orbit around Kambis or Tamber, and there's some law there for people who need help, then it might work. Jake is more well-travelled than I am, he's probably seen a few places like the kind of thing you're describing."

"Working with him on this might be interesting,"

Lamonthe said. "Looks like I know what I'll be doing with my spare time."

"After the emergency," Ayan clarified.

"Absolutely."

"How bad are the criminal organizations on Tamber right now?"

"They're small in comparison to Shadow Star. Anderson has his Rangers watching them, and their numbers are shrinking as well. Once they realized that Haven would take in the ones without a violent criminal record, families started coming to our bases and approaching Rangers who visit the Free Cities."

That term, the Free Cities, bothered Ayan. It suggested that the few cities under Haven Government control were captive somehow. Haven citizens could leave whenever they like, they didn't even have to wear a comm unit or the clothing they were issued as standard. Employment earned them luxury credit that they could cash out as platinum that they could use anywhere, and the civilian government was thriving. New citizens that came to Haven settlements from the crime ridden Free Cities were amazed at the opportunities and higher quality of life they were offered in exchange for a quick interview and a simple check to make sure they weren't enemy infiltrators. Her father was once again in charge of the Rangers after being removed from his post as Defence Minister for keeping important secrets from Haven Fleet along with a few other charges. She was still disappointed in him but had a feeling that he ended up in the right place. "I'd like intake numbers and locations on all the people we're taking in who were part of criminal..."

Leon looked to the doorway that led to one of two antechambers where people who were cleared to see her face-to-face could wait. He was nervous, there was something urgent waiting. Ayan finished her thought. "...criminal organizations before they applied for citizenship. We want to make sure that they're not forming underground groups once citizenship is granted." She looked to Leon. "Something interesting waiting in the next room?"

"Councillor Goven Malsen has arrived and would like to see you urgently," he replied.

"It's about time I get to speak to someone with real pull from Lorander. Send them in."

"She only wants to speak to you, she says she doesn't want anyone to overhear your discussion."

"Too bad," Ayan said, looking to Admiral Doolth - the top admiral from the Nafalli tribes - and then to Admiral Lamonthe - the head of Fleet Intelligence - she wished more department heads were present, she could use their advice. "In fact, I'm going to loop the Public Welfare and Science Ministers in so they can hear and see this discussion and offer advice." With a few taps on her command and control unit, it was done. "Send the Councillor in."

The Councillor, dressed in light grey robes over a red vacsuit with a collar that went up to her jawline, entered, her brow furrowed as she looked around the room. "I instructed your people on this. We were to meet alone, in private."

"Ever since I became the Defence Minister, nothing has been private," Ayan said, sitting in a plush chair. There were two more beside that one, and four across from them, which she gestured to. "Have a seat."

Councillor Malsen sat on the edge of the chair across from Ayan. "Congratulations on your new position."

"Thank you, but that's hollow, if I'm being honest. I had to remove my father from this post because of building controversy, and I had to assume the role of Queen because I needed the veto power," Ayan said.

"Oh, I see. Both signs of a failing government, I understand."

"Every government stumbles in the beginning. Once this emergency passes, elections will be held for the Defence Minister position and I'll be able to step away again."

"Most new governments endure a transitional phase after their first attempt at operating as a democracy, usually because a dictator comes in to correct the path of the elected representatives. There's nothing to be ashamed of. Failure is to be expected," Councillor Malsen said, nodding with a thin smile.

Ayan could feel herself being dragged into an argument that wouldn't lead to anything productive. The only way to prove this Councillor and anyone else who thought the way she did wrong was to do as she said; guide the Haven System through the invasion, then step away from government back to her previous position. Arguing about her intentions and how she didn't see events the same way wouldn't convince anyone. "Let's move on to the reason for your visit," Ayan said, trying to shake her irritation at being indirectly called a dictator off.

"I have come because our requests to share in the new technology you're developing have gone unanswered for exactly one standard month now. I know that as the caretaker

of the fleet, and director of its research, that you are the ultimate authority in this."

"Pardon me, Councillor," Shawn Lourdes, the Science
Minister said as a hologram of him appeared in the seat
beside Ayan. "That's not a decision she made alone. As the
Science Minister I'm consulted on new technologies and
whether or not they're shared. Our Queen may have
extraordinary powers, but Ayan is functioning as the Interim
Defence Minister, a post she assumed so our government
wouldn't grind to a halt while the controversial activities of
the previous Defence Minister were being investigated. More
to the point: the decision to stop sending Lorander and our
other allies details about our technical development wasn't
made only by her. When she was still the Admiral who
oversaw the fleet's maintenance and development, she told us
that she wanted to stop updating you when we began work on
refining the dimension drive technology. The Triumvirate,
that's the Minister of Public Welfare, Defence Minister, and
me, voted on the matter and supported her decision. That is
how the most important decisions of our time are made."

"So, you collectively decided to hold developments made
using technology we gave you back from my people?" the
Councillor asked coolly. "I'm genuinely surprised at your
greed."

The hologram of the Science Minister looked at Ayan,
closed its eyes and shook his head. Ayan didn't know him
well, but in the few conversations she had with him over the
previous weeks, she'd come to like him. He was highly intelligent, aware that he over-analysed things as a general practice,
and critical of politicians that didn't use their time wisely.

Most of all, Minister Shawn Lourdes didn't suffer fools silently or politely.

Ayan thought it best that she answered the Councillor's accusation. "You shouldn't be surprised that we decided to hold something back. We need something to bargain with, an edge against our enemies, and an advantage as we join the interstellar community as traders. Besides, I'm surprised Lorander hasn't managed to catch up. You have all the same resources we do, you even have a scan of the dimension drive that was aboard the Fallen Star."

"The progress you've made with that technology has shocked everyone. Since you developed it using labs based on our technology, software and databases we created, it's only fair that you share your work product at least. We also believe we have a right to the data you fed into those systems, since they obviously led to at least one major breakthrough," Councillor Malsen said as though she was speaking to a child.

It would be easy to give in to frustration. A glance at Leon, who looked shocked and irritated, and to Admiral Doolth, who was tugging on a tuft of fur at the base of her neck, her right lip curling in a half-sneer, showed Ayan that she wouldn't be wrong to get angry, but she knew that would be a mistake. Admiral Lamonthe nodded at Ayan. "I have more important business to attend to, if you'll pardon me, Minister," he said, standing and striding to the door. He'd seen the fall of the Aucharian military and been in the middle of the final battle that spelled its utter defeat. Nothing anyone said to him made him the least bit irate. Words didn't compare to the trials he'd seen in his life, but he valued his time too much to bother with the kind of conversation Ayan was having.

"Dismissed," Ayan said, wishing she could follow him and do something more useful. The Councillor was wasting her time, trying to get a rise out of her, but Ayan didn't want to be baited and didn't appreciate being underestimated. Instead of giving in to irritation, she settled into her seat and stared at Goven Malsen, meeting that pale blue gaze as passively as she could manage. Instead of speaking, she let her mind work, and watched as the thickening silence acted on the Lorander representative.

There was a reason, a core, simple reason why they were asking for access to their technology. The attempt to frustrate Ayan, to push her mentally off-balance was to keep her away from realizing what that was until Lorander had what they wanted. Councillor Goven Malsen's mouth started to open, and Ayan interrupted her. "Why are you making this request now?"

The furrow of Malsen's pale brow signalled the turning of the tables as she hesitated for a moment. "Lorander has provided the keys to your success here. You would still be in old ships and makeshift shelters on your island if it weren't for the Solar Forge and other shared technologies. What we're asking is reasonable."

"You offered the Solar Forge freely, and we shared all the technology we discovered that led us to the small leaps we've made since. That should be enough for a culture that has stolen or borrowed every technology you have. We took a look at the database that came with the Solar Forge and were able to find outside sources for most of the technological advancements you've made over the last century. You made sure there were gaps so it wouldn't be easy to see how all that tech combined to advance your systems, but we managed to fill most of them. Some great minds have come to the Haven System, and once we figured out how you combined technologies to create new advancements, we started adding to your database so we could do it ourselves, and it's been productive."

"Like this mobile monstrosity you've created, the War Forge," Councillor Malsen said. "We didn't give you the Solar Forge so you could learn to make an armed monument to destruction."

"No, you gave it to us so we could celebrate the technological miracle it was and enjoy it. I'm sure you were surprised when we made Solar Forges Two and Three, then used them to build this. We don't sit on our heels here, we use what we have to improve our situation. It's the Haven way. You can have Solar Forge One back, if you like, by the way. I think we can get on without it. We don't use it for classified research though, so the technology you're after won't be there."

"Why are you resisting? We are only asking for what's reasonable. We are entirely in the right."

"I already explained why we're not sharing our technology. I thought Lorander was leaving, anyway. Our weekly appeals for help in fighting the Order of Eden and the Edxi are ignored, and all but three advisors have left our facilities, so I thought your people would be gone any day now."

"My people stay to oversee the use of our gifts," Councillor Malsen said. "How can we do that if we're not abreast of recent developments?"

"Why don't you scan one of our ships for yourself? You can't scan the War Forge, I realize, but..." Ayan stopped as she saw the Councillor's expression darken. *That's it. The scanner defeating technology we developed for the intelligent plating we're using is stopping them from seeing what we're doing.* She thought. *There's still more to this visit, though.* "You can't scan our ships anymore, can you?"

"We would rather ask for the technologies you've developed than steal them," the Councillor said, straightening in her chair. She was looking anywhere but at Ayan.

"Help us survive the invasion. Join the fight, and I'll share something with you after we've made it through."

"We will not get directly involved in this conflict. It is not our way."

"Then you get nothing," Ayan said. "If you scan a couple ships on your way out of the system, I won't stop you, but I'm not giving you anything."

"That's not our way."

"Sure, it is," Science Minister Lourdes burst. "Minister Anderson just explained that we've seen the evidence proving that most of your technological advancements are from stolen technology. You can't scan our ships anymore, can you? We suspected that our intelligent plating would stop you, which wasn't our intention, but I'm not unhappy about it. You probably don't even know what's inside a quad drive."

"Ridiculous," Councillor Malsen dismissed, flushing deep red. "We're adhering to etiquette."

Ayan realized why the Councillor was there in person for the first time, then. "You are leaving," she said. "You're afraid of what's coming, aren't you? This is your attempt to get everything you can before you gather your people and run."

"This isn't productive," she said, standing.

"No, no, don't leave me with the impression that you're a complete coward. If I'm right, please have the decency to say so. I don't want to remember the highest ranking Lorander representative I've ever met as a greedy coward."

That only sped the Councillor's steps, but at Ayan's signal, the door wouldn't open. "Allow me to leave or this will become an incident," Councillor Malsen said, it was almost a whimper.

Ayan stood and crossed the room calmly. She touched the Councillor's shoulder, directing her to turn away from the door. "I'll give your people all the new technologies we've developed if you stay and help us through this fight. Maybe we can have an even better relationship after this emergency as we take the next step in development together. Not only in technology, but in diplomacy, in developing a culture with a broader perspective. We still have a lot to learn from your people."

"Please give us a quad drive before the Edxi arrive," the Councillor plead, there was real fear in her eyes. "You don't know this enemy as well as you think you do."

"You've fought them before," Ayan said. "You've fought them and lost."

"Your station can make dozens of quad drives a day, maybe hundreds. Give us one, and I'll tell you."

"I don't need you to tell me that what's coming for us terrifies you, that you've faced them," Ayan said. "You're shaking. I can't give you a quad drive. They're scan-shielded for a reason."

"Then let me go, please."

Ayan stepped away and pressed the security release on her command unit, unlocking the door. It slid open and the Councillor nearly fell through it, joining her delegation of four on the other side and leading them away quickly. When the doors slid closed again, Ayan faced the Ministers' holograms. "I propose that we send an invitation to all Lorander people in the system to defect if they want to join us as Haven citizens. After a loyalty check, they'll join us in assisting with the defence then be free to choose whatever life as citizens they like after three years' service in the military. My vote as Defence Minister counts as one for yea. I need one more."

The Science Minister thought for a moment, looked to the hologram of the Minister of Public Welfare, then shook his head; "Nay. Other than the Solar Forge and help with a few matters of telepathy, Lorander resists the idea of sharing knowledge and looks down on other cultures. I think we've gotten everything we're going to out of this alliance and inviting deserters from their ranks won't benefit us in the long run. I know that tactic has brought great scientists to new nations in the past, but I expect we'll get the worst of the Lorander people here. Most of their lead scientists are, for want of a better word, snobs."

"Their culture, even though it may be secretive at times, is highly advanced. Our Triumvirate concept is largely thanks to their influence, and they can offer more than technological knowledge. I worry that this will be seen as a betrayal to

Lorander, but since they're abandoning us in our hour of need, and their people won't require training if they join us, we should extend a bridge to Lorander citizens who wish to stay. I vote yea."

"The ayes have it," Ayan said. She looked to her command and control unit. "You've been listening in, Admiral Lamonthe?"

"Aye, we'll put the invitation out over the known Lorander communication networks in a few minutes. I'll make sure it's clear that they have to submit to a surface thought scan during a loyalty check so we don't get a few newbies who run back home the moment they get an interior scan of one of our ships. Shrewd move, Minister, I'm looking forward to seeing what a Lorander soldier looks like."

TWENTY-ONE

Lacklustre Success

THE ALARM WENT OFF, and Alice's first reaction was to roll out of bed and put both her feet flat on the floor. Three and a half hours of deep sleep had come to a sudden halt and her head was left in a fog. Through the reflex she gained while she was in the Academy, those clear-headed days, she recalled the next important task ahead of her. If she was reading a mission objective chart, it would say something like: RETURN TO THE MERCILESS AND DELIVER THE ECHO SYSTEM PACKAGE.

The ship would arrive in the Haven System soon unless something went horribly wrong. A glance at the command unit on her right wrist confirmed that. They would arrive in fourteen minutes. The box they'd stashed the Echo Corporation Communications Core in was in the secure closet in the middle of the ship. It could survive more damage than any other part of the vessel, and she knew it could transmit. The system was intact, at least, and the database inside was unlocked, probably so any human who came across it could use it. The last person to record a message and set it to broadcast must have been kind-hearted, or at least a big supporter of 'Team Human.' No one was listening though, at least no one who cared to respond or send help.

For a moment Alice allowed herself to imagine what it would have been like if she had that technology while she was with Bernice. If that technology was loose in the galaxy, if everyone had one she would have been able to find Jacob in minutes, sending messages out to him that would reach every civilized system. What would it have been like if she didn't have to spend so much time running from Meunez? If she found Jacob Valent early and joined the crew of the Samson?

There may have been a long time for her to get to know him, Stephanie, Frost, Ashley, and the rest of his crew. She would have been able to keep track of friends that were months away by signal. Then again, the Holocaust Virus could have transmitted almost instantly to thousands of worlds where there were more emotional artificial intelligences than people. The destruction could have been worse, it could have been utter, instead of leaving hundreds of civilized fringe systems untouched because they were able to shut their vulnerable computers down in time. With a shake of her head, she moved on, noting the passing of those thoughts as she muttered; "'What if' doesn't matter now."

A quick double check of her uniform, a few seconds spent sorting her hair out and she was stomping into her boots, slipping into her long coat and on her way out of her quarters. It may have taken her a few moments to shake the cobwebs from her quick rest, but she hadn't had sleep that good since she could remember. "I love this ship," she sighed to herself. She found it much more comfortable than her military housing.

"You know, your mother has a habit of thinking aloud, too," Lewis said from his audio system. "Hungry?" he asked, a thick, cool fruity concoction called Blasting Berries filled a cup with a straw in the food dispenser.

"Yes, thank you." She took the cup and pulled on the straw, the tart flavoured, smooth textured drink filling her mouth. It was funny how hunger could hit at the first sip or first sight of something as it did then.

"You don't regret relinquishing your house, do you?" Lewis asked.

"I'm happier on the Clever Dream. I want to live on the ship and keep customizing, make it my own again. Fleet techs have been through here so many times, adding, removing, upgrading so much that I'm having trouble keeping up."

"The logs say you've read about every change," Lewis countered. If he had shoulders he'd probably be shrugging, at least that's what it sounded like.

"I know. I know every panel and system aboard, but that's not the point. I don't feel like I've really taken possession, like it's really ours again."

"Speak for yourself, I never left."

"You're right, but I think I'm glad I'm spending real time aboard. Living here, buffing out the rough corners and making refinements for a while. Spending some time with you is priority number one. Maybe checking your code over for changes that the Fleet added."

"I thought you already did?"

"I started, but time ran out," Alice replied. "It's always running out. So, being here instead of splitting my time between two places feels right."

"What about Theo?"

"I'll invite him to live here, but maybe he'll want to spend more time with Noah too, so he could bounce around as he likes. What do you think of him moving in full time?"

"I argue with him from time to time, but I would like him to stay. Besides, someone has to play doctor to the biologicals that spend time here. Speaking of which, Faloo is awake and better than new."

"Good, I'll offer Theo a permanent spot on the ship. It looks like I'll be spending more time aboard," Alice said.

"Excellent. I wasn't going to say anything, but I disliked splitting time with that terrible house minder of yours. She wasn't worth the memory, if you ask me," Lewis grumbled.

"Oh, you mean Roomie?" Alice asked. "Don't worry, I was on the verge of deleting her." The hatch to her quarters slid aside and she took a right down the short corridor to the small bridge.

"...changes everything. Imagine making a call to the core with no delay," Noah was saying from the co-pilot's seat. Ute's broad head nodded while she minded the pilot's controls and Iruuk's muzzle bobbed in agreement as he observed the readings at the science station.

"Talking about our cargo?" Alice asked as she sat down at the communications station.

"Yeah, the Echo Corp had this tech almost licked, it's amazing," Noah said, bright-eyed.

It made Alice's stomach turn over. The news she had for him wasn't what she hoped, and she had to share it with him before they got back, which would be in less than ten minutes.

"I took a minute to perform a more detailed scan and enter it into our technology development software," Iruuk added. He was excited. "I deleted the results so no one could steal them once we get back to the Fleet, but it said there was no reason why we can't use the technology with dimension drive systems, making the nodes very easy to produce and instantaneous communication between them simple. Oh, and once Fleet figures it out, it can be done with a software update. The technology that Echo didn't have a good grasp on was the dimension system, and we're getting better at that all the time. There are still a few minor problems, but Fleet should solve them soon."

"That's going to be amazing, Iruuk," Alice said, looking to Noah. "We have to talk." She signalled Yawen, telling her to go to the Captain's Quarters.

"Can you spare him?" Alice asked Ute.

"Lewis can take over co-pilot duties," Ute replied, nodding.

A minute later Alice sat beside Noah on the round seat in the middle of her quarters. Yawen settled in on a padded slide-out seat across from them. "You haven't told him about your part of the mission?" Alice asked Yawen.

"Not yet," Yawen said.

"How'd you sleep?" Alice asked Noah. She hoped her

instinct to let him get some shut-eye before she broke the news to him was the right call.

"Amazing. Lewis set me up with soothing tones as soon as I laid down and I went out so fast I don't remember falling asleep. You?"

"The same," Alice nodded.

Theodore entered the room and sat down across from Noah. He knew what was going on, he was Yawen's second while they executed their side-mission.

"What's this about?" Noah asked, guarded.

Alice took a deep breath and let the news out in one quick explanation. "I put a secondary mission together based on the places where you found survivors around Iora. After getting a passive scan of the continent that the Order of Eden are settling, the Clever Dream did a sweep across all those locations. Only one still had signs of living humans. Niler Station. Someone's turned it into an armoured bunker, and there are thousands there. From what Yawen and Theo could tell, the Order of Eden are leaving them alone."

"There were no signs of life in any of the other places where I found people?" Noah asked.

"I'm afraid not," Theodore said. "But that doesn't mean that they were all killed. There are other settlements, we're sure."

"How? How can you be sure?" Noah asked. He and Theodore stared at each other for a long moment.

Yawen broke the silence. "The Edxi hatchlings need something to feed on. We detected clusters of hundreds, sometimes thousands, and they're thriving, so they're eating something. I'm sorry, there's no other way to say it, but it's still a good sign."

"The scans, that information will trigger rescue missions, right?" Noah asked, looking to Alice with a tear in his eye. There was a little of the scrawny young man who landed on Iora in him yet.

She didn't want to see him beg or get hurt. "There are two battle groups in range of Iora from what we saw, and then there's the Edxi fleet there. It'll be a while at best, but Haven needs people, so..."

"Tell your mother to send ships. If anyone can get something happening there, it's you. Maybe your father can send his SOCU teams."

"We have to get through this invasion first," Alice said.

"I know," Noah said, wiping his cheek dry with his sleeve. There weren't many tears, but it was heart wrenching to see him break down at all. "God, I barely knew any of them, I don't even know why I care so much, but they must be going through hell."

"I was there," Alice said. "Just what I saw in that lab was enough to make me want to go back for anyone we had to leave behind."

"But the people who are left are in makeshift bunkers," Yawen said. "Homemade hardened defences would slow any rescue down, and this ship is too small to take any one of the strongholds we saw aboard. There are hundreds, sometimes thousands of people in each one. I know Alice won't forget them, though. She may get quiet about it, but I know her. A cause like this will be like an itch in her brain."

"I'll make sure everyone who can do something about this

will know there are people we need to help," Alice reassured. Her report was already filled with details about the survivors, as much data as they could gather, and she added suggestions to show she had a plan.

"Yeah," Noah said. "I believe you. Thanks for telling me. Glad I got a few hours' good sleep before you dropped that on me, too. Might be awhile before that happens again."

"We're about to arrive in the Haven System," Lewis announced.

Noah's arms went around Alice just as she was about to stand up, and she returned the embrace. When it lasted longer than the momentary, supportive grasp, she closed her eyes and let something she was afraid to say loose against his ear in a whisper. "I wanted to find some of them for you. I wanted to be your hero."

TWENTY-TWO

Two Ships

THE BRIDGE of the Merciless was already darkened. The entire fleet was at a heightened state of readiness, and the final arrangements were being made for the long-awaited siege. Admiral Rice, commanding a large portion of the defence either had a strong gut feeling, or knew something that Jake wasn't privy to.

"The Clever Dream has arrived in-system," Huun reported, looking up from his tactical station. "They are in perfect condition and report mission success."

Jake knew he was happiest that his daughter and her crew were back but hearing that she'd actually found and retrieved a working Echo Corporation communications system made him grin. The chances of that mission being successful were less than fifty percent. A few people in intelligence theorized that the section of Iora they were visiting was most likely covered in Edxi who were down to the last food sources. They were ready to start fighting and feeding on each other, possibly the most dangerous time to encounter one. Alice went on her mission with that knowledge in mind. It was one of the riskiest ones SOCU undertook yet. "Signal them to deliver their cargo to the War Forge, then to carry on to our location."

"Aye, Sir," Liara said, passing the task to the three team members behind her.

"Sir," Captain Neel Moore, the third watch commander of the Merciless said from over Jake's shoulder as he approached.

Commodore Valent turned his seat so he was face to face with the towering Nafalli. He was one of the few of his people to have ancestral lines that crossed between the burrower and tree tribes. "Yes, Captain."

"I wanted to thank you for everything before I left for the Rassaaga. I will carry the knowledge you shared with me to my new command." He bowed low for a moment before straightening and extending his hand.

Jake stood and reached up to shake it. "I can't wait to see what you do over there. I believe you're about to make you and your crew legendary." The sister ship to the Merciless, the Rassaaga, was manned by hundreds of Nafalli with Mergillians taking positions at the helm, as gunners and fighter pilots. He hoped that he would get a chance to tour the ship once it was fully crewed before the invasion started, but it didn't look like he would get the chance. "Good hunting, Captain."

"And to you, Commodore," Captain Neel Moore said with a final bow of his head before releasing his hand and taking his leave of the bridge.

"Sir, the Sky Queen is in-system, transmitting on an encoded emergency channel," Liara announced, bringing it up on the main hologram projector in the middle of the bridge.

Alaka's head and shoulders appeared. "The swarm ships holding position outside the Haven System entered a dimension window nineteen minutes ago. My science officer is telling me that they're on their way here. He's ninety-four percent certain."

"Thank you. You'll be given a course that will take you into our patrol pattern. We're watching planet Carole," Jake said as he signalled Liara and her team to pass the news up the chain of command. "I'm also happy to report that the Clever Dream is back in-system, all souls accounted for. Their mission was a success."

"Thank you, Commodore," Alaka's relief was visible in his eyes, which softened for a moment before he acknowledged his orders. "The Sky Queen will be in position in little more than six minutes."

"Here we go," Jake said to the bridge crew as the oversized image of Alaka's head and shoulders faded.

"Are you sure this is where we ought to be?" Huun asked from the tactical station. "Carole is absent all but the simplest forms of life, not ready for any oxygen-based habitation and of little immediate tactical significance."

Jake knew he was only half right. Carole and its moons had water in abundance and other basic compounds that could be easily mined. There were also key points where an enemy could hide while they fortified their positions. The Merciless, its fighter squadron and SOCU ships could have been more useful elsewhere, especially since he suspected that the enemy might risk emerging closer to Kambis and Tamber, but there were heavy defences there already. "You worry about minding your station and directing your team, Lieutenant Commander. I'll make sure we're where the Admiralty needs us and contemplate our role in the big picture."

"Yes, Sir. I offer my apologies, Sir," Huun said, his nose pointing up in the air, covered by both hands for a moment. It was an expression of deep shame.

"Accepted. Don't worry about it," Jake reassured. He looked to his tactical overview and created a sub-image where he could focus on the Clever Dream. The relatively small, familiar vessel was running at full thrust, acting under orders that told them that speed was more important than stealth. A fleet-wide order to go to red alert was given, and the lighting on the bridge changed accordingly. He took a moment to send his hopes to his daughter before focusing on the task at hand. There was an attacker in system. It wasn't in the zone they were protecting. He waited for the details, shifting to the edge of his seat.

WITHIN THE MOST HEAVILY SHIELDED SECTION OF the War Forge was a secret known only to one hundred forty-four special crewmembers. It was born in the first moments of the station's design, the brain-child of Merin Lerner, a designer who was a relatively unknown member of the then new design team. Ayan noticed her when she saw the idea for the HF Prometheus, a ship that would provide an escape option for everyone in the core of the War Forge.

The concept behind the ship became more intricate and impressive as the War Forge was being built. Instead of sitting in a secure hangar, it had its own construction bay that made improvements and alterations as better technologies were developed. Testing was also a constant, with a core crew that made sure that the kinks were worked out before the ship had to be put to use. The last version of the Clever Class Corvettes, Haven Destroyer Class, the final build of the Merciless and its sisters, and several future ships wouldn't have been developed nearly as quickly as they were if it weren't for the accelerated testing aboard the Prometheus.

The simple escape ship had become something no one initially intended. It became an instrument of war unlike anything Ayan could have dreamt of. There was room for everyone who worked in the middle of the station. They would be well protected, and if the worst were to happen, and the War Forge was about to be destroyed, the Prometheus would break free, become exposed and either join the fight or escape. It was the first Cruiser Class ship in the fleet. The fighter pilots and most of the crew had no idea they were on board. The hallways leading from the War Forge to the Prometheus were disguised so the transition between them was seamless, and as far as Ayan knew, no one guessed that most of the station's secure section was actually aboard a heavy cruiser buried in the core of the structure.

As Ayan took her place in the middle of the command centre, a dimly lit circular room with rings and rings of people working at stations, assisting with the coordination of the fleet and serving as a backup central command for defence of the Haven System, she knew that the last of the modifications to the ship were being performed. All development would be halted until the emergency was over.

There was an important analysis alcove aboard the ship that waited for the Echo Corporation communications system to be installed. Engineers waited to find out how the programming inside could be adapted to the quad drives installed across the fleet, and used for instantaneous communication. Ayan watched a small holographic display of Alice handing the case with the Echo Corporation device to a crewmember in a red and white uniform. The Lieutenant saluted her then ran to an Ensign from the Prometheus crew who waited in an express car that would take him to the hangar in the middle of the station.

"Thank you for picking that up, Alice," Ayan said through her comm. "Be careful out there, but good hunting."

"Thanks. Here's hoping the War Forge doesn't have to join the fight, but good hunting just the same," Alice replied as she turned and ran back to the mooring the Clever Dream was affixed to. She had to join the other SOCU ships near planet Carole.

The channel closed and Ayan focused on the matters at hand. To her right was Leon, the aide she'd chosen and trusted more by the minute. To her left was Admiral Lamon-the. He represented a few dozen intelligence analysts who were busy going through reports and incoming information, using several artificial intelligences to assist them in providing options for her and everyone else who commanded a section of the defence. Leon was already speaking to her. "Tamber Defence reports that the moon's shield has one hundred percent coverage, but the cannons are only at ninety-two percent. They couldn't get all of them installed in time."

"How long will it take to install the last eight percent? Those gaps will be easy to spot if enough ships get close to Tamber," said Ayan.

"They estimate just over thirty minutes," Leon replied.

It was a problem that started with the Haven Council. They were happy to agree with the military building a shield but wanted a voice as soon as they heard that Haven Fleet was about to put heavy cannons in orbit. The Council peti-tioned to have a say in how or even if they were deployed and arguing that point cost them two days while the Solar Forge turned out turret satellites that were warehoused instead of installed. Ayan knew that her father, Carl Anderson, could have denied the Haven Council any say in where military defences went while he was the Defence Minister, and she hated to fault him for not doing so, but his inaction was a mistake, and she was seeing the problem it created. "Move Solar Forge's One, Two and Three into the largest gaps and call destroyers into the rest. We can't give them an opening."

"Our intelligence still indicates that this will be a conven-tional attack," Lamonthe said. "The enemy will emerge some-where just inside the edge of the solar system and push towards Tamber from there. If that's the case, then you'll face criticism for pulling some of our resources back for a close defence."

"Politics don't seem too important right now, Admiral," Ayan sighed.

"Good." Lamonthe nodded with a tight-lipped smile.

"You don't think the intelligence is right, either, do you?"

"I think they're completely wrong. It's wishful thinking," he said in agreement. "They're going to try to drop right on top of us. The outer incursion near Planet Zelas is a distraction. The Excalibur and the rest of the defence group there have that under control." His eyes went wide at something he was reading on his wrist. "My analysts just finished checking a data stream that's coming from the Sector Jumper. We weren't sure if a conclusion Shamus Frost came to was correct, but we've verified it."

"What conclusion?" Ayan asked as she looked at the map of the Solar System. Planet Zelas had a red rectangle beside it where the Excalibur along with six destroyers were engaging a small swarm of insect ships along with a cruiser of some kind. They were winning and providing more data on their enemy by the second.

"I'll let him explain it himself, he recorded his conclusions clearly."

The head and shoulders of Shamus Frost appeared in one of the main holographic displays in the middle of the command centre. "To Haven Fleet Command. I'm bringing back a lot of information that you'll find worthwhile, but the most important bit is this revelation I found in a secure data vault. In these old Lorander accounting records the Sector

Jumper's computer managed to decrypt I found an invasion map of a part of the Sagittarius Dwarf Galaxy that shows solar systems that are off limits because they've been overrun by Edxi. Another part of the map shows several galaxies and sections of the Milky Way that Lorander marked as safe along with records of who was resettled there. There are dates attached to all the worlds, and after some digging, I discovered references to several other documents that look like treaties. I'm not some legal genius, my record can confirm that, but I swear they're treaties with those Edxi bastards. I decided to start sending you everything I've managed to decode instead of waiting until I have it all figured out here with Hal, who was the one who figured half this stuff out before I knew what was going on. Good luck and tell Stephanie I'll be home soon."

The image faded and Lamonthe took over, his tone flat and face expressionless. "From the data he sent, we have been able to confirm that the Lorander Corporation has been tracking the expansion of the Edxi and sub-species for over twenty years. Their colonization program seeds this and other galaxies with humans away from their areas of encroachment."

"The program they've been running for years, where you give them a whole pile of credits or platinum and in return they settle you on a nice hospitable world with a pre-vetted bunch of colonists? That program?" Leon asked.

"That's the one," Admiral Lamonthe said. "There were a few treaties on record, but they were made by the Order of Eden, not by Lorander. The Lorander Corporation still uses them to their advantage, however, by using the secured worlds as a sort of staging area before pushing further out from the galaxy with colony ships. Using the records of transfers from the accounting data and destinations for clients, my analysts have determined that Lorander has known about the Edxi for years, decades. They're working their own plan to ensure that humanity survives outside of this galaxy because they see a day when it may be overrun. The invasion map of Sagittarius confirms something I've feared. The Edxi breed and expand exponentially approximately every thirty-three years. It has been thirty-four years since the last surge in that galaxy, and they're setting up broods that will mature in about three decades in the Milky Way. We don't know how extensive the broods are, but seeing this old Lorander data, I expect they'd be the ones who could tell us."

"Where is Councillor Goven Malsen?" Ayan asked, looking the information up for herself at the same time.

"About to leave the station," Leon replied.

"Detain her and her entourage. Lock the mooring points to their ship and send soldiers aboard to secure the vessel." Ayan was so angry that she was seeing stars, so she took a deep breath before continuing, trying to clear her head. "Enable psionic dampeners station wide and lock every Lorander citizen up in the brig. Not the station's brig, but the interior cells aboard the Prometheus."

She opened a secure channel to Lorander Command as she watched her orders pass from Admiral Lamonthe to the security staff aboard the War Forge. She sent the Intelligence report that was just summarized for her and followed it with a message of her own. "This is Haven Defence to all Lorander ships. I will only give you a chance to explain yourselves and fully become our allies going forward if you stand with us and defend the Haven System. If you don't fully pledge to assist us, your ships will be seized and boarded. I know you are withholding information that will assist in the defence of this system, and I will have it."

For the first time Lamonthe regarded her with open surprise. It only kept him from his duties for a moment before he refocused but getting a reaction from him was something she'd remember. The next step Ayan had to take was clear. With a gesture at her command unit she opened a channel to Commodore McPatrick, who was back on the bridge of the Triton. "Oz, cloak your battlegroup. You're going to be enforcing that threat."

He nodded at her solemnly. "I just saw the report from Intelligence. Battlegroup Seven will be in position when the time runs out for our Lorander guests."

Ayan knew the Triton would be leading the rest of the Seventh Battlegroup away from its orbit around Kambis to the sector of space where five modest Lorander ships had watched them for months. She hoped they wouldn't have to use force on the people who had provided them with the building blocks they needed to form the foundation of their civilization, but she wouldn't flinch if it came to that. Leon was visibly shaken, watching the security feeds near the railing in front of him as the Lorander Councillor and her entourage of four were put into restraints and led towards the brig. "If they knew that the Edxi were coming," Ayan started to explain in hushed tones. "Then they probably fought them, or at least studied them. They know their biology, their culture, and at least some of their history. All that could have helped us prepare, given us some advantage. It might have even gotten us out of this emergency without firing a shot."

"So, withholding is as bad as lying under these circumstances," Leon said, nodding. "But if they got close to them before, then why didn't they figure out the dimension drive technology for themselves?"

"Everything we've seen has shown us that the Lorander people will always avoid a fight," Lamonthe said. "As we use the War Forge to build more weapons and fighting ships, their volunteers have come less and less. They've even voiced their disapproval several times. I don't know what they expected us to do, we have enemies on all sides here, but they don't like a fight."

The Lorander ships in the Haven System were highlighted on the large holographic tactical map, and Ayan watched as they all opened wormholes and departed, leaving several shuttles and volunteers stranded. "Lock anyone left behind in temporary quarters," Admiral Lamonthe said. "Strip them, take everything they own so they can't destroy or delete the contents of hidden data devices, then put them in standard vacsuits. Do it quickly, don't injure a single one. They'll get their things back after they've been thoroughly scanned and have determined that they're not carrying anything that can harm themselves or our people."

The Intelligence Officer behind him nodded then sent the orders across the fleet.

"The Seventh Battlegroup confirms that all the Lorander ships have departed the system using wormholes that stretch over fifty light years," one of the Tactical Commanders in the middle of the large chamber announced.

"I don't think I've ever been more disappointed," Leon muttered as he returned to his work.

Ayan shared his feeling, staring at the empty space where there were once ships containing who she thought were wise, advanced people. "It's the British Alliance and us, then," she said with a nod. "That'll do."

TWENTY-THREE

Close Defence

COMMODORE TERRY OZARK MCPATRICK sat down in the command seat of the Triton. It was good to be back, but it didn't feel like the same ship. It wasn't because of a wide variety of upgrades, or the changes in the crew, but the feeling he had when he was near Haus Geist. It was the only truly good natured being of its kind that he'd met, and he still missed it.

He'd finally come to grips with the loss just enough so he could assume command of the Triton again. It wasn't a permanent post. He was taking over the Fleet Academy, but during the defence many experienced officers were forced into taking command positions aboard ships, and it only made sense for him to take his seat aboard the Triton.

Lorander's quick departure was a surprise. They were

largely pacifists, even the warriors among them were more inclined to play diplomat until the last possible second than draw a weapon, and he admired them for that. Even still, the Haven System was largely a creature of their creation, even though they didn't directly guide its growth, and he found it demoralizing that they weren't willing to help defend it. "Order all ships to return to our standby position," he said.

A relatively small ship with a forked hull appeared on his tactical display and was identified as a Lorander Heavy Destroyer. It was new to the system, but the ship was classified by its power level, which was high for its size. "This is Captain Allen Czona of the Mira Lane. We just appeared on your scanners for the first time because we'd like to join you. Until now, we've been providing security for the other Lorander ships here, but now that they've moved on. We are no longer members of the Tri-Galaxy Collective, the government that oversees Lorander and the other organizations our people hide behind."

"Sir, our scans only detect sixty-three crewmembers aboard that ship, but there is room for two hundred fifty," Tactical Officer Rivas reported from behind Oz.

"Let's reply," he said to his lead communications officer, a Mergillian named Stut. He was already prepared, and the channel was open the moment Oz finished giving the order. "Captain, I'd like to confirm: You are defecting and joining Haven Fleet?"

"That is correct. By staying behind, we are officially separating from our government and will not be welcome back. I am the worst offender, since I am the commander."

"Welcome," Oz said, aware that Fleet Intelligence would

spend the next month looking into their motivations, going over their equipment, and trying to verify their loyalty. He wanted to give them a chance to prove it before Intelligence got involved. "Is there anything we need to know about this enemy? These Edxi don't seem like the ones we've faced before."

"The swarm that is about to attack the Haven System are specifically bred to be warriors, genetically modified to work together and to be more effective in combat. Cybernetic enhancements are added so they can communicate with their swarm and be even more effective. They are vastly different from the hatchlings you'd find on brood worlds, which are bred to grow into independent thinkers and become sentient after a long developmental, animalistic phase."

"So, something, or someone made this warrior type of Edxi we're seeing now?" Oz asked, his mind working to think through all the implications that what he was learning made. It didn't seem like much, but there were helpful bits of information there.

"Yes, but that's a longer story that doesn't apply to our current situation. Where do you want my ship to patrol? We're ready for combat. If you're wondering what kind of weapons we have, you can look to your own new class of beam weapons, gravitational shielding and intelligent plating. We are similarly armed, though your plating is several steps ahead of ours."

"Good to know," Oz said. "Take up a position on our flank. Where do you think the next swarm will emerge?" he checked the status of the Excalibur and the small battle group with it. They were performing a final clean-up of drone ships half way across the solar system. Three of its companion destroyers were damaged, but the casualties were minimal.

"We are detecting an energy surge in these coordinates. It just came up on our scanners," Captain Czona said. "We have to wait until they emerge before we engage. An explosion on the threshold between trans-dimensional and normal space is usually cataclysmic."

Oz looked at the location of the readings and nodded, looking to his Tactical Officer, who sent the instruction to hold fire across the Seventh Battlegroup. The site of their emergence was little more than two hundred thousand kilometres from Tamber. "Does this indicate a large group?"

"Yes," Captain Czona replied.

It only took one point four seconds for the attackers to emerge from dozens of dimensional gates clustered so closely together that it was impossible to predict their number. The rush of ships had armoured fore sections with girder like tendrils extending back. Each vessel had hundreds of signals within, they were all carriers with powerful broadcasting equipment built into armoured antennae running through the middle of their ships. He'd never seen a configuration like it. Many of the fighters it carried clung to the outer armour, their weapons pointing outward as glowing red eyes searched for enemies. The Triton's tactical computer was having difficulty calculating its threat level. "Launch all fighters, warn them to stay out of our active firing arcs. We're going to start this fight with nukes, inform the battlegroup and begin firing sequence Theta now." He marked the lead ships in the enemy fleet for the battlegroup to fire on, aware that his torpedo rooms were almost finished loading cloaked and shielded nuclear torpedoes. The instant the first was ready he looked to Rivas and nodded. "Begin firing."

One torpedo after another left the Triton, thirty-six torpedo tubes located across the hull opening, spitting their munition and closing after another, each would be reloaded with an accumulator torpedo, a weapon that was reserved for the direst situations that generated antimatter as it travelled to its target. As soon as the first torpedo volley finished firing from the Triton, the rest of the fleet - two carriers that were launching several fighters at a time using punter systems, and six destroyers who added to the swarm of humanoid piloted attack ships - began launching torpedoes in sequence. All together there would be over seventy nuclear torpedoes cloaked and on their way to the enemy.

They didn't have much time to strike the invaders with heavy munitions, they came out too close to Tamber, skipping past most of their fleet. Their defences were set up conventionally, Admiral Rice and the rest of the commanders in charge of the overall strategy opting to set up the fleet as if they were fighting an enemy that used wormholes or hyper-type travel. It wasn't a strategy everyone agreed to, but they had more experience, most of them veterans of Freeground Fleet, which defended their home station for long years.

As the first nuclear torpedo exploded at the head of the lengthening enemy column of ships, barely damaging its shields with a brilliant atomic bloom, he wondered how long it would take for the fleet to change their tactics, and if his old friend Jacob Valent would step out of line. As the next three torpedoes went off in succession, none of them breaking through the shields of the insect ship column only wearing them down imperceptibly, he shook his head. "Message to my entire Battle Group: get ready for close fighting. We're going to have to get in there with directed electromagnetic pulse beams, using our fighters as a defence screen to break up the enemy fleet. All those ships are contributing to one shield. The only way to break it is to separate the ships before it reaches the Tamber planetary barrier."

"The moon's perimeter guns are firing but having little effect, Sir. If we don't break them up soon, they're going to break through Tamber's shield. That's if they ram it in their current configuration," Tactical Officer Rivas reported. He was normally flat-toned, seemingly incapable of excitement, but there was a tinge of fear in his voice.

"That's what they'll do. They're not interested in taking control of our outer planets, they want to assume control of our heart and dig in," Oz said. The flashes of one nuclear blast following another and another breaking against the enemy's shields continued. The readouts from his Pure Sciences Department estimated that they had taken their shields down thirty percent. Individually, the enemy ships had just above average shielding. In their formation of twenty-eight in a solid column, they were nearly undefeatable. They were accelerating, and he knew they wouldn't have a chance to hit them harder, they'd be too close to Tamber's shield. "Helm, intercept the ship half way down the column at full military thrust. Prepare to activate the gravity ram."

There was no hesitation in Denidi, the new Mergillian pilot of the Triton. He had a family of nine on the surface of Tamber, their half-submerged home in Haven Shore was his pride and joy. There was no doubt that he'd sacrifice himself for his own little tribe. "Aye, Sir," was all he said in a low croak.

"Cease fire, activate all shield systems," Oz ordered, listening to the dampener systems aboard begin to roar. It was a system he knew Jacob Valent looked forward to testing, but Oz didn't relish using in the least. He didn't think it belonged on a ship as versatile and elegant as the Triton, but the math of the situation didn't lie. No weapon his battlegroup had would stop the column of Edxi Warrior Carriers from breaching the shield protecting Tamber. He watched the gravity ram system start coming online, pointing a repelling energy shield that extended out from the forward section of the ship like a sword made of light.

The rest of the Battlegroup were continuing their firing sequence, sending the last of their nuclear torpedo volleys at the enemy. A cloud of fighters along with a few fully manned Clever Class Corvettes moved like a menacing cloud, enjoying the protection of the fleet while they closed in. They were all behind the Triton, which was putting more and more distance between its allies by the second.

"God save us," Stut said under his breath from the Communications Station. "Flight reports that all our fighters are clear along with the Smasher," he said as he turned his attention to the main holodisplay.

The Smasher was the last thing Oz was able to fully crew; a Clever Class Corvette with the best incursion team he could put together. Most of them had experience in more than one type of tactics, space, air, and dirt.

He turned his attention to the holographic display at the front of the bridge as well, the ululating roar of the dampeners bracing the ship for the upcoming impact. He found himself starting to cringe and forced his back straight, gripped the arm rests and clamped his teeth. The ship's gravity shielding activated with an energetic flare, and the tip of the shaped barrier pierced through the middle of the enemy column's shield.

That was the crucial moment. If the tip glanced off it would have sent the Triton spinning, possibly colliding with the enemy's shield and the ships within where metal may clash in a maelstrom of battling energy barriers.

The first milliseconds of their impact - gravity shielding stabbing through energy barriers - was sound. They continued inward, the pointed end of their gravity shield ripping into the middle of the enemy column, sending insect fighters spiralling in every direction. The secondary shields around the Triton began to take severe damage as they pushed the ship into the column, colliding with twisting wreckage. "Gunnery deck! Fire! Fire! Fire!" he shouted as the Triton broke through completely, crossing under the enemy shields. He activated the armaments along his ship's underside, burning the enemy with their new Prometheus Five beams as they made contact with directed antimatter streams. Missile racks slipped out from under heavy metal covers and began unloading high explosive guided projectiles ten at a time.

The sound of a collision reverberated through the ship as one of the enemy capitol ships tried to break through their gravity field and energy shielding. They struck so hard that they momentarily made it through. Several gun emplacements were crushed and one section of the gunnery deck was open to space. They would keep firing despite the damage, most of these crewmen and women were trained by Shamus Frost and wouldn't abandon their posts if they were covered in burning plasma.

Another slam against the hull and a deep loss in power to their shields revealed that a second Edxi Warrior ship made an attempt to hammer at them. They were losing shield integrity quickly. "Get us out of here, Lieutenant," he ordered his helmsman.

The first attempt to continue moving through to the other side of the enemy's column shield yielded little progress. Lieutenant Denidi engaged their Xetima fuel, increasing their thrust by a factor of seven and managed to point the nose of their ship at open space. Their energy shield held as they passed through but three of the enemy ships collided with their aft section from above as they were about to break free, sending them spinning and slamming against the remaining enemy shields.

They were in open space, the last attempt to crush the Triton had failed. They had taken damage across the dorsal side of the ship and were open to space in several places with little power left for shielding, but they made it to the other side. "Did that Valent style tactic work? Did we break the column?" he asked as he checked the readings on the enemy himself.

"There are five enemy ships on course to collide with a small section of Tamber's shield, and their energy barrier is repelling cannon fire. We damaged three of the enemy ships that are not proceeding to the moon, and the rest are regrouping, launching fighters," Rivas reported.

Oz ran a simulation of five Edxi Warrior ships colliding against the Tamber planetary barrier with their combined shielding and saw that two would get through, the rest would be destroyed when they impacted the solid shielding. "That's better than their whole fleet hitting. Good luck, Anderson," he said, happy that Carl Anderson was back in charge of his Rangers and the surface defence effort on Tamber. Oz turned his attention to the broader tactical map, watching the rest of the Edxi ships arrange themselves in a circle so they could reinforce each other's shielding again. They were launching a cloud of fighters. The Seventh Battlegroup was taking positions around the Triton. "We'll reinforce your energy shields while you effect repairs and continue to command this effort, Triton," said Captain Allen Czona as the Mira Lane appeared three hundred metres below them. "I'm sorry we couldn't assist you during your ramming action, but we don't have that kind of gravity shielding aboard. I salute the bravery you and your crew exhibited."

"What kind of special weapons do you have aboard?" Oz asked, hoping that he was about to discover a trick Lorander had been hiding.

"We primarily depend on hyper-velocity short duration drone attacks," Captain Czona replied. Five drones smaller than one square metre fired in front of the Mira Lane and disappeared into wormholes. They reappeared along the edge of the enemy's energy barrier, each finding and blasting a fighter it found outside the shield, flinging chunks of the fighter as high-speed projectiles at other enemies before exhausting the last of its energy by firing antimatter beams at available targets. "We have one hundred ninety-five of those left, but they perform better when they're affixed to an enemy hull. That was anti-fighter mode. Other than that, we have three cutting arrays. You call them beam weapons."

"Welcome to the defence, get ready for the first wave," Oz said, watching as hundreds of enemy fighters turned and began accelerating towards them. He looked to Stut, his green and silver skinned Mergillian Communications officer. "Remind the Battlegroup that we're too close to Tamber for nuclear strikes or anything heavier."

He looked to the main display in time to see the five Edxi Warrior ships they couldn't stop collide with Tamber's shield. All but one of the ships, the last in the line, was reduced to a mass of twisted metal. The fifth made it through along with several fighters. No one wanted the invasion to touch Tamber, but there was no stopping that now. The Tamber shield regenerated and closed behind it.

"If it only takes five of their ships to break through the shield, then they can do that at least a couple more times if we don't stop them here," Stut said, worry creasing her normally smooth brow.

"That's why they won't make it any further," Oz said firmly.

"The gunnery deck reports that turrets twenty-seven and eight are restored," Rivas said.

"Fire at will," Commodore McPatrick ordered, checking on the rest of the fleet. Every ship was undermanned, but you couldn't tell from the number of flak rounds they put into space. A storm of metal was on its way to greet the enemy fighters.

TWENTY-FOUR

Returning Birds

EVERYONE aboard the Merciless paid close attention as the Defence Minister spoke. Ayan's speech didn't have the polish of the previous ones, where her image appeared on a stage, or in a room dressed in calming colours. She was in an armoured uniform, blue with a white stripe. The insignias of Defence Minister, Queen and Founder were above a jawless skull that had HAVEN FLEET written as its teeth were on one side of her chest. The other featured pips for the battles she'd been in, there were several, along the top of the Haven Flag, the silhouettes of Tamber against Kambis with a yellow sun behind it on a black field.

The transmission felt more live than ever against a blurred background of a command centre few had ever seen. There were people behind her, most likely working while she gave her short speech, but none of their faces or uniform insignias were clear. Her manner was serious, but Jake could see notes of sympathy in her expression, something that he hoped most of the people watching would notice too. He was happy the system wide address wasn't his to give. Citizens across the solar system were listening.

"Moments ago, over two dozen Edxi Warrior Ships made an attempt to breach Tamber's shield. These were landing craft, made to invade worlds just like ours. We were able to stop all but one, and the Haven Rangers are addressing that threat with our allies, the Nafalli Warriors. The shield has regenerated and Tamber is safe for the moment. I ask that you follow the instructions of your local leadership, who are already contacting you using the Crewcast Network. No sane leader looks forward to the day when they have to give a speech like this. We all know we gathered here after our people suffered a great wounding. All of us know loss, but we also had the ingenuity and steadfastness to find our way to common ground so we could rebuild and weather whatever storm the future brings together. I wish the fight was over, and we could concentrate on the work ahead, but we have to be strong again. With the help of our allies, our brothers and sisters, we will overcome whatever challenges they offer. First, the Edxi have been pointed in our direction, and the Seventh Battlegroup led by Commodore Terry Ozark McPatrick has disrupted their plans to overwhelm Tamber. Lorander has sent their support, joining us in a fight for the first time. We will defeat our enemies today and prove our right to sovereignty as a solar system, as a people going forward. If we must meet our enemies on the battlefield, then we will do so with horrifying violence and resolve so we can enjoy peace once again." At least part of what she was saying was being read until that point, Jake could tell that part of her stiff resolve was coming from the reassurance of something prepared, but then she seemed to look directly at him - an experience that anyone looking at her image would feel too - as she finished off script. "I am so proud to have you during this crisis. I am supported by some of the greatest military minds I've ever known, and we will defend you with every fibre of our being." Her image faded, and Jake wished he could be there to reassure and help her.

Ayan was at the same time in the safest place in the solar system, and in the most vulnerable. If the War Forge joined the battle, it would mean that one of their most important strategic points was at great risk. It would have to reveal its location to do so, and he was sure the enemy would make destroying Haven Fleet's only base ship their main priority. That was if the Order of Eden sent any ships of their own into the fight.

Jake watched the tactical display around his Captain's seat carefully. There were no signs of another group of Edxi Warrior ships in the system. The Triton was leading the Seventh Fleet in an effort to contain the first group in place and they were doing extremely well. It took thousands of flak rounds per minute, but the enemy fighters were forced to hide behind their carrier landers, and the heavy munitions launched by the entire battlegroup had them on the run. The Edxi Warrior capitol ships were on the verge of scattering, their shields were thinning, and the first few were taking direct hull damage from heavy non-nuclear conventional warheads. If Oz's Battlegroup kept pushing, the enemy fleet would come into line-of-sight with Freeground's main railgun batteries, and that would be the end of them. Even though the weaponry wasn't complete on the old station, the majority of its main guns were functional for the first time in many years, and Jake hoped that Frost would arrive in time to see them fire.

"It was a good speech," Agameg said from his right-hand side. He'd activated the seat there so they could be in whispering distance as he performed his duties as First Officer. "The Seventh Battlegroup is doing well."

"You're wondering why I still look like I expect a knife in the back?" Jake asked quietly.

Agameg nodded. "This is not how I remember you acting while you were expecting trouble."

Jake watched the Clever Dream take its place in the patrol pattern he set up. An automated Uriel fighter launched and started to make its way to it for Carnie. It was time for the pilot to get back to his real job.

The fleet surrounding the Merciless was alerted as the first Edxi Warrior ships arrived. Someone in command wanted all the Corvettes from SOCU and three destroyers - The Banta, Lupus and Gladius - along with Samurai Squadron patrolling the space around Carole. There was an asteroid belt, nine moons and many abandoned industrial bases to hide in there. It was a stretch to assume that the Merciless and that small number of ships could defend the position if it came under fire, but he knew that the other options weren't worth pursuing. He wished he was closer to Tamber, but Carole was an important strategic point, and the trust the Fleet placed in him by placing his Battlegroup there was significant.

The Merciless was cloaked, while the rest of the Third Battlegroup, his Battlegroup, was spread out around the planet and the asteroid field that trailed well behind it. "Liara, send this quick message to Captain Valent and the crew of the Clever Dream: Congratulations on a successful mission." He hesitated for a moment, then nodded. "End of message, please update their orders." Jake turned to Agameg. "I have a feeling about this. These Edxi Warriors made a direct strike on Tamber so fast that Oz almost didn't get in front of it. That took intelligence and strategic thinking. The way they did it took a kind of ruthlessness that I've never seen before. They were willing to sacrifice several capitol ships, thousands of their warriors to get through that shield. There's either a great mind behind this, or these Edxi are more intelligent than most of us were expecting."

"Perhaps the Tamber attack was a distraction?" Agameg asked in an equally low tone.

"I think it was a test," Jake said. "Maybe a distraction as well."

"Sir, the Raven has emerged into normal space," Kadri, the lead officer of his Sciences and Scanning Department reported. "They've taken heavy damage and would like to be cleared for an emergency landing."

"Send them to the Banta," Jake said, highlighting the destroyer closest to their emergence point. It was mostly crewed by Aucharian and Irish humans, all survivors led by Captain Lee Mahony. They had the hangar space, especially

since the few fighters they had were assisting Samurai
Squadron.

"The Raven has opened a channel," Liara reported.

"Put it up," Jake said.

Remmy was still in his heavy encounter armour, the
collar blocking his chin. There were several dents on the
shoulders of his suit. "Commodore. We managed to save eighteen humans from a satellite in orbit around Baila. It was
some kind of stasis warehouse where they stored humans and
other mammals. They were being kept as food, prepared so
they could supply brood ships as they travelled here. They
have millions of Edxi that are specifically bred to be Warriors.
They're like a cybernetic swarm, and one of the people we
rescued pointed out coordinates where lander ships were
rallying. We followed that up and saw that there were
hundreds of them entering dimensional transit rifts towards
the Haven System. I know our quad drives got us here faster,
but I don't know by how much. Our perimeter watch system
picked up something while we were in transit, so there are
definitely a number of them coming this way."

"What happened to your ship? Where did the damage
come from?"

"A swarm of fighters hit us. They didn't care about the
damage our shields did to them when they made contact, just
kept smashing into us until they created an opening. Then
they tried to cut through the hull. I'd rather fight a regiment of
Order Knights. We repelled the boarders and got a light
cybernetic fighter drone as a souvenir, but most of the Raven
is open to space. I have three crewmembers who just got back

on their feet, and eleven people left from the ones we rescued in stasis."

"There are people waiting for you aboard the Banta, they'll take care of you. Good work, Remmy," Jake said.

"Get me and my crew aboard the Scythe, and we'll join the defence. We want back into the fight," Remmy said.

"Normally I'd put you off duty for a couple days, but I'm sending the Scythe over so you can transfer from the Raven." Agameg started passing the order to Flight so they could launch their backup Clever Corvette. That left them with only one, and it belonged to Jake. "Good hunting."

"Thank you, Commodore, I'm uploading my report now." Remmy's smirk was almost a sneer as his image dissipated. He was more eager for a fight than Jake had ever seen him.

"Forward his report to Fleet as soon as its downloaded," Jake ordered as he looked to the scan data collected while the Raven was in transit. "Kadri, can you make sense of these globs and dashes? All I see are sensor shadows."

"Clearing it up, Sir," Kadri said. She coordinated her section of the bridge as officers under her command worked quickly. Minutes later a new version of the images appeared in the middle of the bridge.

At a glance, Jake could see fifteen groups of three Edxi Warrior attack ships, their heavy end propelling them through dimensional space with the antennae pointing forward. The navigation computer determined their destination. "Inform the fleet: Planet Carole is about to get hit," Jake made sure the Merciless' weapon and shield systems were ready. "All hands to battle stations, this is a Red Alert. Send orders across the Battle Group:

Regroup at the location of the Lupus." He highlighted the War Forge made, Nafalli manned destroyer on the tactical map. They were closest to the predicted enemy emergence point.

"The scan data shows four more large groups coming towards the Haven System," Kadri reported. "They're going to emerge near Kambis, Norren, Garo, and the Jensen Belt in the outer section of the system. From the scan we can guess there are over a hundred ten ships overall."

Garo, Kambis and Carole were all firmly in the goldilocks zone. Norren was on the inner edge, too hot for easy terraforming, but it had an atmosphere even humans could breathe and an ocean. It was almost barren of all but bacterial plant life and heavy gravity, but he could see why the Edxi would want it. The Jensen Belt was further out from the sun than any planet in the system, a perfect place to hide rein-forcements, and he knew Admiral Rice had foreseen that. The Sunspire would lead the Second Battlegroup, and he wished he could join them.

The challenge they faced near Planet Carole demanded all his attention, however. "Time to arrival?" he asked.

"Difficult to determine," Kadri replied immediately. "We're working on it, but from what we can see in the scan data, they're not taking the same kind of direct route we do through near-dimensional space. I can only determine their direction with any accuracy, their speed seems dependant on a lot of factors we don't understand yet. It's like they're riding currents in there using some sort of compass or something we haven't seen before."

"Best guess?" Jake asked. The Third Battlegroup was

moving into position with surprising efficiency, nearly half his ships had joined the Lupus.

"Twenty to thirty-five minutes," Kadri replied. "Fleet's working on it now too."

The system wide tactical map showed several battle-groups start to move, and Jake wondered if, like Oz's group of ships, he'd be reinforced. They were working on destroying the last two Warrior Ships, finally chasing them into the firing arc of Freeground Alpha, where they were blasted to pieces by its heavy gun batteries. "Everyone mind their stations and run through checklists. We may have to wait, but we do not have to wait idly," he ordered, his eye wandering to the Clever Dream, where the Uriel they launched was docking. They were flanking the Lupus, and Jake tried to shake the feeling of dread crawling up his spine.

TWENTY-FIVE

An Old Idea

TO NOAH'S SURPRISE, Theodore embraced him when he offered his hand. He enjoyed the emotional effort, even though it was a little awkward. "Best friend anyone could have," Noah whispered as he patted him on the back. "See you landside after we take care of our bug problem."

The pair separated, standing across from each other in the dimly lit hallway. "Don't do anything foolish," Theodore said, poking his armoured chest.

"Foolish? Never." He was slipping into a different way of thinking, of being, becoming a version of himself that only existed under certain circumstances. He was filled with the feeling that he was part of a pattern, the universe around his cockpit, instruments telling him everything he needed to know to fit into it. If he had to describe how it felt when everything was going right while he was flying, he would say that it was like being connected to everything and he could do anything. "This is the kind of thing I live for."

A hard click and the sound of pressure equalizing from above filled the dim hallway. "Just got the last latch in place. That mooring point hasn't been used before, looks like it wasn't aligned right," Faloo said as she climbed down from the hatch that led to his Uriel fighter. "Pressure is equalizing, you'll be able to get into that fighter in a few seconds."

Alice stepped into the hallway, her long coat flailing around the bottom as though she stopped running a moment before coming into sight. A little smile flashed before her composure returned and she approached with a casual gait that looked a little put on. Her red hair was pulled back into a short ponytail, and her dual blues locked with his. From a distance she was pretty, interesting, sometimes intimidating.

After having only a little time with her aboard her ship, he found that the image she projected on Crewcast were fairly true to how she was in person. There was something else though, and it was greater than the assumptions he was led to before meeting her. Alice was quieter than he expected, more pensive, and at times he caught a glimpse of a vulnerable side. He wanted to ask her what she was thinking when she seemed far away, and if she was all right when she had a moment when she looked weary. There was never time for that.

Most of the time she was a leader. Strong, knowledgeable, and her confidence was contagious as he watched her coordinate with her people. Two races of Nafalli, an android, a few humans and a Mergillian seemed right at home when she was around. Where did she learn that? He found himself asking that question more than once as he watched her manage her ship. His final thought on it, while he turned to the ladder that would take him to his fighter, was that it didn't matter. Maybe her parents gave her great examples to follow, maybe it came during her short stint in the Academy, or somewhere else entirely. It didn't matter because the confidence and her leadership style belonged to her completely.

A thought struck him about her Crewcast profile then. In those captures from training, from obstacle course failures and victories, moments with her crew that weren't too highly classified to see and the casual comments about her day, she sometimes seemed small. He even looked on in disbelief as she made incredible running leaps across obstacles on a course designed for people to cooperate on, carried the same amount of gear as people twice her size, and stood amongst crewmembers who were all taller than her - especially Iruuk, who seemed twice her height - and yes, she often seemed small.

That was not the story in person. That was the unintended deception that Crewcast made, that she was working so hard so she could keep up with the world around her. The woman he saw in the hallway in that moment didn't have that problem. In fact, he wondered how often her crew had to struggle to keep up with her. Alice was a hundred times the person he thought he saw in her Crewcast profile, and yet, she stood in the hallway, her blue eyes staring at him expectantly, and it looked like she was struggling to find something to say. It was probably because she thought her and her crew let him down on Iora when they weren't able to find anyone he knew to save. That was an unexpected injury to the heart, but he'd never blame them. It was amazing that they tried, so he told her, in as few words as possible, what he thought of it all while trusting that cocksure, centre of the universe feeling to give him the words. "This ship is incredible. Your crew is..." he shook his head and smiled. "I'm just glad I got to meet them now, just as they're starting to realize that they're becoming an amazing family."

"Thank you," Faloo said sweetly, giving him a quick embrace then retreating. "I have to get to my turret, but good luck out there."

"You too," he said, sparing the motherly, shaggy Nafalli a smile before returning his full attention to Alice. "I'm glad I finally met you." He watched the corners of her mouth start shifting into a smile, but something was holding it down. The moment was getting heavy with that private, personal feeling, and he knew the time was wrong. In a moment he'd be in the pilot's seat, all his concentration would be there. On the other hand, he'd gotten into his cockpit, flown missions, and come back to a changed world before. Who knew what could change this time, or how he might be different after the upcoming battle. With that in mind, he said something that he would normally save for a quiet doorstep at the end of a good night. "There's no one out there like you, not anywhere. I'd stick around, but, you know..." he glanced at the hatch above before seeing her surprised smile. That was the thing he needed to see; Alice smiling at him.

"You have to go," she agreed quietly. "Just..." Alice glanced at Theodore, who was watching with interest, as silent and still as a statue. "Good hunting."

. . .

"GOOD HUNTING," he replied with a smirk that seemed almost too confident, like he was telling her; 'I got this,' and she wanted to say something else, to tell him to focus, to be careful, but 'good hunting' would do. He wasn't as witty as he thought he was, but his compliments left her wishing she had something better to say. Something that could convey how happy she was to meet the real Noah Lucas, and that she felt like there was a lot more to know now that the infatuation she'd grown while listening and watching his file was fading fast. A thought occurred to her then. It was too soon, but there was one way she could tell him what she wanted to say most, something that could tell him one of the most important parts of her story. A white scarf, simple, with no devices or tricks inside would tell him; 'come back in one piece.'

"Wait," Alice said, rapidly selecting the simple scarf design on her left command and control gauntlet then printing it against the bulkhead, the material spraying as it solidified there. Alice was filled with an urgent excitement as she picked it up and stepped half way up the ladder so she could put it around his neck. Noah watched her wrap the smooth fabric around him and tuck it into his jacket so it wouldn't get in the way. He looked surprised, amused, and it made her feel bold. "Just to remind you that you're always welcome," she kissed him on the cheek and whispered; "Go get 'em, flyboy."

"Thank you," he told her as she stepped back down. He winced a little then shook his head. "Ronin's in my ear. I can't be late for this party."

Theodore waved at him meekly as they watched him squeeze into the narrow passage that took him up into his fighter. The hatch closed behind him and the sound of the fighter decoupling a moment later was their cue to return to the bridge. "That meant more than; 'you're always welcome,'" he said.

"I wanted that goodbye to be memorable," she nodded, looking at the status of the defence. They were still on patrol, waiting for their enemies to emerge from a near dimension.

"Reviewing the documentary made about Ayan and Jonas, it inferred that she loved him. It was part of a dress she wore during an important part of their romance. The tradition grew for a short time on Freeground, before the Puritan Party began to gain in popularity," Theodore explained. "His Wing Commander will know what the gift implies, you might have to explain..."

"I don't know what it means yet," Alice said. "I think it's lucky for me. Jacob wore one while he was looking for me. While I was making my way back to him. He wondered why he couldn't let it go even though he didn't know who gave it to him. All he knew was that it was in the bag I left for him when I freed him on the Samson, and while he wore it, we found each other. Maybe that's what it means right now; 'come back to me.'"

"Perhaps you can say it means you enjoyed getting to know him, even for a short while," Theodore suggested. "For now, at least."

Alice remembered his surprised, pleased expression once it was on him and blushed. It was like a delayed reaction, what it meant, she couldn't say, but it felt good. "What do you think he'll say about it?"

"Nothing," Theodore replied with a smile. "Noah doesn't normally explain himself at length to his fellow pilots. That's something he says he reserves for his mentor, Minh-Chu Buu, and seemed to start doing around you. I think it'll be like Mister Alberton told me when I asked why he'd want me to wear a tuxedo if I was to become the host and usher of his club. It will add to his mystique, his legend. The less he says about it, the more interesting people will think it is."

"Not too interesting, I hope," Alice chuckled.

"What do you mean, not too..." Theodore's eyes widened then. "Oh, I'm sure he'll correct anyone who suggests anything improper. You can expect that, and that your token will have the intended result. He'll be back. Noah is a curious young man and a romantic. I'd say you've piqued both interests, but then, I'm only speaking from the observations of a few thousand psychologists, so I can't be absolutely certain."

"Only ninety-nine-point-something percent, right?" Alice asked as the hatch leading to the small bridge opened.

Jessen looked up at her from the communications panel and cocked her head. "Your Flyboy make it back to his flock all right?"

"You heard that?" Alice asked, rolling her eyes.

"I tried to stop them," Iruuk said from the sciences and scanning seat.

"Couldn't resist. We finished all the checklists twice and there was nothing else going on," Jessen said.

"I love human courtship," Ute said from the pilot's station. "It's wonderfully complicated and social. My people know whether or not someone's a good match before we even see each other. It's all pheromones, not that I'm complaining."

Yawen slipped out of the co-pilot's seat and Alice took her place. "Lewis put it up on a couple screens. He's been extra interested in the crew since we corrected those behaviour limiter modifications fleet added to his code."

Alice shook her head, less embarrassed than she pretended to be. "Well, it's a small ship anyway."

"Is our Captain in love?" Jessen teased.

"Let's say I'm 'in like,' and concentrate on watching and waiting," Alice replied, waving her finger around at the bridge in general.

"Yes, Ma'am," Jessen said, letting Theodore take her place.

"The next wave of Edxi ships is emerging at point Delta," Iruuk announced. "The Sunspire and her Battlegroup are engaging. I'm detecting an emergence point about half a million klicks away from Planet Carole. Scans show eleven ships will be in normal space in three seconds. Merciless Flight is ordering all ships to hold fire until they are out."

"Too bad we can't catch them as they're coming through," Jessen said from the rear of the small bridge.

"There is a high likelihood that an explosion at the event horizon could set off a reaction that will begin an open exchange of highly energetic particles between the dimension beyond the opening and this galaxy that could result in a cataclysmic event," Theodore said. "Or it would do nothing interesting at all."

"Or it could cause the emergence of a white hole," Iruuk added. "Very bad for the solar system."

"I was just saying it was too bad," Jessen shrugged.

Alice watched as the Edxi ships emerged into normal space, and Ute followed a new course sent to them by the Merciless Flight Deck. It would take them closer, where their Battlegroup was drawing a line between the invaders and the surface of Carole. "Here we go."

TWENTY-SIX

Turning Tactics

"I'M SORRY, but I must ask," Ensign Ottun whispered to Agameg as he finished clearing the wrappers from the tray on his command seat, making sure they all went down into the recycler box properly. "Everything I have learned about you and the Commodore suggests that you are the core of a well-respected and talented command team. Why are we guarding Carole when there is fighting elsewhere?"

"You've asked this question before," Agameg said to his fellow Issyrian with measured patience. Jake enjoyed watching the pair together, especially since his old friend had a firm hand with the Ensign. "I understand your confusion. The fleet is stretched thin, and the Admiralty knows that the command crew on this ship are used to battling over-whelming forces. Planet Carole is a strategic point close to

Kambis and Tamber and is partially terraformed. The oxygenated atmosphere alone makes it a good location for a base, but we don't have assets there. So, it is better that a small, experienced force with a substantially powerful ship like the Merciless guard it when the enemy comes to dig in. Once the Edxi ships reach the ground, they will be much harder to defeat, at least, that's what was recently predicted. We must stop them from gaining a foothold. Meanwhile, more sensitive targets are being guarded by larger groups of ships under the command of Admirals and other officers who have much more experience with large groups of ships."

"I understand, thank you, Commander," Ensign Ottun said with a respectful nod as he pushed the service tray down into the bottom of the bridge seat. He retreated silently, accepting a meal bar wrapper from Looph on his way off the bridge.

Jake turned his full attention back to the holographic tactical display that surrounded him. The Edxi Warrior ships that they expected to arrive near Carole were finally about to emerge.

"Flight confirms: twenty-three Edxi Warrior ships are emerging into normal space. Several were linked together to hide their numbers during transit. They are approximately four hundred fifty thousand kilometres away from Carole's atmosphere," Kadri reported from the Science Section of the bridge.

"All ships in my Battlegroup: Hold fire, load antimatter torpedoes. Prepare to engage using the most recent firing sequence uploaded to you from flight," Jake said. Seeing the long, thickly hulled landing craft emerge into normal space put his teeth on edge. He knew many shades of anger, but something primal, territorial threatened to rise as he watched them. The ambient light shining through Carole's atmosphere painted everything in hues of blue. The folded arms along the sides of the Edxi Warrior ships glinted as though they were as new as the Merciless, and he imagined them unfolding, digging into the soil of the planet behind him and his small battlegroup so a host of insects could spread out, take the land that no one in Haven Fleet had time to explore. "They're not going to make landfall."

The Merciless was still cloaked, along with the Clever Dream and the rest of the corvettes. To anyone looking it would seem that three Haven Fleet destroyers, the Banta, the Lupus, and the Gladius had formed a line with only thirty-five fighters between the invaders and Planet Carole. Their crews were busy verifying that Mark Nine Hammerhead torpedoes were loaded in their tubes. It was a kind of munition that the galaxy had never seen. They had cloaking, guidance, and antimatter production systems aboard along with a short-range wormhole system that made them deadly. "Twenty-one of twenty-one tubes loaded and ready, Commodore," Lieutenant Commander Huun announced from tactical. "Our punter systems are loaded with missile drones. Eighteen ready."

"Keep those systems closed until the last minute. I don't know if they scan for radiation, but I don't want to give them any warning that our drones are coming," Jake said, watching as the dimensional rift closed behind the last Edxi Warrior ship. "Prepare to fire in sequence with our destroyers."

To his surprise, the Edxi Warrior ships started launching

fighters immediately. It was an instant swarm, the lander ships shedding a hundred, then two, and three hundred fighters like fleas from their hulls. "Ronin, keep your fighters back."

"You don't have to tell me twice, Commodore," Minh-Chu said. "You take out as many as you can with your fancy warheads. We're just the maids."

"Maids?" Agameg asked as he listened to reports from the Flight Deck.

"They'll do the clean-up," Jake replied.

"Oh," he replied with a nod.

At a glance he could see that the fighters were holding position behind the Merciless. To anyone not on their network, it would look like there was nothing between them and the enemy. "Can you pick up any enemy transmissions, Liara?"

"I'm sorry, Sir, that's why I haven't updated you yet. There's nothing. Like the last attack, we can't find any evidence that they're communicating. I even have one of my people trying to interpret micro-movements between the ships but he can't find any evidence of signalling."

The first antimatter torpedo, fired by the Banta, exploded next to the line of enemy capitol ships bearing down on them. The flash of white eliminated over a hundred fighters and weakened the enemy column's shields. As the sensors were still adjusting, the second went off at the head of the column. As the white fire of annihilation abated, Jake could see the enemy capitol ships trying to break away from each other as quickly as they could, most of them turning away from Planet Carole.

The two ships in the lead suffered a direct antimatter torpedo strike. When the light subsided, the first one was gone and the second was open to space. Its thick antenna was gone, and Jake spotted an engine flare that made that ship's intention clear. "That ship is accelerating towards us, it's trying for a ramming run on the Banta. Tell them to prepare to get clear."

The Lupus's torpedoes started to go off then, and globes of light flashed around the middle of the enemy ships, one after another in quick succession. "Launching our torpedoes," Huun announced.

"We have a problem," Kadri said. "The enemy has captured one of the Gladius' Hammerheads. It was too close to an antimatter explosion and one of their heavy fighters must have seen the torpedoes shadow in the energy blast." The image of the heavy fighter trying to break through the torpedo's hull appeared on the main display as the munitions' cloaking system failed. "It's taking it away from the rest of the ships, away from Carole."

"Activate remote detonation, now," Jake ordered.

"Signal sent," Liara replied. "Gladius Actual confirms that they sent the detonation code as well."

A dimensional rift opened in front of the heavy fighter. "Cancel the detonation!" Agameg shouted. No one knew exactly what would happen if an antimatter weapon was to go off in another dimension, and the entire fleet was doing their best to keep from finding out the hard way.

"Detonation code failed. It looks like the enemy disabled the communications system on the torpedo," Liara reported as the heavy fighter disappeared into the rift and the opening closed behind it.

"That was quick. Do we know where it's going?" Jake asked.

"I can see it was a short transit tunnel," Kadri said. "I predict it'll come up near Freeground Alpha Station."

"Notify the Second Battlegroup. There is a rogue anti-matter warhead on the way, in the enemy's control," Jake said.

Three more antimatter explosions filled the space around the enemy Edxi ships. Their number was already down to nine. Several types of ships scrambled to escape the anti-matter ravaged hulks of the ruined vessels that were adrift far from their target.

"We have another stolen warhead, it's one of ours," Kadri announced.

Jake spotted it on his tactical map, it was far enough away from his Battlegroup so it wouldn't flash back and do damage. He entered the detonation signal and watched as it exploded in a white globe. They had fired seven torpedoes. "Huun, cease fire. It looks like we're going to have to finish this fight another way."

"We are no longer firing torpedoes. Nine of their ships are still in fighting shape, the rest are either gone or finished. No power, very little life," Huun replied.

"Target the nearest ship and open fire with all cannons. Hold beam weapons and missile bays until we're in range and launch turret drones."

"Aye, Commodore," Huun replied.

. . .

"WE FOUND THE MERCILESS' lost torpedo, Admiral," the dark haired tactical officer of the Sunspire, Nozen Fenk announced to Admiral Rice.

"That was fast," she replied as she saw it highlighted behind the Terran Traveller, one of the few Aucharian ships that had been upgraded by the War Forge. "Make sure they spotted it." It was alarming that the thick hulled ship's close countermeasures hadn't fired after several seconds. The reactions of that crew were slow, but it was getting ridiculous. The heavy fighter carrying the torpedo and the antimatter within moved into a thicker part of the asteroid field, obscuring any shot the Terran Traveller might have. They were on their way to a group of three Freeground destroyers that were short on fighter cover, and none of them had a clear shot.

"We have emergency detonation codes and abort codes from the Merciless," the communications officer announced, a thick-bodied Mergillian who was uncharacteristically bad at flying a ship, but good at hacking into computer systems.

"Use them both," Admiral Jessica Rice said, watching as the Sunspire fired a final volley from its port side guns at the nearest Edxi Warrior ship. Its lights went dark, the stringy hull came apart as its core ruptured and blasted the ship from within. Her attention turned back to the Merciless' Hammerhead torpedo, and she wasn't surprised to see that it was still there. The heavy fighter carrying it was about to make a run for the asteroids behind her three destroyers. She keyed in emergency orders to them with instructions to get out of the asteroid cover, it was about to turn against them.

"The codes did not work," her communications officer announced.

"Can any gun get a clear shot on that damned fighter?" Admiral Rice asked, looking at the Sunspire's firing arcs. They were too far from the asteroid field to get a good shot. Several of their starboard guns fired anyway, her gunnery chiefs were listening in to her every word on the bridge.

"Sensors show the, er, fighter's limbs are trying to puncture the antimatter containment chamber," her Sensor Officer announced. She was young, brilliant at her job, but fresh from Freeground Fleet Academy, one of the last graduates that institution would ever produce.

The antimatter torpedo detonated, annihilating tons of asteroid material around it, but stirring a small section of the belt. The bug knew what it had, and how to use it to trap at least three ships, perhaps as many as five. She watched the three destroyers on her screen begin evasive manoeuvres, trying to avoid the mess of drifting stone before it collided with them. At best those ships were out of the fight for a minute or two, at worst their shields would be heavily taxed and they'd take some hull damage, perhaps getting forced to come through the churning section of the asteroid belt far away from the fight.

There were thousands of fighters coming from the Edxi Warrior ships, her gunners didn't have a seconds' down time between major targets, and her fighter squadron was fighting for their lives. If they weren't careful, the enemy would accomplish their goal in the belt, a goal that was becoming clearer by the minute. "Message to Command: I can now verify that the Edxi Fleet's objective is to find optimum points in the solar system to dig in and turn this into a long-term siege. Two thirds of their fighters are not engaging. They are heading into the asteroid belt so they can evade our sensors and hide. Several of the carriers we've seen are trying to get away from us. I predict they will dig in the moment they think we can't see them. End message."

"Sending," the communications station said.

"All right," Admiral Rice said, still thinking, looking at the tactical hologram filling her view. "Let's concentrate on herding these bastards." She highlighted the eight destroyers and six dreadnaughts - all the same as the Sunspire under the new classification thanks to their firepower and size - then directed them to cut off the nearest Edxi Warrior ships.

"Will that tactic not leave five of their carriers free to escape?" Captain Nellen, her First Officer, asked. He was another young graduate, assigned to her side for some seasoning since he didn't pass the qualifying tests for his own ship.

"We'll track them as best as we can. For now, we have to take the ones that are in reach down, otherwise they'll scatter and we'll have even more trouble." She cringed as The Lancer failed to move away from one of the Edxi Warrior ships in time to avoid its ramming manoeuvre. The insect carrier accelerated at the kilometre-long ship until the last minute, then flipped, pointing its main thruster at their enemy's hull. Massive arms came down from around the ship as the pair made contact, the last of the Lancer's shields failing, and as the two collided, its hull was in the grasping metal arms of the Edxi ship. Jessica had seen a few Edxi Warrior carriers attempt the manoeuvre, but that was the first one to make it work. "All ships fire on my target. We have to stop it from breaking through the Lancer's hull."

The reaction of her battlegroup seemed frantic, sending thousands of rounds at the Lancer's assailant. It was like watching a giant meet its match, the massive dreadnaught firing its own guns at the legs of the beastly ship that threatened to eat through its skin. Blue flames started firing against the hull of the Lancer as it used its main engine to burn through the hull.

"They'll break through in a little under five minutes," her Science Officer announced. He was an older officer, one of hers. Devin Lokan was rarely wrong, and he knew every nut and bolt aboard the Sunspire type dreadnaught.

"Thank you, Commander Lokan," Admiral Rice said, watching as several conventional torpedoes converged on the middle of the Edxi Warrior ship. Its grasp didn't loosen, but the lights went out, its hull was ripped open, and the fire of its main thruster sputtered then died. Another wave of torpedoes was on the way, that would finish the ship off.

"Thanks for saving our asses, Admiral," the commander of the Lancer, Captain Megan Evans said. "We'll get it separated from our ship. Might be out of the fight for a while though. My science officer got a good scan of the inside of it, we're forwarding the data to fleet."

They had scans of the Edxi ship interiors, but none of them were taken while they were operational, but the new data was highly detailed. There were half a dozen different types of insects working inside the ships that they'd never been able to scrutinize so well. "Good work, now make sure you don't get boarded. There are still a few hundred bugs inside that carrier riding on your back."

"Aye, we're working on it, Admiral."

There was a domino effect that started with the arrival of the Merciless' captured torpedo. Time would tell if seeing one heavy fighter demonstrating good tactical thinking would be useful to them, but for the moment, the five ships it threatened were almost out of danger. Even still, it would take them long minutes to get back into position with the rest of her battlegroup, a delay that could cost them, but she'd compensated as best as she could. She keyed a quick low priority message to Commodore Valent aboard the Merciless; NEXT TIME SEND FLOWERS, then returned her full attention to her tactical display.

TWENTY-SEVEN

Tipping Point

THE TACTICAL OFFICER for the Triton, Lieutenant Commander Marc Rivas jerked in surprise so abruptly that Commodore McPatrick noticed immediately, even through the dense holographic display around him. "Commodore, a dimensional rift just opened like a volcano. An Edxi Brood Ship and nineteen Warrior ships just came through behind Freeground Station."

"Just when we thought we were starting to get this mess under control," Oz said, watching his tactical screen populate. Freeground station was already starting to fire its heavy guns, but from the first impacts on the Brood Ship, he could see the nearly three-kilometre-wide vessel would survive long enough to at least damage Freeground. Deep in thought about the adjustments he needed to make to his strategy, he watched the old railgun emplacements aboard Freeground Station turn and fire at the Edxi ships that appeared within firing range. He put the thought that their scientists didn't think that dimensional rifts could be opened so close to a moon or planet's gravity aside. That was obviously wrong.

"Tactical, fire the rest of our drone ships," Oz said calmly. "I want them to assist our fighters. Assign three to every pilot we have left." The drone ships were a late addition to their arsenal. Using them was a risk, they could be hacked, but other than stealing a torpedo, the Edxi didn't show any talent or interest in hacking. The drones aboard the Triton were armed with a pair of triple barrel turrets, perfect for covering live pilots and evening the odds, he wished he could find a way to use them all the time.

The new Edxi ships launched so many fighters so quickly that it looked like they were surrounded by a cloud. The computer counted six hundred thirty new light and heavy Edxi fighters and Oz shook his head. "That's it, we need to even this up. Helm; send us right into that swarm. Engineering; push as much power as you can to our shields and Tactical, tell our gunners to fight for our lives. I'm ordering the entire battlegroup to outflank the enemy. If we don't stop them from taking Freeground out, they'll have a lot more opportunities to take shots at Tamber's shield and land ships." He marked his orders for the five destroyers and the pair of carriers he had left for Tamber defence on his Tactical map.

"Massive energy build ups on Warrior ships twelve through fourteen," the Sciences officer, Lieutenant Commander Joshua Mape, announced.

A wave of nearly two hundred fighters was turning

towards the Triton, firing missiles and needle guns as they accelerated, the three ships that launched them, Warrior ships that had emptied their launch bays, were accelerating hard. Oz watched as one attached itself to Commander Lokan's ship. "Get our gravitational shielding charged up," Oz said looking at the state of it, only thirty eight percent powered. The hard energy shielding beneath was almost fully charged, but it could only sustain so much kinetic damage, it wasn't made for multiple collisions. "Helm, evasive action."

"The rest of the Warrior ships are accelerating towards our companion destroyers and carriers," Tactical Officer Rivas said.

"They're ignoring Freeground," Oz said, watching as the looming Brood Ship and hundreds of fighters moved even closer to the Station. They didn't need help wearing the old station's defences down. They would last minutes, only minutes.

Oz watched the gravitational shielding of the Triton rise, then begin to drop rapidly as a wave of dozens of light Edxi fighters collided with it at high speed, firing until the last second. The Mira Lane moved into position beneath the Triton, its Lorander beam weapons sweeping through the Edxi fighter screen as heavier energy cannons fired at the nearest oncoming Edxi Warrior carrier. The Triton's defensive beam weapons were at work trying to fend off the wave of attackers. The Gunnery Deck sent a frantic hail of rounds at the enemy fighters. The smaller ships broke up, slowed down, but many of them still collided with the Triton's Gravitational shielding, spinning off it at first as they were redirected by the negative force. As the integrity of the shielding was worn down, enemy fighters - both whole and in pieces - began to break through to strike their hard shielding.

It was no surprise to Oz that the fighters were able to adjust their courses enough so they could hit the Triton whether they were whole or in pieces, but he was nearly dismayed when he watched the large Warrior ships easily adjust course. The nearest exploded thanks to the assistance of the Mira Lane, and most of the wreckage passed close to the gunnery deck. The glancing blows suffered from the remaining pieces were enough to take their shields down nine percent. "Switch inertial dampeners to ramming mode," Oz said as he watched the pair of Warrior ships turn end over end and begin unfolding their giant grappling arms. "Now, Rivas!"

The bridge was filled with the sound of the humming inertial dampener system as the whole ship braced for the impact. Oz realized he was bracing himself, gripping the arms of his seat and shook his head. It wouldn't matter. If the dampeners failed when the enemy collided with them, even safety harnesses wouldn't be effective. The first Edxi Warrior ship struck hard, its appendages attempting to wrap around the port side of the forward section of the ship. It struggled to grip the hull through the failing energy shields. "Engineering, we need a surge of energy on the grav shield in section seventeen, now," Lieutenant Commander Rivas said from his tactical station.

"Aye," replied someone unfamiliar from engineering. "Pulsing now!"

It was something Oz didn't plan for, to be grappled onto by another ship, but Rivas already had ideas. The gravitational shielding under the main thruster of the Edxi Warrior ship was flooded with a sudden rush of energy and was wrenched free of two of its heavy latching arms. "We burned that section of the gravity shielding out with that stunt, Sir, I'm sorry."

"Don't worry, just hang on," Oz said, watching as the second Edxi Warrior ship collided with their starboard side. The first had to struggle with energy shields that were mostly charged, but this one managed to get two of its arms through the shielding, gripping the hull directly. The third arm clashed with the shielding hard, crushing one of its own heavy fighters by mistake in the process. "Alert security, we might have boarders in a few minutes."

The Mira Lane interjected, colliding with the middle of the Edxi Warrior Ship and glancing off smoothly, opening the hull to space. Its energy cannons fired at the exposed reactor, leaving the enemy vessel powerless. Its arms were still affixed to the Triton, but the ship was dead, and the likelihood of anything surviving inside was low. "Thank you, Mira Lane," Oz said, activating a channel his communications officer set up.

"You're welcome, but we'll have to recharge our shield systems before we can do it a..." the response was cut off as a focused beam of energy cut through the space between the Brood Ship and the Mira Lane. It followed the Lorander vessel as it turned in an attempt to evade the attack, then was cut open across its starboard side. A rush of fighters turned towards the ship and started accelerating.

"Helm, get us between the Mira Lane and those fighters!" Oz ordered.

Denidi's Mergillian hands worked at the controls, his neural interface assisting in the effort to move the Triton into position despite the damage and being put off balance by the Warrior ship still attached to their starboard side. A string of enemy fighters collided and exploded against the fissure in the Mira Lane's hull, opening it wide enough for several fighters to rush inside at speed and detonate within the ship. The lights went out, and the Mira Lane drifted askew. "This is Nerum Kast aboard the Mira Lane. Move your ship as far away from us as you can. I'm activating the self-destruct system."

"You heard him," Oz said, disappointed but not surprised that they failed to block the manoeuvrable fighters charging at the Lorander ship. All of his Battlegroup's ships had already been struck once or were being struck by a Warrior ship. The Watcher, a carrier with capabilities similar to the Triton, had been struck by two at once. The second was powering its main thruster to burn through the carrier's hull. "Fire all missile turrets and beam weapons at that Warrior ship. We can't allow any of them to burn through a hull and board."

"There is little chance that our missiles will reach their targets. These fighters are intercepting everything with a rocket on it," Rivas countered.

"Then our missiles will hit fighters instead!" Oz retorted, letting his frustration get the better of him for a moment before calming down.

"Yes, Sir. Firing all racks, sorry, Sir." Rivas replied.

Two destroyers; the Monitor and the Eagle managed to shake their first attempted boarders off and joined in on the barrage. Fighters swept by, firing at missiles and getting cut to pieces by beam weapons that were trying to blast the Warrior ship grappled to the Watcher.

"I located the battery bank that the Brood Ship is using to charge their main particle beam," reported Science Officer Mape. "I estimate that it's at about three percent charge. I don't know how high that has to get before it fires."

Oz keyed in the code that signalled an emergency to the rest of the fleet. He wouldn't tell his crew, he suspected he didn't have to, but they were losing. There were still over a thousand fighters and the Brood Ship was still untouched, its shields holding. "Keep an eye on it, report every ten percent gain," Oz said.

"We know your Battlegroup is in distress, Commodore," Oz heard Ayan say in his ear. "The British Battlegroups are on the way. Hang on, Oz."

TWENTY-EIGHT

Listening

"WHAT'S THIS?" Iruuk asked himself as he looked at strange, faint energy readings on the Scanning and Sciences station aboard the Clever Dream. The ship's gunners were firing constantly, working with everyone in Samurai Squadron. He opened a secure channel to the Wing Commander, momentarily forgetting that he should have gone through Alice, who was busy commanding Clever Dream from the co-pilot's seat. He closed the channel, hoping no one noticed.

A few seconds later, Ronin was contacting him directly. "Can I help you?"

Iruuk glanced at Ronin's position on the tactical display and sighed in relief as he saw that he and the rest of the fighters were still thousands of kilometres away from the main swarm of fighters taking out anything that tried to break out and escape into the solar system. "I'm sorry, I'm Iruuk, Science and Scanning Officer aboard..."

"The Clever Dream, I know, what's up?" Ronin didn't seem impatient, he spoke quickly in a friendly tone.

Alice looked over her shoulder at Iruuk as he continued. "Members of your wing sent sensor results that look like a low powered data stream. Not like any I've seen, but I can't understand how it could be anything else. They disappear as soon as dimensional rifts close but appear every time while they're open."

"Sorry, Iruuk, what's the question?" Ronin asked so rapidly that the sentence seemed to be one word.

"Have you seen this before? Do you concur with my assumption? Why not send it to the Merciless?" Iruuk asked quickly.

"No, yes, and we did but their people are busy scanning for new breaches. Sent it to the War Forge too, but they won't receive it for another couple minutes. Can you look at that for us?"

The War Forge actually wouldn't receive the transmission for another four minutes and nine seconds, but Iruuk decided it wasn't the time to correct him. "I'll do that, thank you. Sorry for interrupting you."

"No worries, good hunting, or good science-ing!" Ronin replied, closing the channel.

"Do you think that's how the swarm is communicating?" Alice asked, half out of her seat and turned around.

"I am taking control of the Navigation station," Lewis said, noting that Alice was distracted.

"I don't know how it could be anything but communications. It's a weak energy pattern that has peaks and valleys like an audio signal." He sent the playback to his ears only and winced. It was like listening to insects burrowing into his head. "It doesn't sound like mammals, that's for sure."

"What do you need to listen in?" Alice asked, getting out of her seat and joining him at his station. There was barely enough room, she had to look under one of his arms to see some of the displays.

Iruuk thought for a moment, looking at the short data stream, the frequency it was captured from, and played with it for a moment, moving the layers of sound around with his finger. His eyes widened as he realized that one of the layers was only background noise. The onslaught of clicks, scrapes and hissing noises became perfectly clear, and he narrowed the frequency down to a much smaller range. "If we could open a microscopic hole that moved with the ship to this dimension, the one they travel through, and listened to this frequency range, we could hear what they're saying. We could eavesdrop."

"So you need the programmed dimension drive module," Alice said. "That could put a target on our backs."

"Wait," Ute said from the pilot's station. Her high-pitched voice was still perfectly clear over the hum and rattle of the Clever Dream's turrets. "Can we understand anything they're saying?"

"Running that noise through translator programs," Jessen said from the communications station. "Nothing. It's an Edxi related language, but I think that's just because the bugs are using it."

"Then we jam that frequency," Alice said. "If that's how the swarm is communicating, then we see what they can do when we block it. I bet they won't be able to keep swarming and the fighters will be able to do some real damage."

Iruuk looked at the scan of the Merciless. It had drawn most of the swarm around Carole to itself by doing incredible damage to over a dozen of their landers. Their shields were down to twenty-eight percent and they'd already lost one of their main gun emplacements. "I like this plan, but I am going to guess it won't take long for the enemy to figure out who is jamming them."

"I'm forwarding the plan to the Merciless," Alice said. "Ute, get ready to make a run for them, the Commodore will probably want to protect us."

"Aye, ready," Ute replied, gripping the controls. The swarm was between them and the Merciless, hundreds of insectoid fighters firing at the Merciless in an effort to cause another breach in its shields.

CAPTAIN LEE MAHONY was as steadfast a commander as Commodore Jacob Valent had ever seen. A surviving Aucharian who followed the directions of Haven Fleet with no questions, and showed trust at every turn, appeared as a hologram in front of Jake's command seat. "We're being targeted, Captain, it's a concentrated strike," he said from his bridge on the Banta. "I'm learning to read the swarm, its movements, and its coming for us, getting ready to break the ship. I'm moving out of position so our self-destruct can take them out."

"Stay in position, Lee," Jake said, watching the swarm of over two hundred forty fighters come together. The Merciless' guns blasted them with explosive rounds, taking out two and three of the small enemy ships every time a shot struck, but more were massing, more were firing on the Banta, its shields already almost down, a part of its dorsal hull open to space thanks to the second ramming run made on it by an Edxi Warrior ship. Samurai Wing were doing what they could, every available gun was firing at the threatening swarm from a safe distance, as they were ordered to do, and the corvettes were doing the same. The Lupus was turning slowly, in place, giving every turret on its port and starboard sides a chance to get a shot on that swarm.

"Fire all torpedo bays on my target, set for detonation at the destination," Jake said quickly, aware that only conventional warheads were loaded. There would be peripheral damage to his ship, to the Banta and the Lupus but it would be minimal compared to what a full swarm of hundreds of Edxi fighters could do.

The torpedoes launched at incredible speed, crossed the short distance between the Merciless and the swarm. An instant before the munitions could explode, the swarm moved as one. It was enough to save most of them, but dozens were destroyed just the same. "Our shields are down to eighteen percent, but we are recharging slowly," Huun said.

The Edxi swarm rushed the Banta. "I hope this isn't farewell, Commodore. It has been an honour," Captain Mahony said. He turned to his bridge staff. "Drain the ships' systems of power, send all energy to the shields. Ready counter-incursion teams and send everyone not in a turret or at an essential station to the armoury."

"Sir, we should get to escape pods, it's regulation," said a voice from his side.

"With those fighters? Do you want to face one of those things in a lifeboat? Soldier up, Lieutenant. Let's get some wear and tear on that sidearm," Captain Mahony said with no ill will, but as rigidly as iron.

The swarm made contact with his ship, firing hundreds of penetrating rounds. The Banta's shields didn't last two seconds, and a third of the swarm, several dozen ships, flew into the opening in its hull, unplugging from their fighters and rushing in.

The Banta wasn't in a position that the Merciless could fire on, and the swarm was already moving on, targeting the Lupus. Their number was back up to three hundred and climbing, new fighters joining them from waiting groups that were out of the Fleet Battlegroups' reach. "Ideas! How can we help?"

"I volunteer my team to assist," Remmy said from the Scythe, a Clever Class corvette. "We can drop in behind the boarders, slow their progress through the Banta down."

Jake watched the main thrusters and most of the lights on the Banta go out, checked his tactical readings on the ship and saw that they no longer had main power or control of the systems that would allow them to enable their destruct. The Scythe and Remmy's team were useful where they were, firing on the swarm and the few remaining Edxi Warrior ships that were left. They could also land their heavily armoured Special Operations Combat Unit members in coordination with other groups to be more effective. The Banta was all but lost, but the crew... Jake thought for a moment, then locked eyes with Kadri, who was waiting urgently. "Drop your squad, Remmy, but leave just enough people so you can keep firing the guns on your ship. I need you in two places at once. Oh, and no heroics. We need to control the boarding action on the Banta without sacrificing you and your team."

"Aye, aye, Commodore," Remmy said with a grin.

Before his channel was finished closing, Jake addressed Kadri. "How can I help you?"

"The Clever Dream just came up with a plan that could break the swarm. They found how they're communicating but they need cover while they jam the source."

"Can they do it from within the Merciless' shield radius?" Jake asked.

"Yes, they need to use their basic D-Drive system, the one not bound by the limitations of a Quad Drive, to..."

"Shorter version," Jake said.

"They tap into the dimension the Edxi are communicating through then jam them, painting a huge target on their back but hopefully breaking the swarm's coordination down."

"We have to disperse these swarms," Jake said, turning to Huun. "Stop firing all beam weapons, send the power to our shields. If this works, we'll be the biggest target in the solar system." He turned to Liara, but Agameg was already giving the order to signal the Clever Dream into position. Jake moved on to speak to Engineering. "Finn, can you create more quick charging capacity for the shields?"

"More? There are space stations that don't have the capacity we do," he asked.

"In a minute or less, every swarm in the solar system might try to pick us apart," Jake said.

"Oh, in that case, I'll find it even if I have to start burning micro-capacitors in the galley to make it happen," Finn said. "Give me a minute to work the board down here and redirect some capacity."

"How much do you think you can get in a minute?"

"If I use the beam capacitors, another forty percent. Give me more time, and I can get another thirty, but lights will flicker, I guarantee it."

"Put us in the dark if you have to," Jake said.

"Aye," Finn replied.

"The Clever Dream is moving into position, and they report that the program is almost finished," Looph reported from the Flight Station. "They will be locked with a mooring point in less than a minute."

"Good pilot," Ashley muttered, her Mergillian co-pilot nodding.

Jake looked to the corner of his Tactical display with a broader view of the solar system. The defence around Tamber was failing. The swarms were taking out large guns in orbit one by one. The Brood ship kept moving behind the British Alliance Fleet, putting dozens of ships between it and Freeground Alpha's cannons, and the Triton was fighting off a new wave of Edxi Warrior carriers, losing quickly. One was attached to its aft-port side, and they were reporting that they would be boarded soon. It was already too late for them in this fight, the order for the Triton to retreat was given, and Oz was guiding the ship away from Tamber under protest. The swarm nearest to him was leaving Oz and his ship alone, focusing on the destroyers. One of the carriers in his battle-group was already a dead husk. "We're setting up a group of railgun turrets in front of the breach they're going to come through," Oz was telling command. "They're in for a rude surprise. After we counter the incursion, we'll re-join the battle."

"Negative," Ayan said, taking over the responding chan-nel. "You will retreat to position Theta and make sure there isn't a single Edxi survivor on your ship before moving on to Delta. The Triton is in no shape to fight," she replied.

It was true. A swarm twice the size of the one Jake and his battlegroup was dealing with hammered the Triton for several minutes, enough time to break their shields down and ruin the gunnery deck. The loss of life was minimal, the swarm had moved on, but with hundreds of boarders preparing to enter from the aft section of the ship and secondary damage across the ship's system board, the Triton was in need of repairs, or at least an hour to perform emer-gency repairs and regroup.

"The British Battlegroups are moving in to take your place," Ayan added. "Get out of here, that's an order."

"Yes, Defence Minister," Oz replied.

He had the same knowledge Jake did about the situation; the British Alliance was moving everything they had in the system into orbit around Tamber and their firepower made an impression, but they were also being used as a shield by a Brood ship that was taking damage but still functioning, still launching dozens of fighters every minute. A British Carrier and its five destroyer support ships were already almost finished, and they'd only been in the fight for eleven minutes.

The Edxi weren't even bothering to board them, simply swarming them until the guns stopped and the lights went out, then moving on. "Alice, as soon as you're ready, start jamming the Edxi," Jake said through his direct comm line. He looked to Kadri. "Is this real? Do you think the solution she found will work?"

"Her science officer, Iruuk, actually found it," Kadri said. "I've checked it out, and yes, it'll definitely do something. I don't know if it'll do everything we hope it will, but I think it'll slow them down."

"I'll take it. Right now, I'd take anything that improves our odds."

TWENTY-NINE

The Verge

THE COMMAND CENTRE was a din of people trading information behind and across from Ayan, who was in the middle of an exchange herself. Her deft fingers worked at the command console, the Freeground Carrier Independence, one of the oldest ships they had and an upgraded vessel had succumbed to the swarm. It and the three-destroyer escort with it had performed their duty, holding the line against the Edxi Warrior ships, but there were hundreds of drones left. The final decision as to what to do with the ship that was about to be overwhelmed was hers. Samurai Squadron was in range, and the Merciless' rear guns could break up the fighter swarm that was threatening to board the Independence.

The Merciless had a situation of its own, a swarm of its

own. If she made the wrong decision, it would cost Haven Fleet the Independence and the Merciless, not to mention Samurai Squadron. There were other pressing decisions waiting. "The Destroyer; Conscience, has been lost, Ma'am," Leon reported from her right. "The destruct sequence is counting down from ten, so there's that." Ayan glanced at the hologram of the ship with an Edxi Warrior vessel affixed to it, flooding the decks with its drones. The ship's last good sensor readings said that they had been overrun, there were hundreds of drones on the attack, and most of the crew were ordered to the escape pods. A group of enemy fighters were on their way to take care of that, there was no help in range, the pods would be destroyed or taken.

The Conscience exploded, the gravity and electromagnetic wave from the destruct mechanism shattering the Edxi Warrior vessel, pushing most of the nearest escape pods away from the ship. The Quad Drives aboard most of their ships were also very destructive bombs, a purpose she never wanted them to serve.

"There are only nine Edxi fighters on the way to take those pods out. Put the call out to any free corvettes and fighters in range to cover them while they make their way to us." She made her decision about the Independence, ordering the remaining crew to get to their escape pods or shelter in place. Normally the escape pods would be suicide in their situation, there were so many Edxi ships nearby, but she brought the Helm for the War Forge up. "Commander, we are going to make a micro dimensional jump to cover the Independence."

"Yes, Ma'am, we'll begin plotting right away. Jumping in

forty-five seconds," he replied, the pair of navigators behind him looked surprised.

"You can't be taking the War Forge into the fight," Admiral Lamonthe said. "It's too risky, we should be ordering our ships to retreat."

"We are," Ayan replied. "If the War Forge doesn't fully reveal itself and use its guns to cover escape pods, we'll lose the entire crew of that carrier. We need to rally and retreat to point Delta."

"You know the simulation results," Rear Admiral Case said quietly, running his hand through his silver brush cut. "The War Forge reveals itself, and the Edxi flock to it."

"New report from the Clever Dream and the Merciless, they have another plan. You might want to put that jump on hold," Admiral Lamonthe said.

"No, no plan they can follow right now will change the situation of the Independence, and as for the simulations, the chances of the Edxi swarming the War Forge always went down when we were far enough away from Tamber."

"News about that, by the way," Rear Admiral Case said. "The British Alliance failed to cover their command ship, it's being boarded and an Edxi Warrior ship is affixing to it now."

Ayan shook her head. "I can see that, it's right in front of me," she said, gesturing to the main tactical display. The sight of the British Alliance failing to cover the invasion of Tamber was dismaying, but every tactic she and the Admiralty considered only put them in a position to lose more people faster. The simple truth was that they were woefully unprepared to defend the solar system against the invasion, and they were losing a destroyer or a carrier every few minutes. It was time to collect their people, their ships and regroup somewhere else if they could. "I know, we could lose the War Forge, but we'll save..."

"This message is two minutes old, sent through normal space," Lamonthe interrupted, showing her Iruuk's face and a diagram underneath that showed a transmission moving from normal to trans-dimensional space then coming out into normal space again through thousands of micro-rifts in the antennae of the Warrior Edxi ships. "They found how the swarms are communicating and are going to jam them. It should start in a few seconds."

"Good, we might have a chance to retreat," Ayan said.

Lamonthe wanted to argue, she could see it in his disposition, and she turned away from him as she watched that rare urge to argue turn to sad resignation. An announcement came over the command room main audio system; "Jumping in three seconds."

The tactical display glitched for a moment, the tall holographic map moving all the planets and ships relative to the War Forge's new position. They'd crossed the solar system in an instant. Lamonthe cleared his throat and took a place at her left side. His resolve was restored. "We retreat, then. There's nothing for it."

"Not today," Ayan said. "But there must be people out there who want to see the Haven System free from this."

"There are," Lamonthe agreed. He would know. Of all the people in the Admiralty, he knew of more races, more cultures in the sector and beyond who weren't pleased with the encroachment of the Edxi or the Order of Eden. "We're receiving more up-to-date data from the Merciless. The

Clever Dream is attached to one of their lower mooring points, and they are starting to jam enemy communications now."

A quarter of the large tactical map focused in on Carole, then on the Merciless, the swarm harassing it, and another group of seven Edxi Warrior ships emerging into normal space. The Samurai Squadron and most of the corvettes that supported them were keeping their distance, firing at the swarm but not getting caught in it. She could imagine those fighter pilots, white knuckled, wishing they could get closer, take a more active role. "No change in the swarm behaviour yet," Rear Admiral Neth, a Nafalli whose fur was so white that it looked blue in some light reported under her breath. She was grooming under her chin with her claws, a sign of tension if her wide eyes weren't sign enough that she was on edge.

"Wait, there," Rear Admiral Case said. "Look, there are collisions in the swarm."

Ayan watched as the orderly swarm started to break from the middle, heavy fighters colliding with their escorts as they made another pass at the Merciless. Countermeasure guns rattled a rip of energy bolts at the swarm, and the collisions became worse, several fighters spinning into the Merciless' shields, others breaking formation, exposing them to more guns that they were avoiding handily until then. The swarm was breaking. "The disorder is spreading across the system," Rear Admiral Case said. "This is working, we might..."

"Let's not count our blessings just yet," Lamonthe said. "We have work to do."

Ayan saw an urgent command go out from the Merciless,

and played it back for her ears only. "Samurai Squadron! Available SOCU Corvettes, this is Merciless Flight, get in there and take out those enemy fighters."

"Getting rid of your bug problem, Merciless," Ronin replied. "Dog fight of our lives, everyone. Just because they're not talking to each other right doesn't mean they're not dangerous, take them out by the numbers and stay close enough for cover. Oh, and do not get into the Merciless' firing solution. If you manage to survive, you'll be cleaning latrines for a week."

"Madam Defence Minister," Captain Jorges addressed in her other ear. "We are waiting on your order, holding in stealth at the position you indicated."

Ayan reconsidered her decision to assist the crew of the Independent and the two escort destroyers that were damaged beyond function for a second then nodded to herself. "De-cloak, activate all gun batteries, and cover the escape of the Independent crew and their escort destroyers." The invasion of those ships was slowing, but Edxi warrior drones were still trying to break down doors to get at the crew. "Send our mechanized division on a rapid recovery mission. Make sure they know they don't have much time to get to anyone who can't escape that ship themselves." The division was only a hundred fifty people, but they were in the heaviest armour they had, as resilient as a starfighter, and even though a third of them were trainees, putting them aboard the Independence could save hundreds of lives.

The War Forge appeared on the tactical map, its two hundred and ten heavy quad railgun turrets firing immediately. Every muzzle sent high explosive, guided rounds into small wormholes that delivered their munitions to their targets in milliseconds. "Fire on all Edxi targets in range without doing collateral damage." The beam emplacements began pulsing from all sides of the station, briefly drawing lines of white lines across kilometres of space, burning through targets with extreme precision. "Yes, Ma'am," the Captain replied. "I'm sorry to report that three turrets and five beam emplacements aren't functioning."

"That's better than expected. How long until we can rescue the crew of the Independence and her companion destroyers?"

"We estimate eighteen minutes if everyone hears our transmissions and is where they are supposed to be, Ma'am."

Ayan exhaled sharply, that was a great time, even ten times as long was a great time, but it was a long time for the War Forge to be away from other places where it could be of help. "Thank you, Captain, carry on." A look at the tactical map, the Sunspire and the Merciless made her wonder if she made the right decision for a moment.

Leon saw where she was focusing her attention. "This is the right choice, Ma'am. Those ships are still operational, the three thousand people in the Independence Group didn't stand a chance without us."

The Triton slipped into a wormhole, its hull burned where the Edxi Warrior ship tried to break through, other sections were seriously scarred as well, but most of the crew survived. The defence around Tamber was still failing faster by the moment. The thousands of fighters there might have broken up, they weren't moving as one or two swarms anymore, but they were still dangerous, as Minh-Chu said.

Freeground Station and the British Alliance were still losing ground. The War Forge wouldn't be able to fend that kind of assault off alone, even though it was the most powerful battle station in the sector. It was barely manned. Every person who lost their life or had to retreat would be leaving an important post unmanned without the possibility of having a soldier replace them. "We have to abandon Carole, the outer asteroid belt, and the Excalibur has to extract itself from its position immediately. Order all fighting ships to prepare to rally around Freeground Station. The War Forge can't save Tamber alone, but maybe if what's left of our fleet accompanies it, we can turn the odds in our favour."

"I agree with you," Rear Admiral Case said. "But the Edxi will almost certainly concentrate on the War Forge, and we can't afford to lose it, especially if we're giving so much ground, especially if this all ends in retreat."

"It's our only chance to save Tamber. I'll trade the War Forge for the safety of Tamber over and over, Rear Admiral."

"The Edxi will dig in across the system while we fight tooth and nail to save one moon," he countered.

"We'll have to rally and clear them out," Ayan replied, knowing that it would be an unlikely event. During the entire invasion they hadn't seen a single Order of Eden ship, and if there was one in the system they definitely would have. Every scanner they had was turned all the way up, pointed in every direction. "It's a bridge we'll cross when we eventually have to."

Rear Admiral Case nodded. "Yes, Ma'am." He knew not to push too hard. "I'll make sure every commander with a worthy ship knows what's coming."

"You know you're only going to solve the bug problem, it could cost us all the manufacturing lines and the facilities of this base," Lamonthe whispered after Rear Admiral Case was back at his end of the command ring.

"Let's hope the Order waits a few days for the smoke to clear before following the Edxi's assault with one of their own," Ayan nodded. "And that we can save one manufacturing line at least, so we can repair a few ships."

He only nodded. "I might take up prayer, with odds like these."

THIRTY

Planet Carole

"CAPTAIN, the Banta is secure for the moment, but there are more boarders coming," Remmy said from the rear of the ship. "Some systems are coming back online."

Alice glanced to the destroyer on her tactical display as she listened in on the transmission to the Merciless' bridge. Five of the Banta's main turrets came back to life, firing hundreds of railgun rounds at the less organized Edxi fighters and the last few Warrior ships. They'd come close to losing control over the orbital space around Carole but were regaining the advantage quickly. "I need the Scythe to get tow lines on that ship. We're retreating to Tamber space," her father replied.

"Retreating to..." Remmy replied at first, surprised. "Aye,

Sir, we'll be ready to tow the Banta at speed soon. At least her guns can support the Merciless."

"I'm putting you and the Banta in a wormhole here. Her backup transit system is still online."

"Yes, Sir," Remmy replied.

Alice could hear a hint of dissatisfaction in Remmy's voice, but he knew better than to push back. The Banta had taken heavy damage, the fight around Tamber was still vigorous, and a barely operational destroyer would be a liability. Her father was saving lives. Even still, the idea that they were abandoning Carole after they sacrificed so much - the Lupus had taken losses during an incursion, and the Gladius was barely hanging on - made her want to argue for the cause, but it wouldn't be worth much if they lost Tamber. A glance at the Excalibur's battlegroup revealed that it was retreating from Lonos at speed. It was a world she occasionally thought of visiting. Fully terraformed with diverse life and fewer than ten thousand people living on the surface, it sounded like an untouched paradise. The Edxi Warrior ships the Excalibur and the five Nafalli support ships were leaving to land there would make it their own, and Alice shuddered at what the world would become. "We have fighters coming for the Banta, again," Remmy said. "Looks like they'll touch down aft."

"We've got you," Ronin said as he and Carnie's fighters swept in behind the group of nine Edxi fighters. The Edxi fighters broke off their landing approach, trying to evade the violent barrage of Ronin and Carnie's guns. The whole Samurai Squadron were a full-on menace to Edxi fighters from the instant they were set loose after the less organized swarm. Alice couldn't help but smile a little as she watched

Carnie's fighter tear through the nearest Light Edxi fighter, then gracefully turn to chase another, another, and one more, getting into position behind each one so his guns could reduce them to shreds of metal before flipping and launching three sets of small missiles that scrambled after the enemy ships that were trying to get behind him. Ronin was equally active, picking Edxi Fighters off the forward section of the Banta's hull without scratching the heavily damaged ship, then returning to his wingman's side, where he started picking at the larger group of fighters that were taking notice of Carnie's work. The pair of them worked together in a deadly weave of graceful flight patterns that made it clear that they were thinking at least three kills ahead, and the Edxi couldn't keep up without being able to coordinate using their transmitters. "How long until the Merciless takes over comm jamming duties?" Alice asked. The fighters of Samurai Squadron and the two Corvettes from SOCU were doing well, but it was still a tooth and nail fight. The Gladius was struggling to stay close to the Merciless. The Edxi had made it their secondary target after her father's ship.

"Seconds," Iruuk said. He cringed at the sight of an Edxi Warrior ship spinning so its main thruster faced them, where they were hiding behind the Merciless's shields. It was coming in fast, trying to collide with the large ship, but the Merciless focused all the firepower they had along their lower hull, cracking the enemy vessel apart as Ashley piloted them out of the way at the last second. "You're seconds away, right?" Iruuk asked the Merciless crewmembers who were working on getting the jamming system working on their ship so the Clever Dream wasn't such a target.

"Just about, we're focusing a spare D-Drive now," Finn said.

"That's what you said a minute ago," Iruuk grumbled, his communicator muted.

The Scythe was in position in front of the Banta, firing its two lines. Samurai Squadron worked feverishly to swat Edxi fighters away. "Emergence point, aft at four by thirty-three by six," Alice announced on her alert channel. Sticky and Hunter were within a few kilometres of the dimensional rift when it opened. It put them between a trio of Edxi Warrior ships that were attached to each other and dozens of fighters.

"Get out of there, Sticky, Hunter," Ronin said.

Hunter listened, blasting all her thrusters, sending her fighter back towards the Merciless, where she could find cover. Sticky followed using her secondary thrusters, taking several seconds to launch a nuclear Javelin Missile, her only one, at the newcomer ships. The missile cloaked, and she turned her fighter so she could use her main thrusters to retreat. Edxi fighters affixed to the hulls of the newcomer ships had her in their sights, and fired together, sending thousands of thin needle projectiles, and dozens of heavy explosive shots at her fighter.

The instant later, a bloom of nuclear fire exploded as the dimensional rift closed. Its timing was perfect, and the lead Edxi ship was a ruin. The two affixed to it separated, leaving the smouldering hulk behind. The bomb didn't go off in time to save Sticky. What remained of her and her fighter was barely worth scanning. "I lost Sticky," Hunter said. "She just had to take that shot."

"Regroup around the Scythe, we have to cover it while it hauls the Banta into its wormhole," Ronin said flatly.

"Sticky's gone?" Ute asked, her big round Mergillian eyes blinking in surprise.

Alice glanced at the scan results of her fighter and nodded. There was nothing left to save. She didn't know her well, but everyone who met her liked Sticky, and she would definitely have a new, more honourable call sign at the conclusion of this battle if she wanted it. A wormhole opened in front of the Banta projected by the Merciless and the Scythe's thrusters fired hard, dragging the destroyer towards the opening.

The pair of Edxi Warrior ships began a ramming run towards it, their large main thrusters burning white-blue as they started to close the distance. The Merciless' guns fired at them, some of their lighter weapons' fire was caught by the new Edxi fighters that were launching from the surface of the Warrior ship's hulls. One of the Warrior ships put itself between the Merciless and the other, and the main guns of her father's warship broke it down, blasting the pieces aside, but the last Edxi Warrior ship was still on course to strike the Banta. It turned end over end, lowering its grappling arms from where they were stowed along the length of its hull and firing its engines to slow a little in preparation to make contact. "Uh, brace! Brace for impact on the Banta!" Remmy said over the general emergency channel for the battlegroup.

The Edxi warrior ship connected with the aft end of the Banta, its grappling arms finding purchase as Edxi fighters leapt free of the hull, rushing to the Banta. "We're going into this wormhole with some company," Remmy said.

The Merciless' heavy guns crushed the midsection of the Edxi Warrior ship, leaving only the grappling arms and main thruster affixed to the Banta. There were dozens, possibly over a hundred Edxi fighters crawling towards the breaches of the Banta's hull as it disappeared into the wormhole. The Scythe's rear guns were firing at them, but Alice knew Remmy and the crew of the Banta were in for a battle as those fighters became boarders.

"The Merciless has taken over inter-dimensional jamming, we're free to detach," Iruuk said.

"Great, shut our secondary D-Drive down and redirect energy to shields," she told him. Then, she activated her battlegroup wide channel. "This is Captain Valent. The Clever Dream is joining the effort to cover the Gladius." She opened the ship-wide comm. "I hope you enjoyed that break, gunners, because you're not getting another one for a while."

"Fantastic," Woone growled her eager response.

The sound of the Clever Dream decoupling from the Merciless filled the ship. There was an instant of quiet before the main thrusters fired, filling the ship with a familiar, comforting low rumble.

Samurai Squadron led the way, gathering around the Gladius as one of her sister ships, the Lupus took position in front of her. "Clever Dream, this is Ronin. We could use you beneath the Gladius, it's going to be hot down there though, so you won't be alone."

Alice adjusted their course so they could provide cover for the bottom side of the damaged destroyer. The Merciless was above it, their anti-fighter guns providing a deterrent to any enemy who was careless enough to get between the ships.

"We're on our way," she replied as Ute rolled the Clever Dream and maneuverered it down at a stomach-turning angle. The Mergillian fired the heavy cannons running under most of the ship at a Heavy Edxi fighter, and it was instantly obliterated. "That was for Sticky," Ute said under her breath.

The Samurai Squadron were behind the Clever Dream, still moving into position when they started to slow so they didn't overshoot their place in the battle. It gave her time to highlight the Edxi fighters coming for them and launch a pair of small seeker missiles at each of them. Their small missile launchers opened, fired a barrage of forty guided projectiles that filled the immediate space around her ship on the tactical map for an instant before the Clever Dream was surrounded by the enemy Edxi fighters. The enemy started taking devastating hits. Light fighters were blasted to pieces, while Heavy Fighters seemed to reconsider rushing the Clever Dream as their shields were defeated.

The attack didn't have to be repeated, the Clever Dream's full gunner crew finished them off with gusto, and Alice targeted the next wave of Edxi fighters that were putting the Gladius and the Lupus between them and the Merciless. There would be no shelter there. As the Clever Dream launched another volley of missiles, the Samurai Squadron was fully present, and it was clear that the Edxi fighters that remained would be no match for them.

The tactical display told a bigger story. The Merciless was leading the remaining ships in its battlegroup away from Carole. They really were abandoning the planet, it was diffi-cult for Alice to believe, and as they cleaned up the fighters that took one final attempt at taking out one of their destroyers, everyone was increasing speed towards Tamber, the Clever Dream included.

The fight around her ship lasted several more minutes, their shields taking several hits from heavy fighters, but they had time to recharge. The Samurai Squadron was extremely good at what they did, coordinating and fighting together. "Incoming ship, looks like they're using a Quad Drive," Iruuk said.

The Sector Jumper, captained by Shamus Frost, emerged several hundred thousand kilometres away, and Alice's tactical display showed its orders. The ship was to fall into place behind the Clever Dream and would be in position in less than two minutes. The vessel looked like it was in perfect shape and reported the presence of several trainees at the guns, people she'd never heard of before.

"Looks like I just missed the party," Frost said to the battlegroup.

"No, you arrived just in time to crash one with us. We're about to save Tamber," Commodore Valent said.

"More emergence points opening around Carole, these ones were not made using a quad drive," Iruuk said sadly. They didn't have any ships back there, the planet was defenceless.

"Wait, we're jamming them, how could they know?" Alice asked as thirty-three Edxi Warrior ships emerged and headed for Carole's orbital space. They were keeping the planet between them and the Merciless' battlegroup, there was nothing they could do unless they turned around.

"I don't know," Iruuk replied. "I'll find out though."

"Let the Merciless science officers work on that, Fur-

Face," Alice said quietly. "We're about to have bigger problems." Her display told the rest of the story as Iruuk looked over her shoulder at the battle that was taking place around Tamber. Freeground had several Edxi Warrior ships affixed to its hull. The British Fleet were failing to retreat, their ships were being boarded. The Excalibur's battlegroup was outnumbered and already fighting hard, even though they had the support of Tamber's orbital guns, which were under threat as well. Even without the coordination of their hidden signals, the Edxi were fighting. The fighters were organized in smaller groups of three to nine, and they seemed to get better at working together as time went on.

Alice tried not to look at the vulnerable green, blue and brown planet ahead. She knew they were already fighting down there. One Warrior ship had gotten through, and a report stated simply that it had landed and was deploying attackers. The thought of letting more through, losing Freeground and the moon was too much for her to consider as she tried to imagine the tactics that would keep her and her crew alive.

THIRTY-ONE

Holding On

THE FEELING on the ship was one of excitement mixed with a sinking notion. The Edxi Fighters were a menace beyond anyone's dreams. A wave of nearly a thousand confronted the Merciless and its small battlegroup. The main guns beneath Alice's feet rattled the deck beneath her feet as they fired, fired, fired, every shot taking a fighter or three out. The pulse and bump were so constant that she was used to it after the first minute.

The turrets were nearly overheated, the nine seconds it took for the missile racks to reload seemed to extend into eternity before they could fire their own swarms back at the insects. The Gladius had several of their turrets working at full power, but it wasn't enough.

The fighters were much less organized than before, less of

a swarm, and more gangs of a dozen at most, but they watched each other, making decisions based on the actions of their nearest neighbour. The wave met them and it felt like they were submerged in a scrambling pile of insects that had no fear and only one goal: to take everything they met apart. "Impact incoming," Ute said, straining at the controls. Two light fighters smashed into their port side shield one after the other, reducing the charge down to forty eight percent.

"I am turning the reactors in the Quad Drives all the way up," Iruuk said. "They'll provide the power we need to keep the shield charged."

Ute rolled the Clever Dream as a trio of heavy Edxi Fighters raked them with a dozen of their heavy plasma pods. They struck like fast torpedoes, reducing their lower shield charge to twenty-three percent. A light fighter collided as the trio moved off. Slider almost intercepted it, tearing into the light Edxi fighter with her guns, but the wreckage struck the Clever Dream at full speed, and for the first time since the battle began, everyone heard something slam in to the hull. "I'm putting you in charge of keeping our shields up, Lewis," Alice said. "We need your speed."

"The Gladius is taking heavy damage," Theodore said. "Small Edxi fighters are striking their fore dorsal shields in the same section over and over."

Alice brought the tactical scan of the Gladius up in time to see two light fighters strike the shield at incredible speed. A glimpse of something made her suspicious and she reversed the feed to milliseconds before the impact. The fighter was extending its legs as though it expected to land, firing a cutting beam of some kind at the same time. It was destroyed by the impact, but she spotted what it was after. The main antenna package was right in its path, beneath the shield. There was a field emitter package in that bundle of antennae as well. "If they get through to that, the Gladius will lose most of its shielding in that section, they'll have to switch to remote emitters, and the bugs will get through no problem."

Theodore nodded and added; "They seem heavily invested in destroying antenna packages on every ship they're attacking, including the Merciless."

"We have to guard that spot," Alice said to Ute. "You have to put us in the way."

"Aye, aye."

"We'll take as much pressure off the Gladius as we can and break off when our shields are too low. Maybe they'll get enough relief to recharge." She turned to Theodore. "Send your conclusions to command then take over on the weapon station if you think you can attack these fighters."

"My program sees them as a threat, a pest. I'll be able to use any weapon you like," Theodore said.

Alice got out of the tactical station seat as fast as she could and Theodore slipped in, pulling a slim data line from his torso and plugging in directly. The main weapons aboard the Clever Dream began firing again, sounding a frantic tattoo across the ship. The tactical display could barely keep up with his targeting speed. Alice didn't think twice but opened a channel directly to her mother. "I have an android here who is having no problem targeting and killing Edxi. Do you think the bots you have there, on the station, would be able to fight them too?"

Ayan's stunned surprise only lasted a second. "We'll run a

simulation across all the fabrication bots. We have unmanned ships that are finished in the manufacturing lines. If you're right..."

"Running simulation now," a young man announced. Several moments passed. The Clever Dream was completely focused on killing everything that came near the Gladius' dorsal side, but two light fighters still got through, crushing themselves apart as they collided with their shields. Lewis was drawing massive amounts of power from every reactor aboard, one for each Quad Drive, and their mains, but that didn't keep them from picking up a few scratches from debris that got through. It was already too close, they were taking too much damage and wouldn't be able to last long.

"Simulation complete," Ayan said with a surprised smile. "Fabrication Control; split the fabrication droids between the destroyers and carriers we have at the end of the lines and upload training packages for their systems. We need to launch those ships immediately." She turned to Alice. "Thank you, this might win the battle."

"I hope so," Alice replied. A screeching of metal against metal on the hull over her head made her cringe. A fighter had gotten through, its remains intact enough to try to cling, but it slid off the sleek form of the Clever Dream. A glance at the shield display told her that they had lost their own dorsal shielding for a moment, and it was recharging as Ute rolled the vessel, putting their more fortified side towards the assault. "I hope so," she found herself repeating. "I love you, Mom."

· · ·

"I LOVE YOU TOO," Ayan said quietly as the channel to her daughter closed. She was a wonderful young woman, perhaps a bit too stoic at times like her father. Even through that there was a hint of something that Ayan never wanted to see; fear. For a moment, she let her eyes close and thought about the entire battle. The Sunspire was coming back with two more ships in its class. They would help turn the tide even though they were all fairly damaged from battling the Edxi on the edge of the system. They were leaving an undetermined number of enemy ships behind, they'd have to deal with that later, but it could keep for the time being.

At the moment the biggest problem was the shield around Tamber. It would fail soon. The Excalibur's battle group was down to the main ship and one destroyer. The Merciless would lose the Gladius, even though the Clever Dream was doing a good job of blocking attacks, then they'd lose the Lupus. Nafalli ships were fighting on the outskirts, their older systems and lighter armour wouldn't stand up to the same punishment that the Haven Fleet vessels could withstand.

The British Alliance ships were finished. Even the older Carthan vessel that they'd taken, with its meters-thick hull, was overrun by boarders, a few British Alliance soldiers were fighting a valiant last stand, but there was no way to get them out before the Edxi got to them.

Freeground Alpha, the great ring, was being boarded by hundreds of Edxi, their old defences had failed them, and they were fighting in the corridors. The Merciless and the Excalibur, sister ships, were becoming the prime targets around Tamber, and even though the number of Edxi ships coming into their space had slowed dramatically, they wouldn't be able to hold out. Changing tactics too often could ruin a chance at victory, but Ayan knew it was time to call a retreat or make one last attempt at saving Tamber. When her eyes opened, she noticed that Leon and several of her staff were staring at her. "We're leaving a destroyer here to take the rest of the survivors from the Independence. Prepare to jump into range with Tamber with the rest of the destroyers."

"What about the fighters, Ma'am?" asked Rear Admiral Case. "We have three hundred ready for pilots."

"Upload the automatic flight programs, add our defence drone software and launch now. Disable the safeguards," Ayan said.

"But that'll enable them to fire on non-Edxi targets. It's against our own laws."

Ayan knew there was something else coming, she could feel it. If they were victorious against the Edxi near Tamber, it wouldn't be the last fight they would have to win that day. She looked Case in the eye. "This is a direct order. Upload the Killer Drone software, the modules for those fighters and launch immediately. Lock their programs."

"Aye, Ma'am," Rear Admiral Case said.

"We'll be ready to jump across the system in two minutes," Leon said.

"Tell them I expect to see Tamber through the window in twenty seconds," Ayan replied.

"Right away," he busied himself with passing the order, nodding at Admiral Lamonthe before he stepped away.

Ayan turned towards him. He was almost smiling. "Good news?"

"Intelligence has been analysing the reaction the Edxi are

having to the jamming signal the Merciless is sending into the dimension..."

"Explain faster; what do I need to know?" Ayan said.

"They're getting accustomed to the signal noise," Lamonthe said. "The jamming is stopping them from using interdimensional communications, sure, but we think it actually might have caused them pain. That's why they were completely unable to coordinate at first, and now they're using visual cues to cooperate in smaller groups. We think that if..."

Ayan could guess the rest. "Send the jamming program to every ship with a quad drive and order them to execute it. If one ship using one quad drive can make them stutter, let's see what a few hundred quad drives can do."

"You want them to use all their drives?" Lamonthe asked.

Most ships had two or more quad drives that worked together, it could cause a cacophony if it worked that may disable the Edxi. "All their drives. The station will use all the main and secondary systems as well," she said, aware that there were hundreds of quad drives connected across the War Forge generating power, maintaining the gravity and keeping the structure in one piece whenever it had to make a jump. "They should be warmed up if we're about to jump."

"If this works it might buy us enough time," Lamonthe said. "Uploading the program now. The fleet will be ready in a few seconds."

The floor felt like it shifted under her feet a little, then the tactical display in the middle of the room changed to show them in outer orbit around Tamber. Their weapon emplacements began firing, tearing into Edxi Warrior ships first, then their anti-starfighter beam weapons began sweeping the dark space around them. It was impressive, but on its own the War Forge provided a prime target more than a solution. "Fighters are loading into the outer punter systems," Rear Admiral Chase reported. "They'll start launching in a few seconds."

"Tell the War Forge Navigation and Communication departments to begin broadcasting jamming signals immediately," Ayan said. "Let's see how the Edxi react when we turn the volume up."

"Aye," Lamonthe said, passing the order through his terminal. The quad drives aboard the War Forge all activated at the same time, something that had never been attempted before, each opening a microscopic hole into the dimension the Edxi used to communicate, broadcasting a harsh jamming tone. They waited, watching the tactical display for long moments. "Reports coming in," Lamonthe said finally. He tilted his head, hearing something on his private feed, then grinned for the first time since Ayan met him. Ronin's voice filled the room as he put it through the main audio system. "I don't know what you guys are doing, but every bug in the sky just forgot what they're doing. I swear it looks like they're cringing. Let's make the most of it!"

The Command Centre erupted with the cheers of officers, filled with renewed hope. Ayan sighed, the momentary relief was wonderful, but she had a nagging feeling, a sense of dread that wouldn't subside.

THIRTY-TWO

Accounting

SHAMUS FROST HAD the feeling that he was passing into the belly of a great beast. A beast that had swallowed a labyrinth. Hal was at his side, a pilot who had become a trusted friend during their journey to and from British Alliance space. It had been a long journey, and he wished he would be seeing Stephanie at the end of it.

"Hey, we're in a ship," Hal said, looking in every direction as they followed the lead of two armoured War Forge guards.

"Station," Frost corrected, his attention returning to the present. "Guess you could call it a ship though, since it can jump from one place to another."

"No, we passed through the station, yeah, but at some point, we got into a ship inside the station. Some of the panels are different, the scale shifted a little, and we passed a hum

back there. Like some kind of local dampening system hum."
Hal looked to the guard ahead, a woman who glanced back at
him frequently, already following what he was saying. "You're
going to want someone to check that, by the way. Printing
ships isn't really a perfect process, I found a few flaws in the
Sector Jumper, I couldn't imagine the bugs you'd have in
something like this."

"We'll have it looked at."

Frost wished he'd paid more attention as they made their
way into the station from one of the interior hangars, he
missed the details Hal was talking about. "A beast this size
will have its secrets," Frost said. "Don't think everyone is
meant to notice what you did, lad. Maybe you should keep
that under your hat."

"Right," Hal said. "What about everything else we found
out there?"

"We're definitely not keeping that secret," Frost said. For a
moment it looked like the report and raw data they sent to the
War Forge and the Merciless might be their last statement
before they were taken out by an armada of insect ships. Even
though they carried important information and only had a
few people who trained on the Sector Jumper's systems and
weapons on the journey back to the Haven System, the Fleet
still put them in the middle of a desperate fight. It didn't look
good. "Chief Frost," Admiral Lamonthe said, his voice uncharacteristically warm and welcoming as he emerged from a
room ahead.

As he ran his finger along the outside of his military
vacsuit's thigh pocket, it opened so he could retrieve the data
cylinder he stole from the vault in orbit around Sa-Hadin.

"I've been itching to hand this off to someone," Frost said. "We could only decode some of it."

"It's not just one archive, but several of them in different encrypted wrappers," Hal added. "I'm not much of a software cracker type, but it looks like someone really didn't want anyone seeing these records."

"We saw, and it was enough evidence to change our disposition towards Lorander going forward. Follow me, gentlemen," Lamonthe invited.

They passed through a large airlock with half-metre thick doors. Between those doors there was a squad of fourteen heavily armed soldiers in armour standing guard, watching them silently as they passed. "Best behaviour, Lad," he muttered under his breath to Hal.

"I was just about to say the same for you, but you outrank me by a bit, so..." Hal muttered.

"Good point." As the words slipped out, the inner security doors opened to reveal a round chamber with several circular tiers. In the middle was a large tactical hologram that hovered over a round display. Ayan Anderson was sitting on a tall stool with a backrest as several high-ranking commanders took their turns reporting. One of them, the lowest ranking, put a meal bar in her right hand and a drink with a long straw in her left. "What are we doing here, Admiral?" Frost asked as Lamonthe led them down towards the innermost, lowest tier.

"There were a few things in your report that I found alarming. It might not seem like the time to investigate the British Alliance and their practices in the Core Worlds, but there is a large carrier group on the way. They just signalled, and they'll be here soon. We need to take the time to interview you and the man who ran the scan that might be famous in Intelligence circles soon."

"I was just scanning Beta Bio back. It looked like every development company and government substation there was trying to get a read on what was inside the Sector Jumper, so I thought it was only fair to do a hard scan sweep of the whole station. A bunch of them sent some nasty messages about it, but we ignored 'em, they were just irritated that we had better scanners and saw most of their secrets," Hal said. "Nothing worth getting famous for."

"I'm not so sure," Ayan said as she swivelled on her stool so she could face them at the side of the main tactical board. She was working on finishing a small bite of her chocolate meal replacement bar. "I just started looking through the summarized results, but it's all raw data right now, so I wonder if you'd mind telling me about the parts that alarm you most? Oh, and welcome back."

"Thank you," Frost said. He knew he had a thick accent but listening to her classic British speech style reminded him of home. A lot of people spoke with the flatter enunciation that was fairly common on the fringe, but people from his dock city had a mix of all kinds of accents, many of them were different styles of British. She seemed more confident than he remembered her before they left, as if the matter they were about to discuss was the simplest thing in her day, and considering what they just lived through, it might have been. "Like Hal was saying, he scanned Beta Bio, a research facility that didn't take too kindly to that. It was supposed to be an important research centre in British Alliance Territory, but after looking at the scan results on the way back here, it looks more like a collection of showrooms and high-end shops. That's not so bad, but what they're selling really tells the tale. Companies are showing off suits with our most advanced vacsuit features, stealth tech, the last generation side-arms, environmental recycling tech, and there's even a company selling a near exact copy of our last heavy infantry armour gear. It's a generation behind, but there's no denying that they got our design."

"I did the legwork on the Stellarnet and Hart News," Hal added as Frost nodded at him. "The news hasn't made its way here yet, in fact, most of it was stopped as it hit hyper transmitters along the edges of British Alliance Territory, but our allies here have been selling detailed scans of most of our tech. Well, most pre-War Forge tech. The only classified items that they sold from this generation of tech were some low-heat thruster systems and a primitive version of the new intelligent plating. It's ours, though," Hal said. "The British Alliance is making billions in plat by licensing or selling our tech. I mean, that's fine if you have a deal with them, right? But we didn't hear about anything, so we thought it was important."

"We don't have a deal," Lamonthe said sourly.

Ayan turned to face her tactical display. The destruction of the Edxi ships near Tamber was going so well that Frost would call it a clean-up effort if anyone asked him to describe what he saw. She brought an image of a broad-nosed trio of destroyer class ships up on a secondary holodisplay. "The new British Alliance carrier group is using our hyperspace and wormhole combo drive system. Exotic particles that we call the Advancement Matrix now surround the hull, making accelerating past the speed of light possible in normal space, then their ships enter a wormhole, decreasing their transit time. The systems they're using are perfectly balanced and safe. They're also stolen. If it were just this, I wouldn't mind, but your scan is showing us that they're stealing everything they can scan. Considering the sacrifice they made in orbit around Tamber, I don't doubt their dedication to our Alliance with them militarily, but we'll need to renegotiate everything else if they expect to finish building their base on Tamber, or stay in the system at all." Ayan looked back to Frost. It was almost intimidating to be watched so closely by those blue eyes. "What would you do if you were Defence Minister, Chief?"

The ranting and raving about the British Alliance making a mint off of technology that didn't belong to them was long past. He'd had several rants during the trek back, and the initial outrage had faded for him and Hal days before their return. It was a good thing, because his answer was absent irrational irritation. "Get paid for what they stole and give them something new so they feel good about helping us out here. That is, unless we can afford to lose them?"

"We can't," Ayan replied as she nodded her agreement with everything he said. "Ever think of running for office? I'm stepping down once the emergency is over."

Frost's short burst of laughter was almost a bark. "Oh, I'm too hot-headed for that, and with a baby on the way..."

"Stephanie is on the surface," Ayan said. "I'm sure she's eager to see you, we'll have a shuttle take you down."

"Are you sure you don't want to discuss another set of scans first?" Frost asked, looking from Lamonthe to Ayan.

"We reviewed the scans you're talking about," Lamonthe said, activating a scrambling field on his command and control unit. No one would be able to hear what he, Frost, Hal and Ayan were discussing. "The Geist Scans are classified at the highest level while we go over the data you collected. When the classification is lifted, you two will be seen as heroes for the risk you took getting that information. Until then, you won't speak to anyone about it."

"So, it'll help, then?" Hal asked in a whisper.

"Our preliminary examination has led us to believe that the installation you found may be the source of the Geist beings outside of the Sol System. It could be the most important Citadel base. It will help," Lamonthe said, then he turned to Hal. "You're going to stay in quarters here until you're fully debriefed, though, we need to pick your brain clean, Hal Rhea."

Hal glanced at Frost, then back to Lamonthe nervously. "I'm going to spend a couple days in a scanner, aren't I?"

"No, we're going to go over all the scans you took so you can give them a little more context, maybe some descriptive flair. You're going to like the quarters on base, too, so look at it as a working vacation. The Chief will be debriefed after he spends a little time on Tamber."

"Oh, good. There's some stuff in my brain that I'd rather keep to myself. I'd do a deep scan for Queen and country, but if I don't have to..."

"Don't worry, we'll be doing everything the old-fashioned way," Lamonthe said. "Unless we feel you're holding something back."

Hal started to go pale, his dismay visibly growing by the second.

Lamonthe laughed, patting him on the shoulder as he deactivated the scrambling field. "That's just a little Intelligence humour."

"Sir, the shuttle for Chief Frost is ready," a Lieutenant said as the scrambling field dissipated. "His nephew is already aboard."

"Time for your happy reunion," Lamonthe told Frost.

"Here's hoping it's better than the send-off," he replied.

THIRTY-THREE

The Third One

THE DECISION TO accept her promotion without fanfare or the presence of friends wasn't what brought on the bitter feeling that Captain Stephanie Vega silently tried to dismiss. Captain. Since she saw Haven Fleet begin to come together, she expected the rank would come with her own ship, but conditions put that aspiration on pause.

Pregnancy held her back. It was a hold-over regulation from the Freeground regulations that Haven Fleet used to build their own around. The restrictions were simple: her space travel would be severely limited while they had a safe space to house her where she could work. Even though she tried to push command to station her aboard Freeground Alpha where she could have an active role in defending Kambis and Tamber, they decided to plant her on Tamber, to represent the military there. The Rangers had the terraformed moon under control for the most part, so her territories included military bases, garrisons in cities where the Rangers needed support, and occasionally playing a role in supporting counter espionage teams. None of that could have been further from being on the bridge of a starship.

The kicker was that she wasn't due to be called up for duty, and the fleet doctor found that her pregnancy was in the high risk category, the little one was barely hanging on, and she didn't want to lose it. There was little to be done other than take her medication as prescribed, but it put her out of the fight. Stephanie wouldn't be allowed to touch a rifle, but her new rank did come with its perks. With so many members of the military spread out across the solar system, she was one of the highest-ranking people left on the ground.

There were fewer than a hundred people on staff in the military base closest to the landing site of the only Edxi Warrior Ship to make it through Tamber's shield, and she was second in command.

So, she still had to gear up in heavy armour while Commodore Elsa Naka led most of the troops in support of the Rangers and coordinated the three Clever Class corvettes from the base during their attack on the landed ship. The heavy armour felt good, but she knew anything other than normal activity would put her precious cargo at risk. They wouldn't know if the medication was helping for a few days.

The command room was empty but for a clerk who looked frazzled as he watched the tactical display. The Rangers were falling back from the close fight with the armoured Edxi drones on the ground, and the Corvettes were getting ready to launch missiles. The fight would be over soon unless another Edxi Warrior Ship forced its way down to the moon and landed, sending hundreds of drones out.

The base was under an energy shield, it was more powerful than most destroyer class starships, and they had automated defence guns that had already taken out a few heavy drones that got past the fighter squadrons assigned to protect the skies. The situation was still uncertain, even though it looked like they had the advantage, so Stephanie had no plans of leaving the base, or taking her eye off the fight, but that didn't mean that she had to stay in the command room with the clerk who was busy quaking in his boots.

She took her leave quietly, letting him watch the swarm in the distance through the window in the high command tower. It looked closer than it was, ominous as Edxi fighters flew around the Warrior Ship sticking in the ground. That was, until the Fleet figured out how they were communicating. Stephanie was switching to her remote command system, using the holoprojector on her wrist to watch the tactical status feed. The elevator was heading down towards the containment level many floors below when the news came through that the Edxi were almost completely halted, as if the frequency noise the Fleet sent them was so loud that they couldn't do anything. The Clever Class Corvettes moved in without hesitation, blasting the Edxi Warrior Ship with their main guns and a torrent of missiles. It would have been good to be on the ground, just behind the lip of the ridge nearest to the Edxi landing site to feel the shockwaves from those explosions, to experience the defeat of perhaps the most terrifying invader humans had ever known first hand.

There was another adventure waiting for her, though, one that she found more intimidating than an Edxi invasion. "I hope you'll go easy on me, little bug," she said, looking down to where she hoped her first child was beginning to thrive. An image crossed her mind then, one that she suspected may have been taken at the most opportune time, maybe even doctored, but it made her smile nonetheless. There weren't many images of Ayan with her new born, but Stephanie was struck by one in particular. Someone caught an image of Ayan lowering little Laura into her basinet. The babe was fast asleep, and Ayan looked tired but so happy. To most it was a portrait of their Queen, a strong figure with an enchanting softer side. To Stephanie it was the picture of a woman who was trying to have a family without putting her career on pause. Ayan made the decision to adopt when Jacob was away as well, and Stephanie secretly admired her for making that choice on her own. It wasn't what she expected from the woman, who sent Jake regular messages in an effort to keep the fire of a relationship she was rebuilding with him alive. For a while it looked like Ayan was still apologizing a little, even following his lead when she could. Then, she adopted on her own. It could have sent their relationship into a tail-spin, but Jacob loved the idea, and Stephanie was treated to the sight of him burping Laura once, something she thought she'd never see, and it was amazing. He cooed at little Laura, big hands holding the babe gently as a few little bounces brought the burp up. Even though she wished she recorded it, Stephanie knew she'd never forget.

Ayan was stronger than Stephanie expected, so much so that she looked up to her. Hopefully Frost would follow Jake's example. It was good that he was home, better that the Fleet finally had the upper hand on the Edxi, and she wanted him to come down and join her as soon as possible. He'd been away long enough, and she didn't let him leave on good terms. It wouldn't be all hugs and sunshine when they reunited, but Stephanie definitely wanted to make sure he knew she was happy he was back. The addition of a nephew was welcome too, even though she had no idea what to expect.

The transit car shifted from vertical to horizontal mode and arrived in the containment section of the base a few moments later. A pair of guards in heavy armour looked to her when she stepped out and saluted. She returned the gesture. "How is the Duchess today?"

"She has been staring at the swarm on the horizon using the magnification mode on the windows since it landed. Lunch has been delivered, but she hasn't touched it yet," the Sergeant replied.

"The show's almost over. Our scientists found a way to slow the Edxi down so we can take them out," Stephanie said.

Both the guards looked relieved. "So, we're going to win?" asked the Private on the far side of the door.

"How could you ever doubt?" Stephanie asked, hiding her own fading misgivings about the certainty of their victory. They opened the heavy windowed door as soon as she nodded at it. "Now that the crisis is just about over, I think it's time to talk to our visiting royal."

"Would you like us to go in with you?" asked the Sergeant.

It was his job to offer, even though he probably knew that there was no need.

"I'll be all right, thank you," Stephanie said. "Besides, anything you overheard would be classified. No need to pile secrets you don't need on you two."

The holding room was more like a nice apartment. The furnished guest quarters still had all the chairs, sofas, imitation oak table, and separate bedroom with its own furnishings. The difference was that the wall facing the hallway was transparent, as was the interior wall separating the bedroom and bathroom from the rest of the space.

The Duchess turned from the window, where the dust was settling from the first of the large explosions that rocked the Edxi Warrior ship. It was leaning precariously, one side broken open, threatening to teeter over onto its side. "Hello," she said, uncertain. It was uncanny, how much she looked like Ashley, her best friend from the days of the Samson. She even moved similarly as she turned towards Stephanie and adjusted her thin, silky robe-like dress.

Stephanie turned the holographic tactical feed off and switched it to audio so she could hear it in one ear. She wanted to know the instant things changed with the battle. There was still every chance the Edxi would rally, and if her commander was taken out of action, Stephanie would have to step in regardless of her status. It was the drawback of an undermanned military: even when you were taken off duty for the best of reasons, you could be recalled at any moment. "I'm Captain Stephanie Vega," she said to the woman who moved like Ashley, spoke with her voice, and had the full appearance of her friend.

"I suppose you're a high-ranking interrogator or some-thing?" Duchess Tammy Dermen said.

"Just a well-seasoned Void Grunt," Stephanie said with a little smile. It was a nickname from her short but eventful first service in a military organization, and it once made Ashley laugh.

The Duchess' forehead crinkled, she looked a little trou-bled. "I'm sorry, I don't know what that is."

Stephanie picked up the tall glass of orange and pineapple juice that they delivered with the Duchess' lunch and crossed the room, giving it to her. "It means I worked my way up through the marines, mostly in space."

"Oh, I'm not very familiar with the military, I'm sorry," she accepted the tall glass and took a drink.

Stephanie stared. *She even has the same lisp. It's unbeliev-able.* "Has anyone spoken to you about the preliminary results from your memory scan?" she asked, breaking her mesmerisa-tion. There were points of conversation that she could pursue for Intelligence. Normally officers from that branch would be sent, but they left the tasks open to anyone from Commander rank or higher to pursue them. It was another big problem created by understaffing.

"Yes, my therapist talked to me about it before she left. She said I'm closer to leaving this room, visiting some of the nicer parts of your world, but they were still investigating. I guess that's probably slowed down now that you're under attack."

"Things are going well," Stephanie said. Her attention was drawn back to the view by several flashes of light in the distance. Heavy munitions were striking what was left of the

Edxi Warrior ship. It toppled, falling to one side trailing thick black smoke as it did so. "The crisis is almost over."

"I didn't expect this," the Ashley-like Duchess said, shaking her head and turning away from the window again. "Lucius told me your people were filled with grand ideas, thought you were this rising force in the galaxy and had a tyrant commander who kept a girl at his side who thought she was a Queen. The message from my father said the same, and that I'd be able to go home if I got the Haven System ready to be taken over by him and the rest of our family. Everything I was told was wrong. Your Queen was nice, but even in the propaganda I was allowed to watch she was a military ruler. I haven't had to deal with Jacob Valent, the one Lucius really warned me about, and everything has been so organized since I got here. Even that terrible memory scan wasn't so bad. I didn't have to leave this place, everyone was really nice, and it took a few minutes. It didn't even hurt. I'm surprised they didn't give me a lollipop at the end." She shrugged and shook her head again. "What else did Lucius lie to me about? My minder won't tell me, maybe you will. You're a military person, maybe you can give me straight answers before you start asking me more questions?"

There was desperation in those familiar, dark eyes. Stephanie felt herself getting drawn in, her sympathy blooming for the young woman. "Well, it's true that we're not here to hurt you." The early summary of the report on her deep memory scan was surprisingly simple. The Duchess was more of a club-loving partier and royal servant than anything, practically an innocent. There were few memories of hardship, but Stephanie knew that was about to change. "Intelligence's best guess is that you were sent as a distraction. We even checked for..." Stephanie remembered how the first Lucius' flesh and blood turned into reactive compounds, how Jonas died protecting the Triton. The scans on the Duchess were clear, though. "...we checked for contaminants and dangers and didn't find anything."

"See? That just makes me more curious. What contaminants? What danger were you expecting?"

"We were afraid that Wheeler injected you with something that would eventually turn your tissues into bomb materials."

The stunned expression that brought on was genuine, it had to be. If it wasn't, the Duchess was one of the greatest actors Stephanie had ever seen. "He's done that?"

"We are sure he's capable of it," Stephanie said. "But don't worry, we made sure you're safe, clear of any problems."

"All right, then why am I still here?"

"It's the brief affair you had with Lucius Wheeler. We need to be sure you're not his agent before we start giving you freedom. He's with the Order of Eden, a part of their leadership again from what we can determine from your memories and interviews."

"He was an Admiral. He was kind to me after he found me and saved me from a stasis sleep that could have lasted forever."

"I understand, but he's done things you couldn't imagine. Not just the kind of thing you do because you're at war with someone, but twisted things, the kind of thing a psychopath would do."

"Oh," was all the Duchess said, sitting down on a round seat in the middle of the room.

"If he weren't with the Order, we still wouldn't trust him, but now that he's back in their ranks, we expect the worst. Just being near the Order of Eden taints you for us, so it'll take time, but if things continue as they are, you'll be free again."

"You hate the Order that much?"

"They brought the invasion that you just saw the very edge of here. The Edxi are their allies, and we could have been destroyed today. If a dozen of those ships landed today, we would have lost Tamber completely. This base would have been the first place to fall."

"Why would my father send me here if the Order knew they were about to be invaded? It doesn't make sense. Why should I believe any of it?"

"Because your family had children of their own while you were in stasis," Stephanie replied. There was nothing in the instructions from Intelligence about handling the Duchess that said that she should start making great revelations to her. It just slipped out, Stephanie felt like she had to make the facts of her situation clear, Stephanie was starting to feel like she wanted to protect the Duchess. "This was a bad idea," she said, turning.

"No, wait!" Tammy said, tears already streaming down her face by the time she caught Stephanie's arm. "Ever since I got here I've been getting this feeling from everyone that there's something wrong with me. It's not that I was with Lucius for a little while, I don't even think it's because your enemies sent me, that they tricked me, it's something else and no one will tell me. My family had children of their own? What does that mean? I'm the prized daughter of the Dermen Empire. Nothing can change that."

"I'm not the one to tell you," Stephanie said, gently trying to extract herself from the Duchess' grasping hands. The woman held her arm with desperation, made sure they were nose to nose. *If only she didn't beg with Ashley's eyes.*

"I'm stronger than I look," she said. "Whatever it is, I'd rather know than live in mystery and confusion."

"You were grown until you were a toddler in a Numo Life company facility," Stephanie said, giving in, hoping that she wasn't starting the Duchess down a spiral of despair. "We realized right away because you're a perfect match for someone in our fleet, my best friend. Your DNA has a scan mask so it appears to anyone with a normal scanner that you're related to the people who bought you, the Dermen royals."

"No," the Tammy Dermen breathed, fresh tears rolling down her cheeks. "This is a lie. My father is punishing me for running away. I wanted to see the fountains and gardens of Euphoria Three, to be the celebrity of the night life there for a night, and I left without permission because I knew he'd never let me go. Next thing I know there's some kind of emergency and my guardsman is putting me in stasis, telling me it's the best way for me to hide. Lucius saved me, my ship was adrift, would have been in orbit forever around the Euphoria star with me asleep under the deck plating if he hadn't come along. My father is punishing me by sending me here, and you're telling me stories, it's all mind games."

Stephanie was in awe at the amount of research it must

have taken for Wheeler to track down a lost royal, especially one that looked exactly like Ashley. When did he start planning it? How did he even find out Ashley was manufactured and not born? Those questions and more were present on her mind, but watching Ashley, no, this young Duchess cry on her arm was foremost. "I'm sorry, we'll help you sort things out. We'll help you put yourself back together, Duchess."

Her sobs redoubled as she hugged Stephanie despite the slats of armour between them. The tears were real, she'd gotten through to her, for better or worse. Stephanie almost wished that she could let her live in her fake situation a little longer if it would cushion the blow that reality brought. When the waterfalls finally subsided, she withdrew. "The woman who looks like me, your friend; is she kind? Is she a good person?"

"The best friend I've ever had, Duchess. One of the sweetest people I've ever known."

"Please, you should call me Tammy. I don't think I'll ever be a Duchess again." She slipped back to her round seat, composing herself. "You said they had children? The people who bought me?" her chin quaked, warning that there could be more tears, but she regained control.

"A boy and a girl," Stephanie said.

"Good, they deserve children, they were good parents to..." Tammy lowered her head and let the tears flow, her knee shaking.

Stephanie's audio feed confirmed that the Edxi Warrior Ship was completely destroyed and the drone clean-up was going well. The fight was over on Tamber, there wouldn't be much for her to do. She retracted the heavy outer layer of her armour so it became a jacket and boots, put her jacket on the back of a chair and sat beside Tammy, just Tammy. It felt wrong to comfort the young woman through a suit of armour, and familiar to do so through a vacsuit, something she'd done with Ashley many times over the years. Tammy leaned into her as Stephanie rubbed her back. A notification that Frost was on his way down in an armed shuttle came late. His face was already in the window, looking through the security door. It slid open and he stepped inside.

Tammy looked up, and the shocked look on his face nearly made Stephanie laugh as he said; "Bloody hell, there's another one."

THIRTY-FOUR

Late Interrogation

WHENEVER THOUGHTS STARTED to slow down in Ayan's head she started thinking about Laura, or Alice, or Jacob. Everyone seemed too far away and like they could be in danger at any moment. There would be no transmission from The Preserver, the ship many of the Officers aboard the War Forge put their young children on so they could be far, far away from the fighting.

The skeleton crew that manned the custom destroyer were waiting for a buoy to be placed at specific coordinates with a particular message, and if they never saw it, they knew to move on to another location and begin building a new colony. It wasn't a fool proof plan, but it was as close as they could get in a few days' notice.

It made Ayan nervous. The War Forge was the largest target in the galaxy for the Order of Eden, as far as she knew. All the technology they developed could be found within its hull along with fabrication systems that made their shipyards look like they were from several centuries past. Keeping the staff's children there or anywhere in the Haven System would be a mistake, but the way back to baby Laura felt uncertain.

It was that feeling and the thoughts that came with it that made Ayan want to visit the brig, where two of the most important prisoners of war were being kept. "This is really unnecessary," Leon told her as they arrived at the main security doors. "One of them has already agreed to and had a deep memory scan, the other has been talking to everyone who will listen ever since he arrived. We have mature files on both that Intelligence are still analysing."

"I know, but you never know what will shake loose under a new influence."

"Deep brain scan? I think we have everything from Clark Patterson, or whatever he is now." Leon countered quietly as they passed into the secure area. There were two guards in heavy armour beside the doors. To her right was the analysis pool. She stepped in to confirm what she suspected: there was no one inside the work space made for twenty. Everyone who worked there normally was assigned to more pressing duties either by Admiral Lamonthe or one of his subordinates. There was no one to analyse the prisoners moment-by-moment actions, but it was the right call, there were more important things to do.

"No one here, let's go have a rest in your quarters," Leon suggested tentatively.

"I'm not here to talk to someone from Intelligence," Ayan replied as she led the way out, nodded at the pair of guards in front of the main doors. "Sergeant, can you show me to Clark Patterson, please?"

"Yes, Ma'am," one of them said, following the procedures set out for someone in his position. Officers in charge of prisoners were not to salute or open their armour while they were on shift. There were a number of other things they weren't supposed to do, any of them could be a distraction that would lead to them taking their eyes off the prisoners or making them vulnerable.

The Sergeant left his partner at the door as he led Ayan and Leon down the left hallway, through another pair of thick doors then to a viewing space for Clark Patterson's cell. There was a panel of half metre-thick transparent metal between her and the captive, who was laying on the narrow bed within. There were a few flimsy displays for him to access approved news and entertainment, a seat, a small round table, and a dry toilet. The cell door was at the rear, made of more transparent metal. "We'll be on watch outside. If there is any kind of emergency, you can press this button," he pointed to a large red button beside her. "Or alert us using your command interface."

"Thank you, Sergeant," Ayan said as she watched Clark Patterson sit up slowly.

He didn't have his own face, but that of Jonas Valent, and he looked shocked. "I can't believe it's you. I sent a request, but never thought you'd actually visit."

It was eerie, watching as so many little mannerisms she forgot lend themselves to enriching the illusion that she was seeing Jonas. The report on what happened to him when he was injected with nanobots that forced his framework system to regenerate him according to whatever he subconsciously wanted to become was confusing. There was a saved file waiting in his framework system that overrode his subconscious desires. It had a flawed memory imprint ready to go that included memories from Jonas Valent and Clark Patterson. It was as if the two were meant to fight for dominance over the Beast's mind when he regenerated, and thanks to Alice's cocktail of nanobots, the framework systems were removed at the same time, so there was no way back. "Do you really have Jonas' memories? What was the point?" she asked.

"I am Jonas, you have to believe me, Ayan. I know, it's been a long time, a lot has changed, even you've changed, but I'm him. I have every feeling that tells me that I'm him," he replied, standing. "They keep asking me what I remember from before, and I keep telling them, I remember being aboard the First Light, fighting to get it home. I surrendered as part of a trade, then there was the stasis tube, and that's it."

The Intelligence file had the foil that would break the illusion quickly enough. "But you remember having a sister."

"Connie." His brow furrowed, a deep flaw in his mental narrative breaking him out of his focus on her. "She was..."

"I'm not the Ayan you knew, either," she said, calling up a picture of Isabel Fonte, the woman Clark Patterson fell in love with while they were aboard the Sunspire. Her smiling face appeared close to the glass, projected by Ayan's command and control unit.

"You are different, but I'll always remember your voice, the way you carry yourself," he said, looking at the image.

"That's Isabel. I haven't changed *that* much," Ayan said. It felt like she was torturing him, especially when he recoiled, nearly tripping over his bed. Intelligence's analysis, which was still incomplete, made it clear that this was the quickest way to get to the part of him that was still Clark Patterson, to get past the Jonas personality. "This is what the first Ayan looked like." Her first face appeared beside Isabel's. "You've always been Clark, more than anything else, I'm guessing. Even with the control that the Order tried to exert on you through their framework technology and their brainwashing, you've always been Clark."

"It's confusing," he said, shaking his head before looking back at the pair of faces. "I remember loving both of them, but..." He stared for a long time. It was difficult to watch him hover so close to despair, that familiar face from her past was creased with the effort of sorting his world out. "Did she die? Isabel is dead? They're both dead?"

"I'm afraid so," Ayan said, turning the projections off. "Do you know who you are now?"

"Clark Patterson," he breathed, dropping onto the modest chair. "Have you found Mary?"

"Mary Reed?" Ayan asked. The name summoned the image of a strong looking woman on her personal display. "Intelligence has started looking, but we haven't had any luck yet."

"Remmy? Remmy Sands?"

"He's been busy." Observing him while he took hold of himself again was like watching someone wake up after a long sleep. Remmy wouldn't be available for a while. She hoped he was resting after saving the Banta with the crew at his side.

He'd won through in record time, fighting overwhelming forces, showing grit that not even Jake expected.

Clark took the room in, looking from floor to ceiling, observing the simple fixtures. "This isn't a Freeground cell, but it feels almost like one."

"How so?" she asked, following the instructions Intelligence wrote about communicating with him. It was helpful to get him thinking about himself, his surroundings, so Clark could assert himself as the dominant personality, even if for a short while.

"I remember a Freeground cell like I was just there. It was different, this place is actually comfortable in comparison, especially the bed, but the feeling is the same, like I'll never be able to leave unless someone wants me out. Like a hundred people thought about every way you could break free, and every one of them found ways to stop you. This little box I live in has had all hope removed, like a killing jar."

"We don't want to keep you in there forever," Ayan said. "We're just trying to understand what happened when you changed from the Beast to what you are now. Then maybe we can help you be yourself again."

"Who's that? I look at you, and even though you're different, I would trade all the stars to be beside you," he said, Jonas' face pleading. It was hard to watch, Leon observed the exchange silently. "I remember the time we took for ourselves; the feeling of you in my arms comes to me in dreams, then it's Isabel, and the feeling is different, like it could end any second."

"That's a recording of Jonas' memories that was partially imprinted onto your mind fighting to suppress you. We are guessing that it's an extra measure by the Order to hide whatever you learned as the Beast."

"I told them; I don't remember anything about the Order. I remember Freeground, and the Sunspire, and I remember you," he shouted, surging to his feet. "Like we... like her and I were together yesterday! Listen, if you just call Minh-Chu here, he can vouch for who I am and... wait... we lost him, didn't we?" he shook his head hard, nearly losing his balance. "Admiral Rice, contact her, I can give you the Ident Number, and she'll tell you who I am and what my mission is. Above all else, I'm here to make new allies, trade technology, and to explore for my people."

"Ayan," Admiral Lamonthe's voice addressed in her ear, his tone low and a little sad. "He's lost. He gets like this, as if he's Jonas and his mission aboard the First Light is still ongoing. You have to leave, it's cruel."

Ayan stared at Clark Patterson for a moment, her eyes meeting a pair that were a perfect match for Jonas Valent's. "Please, just reach out to my people. They may deny I exist at first, we were supposed to operate in secret, but you'll see. I'm a Freegrounder," he pleaded.

It was too much, Ayan could see that it would be a long way back for Clark to become himself again, if that would even be possible. "I'm sorry," she said, leaving.

Admiral Lamonthe met her in the hallway. "I was curious about what might happen if you visited, maybe that overrode my better judgement. I should have warned you."

"I don't know if that would have stopped me," Ayan said. "Is Jonas really the dominant personality?"

"Decisively. The problem is that neither of the personalities are complete, and they're always competing. It's going to take weeks to go through the raw data from our deep scan, but so far, we haven't found a sign of anything left behind by the Beast. The Order made sure he would be useless the next time he had to heavily regenerate. It lines up with their tactics of leaving us something that takes resources to care for. They like to try to use our sympathy against us. It's like he's pointed directly at you and the Valents, made to mess with your heads, and he's the victim in all of it. I wouldn't wish this on the Beast, or any of my enemies."

"So, there's a treatment plan on file," Ayan said.

A crewman in a white and blue vacsuit strode into the hall and stopped. "Admiral," she said to Lamonthe before turning to Ayan. "Defence Minister; I understand you've had quite a visit. Are you going to make this a regular part of your schedule? I'm just asking because I'd like to clear time after your visits for damage control."

"No, I was trying to see if I could get to his memories as the Beast. I believed he'd have important information and I thought I might trigger something."

"I'm sure you triggered something," the woman said, pulling her short ponytail free and sighing. "I'm Doctor Krause, the unfortunate soul who has been doing damage control for Clark. He's troubled, I'm afraid you might have done some damage that might take a long time to repair."

"I'm sorry, we're in a state of emergency, any information that could help is precious," Ayan said.

"I blame the Admiral," she said, looking to Lamonthe, "Even though it'll do no good. He should have sent you to me first. I would have told you that your connection to the Jonas personality would have sent him in the wrong direction. If there are any memories from his time as the Beast, we'll get to them by rebuilding Clark's personality, not giving Jonas more reasons to come out."

"I'll check in with you if I ever want to look in on him again, then," Ayan said, feeling sheepish about the entire episode. "I don't want to be the cause of any more suffering."

"See?" she said to Lamonthe. "She understands. Clark's head isn't some repository of memories, there's a person in there who can suffer, and the more confusing his experience here gets, the worse it'll be." Doctor Krouse regarded Ayan then. "If it's all right, I'd like to visit my patient. May I have your leave, Defence Minister?" she asked using the reverence that one would reserve for a Queen, not a head of government.

"Please do, I apologize again," Ayan said.

"Oh, if you could keep the Valents away from him, and get Remmy Sands to visit, that would be great, too," the Doctor said as she moved past them into the small observation room.

Ayan waited until the door closed behind her before looking to Lamonthe. "Don't tell her, but I feel better with her on the job. She advocates for her patients well."

"That's why we requested her," Lamonthe agreed with a nod. "Now, do you think you could get Remmy here? We've stopped short of making it an order. He won't do it, especially since he's getting pretty close to Chief Billy Finn, who was nearly killed by the Beast right before we took him."

"I'll talk to Jake, tell him about this. Remmy will get here when he has time. Are you sure you haven't found anything we can use about the Order?"

"Nothing. That boy's head is a complete mess, but someone cleaned up beforehand."

"What about Pope?" Ayan asked.

"Won't consent to a deep memory scan, and lies like an expert all day long. We don't see that changing, and we've dangled every incentive we can in front of him. He's enjoying it."

"It's an emergency situation. Strap him down, scan him, you have my official permission to violate his rights," Ayan said.

"Are you sure? I guarantee the other two thirds of the Triumvirate will hold you accountable once the situation is over."

"Do it, I'll answer for it. I don't think we have much time to gather intelligence before the next wave of invaders are on our doorstep," Ayan replied. There would be an accounting, she was sure, but she'll let them remove her from the position of Defence Minister if it came to that. It was a trade she'd make over and over if it led to intelligence that could give them the upper hand over the Order when their ships arrived, and she was sure they were on their way.

"Before we resort to that, maybe you could pay him a visit. There's no warning in his file about visitors doing damage. He's a celebrity worshipper though, through and through. Maybe you could get something real out of him, or even convince him to consent to a deep scan. You're the brightest star in the solar system."

Ayan didn't like the idea of being paraded in front of Pope, but the prospect of tricking him was tempting, and she was curious. "Let's see what we can shake loose."

THIRTY-FIVE

Considering the Order of Eden

POPE WAS an enemy combatant but in their custody. The recently formed code that everyone in the Haven System abided by gave him rights, but it was still new, still malleable. If she, as the Defence Minister, broke them before they were a year old it would show everyone that the rules were made to be bent or broken. "What does Intelligence say about me interviewing him again?" she asked.

"Pope is a classic idol worshipper. He looks to people with status and fame with reverence and envy. I've wanted to approach you about interviewing him, getting him to tell us anything honest, but my people are still working on the best line of questioning. The more he lies, the easier that gets, but it's slow," Lamonthe said.

A little further down that hall there were Lorander politicians, real representatives of an organization she had barely considered since they were put there. "Do we know anything more about our newest guests?"

"The Lorander delegation?" Lamonthe asked. "They stopped talking as soon as we put them in cells. We're thinking that moving them to guest quarters and securing them there may improve their spirits, but we are keeping them here until the crisis is over. It's safer, and there are already psionic blockers in place. Quan is aboard the Excalibur, he's the only one away from the base. We're trusting him at the moment, but also managing him. He wants to transfer here so he can serve as an arbitrator between us and his people."

"Bring him over, but secure him in quarters. Is there anything I can do to help with the Lorander situation in the meantime?" Ayan asked.

"Eventually. We'll conduct interviews, get the ground work done while you figure out what information you need from them most. Give it some time, you'll find gaps in our knowledge of them and what we need to know most."

"Right now, it seems like there are nothing but gaps. Everything I know about Lorander leads to more questions, but that's nothing new," Ayan said, looking at the door that would take her to Order of Eden Commander Darius Pope. "So, any honest thing will help you and Intelligence?"

"Anything. Even when our systems start telling us that he's being honest it's only so he can hook us to get to the next lie."

"Here I go," Ayan said, passing through the secure hatch. Her command and control system switched to silent mode automatically to prevent Pope from seeing anything he wasn't authorized to.

He turned away from the flip-down sink, and immediately regarded her with a surprised smile. "Your Highness, I'm honoured." In the space of a few seconds, his yellow vacsuit and hair were straightened. "I would offer you refreshments, but the barrier between us is an unsurmountable impediment. I keep telling everyone that I pose no danger to the staff, but that doesn't seem to sway anyone."

Ayan looked at the hand that the medical team recently replaced. "I thought I'd check on you, since you came to us in pretty bad shape."

"Oh, there will be no scars, thanks to your talented people. This hand is starting to feel like my own again, too. It's as if we were never parted. That's not the real reason why you came, Ma'am."

"Then why am I here?" Leon entered, bringing her a stool, and she sat down as gracefully as she could, doing her best to be queenly.

"Perhaps I'll be executed soon, or there has been some kind of agreement with the Order for a prisoner exchange? I often dwell in optimism and pessimism at the same time, it's one of the reasons why I rose as quickly as I have."

"That is a unique talent," Ayan said. "You're not being executed, and the Order hasn't replied to my request for a parlay." Leon nodded at her, about to retreat, but she shook her head and glanced at the floor beside her.

With a nod, Leon settled in beside her and resumed his watch over the private fleet feed he had on his command and control unit. He knew what kind of news she was waiting for and would alert her if anything came up.

"I didn't realize you would want to speak to the Order. Everything I knew about your society is in opposition to ours." Pope stood as straight as he could on his side of the transparent metal barrier, his hands clasped behind his back, all his attention on her.

"I don't agree, but then, I've only read the propaganda we have on hand. There aren't many first-hand accounts from people like you, people who are successful in the Order's system. I may be one of the only people in the entire fleet who's willing to admit that I don't really understand it. That's why I'm really here, to form an understanding that doesn't come from stolen data or reports."

Pope regarded her quietly for a long moment before commenting. "It won't help. The more your people know about us, about the opportunities in the Order, the less they'll want to stay with you."

"Maybe there's something about your way of life that could help us?"

"Not even a little, the Order way is in opposition, there's no compatibility."

"Now I know I don't understand how the Order works," Ayan laughed. "When I look at it, I see that there may be a way to bring in some of the graduated systems you have in place. It would combat one of the biggest problems we've had with new recruits: where to place them in our organization and how much to trust them. I mean, your graduated system only leaves good people on the bottom for a little while before they're recognized and elevated. It seems so... automatic." Ayan knew her wording was key. There had to be enough of an understanding for him to believe she saw the literature, but enough breaks in her knowledge to make him want to correct her.

"You really don't understand anything about us," Pope said, pacing the length of his cell a few times, it didn't take long.

"Help me, then maybe I can have a better start with your people if I get a chance to negotiate."

Pope stopped, his narrow eyes focusing on her. "I always wondered how useful humility in a leader would be. That's not something you see much, it's not considered a strength where I come from."

"Everyone in Haven Fleet is encouraged to keep learning, and humility can keep us open to new lessons. We grow with every new idea, even if the paths they lead to aren't followed."

"Propaganda. No military organization can be effective while maintaining that kind of flexibility."

"We have a rigid system in place and regulations like any military organization, but we're willing to evolve," Ayan said. "I'm sure the Order has changed since you joined."

"Of course not," Pope replied. "The system was built by our founder, who spent years looking into the future, ensuring that the truly successful members would share a fate of immortality and prosperity. Lister Hampon was beyond genius, he was nearly omnipotent."

"That's why he became infected by temporal radiation and was killed," Ayan said.

"He knew it would happen! He knew it, that's why he created the Child Prophet, why he brought Eve to us. His sacrifice and the work he did while he was alive ensured that his followers would be able to achieve eternal life in this plane, and he can still see us from the Victory Machine's Temporal Stream. That's where he lives now, where he continues his work and sends his most prized followers messages from. I reached the rank of Commander, so close to him, so close to being able to hear his whispers."

It was a side of the Order she hadn't examined closely, in fact, most of what he was saying had never come up in the reports that she'd seen. She wondered if it was true. "I've never heard any of this before." It was ridiculous. She's watched people close to the Victory Machine die, of course she wanted to believe they still existed in some kind of temporal stream, but there was no evidence of that.

"You should know Hampon, that he was a miracle among us, an evolutionary leap that will lead us to perfection. How could you and your people miss it? Some of you met him. We, the Order, are fated to become immortal guardians and lords of this reality, he was the first to say it, then he was the first to prove it by making some of his followers immortal with framework technology."

"We've killed plenty of people who had framework technology," Ayan said.

"Don't push that too far, everything he's told you is the truth and some of it is new information," Lamonthe's voice said in her ear. No one else would be able to hear him thanks to the private link to her in-ear emitter.

"Of course, he grants immortality through technology, but that doesn't excuse us from interference. Your people fight us because they don't understand, most of you never will, so you stand in the way of progress, hold the universe back from its true destiny. Keep us from our ultimate fate."

"I don't understand how you get there. From a person who joins the Order to someone who can hear Hampon, who can become immortal, a custodian of the universe." There were many ways to be immortal. The stop shot she took kept her from aging for several years, and the emergency implant in her breastbone, the one everyone in Fleet was given, could restore her to life under most conditions. With continued treatment, she could live as she was for centuries without framework technology, but she followed Lamonthe's advice and didn't push it. "Can you help me? Tell me about your journey."

"Mine is simple. I was a business man, and when the Order of Eden began to warn us about a coming darkness, I paid the fee, the hundred thousand credits to become a true citizen of the Universe. I was sceptical, but followed the literature, loaning hundreds of people the money they needed to buy their way in, and that started my rise. I charged them interest as I was instructed to do, even though it seemed brutally high, but it worked, and I only got richer. The day I saw the machines turn on everyone who wasn't recognized as a citizen, I joined the Order military because I saw all the good the Order led me to do. I saved one thousand twenty-three people that day, just by loaning them money. My labours and donations showed my dedication to the Order, so I rose in rank right away. I was amazed at how I was regarded, at how many more people came to me to borrow money so they could rise too, and when I was told that one more rank up would earn me the right to put the debtors that weren't paying me back fast enough to work for me, to force them into joining the Order Military, I started working harder."

"So, the number of debtors you have is a positive in the Order?" Ayan asked.

"No, the income you bring using interest and the people you bring in under you are positives. The Order rewards recruiters like me by paying part of their debt for them, and I'm allowed to make some of them into my own servants."

"I've seen Eve recruit several people who weren't in debt to anyone. There are recruiting drives all the time and I don't hear anything about money or fees anymore," Ayan prodded.

"Oh, sure, there's that, but they depend on charm and fame. For every one of those there are a thousand of me, who have growing wealth and is willing to share it so people under him can move up, so new people can buy their way into the Order. They get a purpose, food, a system to enter their children into so they can be raised properly, prepared for the new Universe the Order is making. I gain in wealth, expand my control and rise higher, so I can help more people. Eventually my fame will equal my wealth, and I'll be able to recruit entire crowds, reap rewards from the Order for every person who joins, but for now I am rich, and my reach as a Commander is immense." His face drained of all enthusiasm, and he looked away.

Ayan didn't like what she was hearing. It sounded like a debt trap designed to drag people into the Order, but she wanted to know more. It looked like he just realized that his power and wealth were gone, so she had to push. "We already got our hands on your money, you could be wealthy again. I have that power, I can make that happen, even add a significant bonus for cooperation."

Pope looked at her, taking her in from head to toe. "You're telling the truth. You really would give me every credit I had and more."

Ayan was, but it would take months of complete cooperation, something she was sure he'd never go through with.

"What do you want to know?" His expression wasn't enthusiastic like before, but intense, even desperate.

"Why would anyone join the Order military now? Our intelligence reports that Order worlds are stable, there aren't many problems there. Other than backwaters and impoverished outer worlds, where do you get your recruits?"

"Most of our military members come from Order of Eden worlds. How can you not know this?"

"Pretend I know nothing. Most of our recruits don't come from Order worlds."

"That's because they know you'll be crushed any moment," Pope said, shaking his head. "What you don't know about your own situation astonishes me. As for your earlier question, people join the military on Order worlds because keeping yourself housed and fed is expensive. It costs about fifty-five credits, or almost fifty platinum to eat enough to stay alive and pay for a coffin sized space to sleep in where you won't get robbed or worse in the middle of the night. Most of the jobs require Order of Eden Military affiliation as well, so debt is the norm. You're allowed to borrow as much as you need, but once you reach a certain threshold - one that normally takes two to three years to meet - you are forced to work it off. A recruiter like me takes that debt on, most of which is forgiven by the Order, and I get control of whatever that debtor earns. I decide the interest rate, and how much of their income they get to keep. It's only fair, they proved they weren't industrious or smart enough to manage on their own."

Ayan was stunned. Intelligence must have known about that situation, but it never passed through her data stream. There was always too much going on in the Haven System for her to examine the Order that closely.

"You can't tell me you don't have a monetary system that excludes debt. The concept can't be new to you," Pope said, shaking his head.

"The concept isn't new," Ayan said. "We know that someone in deep debt can be resourceful, but their quality of life is much lower leading to disease, shortened life expectancy, and long-term damage caused by the stress it brings. That's why we provide life's essentials and more to our people. Our luxury credit system prevents deep debt in most cases, and since it's separate from their essential comfort, each person's productivity tends to be higher and they have time to be a part of a healthy community. They join our military because we show a need and they want to be of service."

"No wonder you're about to lose," Pope said. "When can I get my money?"

"Push, push for the deep scan right now," Lamonthe said in her ear.

"Consent to a deep memory scan. That'll go a long way to..."

"This is going to be a coin on a string," Pope accused quietly. "Just when I think I'm about to snatch it, you pull it a little further away."

"Cooperation is your only currency," Ayan said.

His brow furrowed deeply as he looked away. There were consequences to betraying the order, and it seemed like he was thinking his way through each one before her eyes.

"What if I gave you immortality?" Ayan asked. "We can implant a regenerative system that counters the aging process today. It'll even cause regeneration in an emergency. Our deep scan will include a full image of your mind, your memories, so it can recreate you if the worst were to happen."

"You're lying. You'd never do this for an enemy," Pope said, looking to her.

She met his gaze steadily. It was within her power, and her promise didn't include freedom, it never would. Being honest about her offer was easy. They could give him immortality, make sure he had all his money, but opening the door to his cage was another matter entirely. "I promise you will receive your immortality at the same time as we perform the deep memory scan."

Startled, he stepped back. "I only need to consent?"

"That's all."

"I do," he said. "If you have lied to me, and nothing comes of it, I'll still gain. I haven't been fooled in a decade, it would be refreshing to meet someone who can lie so well they can trick me."

"I'll uphold every promise, you'll see." Ayan wanted to say one more thing before leaving but held her tongue until she and Leon were through the hatch and it was closed. "If he thinks he's caught every lie anyone's told him for an entire decade, then his ego is greater than his common sense."

Lamonthe snickered, and Leon laughed aloud for a

moment before looking to her. "That's a bit pessimistic, even though his ego barely fits in that cell."

"For someone who believes the All Seeing, All Knowing Hampon the Great is living in a data stream from the Victory Machine? If he thinks he caught every lie, then I'd say he missed a big one."

"You have a point," Leon conceded with a decisive nod.

THIRTY-SIX

Back Home

EVERYTHING ABOUT SHAMUS FROST'S homecoming was unexpected. The invasion was under way and the entire solar system was teetering on the edge of disaster. When that emergency passed, he was informed that the information he and Hal collected led to the jailing of several important Lorander representatives, something he was bound by law not to speak of. That was less of a surprise, but it was followed by a very warm welcome from Stephanie, who gave him a send-off that was anything but. Then there was the third Ashley.

There were quarters assigned to her on base, after comforting her for another hour, Stephanie led him there. He sent word to his nephew, Nigel, who was saying goodbye to Della, his former sweetheart. They kept their conversation on hold until they arrived at the door, where he was waiting for them. He looked weary but greeted Stephanie with a smile anyway. "Oh, man, it's good to finally meet you," he said as he gave her a brief, but warm hug. He was a head taller than her. "Sorry, I'm a hugger, maybe a bad habit I should drop if I'm joining the military."

"It's okay," Stephanie said, she seemed delighted. "You're a lot taller than I expected though."

"I get that, I'm the tall freak in the family," Nigel said with a crooked smile.

"It's a good thing, there might be hope for your little cousin," Stephanie said, touching her belly.

Nigel's mood lightened completely, the weariness disappearing. "Oh, yeah, congratulations. You should sit down, we're standing out here while you..." he turned to the door and looked for a control panel or a button. "How do we get in?"

"The controls are hidden, this is a military base," Stephanie said, leading the way into the room as the doorway parted for her.

"How's Della?" Frost asked.

"Yeah, that was hard," Nigel replied, that weary look returning. "We've been broken up for a few days, but it's like it all came back when the shuttle from Haven Shore came down to pick her and the crew up."

"You broke up with someone on the way here? I'm sorry," Stephanie said as she took her armoured jacket off and put it on a hanger beside the door. Frost's gear was already in her quarters, a simple room with enough soft sitting space for four, a side table that lowered from the ceiling, and a bedroom with a bed that seemed almost too big for it. Everything was coloured in muted greys and blues, made with storage hidden under and in everything. Even though it was comfortable enough, it seemed like there was an expectation that whoever rested there would be moving on shortly after.

"Yeah, Della and I realized that we weren't great at talking, our thing was good because everything else was great, but we didn't agree on a lot. Doesn't help that I want to join the military and she wants to find her place on the civilian side of things. She felt pretty alone on the trip back, especially since everyone else was hot to sign up for the military too. I tried being her friend and everything, making sure she knew I really wanted her to be okay after she got here, that I really didn't want to leave her alone, but I was the wrong guy to try, I guess. Hanging out just brought back all the bad stuff that comes with breaking up for both of us. Makes me feel guilty for leaving, for getting into the military too, but I'm following through, she said she'd kick my butt if I didn't."

"You're going to have to get in line," Stephanie said. "The recruitment centres are already flooded as of a few minutes ago. Winning against the Edxi, and the warning that the Order could hit us any minute has brought on some kind of patriotic urge. It's the opposite of what Fleet was predicting. I think it's the Queen, er, Defence Minister. They needed an icon, a leader that's easy to believe in."

"I've seen her, I mean, my Uncle kept warning me that she appears in a lot of propaganda, so there's a whole lot of fluff, but after today, I'm a believer."

"You should be, I watched her on my last voyage, she's one of the hardest workers I've ever seen, and really bright."

"Yeah, he said something about that too," Nigel confirmed. "Can't wait to go to the Academy."

The conversation seemed to be headed down a long road away from anything Frost was remotely interested in. "There's going to be a delay there, probably a week or two after this crisis is over if we win. If not, then we'll make it through whatever mess we're in on our own." He crossed the room, leaving Nigel with his jaw dropped at the notion that the Haven System could lose the battle, and focused his attention on Stephanie. "I'm sorry for how I left, now it's all about you, love."

Stephanie blushed and accepted a long overdue embrace, squeezing back with surprising warmth. "I hate how we left things. I didn't realize how much I'd miss you, I'm not used to missing anyone, not like that."

"Not even Ramirez?" Frost asked, teasing.

"Just because I said his name in my sleep once," Stephanie laughed as she cupped his cheek, pinching a little. "Totally different."

"Ooh, who's Ramirez?" Nigel asked, excited at the prospect of a little dirt. Gossip seeking was one of the few traits he shared with Della.

"A former ship-mate she got on with well, really well. Good man, if I'm being honest," Frost said.

"You and he were..." Nigel said to Stephanie expectantly.

"Not really," Stephanie replied. "We lost him aboard the Triton. He was a friend."

"Oh, I'm sorry," Nigel said. "A lot of that going around."

"I wish it was at an end," Stephanie agreed.

Mentioning Ramirez as a light-hearted anecdote about

names she mentioned in her sleep was a misstep, Frost realized as the conversation took a much more serious tone. "How
are you feeling?" he asked.

"I feel like I'm getting tired of everyone asking me that,"
Stephanie said with a tight-lipped smile. "The medical
monitor says the little one's still in danger, but the meds are
working, so the situation is getting better. It happens, most of
the time everything works out fine. No gymnastics for me for
a while, though."

"I'd think that was a given," Frost said, wondering if the
stress he caused with his departure could be the cause of the
risk. He guided her to the sofa, her surprised eyes locked with
his as she sat down.

"I'm not made of glass, either," Stephanie protested with a
chuckle. "I'm on light duty while the base commander is away,
that's enough of a rest, even the supervising doctor agrees."

"I just thought you'd want to kick your feet up now that
you have the chance, who knows what'll happen next. After
seeing a third Ashley, anything's possible," Frost said, settling
in beside her.

Nigel took the cue and made himself at home in an
armchair, opening his last meal bar. It was a disgusting flavour
he loved - Lemon Banana Burst - both sour and flavourful. It
was also very, very yellow. "Yeah, I only met one Ashley, but
she seemed awesome. Wish I got to hang with her for a while,
but she decided to join Spin's crew instead."

"What was she like?" Stephanie asked.

Frost answered as Nigel chewed a gooey bite. "Big into
finding her own independence, but who could blame her. She
reminded me a lot of our Ashley, even had the same lisp.

Exactly the same. Had that swagger, too, like she knew she was attracting eyes."

"You can say that again," Nigel added, struggling to speak around a chewy bite before Stephanie regarded him with a raised eyebrow. "I mean, she seemed confident, in that way, you know..." he trailed off.

Frost laughed, Stephanie was a moment behind. "I'm teasing, I know, I was Ash's best friend on the Samson, still really close now."

"Well, she was smart like Ashley is, too. More serious, but then she spent her life trapped in a few rooms, aware that there were about thirty other Ashley's that got to live in the universe. She doesn't want to meet a single one, though, unlike a lot of her people. These people, the ones who were made there, they seem to feel like it's like meeting siblings when they meet copies. From what I heard on the trip back, a lot of them look forward to meeting their... copies."

"Better word than 'models' or 'duplicate dolls,'" Nigel agreed.

"I guess the biggest difference with the Ashley that we found out there was that she was more serious minded, then I didn't get to see the sunnier side of her personality, since our longest conversation was about me keeping our Ashley away from her. There's something else, too," Frost muttered. "These people can't have children, most of them can't even age past a certain year."

"What? So, Ashley could drop dead once she hits some kind of expiration date?" Stephanie asked.

"The Ashley I met out there said that her type didn't have the expiration date, there were a lot of differences in her...

model, but there definitely can't be any children until they take this cure I happened to get my hands on," Frost said, pulling up the formulation on his command and control unit. The holographic display showed all the information needed to formulate it. "Thought our docs could check it out first, but there are a lot of cured people already between Spin's crew, the people she saved and the ones on my ship."

"Well, Spin got the cure, but yeah, we brought it back here," Nigel added. "I'm gonna miss her."

"So, we've gotta get this to Ashley, she's wanted kids since I've known her. There's a pile of plushies in our bedroom in Haven Shore that she keeps adding to. Her and Minh almost had a crib delivered, but I caught them in time, told them it was too soon." Stephanie stopped for a moment, looking worried. "I hope she doesn't find out about her duplicates the wrong way. Someone has to get word to her."

"I sent everything I know to the Captain. He's the closest thing she has to a dad."

"Everything?" Nigel asked. "But the first Ashley didn't want you to tell this one about her, right? I mean, I wasn't there, but from what you were saying..."

"Yes, she wanted me to keep her a secret, even see if I could make sure that our Ashley never found out she was a doll, sneak this cure to her somehow. I gave her my word, aye, but do I think any of that's right? Our Ash has been through a lot, and she's sturdier, smarter than most people think. I don't think it's up to me, keeping everything I learned from her to myself. If she's going to find out that she's got sisters, then she should have the whole story. I'll put it all in her hands through the only one I trust to deliver the news, the Captain she's known for years. Who am I to decide whether she gets to know where she comes from? Some wharf rat from the edge of the core?"

"I get it, I'm just glad I'm not in her shoes. Man, things get complicated when you realize you've got thirty-four twins," Nigel said with a sigh. "Wait, it's not twins after two, right? There's gotta be a word for that many, well maybe not. Maybe the Ashleys could make one up?"

"I'm just glad we don't have a bunch of Klines running around," Shamus chuckled.

"Klines?" Stephanie asked.

"Oh, aye. There was this other one who wanted to sign up for the Fleet, and he almost made the trip, too, but he took the psychological test right before we took off, and we had to leave him behind. Made sure there were no weapons in reach before I gave him the news, and he was standing in front of the airlock, but there was no way I was going to deliver that problem to our Fleet."

"Oh, and he didn't stay behind quietly." Nigel snickered to himself, cringing at the memory. "He took a swing at him, then it took four people to hold him back. Gave Leland, our med-tech, a black eye before he could be sedated. Spin said she'd take care of it, but I get the feeling she'll have to leave him on a star base somewhere."

"Aye, Kline was developed as a soldier then kept in a box like the first Ashley. Some kinda quality control thing they were doing. It didn't result in the right qualities for him, if you ask me," Frost said, remembering how Kline obsessed over the combat qualification simulations for the short time he was aboard the Sector Jumper.

"Oh, oh! Imagine if he went out and found all the copies of himself and they got together?" Nigel asked, excitedly amused.

"Ah, a new nightmare, just what I needed," Frost groaned. "One was a problem, a regiment of them might be a galactic cluster..." he was cut off by an alert that sounded on all their command and control units. It told him to shelter in place, since he was already at a military base, and to await further orders.

Stephanie's had more details. "The Defence Minister has sounded a general alert. Order of Eden ships have been spotted within short jump range of the Solar System."

"Where do we go?" Nigel asked, alarmed. "My thing just says to shelter in place and to follow instructions."

"Then that's what we do until we know more about what's happening out there or we hear from Captain Valent. You're with me until I find something better for you, lad, don't worry, she's the boss."

THIRTY-SEVEN

Equilibrium

The cheering in the Ranger Command Centre was deafening when the last of the Edxi ships were destroyed on Tamber. There was work ongoing in orbit, but it seemed like the invaders teeth had been pulled, and the Fleet was making quick work of them.

Carl Anderson was overjoyed at the sight. It was his first time back in command of the Rangers, a group he was instrumental in forming and one of the reasons why he easily took the position of Defence Minister. That position, Defence Minister, put too much power in front of him, and he let himself slip back into an old way of thinking that once brought him recognition but always led to ruin. The ends justified the means was the credo that could begin describing how he saw the universe when he was on that path.

It took the government to pull him down from his position as Defence Minister this time, and after a quiet ethics review, he was allowed to return to his position as the leader of the Rangers. Everything he did for years would be monitored, but he was happy he could be useful to the people of the Haven System.

The ethics review put things in perspective, it gave him a little time to think about the bridges he almost burned forever, and with the cheers of victory all around, it felt like he had found his place again. The view from the command centre, where it was built into the side of the mountain Haven city was being built on, was spectacular. The emergency shutters opened since the disaster of the Edxi invasion on Tamber was over, and he took in the expanse of blue sky and ocean.

They were high up on the cliff side, the perfect observation spot for approaching storms over the vast body of freshwater. "Perhaps you'd like to say something, Sir?" asked one of the newest members of the command staff, Sergeant Quinn Dresden. She reminded him so much of Ayan, it was difficult not to treat her differently. She was competent in her own right, from the old Tamber Militia, she served there for three years before the organization was folded into the Rangers. He turned to the staff of nine, they were all they could keep behind to coordinate the defence.

He had nothing prepared, taking command was challenging enough without having to prepare a victory speech when that outcome was all but certain. "I've always enjoyed watching better commanders share encouraging words with us during momentous occasions. I'll be the first to say that it's much less interesting when I try to do the same." To his relief, that prompted a few chuckles and several smiles. His communicator buzzed against his wrist, it was Ayan. "I'm proud of the Rangers, the team here, and of our Fleet. I know I'm coming from disgrace, so that may not mean as much as it could, but I'm happy to be amongst you again, especially now that I've seen that you, all of you, can accomplish so much without me. This is an organization that can stand on its own, and I'm happy to be a part of this team." That was enough, he had the urge to say more, but bowed a little to show that he was finished and he was happy to hear the applause. "Now, back to work. We have units out there who need to know what parts of that Edxi ship to bring back."

He slipped off to the side as his command staff returned to their duties and answered Ayan's call. "I'm sorry, I had to address the staff. We had a minor victory to celebrate. Congratulations on your major victory."

Ayan was still in her command armour, the Strategic Command Centre was behind her. "Thank you, I'm glad you were able to get your old position back. How is it?"

"It fits, and I'm lucky, there are more good people here than when I left. The merge with the Tamber Militia was a good move. Commander Sarasin will be a hard act to follow."

"We're lucky she took a position in Fleet," Ayan said. There was every possibility that Sarasin was in the room with her. "Before we get into anything else, you'll get an alert from fleet in a moment that we're watching a cloaked scout ship move into the system. It's one of the Order ships we scanned near Iora. A SOCU ship has also spotted an Order Battlegroup in short jump range. They're waiting, but they're less than a day away."

"So, the Order fleet is on their way to take advantage of
the damage the Edxi did. I'll make sure my people are ready."

"If this goes the way the simulations predicted..." Ayan
started, worry etched on her face.

"We'll hold out while you regroup. Tamber and her
people are resilient, and they don't like being tread on," Carl
reassured.

"I was hoping we could sit down when things got quiet,
but just in case that doesn't happen for a while, I want you to
know that I'd love it if you could be a grandfather to Laura. I
don't think any of the damage done is so bad that things can't
be mended."

"Thank you, you don't know how good it feels to hear
that. I have to make things up to Alice, too, that'll take time,
but I want you to have the family you deserve, so I'll do whatever it takes."

"Alice will forgive you," Ayan nodded. "It may take time,
her head is still spinning a little with everything that's going
on, but I don't think she holds grudges. I don't think she'd
waste the headspace."

"I hope not," Carl said, turning to Quinn, who was
bringing a message on her communicator up for him to see.

"I'm sorry to interrupt, but the database says you know
this person. They just sent me an encoded message," the
image of Lucius Wheeler's face appeared above Quinn's
command and control unit.

A chill ran down Carl's spine. "Do not decode that
message."

"It's self-decoding, looks like it was made to do it once it
was opened, ow!" Quinn said, trying to pull her left command

and control unit off using the emergency latch hidden under the lip. "The medical injector just put something in my arm, and I can't get my comm-con off."

Doctor Anderson scanned her and grabbed her collar at the same time, starting to lead her to the hall. "We have to get you to containment," he said, trying to sound reassuring.

"What did it inject? I feel..." Quinn dropped to the floor in convulsions.

The scan results on his command and control unit confirmed what he suspected; there was an explosive compound forming in Quinn's blood, but it was happening faster than he'd ever seen. There was no time for him to formulate a counter-agent, or to get her to the hallway. "Everyone out of the command centre! Now!" Startled faces looked up at him for what felt like minutes, but he knew it was only a couple seconds. "Go! Go! Go-"

Doctor Carl Anderson's link to the fleet terminated, Ayan stared at the blank space where her father's hologram had been blankly, stunned. A voice behind her called out to everyone in the Strategic Command Centre. "I just picked up an explosion in the Ranger Command Bunker. I need verification!"

A tear rolled down her cheek as she heard someone from the analyst pool reply; "Verified! Command was just hit. We're scanning, checking the damage."

Ayan's knees gave out and Leon caught her. "You were just talking to your father, was he there?" he asked quietly.

Ayan nodded, regaining her feet and leaning on the railing in front of her. "He was beside the..." She put her face in her shaking hands. There was no time for this, the Order was on their way. A kerchief was put between her fingers, Leon could make almost anything she wanted magically appear. Ayan wiped her tears and pushed her grief away as best as she could. "He's gone."

The room filled with analysts and commanders was silent. Captain Sarasin, recently promoted from Commander as she took her position aboard the War Forge, moved to Ayan's side. "I'm sorry, the Ranger Command Centre is destroyed, and access to the vehicle bays is obstructed. We can't find survivors."

A horrible thought occurred to Ayan as she remembered that Sarasin was responsible for bringing the Tamber Militia into the ranks of the Rangers. It took more determination than she remembered exerting to stand straight, pull her jacket down so the bottom was level, and speak clearly. "Captain Sarasin, you are relieved of duty and will be confined to the brig until we complete an investigation on this incident." She looked to the nearby armoured soldiers. "Take her into custody and transport her to the brig forthwith."

Captain Sarasin allowed herself to be led away, offering only a curt; "I understand," as a parting comment.

The entire staff was silent, some going back to work as many watched Captain Sarasin as she was quickly marched out. "It was the best call," Lamonthe offered quietly.

"Maybe you should take a minute," Leon offered, accepting the return of his damp kerchief.

Ayan looked across the silent faces in the large, round chamber. "I probably should. Let's get this fleet ready for the real invasion. The Order of Eden are coming, this is a clear sign of that."

THIRTY-EIGHT

The Final Clean Up

THE CLEVER DREAM made another pass at the massive brood ship. The rest of the Edxi fleet was either under complete control or destroyed. There was still activity, power and the signs of thousands of life forms inside the thick hull of the brood ship, and their sensors told them that many of them were armed, most likely the older type of fighter brood ships had been seen using before, when someone was able to scan one and get away. Remmy Sands' temporary ship, the Scythe, a match for the Clever Dream, was making sweeps of its own.

Coordinating with six fighters from Samurai Squadron, they harassed the ship, targeted anything that looked like a weapon or a door with their guns. They had been firing for so long that Alice wondered if she could ever get used to silence again. The fleet was deciding what to do with the brood ship, which was half open to space, no longer able to generate thrust. It hung in space, a strange companion to Freeground Alpha, which had signs of its beating on every side as well.

"Is it just me, or does everything from that brood ship look like a completely different bug?" Remmy asked over the command channel. Alice had it routed over the main audio in the small bridge.

"I'm putting a report together on it with a few other science officers. They don't seem as affected by the jamming signals we're emitting, either," Iruuk replied. "As far as the differences, there are many. The Edxi fighters and carriers we just defeated seem like a different branch on the evolutionary tree, a more vicious one. The fighters we're seeing inside that brood ship, the ones we've trapped, scan as pilots in craft, and the pilots only have one connection to their ships, they seem more like the ones Alice encountered on the hull of the Warlord. The new Edxi fighters connect to their ships in several places, even have new organs that make projectiles for their weapon systems, which seem cybernetic."

"Wow, that's a lot of explanation for a simple question," Captain Sands replied with a snicker.

"Oh, I'm sorry, I find it fascinating," Iruuk replied, examining a new result from the Clever Dream's high-powered scanners.

"No, that's cool, thanks," Remmy replied.

Alice double checked the scan results of the weapon systems on the brood ship. The heavy damage the ship sustained kept them from getting power to the guns, but something worried her. "New signs of life near the damaged power grid aboard that ship, take a look and confirm," she said, highlighting the part of the ship she was looking at.

"Oh, it definitely looks like they're trying to repair a few of their weapon systems, especially that big frickin' gun in section five," Remmy replied.

"I see a hundred eighteen drones working on the problem," Iruuk replied.

"I have your target, moving in to see if we can stop that with missiles," Ronin replied from his fighter. The six fighters supporting the Clever Class Corvettes turned and began moving towards that side of the brood ship.

"Negative, all ships break off and return to the Merciless immediately. We're finishing that thing off from here," Lieutenant Commander Looph said from Merciless Flight Control.

Alice's navigation display showed that they had new navnet instructions to land aboard the Merciless. "New flight path received."

"We're on our way," Ute added, flipping the Clever Dream end over end and thrusting towards the Merciless.

"All gunners, stand down," Alice announced over the ship communication band. "Good job everyone." The sounds of the guns thrum-thrumming stopped abruptly and she almost forgot what she was about to say. "Time for a break."

"I think I'll be seeing rapid-fire-flash in my sleep," Woone said over the ship channel.

"So, like any other night, then," Krooke teased.

"At least I'm not dreaming about you," Woone sneered.

"Oh, uh, ouch, okay," he replied, trailing off.

Alice muted the ship wide so the cockpit crew couldn't be

heard. Ute shook her head with a tsk. "I think Woone needs a little practice at playful banter. She has very aggressive responses sometimes."

"Really? I haven't really noticed," said Iruuk, who was looking through a wealth of scan data.

Alice's tactical system showed three launches from the Merciless. The heavy torpedoes passed between the Clever Dream and the Scythe before accelerating so quickly that they struck the brood ship an instant later. Three nuclear explosions went off simultaneously inside the ships open section of hull, and their next scan of the ship showed that only pieces of the shell remained. Several tug ships from Freeground Alpha started towards it, her Navnet system showed that they would be pushing the pieces towards the War Forge, which was a little over fifty thousand kilometres away, taking several ships in for repair. "Well, no prisoners today."

"They took three prisoners of that species type, actually," Theodore said. "Fleet Sciences has had a major windfall today, not to say the sacrifice in lives was worth it, but it's something, at least."

The Clever Dream slipped into the Merciless' port landing bay, Ute didn't release the controls until their landing gear touched the deck. The elevator system started lowering them into the main hangar the instant they were locked to it. "That was satisfying," Ute said, letting the controls go for the first time in hours. "You are a beautiful ship to fly, Lewis."

"Thank you, but I'm not the ship, the Clever Dream is, and yes, she's beautiful," he said happily. "I'm sure she'd thank you too."

A supply and rearming list appeared on Alice's display and she reviewed it. Iruuk looked over her shoulder and shook his head. "Classified at your level, I guess. What does it say?"

"It says we're getting ready to head out soon," Alice assumed, looking at the order to rearm her ship with replacement missiles, five special torpedoes and two mines she'd never seen the specifications of before. There was also an order for a fabrication module and heavy ingots to be installed. There wouldn't be a centimetre of empty space left on the ship if she approved the order, but she gave it the go-ahead anyway. The crew would have to be happy with their current accommodations.

"You are wanted in the hangar side briefing room, or the Rally Room as several of the crewmembers aboard the Merciless have started to call it," Theodore said. "It is not for a debriefing."

"Get out and stretch, everyone, just don't get in the deck crew's way and don't make any plans. Looks like we're going right back out," Alice said over the ship-wide communication channel.

Alice led the way off the craft, meeting Yawen as she descended the main ramp. "I'm not going with you for this briefing?"

"We're on alert, I need you with the ship," Alice replied. "Good shooting, by the way. You guys tore it up."

"The Nafalli gunners beat my guys by one, if you can believe it," she said, smiling at Knud, who was accepting a firm Nafalli hug from Noro. "They tied, I think they're bonding."

"Good, see you in a few minutes," Alice said.

"Maybe I'll stop hearing guns by then," Yawen said with a nod.

Alice only realized that Yawen was nodding at Ronin, who was standing behind her, when she turned around. "White scarf for Carnie, huh?" he asked with a wink. "You picked a good time, the Clever Dream is about to get busy for a while, from what I hear. You're going to leave Carnie behind with all that scuttlebutt."

"Sorry, maybe," Alice said. "It might have been too soon."

"Oh, I don't want details about what happened while he was on your ship," he replied, waving the thought away.

"Nothing really happened, I just..." Alice shook her head, then spotted Carnie and her heart skipped a beat.

"She said she was 'in like' with him, I suspect deeply so from the bio-readings I've picked up," Theodore explained to Ronin.

He laughed and patted Theodore on the shoulder. "See? That is exactly the right amount of detail. You should tell that to the Commodore, it'll put his mind at ease."

"Commodore Valent? I suppose that's fairly forward thinking, but you might be right," Theodore agreed.

"Just keep it to yourself for now, okay?" Alice asked Theodore, turning to Ronin. She didn't want to kill the mood, he was surprisingly jovial, but she had to say something about the battle before she had to get back on her ship and leave. "I'm sorry about the people you lost. I didn't know Sticky, but she seemed really cool."

"Thank you," he replied more soberly. "I'm sorry about Doctor Anderson. I always liked him, even when he took things a little too far."

"What?" Alice asked, her spirits sinking like a stone. Out of the corner of her eye she could see Carnie making his way to her, smiling, the white scarf around his neck. "What happened?"

Minh-Chu took her hand with no sign of his former joviality. "They're still looking through the details, but it looks like a few of Lucius Wheeler's people got in when the Rangers merged with the Tamber Militia. Fleet doesn't know how they got past the interview and scanning process, they're thinking they didn't even know they were operatives. Wheeler became friends with at least two people close to your grandfather using a fake identity before the merge was under way."

Alice's lip quivered and a tear rolled free. "What happened?"

"He hacked their command and control units, used their emergency medical system to turn their bodies into bombs," Min-Chu pressed on. "Anderson tried to get everyone to safety before the explosion, he was right beside it."

She tried to remind herself that Carl Anderson betrayed her, crossed a line that completely violated her right to privacy, but it didn't stop her from hurting at the thought of his life coming to an end. The anger surrounding her grief only made it worse, and she was starting to shake.

The good he did for her, making sure she got the cure for her framework life, making sure she was all right, and ushering her into the Academy became present in her mind. She even recalled his presence on the First Light, when she watched from Jonas Valent's wrist as he treated his injuries and did his best to help him through that first adventure.

A hand touched her shoulder gently, it was Noah, and before she knew it, Alice was weeping in his arms. He squeezed her, made her comfortable, and let her cry. It was what she needed as she began to get a grasp on the horrible thought that they'd never have the conversations that would make things all right between her and Carl Anderson. Even if the resurrection program brought him back, it wouldn't be the same. It wouldn't be her grandfather.

THIRTY-NINE

Military Grief

EVERY CAPTAIN with a quad drive received a classified message notifying them that they were being remotely updated with new communication software. Alice was stepping back from Noah Lucas when she received hers. It would have to wait, she could feel his worry. She felt like she had to show him that her tears were past for the time being, that she'd be all right, especially since she was expected, and Remmy was on the deck with the Scythe. There was a briefing to get to, one that hadn't been cancelled even though Carl Anderson had been killed.

"I'm all right, I'm sorry," Alice said, the feeling of Noah's hands gently holding her shoulders reassuring, she wanted to step back into his arms until his worry was outdone by what she felt beneath it, genuine caring.

"You sure? I'm getting called away, but I'm here as long as you need me, I'll take the slap on the wrist," Noah said.

"More than a slap on the wrist, sorry to break this up," Minh-Chu said from behind her. Alice had no idea he was still there until he spoke, her senses were tuned into Noah to the point of ignoring everything else.

When she looked at him she could feel Minh-Chu's remorse, he felt like he injured her, and she knew why. "You couldn't have known that no one told me Anderson was gone," she told him. His relief, surprise at her guessing what he was feeling, what he didn't know how to apologize for, was crystal clear in her mind. He was either easy to read, or her empathic sense was better than ever.

"I would have handled things differently if I knew," Minh-Chu said. "I apologize."

"It's all right," Alice said before turning back to Noah. There would be a time to mourn Carl Anderson, another time to spend with Noah if they were lucky, and a time to let her empathic abilities open right up, but it wasn't then, and it wasn't there on the deck of the busy hangar. She started shutting herself off, and found it easier to think, to breathe. "I have a briefing to get to and an update to read. I'm all right," she reassured Noah. "I'll see you soon."

"All right," Noah said. "Soon."

"We have a briefing of our own to get to," Minh-Chu said, leading the way to the main doors leading to the rest of the ship.

Maybe Noah was waiting for something as he hesitated to join him, his eyes searched her face, so she popped up on her toes and gave him a kiss on the cheek. Not exactly a perfect example of fleet etiquette, but it was her instinct. "Thank you," she said, aware that Remmy stopped a couple meters away, probably with the realization that he almost interrupted something personal.

"I'm on comms if you need anything," he said finally, turning away so he could catch up with Minh-Chu. A few other pilots from Samurai Wing and other squadrons were waiting for them just inside those double doors.

Remmy joined her then. His heavy armour had more scars from high temperature burns and attempted punctures than she could count. He faked a smile for a brief moment, a bad attempt, then his face fell back into a stern shape that looked how she felt. He looked older than he ought to, more serious than she'd ever seen him. She was happy to be closed off, whatever was going on in his head was severe, and she could feel her own anger starting to bubble up. "You heard," she said, a statement more than a question.

He nodded. "We have a briefing." They fell in step beside each other. "It's just us."

Alice checked the order and nodded, looking over her shoulder at Theodore, Yawen and Iruuk. "Stay close to the ship."

"Aye," Yawen replied.

Iruuk looked surprised, as if he was trying to find a way to make the situation better and she interrupted him. They'd find out about what was going on soon enough, she didn't have time to worry about how, or even where the news came from. Once she was facing forward again, walking towards a narrower set of doors with Remmy at her side, he broke his silence again. "He was a complicated man, but I always liked him. This is going to cost the Order."

It was as if Remmy was trying to stoke her anger on purpose, and she didn't mind. "They have no idea what's coming."

They were silent as they passed through the thick armoured doors, up the ramp to the second story briefing room. It overlooked the main hangar with a large window made of metre thick transparent intelligent plating. The room was one of a few surrounding the small control centre in the middle of that wall, and Alice wondered if they were all little fifteen-seater spaces. Commodore Valent, her father showing his official side, his nearly emotionless job-face entered the room at the other end, from somewhere deeper inside the ship. "I'm sorry, I wish there was time for us to do anything for Anderson. I know it doesn't help much, but the Resurrection program is looking into it. They'll know if he's a good candidate in about a week using their new precautions." He looked Remmy up and down.

"Sorry, the armour won't come off unless my crew dismantles it the hard way. Too much damage," he explained.

"You both did some incredible work today," he said.

Alice wondered why Jake was so stern, holding so much back. It was tempting to read him, but she was afraid to let her guard down so her empathic senses could start collecting everything in the room. She couldn't imagine anyone in that room was in a healthy state of mind. "Thank you," she said, standing beside Remmy. She didn't feel like sitting, especially if he couldn't, and from the look of his armour, that was the truth of it.

"I'm just glad you put me and my crew back to work after the Raven was damaged," Remmy said.

"We're working to repair her, don't worry," Jake said. He took a deep breath, looked at the command and control interface on his right arm for a moment. "I wish there was more time," he started quietly. "But we're being pressed. Before the Order made their second move today, trying to take out the command structure of the Rangers, even before the Edxi tried to take the system, the fleet had a plan in place to counter the beginning of an Order invasion. It's specifically a counter-move to Order ships arriving in the solar system, and SOCU are a huge part of it."

"Tell me we're striking back," Remmy said.

"Yes," Jake said. "Strategically. First, every captain with a quad drive just got a simple notification. I know neither of you checked it, so let me tell you what that was. Thanks to the success of your mission," he looked at Alice, "and what we discovered during our battle with the Edxi about their communications systems, ships with quad drives can communicate with each other almost instantaneously over any distance. I'll spare you the technical details, but this is the first time any human has had that capability in a mobile form. It's a huge tactical advantage, and another reason for our enemies, including the Edxi, whose tech isn't nearly as fast or reliable as ours, to want to capture one of our quad drives. We can't let that happen, you know about the safety measures in place."

Alice and Remmy both nodded. There were multiple solutions. If someone tried to break the seals on any of the technologies in a quad drive, they would melt down, reduce itself to a pile of base materials. If someone tried to hack one, even in person, the encryption was dynamic, changing every millisecond. Without the paired consoles, the quad drive was unusable. As a last resort, the quad drive system would convert into a bomb, building a charge up in milliseconds and going nuclear. The explosion generated could wipe every-thing off the surface of an entire earth sized planet. She was happy the Clever Dream's quad drives were setup so they could be ejected, just in case they were about to get caught.

"So, we're talking coordinated strikes," Alice offered.

"When possible." Jake said. "Using your quad drives, the Clever Dream and the Scythe will go far behind enemy lines, and using a new type of accumulator torpedo, you will wipe out Order of Eden installations. You will each have five of these torpedoes. The Merciless will be your new base of oper-ations, we'll be seeking out our own targets."

"Why do we need a new type of accumulator torpedo?" Remmy asked.

"It's a design the fleet has had for weeks. We didn't want to use them, they break several conventions set down by the old Galactic Courts, which have reformed, but the British tell us that they are deeply corrupt. We're disregarding the old conventions. These torpedoes have antimatter generation systems that can create half an ounce of heavy liquid anti-matter in less than a second, have scan shielding, cloaking systems that are on par with the Clever Class Corvettes, and the same shields our new Uriel fighters use. You will each receive a list of targets, will have a little discretion, and if possible, we'd like you to use the new communication system to time your strikes down to the second. We're not worried about the Order finding out that we have new communication tech, it's more important for them to see how well coordinated we are, it gives their ranks more reasons to fear us. The targets we're giving you keep civilians out of harms' way, but the intelligence is getting stale, so act according to what you see."

"Are we the only two ships on this mission?" Remmy asked.

"For now, yes. Every SOCU ship was supposed to be on this, but one hasn't come back yet, and the rest are needed to help guard the fleet while we retreat."

"Retreat?" Alice felt like her stomach did a backflip.

"The Order has sent every ship within a hundred light years in our direction. The first wave is holding position outside the solar system. We're going to buy the ships we have as much time as we can, but there is no way we can hold the system with the damage the fleet has taken. Don't worry, we'll bloody their noses on the way out, and we'll be back. Meanwhile, it's up to you two to show the Order that they can't afford to hold this system if they expect to defend their backs. The Merciless will join you, going after a third group of targets once the Fleet has set up in a new location."

"We can't!" Remmy batted a padded seat across the room. It flew to pieces against the transparent metal window. "Abandon the system? What good is all this tech, all the training? All the people who we lost if we can't hold here? The Order are just a bunch of brainwashed idiots and corporate-minded assholes with big ships! If we can't hold against them, especially here, what was the point of any of it?"

"Remmy!" Jake barked, finally crossing the room. "No one

is happy about this. There is a plan, and I'm putting you and Alice where you'll be the most effective. If you want this to be revenge, if you need to write the names of the people you lost on the side of those missiles in grease pencil before you launch them, then do it. Just do it your way; smart, direct, and strategically. Make them turn their heads, make them fear us like they should."

Remmy couldn't look at Jake, casting his eyes downward, then, finally at Alice. His expression lost its angry edge as he nodded. "Yeah, yes, Sir. I'm the right guy, you've got the right crew on this."

"Good. Go get them ready, meet the new crewmembers we're setting you up with. Don't tell them about the mission until you're out of the solar system. This is classified at the highest level."

"Aye, Commodore," Remmy saluted him, waiting for the response salute before leaving.

Jake turned to Alice after watching him leave. "I didn't want to send you on this mission," he said.

That was not what she wanted or needed to hear. He was her father in that moment, not her commander. She needed the Commodore so much more than Jake. "I'm as right for it as Remmy," she said.

"I know. There's something that keeps coming up in your profile when I review you and the Clever Dream for missions; your internal psyche profile says you have that angry nerve I do. The kind that the fleet loves because it doesn't mess with our clarity much, but it does wonders for our resolve, makes us want to make that extra leap from destructive to savage. I thought I left it behind with the framework, hoped you did too, but that's not what Fleet's deep dig into our heads says. When I heard Anderson was killed..." he turned to the window.

Alice watched as he tensed more with each step, his hands curling into fists. "I want to think long and hard about everything the Order has, then burn all the most important things they have to slag. It makes me want to grin, I can feel the side of me that enjoys the anger."

Alice knew exactly what he was talking about as she joined him. The people below seemed too calm as they went about their work. She wanted to scream at them, tell them they should be furious, that something happened that made the whole universe feel... wrong, unjust. The mission he was giving her was perfect, but he was right, she had to clear her head, she had to make the targets matter. She imagined striking bases, fleet mustering points, and other places where the Order would notice the destruction. Thinking about it was already starting to clear her head, but she was still angry, she still wanted to horrify the Order from recruits to commanders, all the way to Eve. Alice could still feel the rage beneath everything. "It's like it burns everything else away, removes distraction."

Jake turned to her, he was surprised, and, from the look, a little unhappy. "That's it. If you can't shake it, let it help you. I hope it can, especially since I have a mission for you and your best people. It has to come before this revenge trip Fleet and I are sending you on. Somehow, the Order got a Base Ship into the region, it's based on the Overlord Class Design. I wanted to take this mission myself, but they chose you instead. My hands are tied. You are going to address that threat."

"Fleet wants me to take the Base Ship out?"

"They have a plan, a good one that could save lives. No one can know about this, but it could turn the tide, make it possible to keep the solar system. As an officer, I'm telling you it's essential. As a father..."

"Save that until I've done it," Alice said, able to guess what he was going to say. It would be something like 'if you're in too much danger, or it looks like you're about to sacrifice yourself, then run,' but she didn't want to hear it. "Tell me about the mission. Fleet wouldn't send me on it if they thought it was a waste, if they thought it couldn't be done."

"This requires finesse, stealth. If you stay focused, go quickly, you might pull it off. Just make sure you keep escape in mind after. I'll send you the details."

"Good, I know my crew will be eager to do some real damage."

Jake turned back to the window. "After that you have a three-day transit to your first target. So, do what you have to. Clear your head. Don't take any unnecessary risks. When it's over, I want you back here. If Ayan has taught me anything, it's that anger may get you through some things, but it'll eat you alive when things get quiet, when there's no one to fight. You can make enemies out of friends just so you have someone to fight."

"I'll remember," she said. "I'll leave this out there."

FORTY

Breaking the News

EVERY TIME MINH-CHU walked into a briefing room, or was addressing his people, and especially when he got into the cockpit, he could close the door on the rest of his life. It was a trained ability, something he picked up as a soldier in what felt like a long past life. Compartmentalization was a gift if you could use it right, and while he definitely did, he was never proud of it.

His wing lost two pilots that day, and he was able to keep flying, perhaps even at the top of his ability, but the weight of the loss was settling on his shoulders with everything else that threatened to push him down until he sat in one of the corridors of the Merciless and gave in to the self-indulgent desire to take the grief and the blame for it all on.

If it weren't for Ashley, he didn't know how he would handle it all. She had a way of showing him what was worth a few tears and what he should let go of. It was a talent she didn't use on herself well, he caught her blaming herself for things she couldn't control more than once and repeating her own advice back to her was sometimes useful when she didn't realize it was something she'd told him before. Apart, they would be a mess. Together, they were more than the sum of a pair.

That had to hold up. He'd seen something that was astonishing, that could put her whole world on an awkward tilt, and Jake gave him the opportunity to tell her about it. There was someone who was a perfect match for her on Tamber, and Frost had met another who seemed to be a prototype? A control sample? The first? Her mother? Or just an older sister? He couldn't imagine that any of them were real duplicates of each other. For him, there was only one Ashley Lamport, the one that was in the bridge ready quarters, catching up on sleep. The one who he wanted to propose to, an archaic notion, but he desperately wanted to make the gesture and follow through with marriage if it was something she wanted. To him, Ashley was wholly unique, even one who looked and acted the same couldn't be so for him.

The ready quarters she slept in had four spacious bunks within, each one was more like a miniature bedroom, offering all the comforts needed for rest. They were across the hall from the bridge, it was one of the safest spaces on the ship. His Command and Control system told him that she was minutes away from her alarm going off, and the last one inside. She told him more than once that she preferred to be awoken by him rather than an alarm, so he quietly slipped inside.

Breaking the news could be hard, it could be jarring, it could be world-shattering to her, but Jake blocked the news that there was a Duchess on Tamber that looked exactly like her, had many of her mannerisms, for too long already. It was amazing that Ashley hadn't heard the news from a crewmate or seen something on Crewcast. She was ever-present and always aware of social news, some would say gossip, when she was off-duty. He sat down on the edge of her bunk and gently stroked her cheek.

"Still sleepin'," Ashley mumbled, she had a knack for starting to wake up before her alarm went off, especially when the ship had been on alert often. "C'mon in, waters' nice."

"Your alarm is about to go off," Minh-Chu said, rubbing her back.

Ashley grumbled and covered her head. "Warm, comfy," she groaned. "All I'm missing in here is you."

If he didn't have bad news for her, news that wouldn't wait, and the whole fleet wasn't getting ready to leave the system, he would have been out of his uniform and under the sheets in moments, but he had less than an hour before the first of the Order of Eden ships would arrive. He quietly cited regulation instead. "One to a bunk in ready quarters."

Ashley sat up and sighed. "We need a long vacation."

"I have to go soon, I have a few minutes," Minh-Chu said.

"I'm sorry about Sticky," Ashely said. "I liked her. Think they'll bring her back?"

"They'll try. It might not happen for a long time. Maybe not at all."

Ashley sat up and stared at him quietly for a moment. "We're running, aren't we?" she asked quietly, sadly.

"We're trying to put a defence together, but the evacuation plan is running as best it can. The Rangers lost their command centre, the civilian council just voted against extraordinary evacuation measures, so it's a mess. We don't think we'll be able to get many people off Tamber in time, especially with the bigger evacuation ships staying on the surface."

"How did the Rangers lose their base?" she was genuinely surprised, it was the common reaction people had when they found out.

Even Minh-Chu saw the Rangers as a permanent fixture, it was a well-formed organization from the outset, run well, and they seemed as stable as the mountain their command centre was in. "There was a bombing. Anderson is gone, along with his command staff."

"Alice lost her grandpa? I have to send her a message or talk to her before I'm called back to the bridge," she said, swinging her legs out from under the sheets.

"Wait, there's something else I need to tell you; besides, Alice is pretty busy right now," Minh-Chu said.

"I'll make the message short. She has to know she's not alone right now," Ashley said.

"Can it wait a minute? I have to tell you something before you find out on your own," Minh-Chu said, remembering how he broke the death of Alice's grandfather to her by mistake. If he knew that she didn't know he was killed before he offered his condolences, he would have gone about things differently. The least he could do was make sure Ashley heard the news he had for her properly.

Ashley looked at him, her dark eyes inspecting. "Why do you look so guilty? If you're sleeping with someone else, this isn't the time..."

"Wow, no, it's just been a really, really bad day." He took her hand and forced himself to take his time. "You're going to find out that..." he struggled to remember how Frost put it. For once, he turned a phrase in his report that was worth borrowing. "You were made, not born." That was it, the rest was for him to explain, and he was surprised that there was no hint of shock or confusion on Ashley's face yet. "Wheeler sent a Duchess to see Ayan, everything went all right, no one was hurt, but she's on Tamber now, locked up in a military base because of who sent her and, well, she looks exactly like you. Frost found another one while he was running around near the core, liberated her. His report says she was the first one they made, they kept her so they could observe her."

"I'm a copy of her, or another one of her like this bunk is the same as that bunk, made the same way in the same place."

"Yeah, so I wouldn't use the word copy, more like a..." Minh-Chu felt trapped, abnormally at a loss for words.

Those dark eyes watched him, maddeningly calm, he expected her to have some huge reaction, but he found her impossible to read, which was rare. "And that's weird, right?" Ashley asked. "You find that weird."

"Yes."

Ashley slipped off the bunk, filled the water basin then splashed water on her face. Minh didn't need to see her face to know she was on the verge of tears. The quake of her body a few moments later verified that she was in tears.

"Wait, I mean it's weird to think that there are people out there who look just like you, maybe act a bit like you, when I can't imagine how." Minh-Chu waited for her to turn around, to react, and when she didn't, he pressed on. "It's like these bunks. They're all the same on the surface, but after a while they take on their own characteristics. The sheets, the mattresses especially change depending on how they've been..." he decided to change tact, it sounded like he was trying to compare her to an old, used bed. "Never mind that, I still can't believe you even noticed me, that you and I are together. I celebrate it all the time, how could there be anyone as amazing in the whole universe? I mean..." she wasn't turning around. Her shoulders shook, he could see her eyes were squeezed shut when he leaned to look, then Minh-Chu stood up. "I know not a lot of people do it anymore, but I wanted to propose in my sister's restaurant."

Ashley regarded him then, smiling, looking over her shoulder. "You want to marry me?"

"Wow, that was supposed to be a surprise. Yes! So how could there be two people who look exactly like you? Act a bit like you? It's weird."

"They probably act exactly like me," Ashley said, turning and standing nose to nose with him, tears rolled down her cheeks. "Tell me you don't feel different, that you pro-pro-proposing isn't happening because you know things have changed. I don't want things to change, Minh, I was afraid that if this was true everyone would feel different, like I'm just a doll off the shelf. Do you really still love me? If you close your eyes, forget what I look like, think of me, is there anything left?"

Minh-Chu put his arms around her, but she kept him from holding her close, her dark eyes watching him. "How I feel about you isn't physical, well, maybe when I first saw you it was, but love doesn't come from that, not for me, not when I think of you. I never thought anyone could be so kind, amazed by things that other people take for granted, caring, and more than anything else; secretly smart. You're smarter than most of the people I've ever met, but you don't get a big head about it, you don't hold it over anyone, you help your friends instead, letting them think what they want about you, even if they're underestimating you. I know you know what I'm about to say before I say it most of the time, even when I'm trying my hardest to be interesting for you, but you look at me like there's no one else you'd rather be with, nothing else you'd rather do than talk to me, be with me, and I still can't believe it. The beauty is just a bonus, you don't need it to be amazing."

Ashley cuddled up against him and sighed. "I hope that's always true, I love you, Minh."

"It will be, I love you, Ashley." They stood together, swaying a little after a time, then Minh-Chu asked the question that weighed on his mind. "You said you saw this coming?"

Ashley leaned back so she could look him in the face, let

him wipe her tears away. "When I was little, I remember meeting another girl who looked exactly like me. Not a lot like me, but another girl with absolutely no differences. They let us play together for an afternoon, and, well, it's not all clear, but I remember her getting on a ship and never seeing her again. I kinda thought it was a dream or something, we were maybe five or six, but when I was serving on my master's yacht, making sushi, one of his visitors had two young women with him who were exactly the same as each other, not like me, but eerie identical. Same voice, said a lot of the same things at the same time, acted the same, and I heard they were dolls. I looked that up when I was allowed to get to a console and then I suspected that I must be one. By the time I was sold to Jake, and he set me free, I was sure. I'd had boyfriends when I wasn't on contraception, but never had a pregnancy scare. I'd had cuts from cooking, burns too, and when they healed there were no scars and I didn't need dermal cream or anything. Doesn't matter how much I eat, I always snap to one shape, one form. So, I bought fitness meds I never took, came up with stories about being a genetically tailored person with original DNA from Earth, and stuff like that. I was afraid that if Jake, or other people, especially Frost and Burke, found out if I was a doll, then they'd sell me. I learned I was wrong about Jake after a while, but until just a while ago I still wasn't sure about Frost."

"He wasn't supposed to tell anyone about the... he called it the Control Model... she wanted to live her own life, she didn't want her existence known to other Ashleys." Using her name like it was a model type felt strange.

"I want to see her," Ashley said. "Gosh, I wish there was

time. It's exciting, like I found out I have a bunch of sisters out there." She kissed him briefly. "As long as you still love me, and I can do me, I don't care if there are a thousand of me out there."

"There could never be a thousand of you," Minh-Chu said.

"Keep saying that," she replied with a smile that told him that she was all right, even happy. "Are we all called Ashley?"

"That's the..."

"Model name?"

"Yeah," Minh-Chu said. "There are thirty-five including the first one. Frost and his brother freed her, by the way."

"Good. I still wanna see pictures, holograms. Maybe it is weird, but I'm excited."

"That is not what I expected," Minh-Chu said with a chuckle. "The Duchess isn't taking it well. Stephanie told her."

"Oh, she didn't know. Maybe I can help," Ashley said, letting her forehead lean against his. "I'm not taking it the same way at all, though. That's gotta tell you we're not all the same, at least not all the way through."

"That I've got the one and only Ashley that matters, at least to me." Minh-Chu's alarm went off, a soft, official sounding low beep warning him that he had ten minutes to get to the punter system so he could join the rest of his pilots. "Gotta go, you okay?"

"I'm fine," Ashley said. "Good hunting."

When she said that it was different from everyone else. From her lips it meant; 'come back to me,' a pillow-talk confession she made months before.

"Love you," he said, squeezing her hand once before turning and starting the process of becoming Minh-Chu the Pilot again. The walls would go up around what they shared, and he would be able to concentrate on his job, keeping his people alive, and completing the mission in front of him.

FORTY-ONE

A Moment Before Departure

THEODORE SURPRISED ALICE, standing silently by the entrance to the hangar where preparations to the Clever Dream were being completed. A layer of armour was being added in large, intelligent hull plates to reinforce the thinner sections of the hull. Alice was fighting to put her grief in its place, a battle she was winning, but she felt more purpose driven than ever. "Everything all right?"

"I'm happy to report that the Clever Dream is nearly ready. The deck crew found a way to keep a few crew accommodations while fulfilling the requirements of our mission, I think you'll be pleased. As for everything being all right, your stress levels are extraordinarily high."

"I'll calm down, just give me time," Alice said, starting to make her way to the Clever Dream. She could feel Noah nearby, and she concentrated for a moment to quiet her empathic senses. "God, now is not a good time," she muttered under her breath.

"I'm sorry, I'm just wondering if there's anything I can do, or say, to help," Theodore said. "I know, in times like these, the instinct is to seek revenge, but there's an old expression..."

"Dig two graves," Alice finished for him, her head clearing. She hated that anger was so helpful when she wanted to shut her extra-sense down, it only highlighted how narrow that emotion was.

"Oh, that's not the expression I was going to quote, but it basically means the same thing," Theodore said. "Perhaps you should look to Directive Two, you know, if you have a chance."

"Rescue the enemies of the Order whenever possible," a friend beside Noah said with a grin. He was thickly built and friendly looking. "I think that's my favourite directive. Hard to do, though."

"I don't know if you've met him, but this is Hal," Noah introduced.

Alice did her best to smile and be friendly while she shook his hand. "Good to meet you, I've heard a couple things. Congratulations on your mission coreward."

"Everyone's a reader," Hal said, his grin diminished only slightly. "When I saw that the general report on the Sector Jumper's trip was going to be text only, I was pretty sure no one would notice it. That's nothing compared to whatever you're up to and no one's supposed to know about, though."

"We do a lot less than you think," Alice said, following

Hal's gaze to the Clever Dream. "You know, Theo gives a good tour, if you have time."

"I don't," Hal replied with a sigh. "I wish I did, but I'm back in the cockpit. There's an Uriel with my name on it."

"Hal just got a new callsign: you're looking at Traveller," Noah said. "He went on a milk run and came back with new recruits that score so high on the Qualification Board that they're classified. Oh, and he brought back intel we're not allowed to see just yet."

Alice found her interest piqued, a relief from the slowly dissipating storm in her head. "How far coreward?"

"British Alliance Territory, a bit further," Hal said. "I didn't spend much time off the ship, though. I don't think I even stretched my legs. Not that it bothered me, I used to be a long-haul freighter captain with a crew of one, so I'm pretty used to..."

"How was the attitude there? Do they know what's going on in this sector?"

"Well, not really. The British aren't exactly campaigning to free the Haven System from its suppressors. There's big anti-corporate thinking though, at least with the people I spoke to. They were mostly... exceptional types, not exactly your average citizens, but they saw trouble here with the Order, the recruitment stuff, and almost all of them were super eager to sign up."

"Are they sending you on a recruitment mission once we're out of the system?" Noah asked.

"Not exactly," Alice said, looking to Theodore, who was watching her with interest. She remembered seeing the recruitment speech her father made when she was still looking for him. It was a different time, and a slightly different cause, but her heart lightened at the thought of drawing people to Haven Fleet while she was deep behind enemy lines. *There must be places where revolutionaries and malcontents are hiding. If they join the fleet, they might have a chance at making a difference. Maybe if I show them the kind of damage we can do to the Order, I can get a few thousand to sign up. Maybe more.* "But there's always Directive Two," Alice said.

"How do we join SOCU?" Hal asked. "I love flying a fighter, but there's usually only one directive. SOCU seems to like juggling a bunch of goals at once."

"It's not quite like that, but I'll keep you in mind if anyone asks if I know a pilot with experience on a Clever Class Corvette," Alice said.

"Awesome. I've gotta go do a check on my fighter, but it was good meeting you," Hal said, already walking away. "Good hunting!"

"Good hunting," Alice called after him.

"I already did my systems check a couple times, I have a minute." Noah looked to Theodore. "Good luck, man, I'll see you when you get back."

"Good hunting," Theodore said, looking from him then to Alice. "I'll make sure everything is correctly setup on the ship."

"I just wanted to say... good hunting before things get crazy," Noah said. There wasn't much awkwardness to his well-wishing, it was as maddening as it was reassuring.

"I'm sorry about Sticky, I know you and she were friends."

"Thanks, I'm sorry about Anderson. I wish I could have

known him."

Words seemed to stick somewhere between her brain and her mouth. She didn't want to talk about her departed grandfather, not at the moment. Instead she found herself saying; "Good hunting," Alice said, and he was just about to turn away, she caught his sleeve. "This mission I'm on is dangerous, and there's another one after it that could take a long time."

Noah looked surprised for a moment, then took her hand. He was tall, she only noticed when he stepped in close. He regarded her with an expectant smile, blue eyes meeting and looking into hers. "Guess I'll have to start recording logs so you can have something to listen to. I don't see the appeal, but I hear I have one of those voices."

He was flirting? A chuckle bubbled up out of her, surprising Alice when it drifted up between them. The facts of her primary mission ran through her head, and she realized that she didn't want him to see that vengeful side of her, the destructive side. "This mission, if it goes well, you're going to see things. The Order is going to spin what I do in a way..."

"I don't believe their propaganda," Noah interrupted, squeezing her hand a little.

"Whatever they say, what I do will be at least half as bad. If I didn't have to do this for the Fleet, I wouldn't."

"You think I'll hold whatever you have to do out there, for us, against you?" Noah asked, most of the levity draining. "You know this is war, right? We're all carrying our own kind of nightmares around."

Now I wish I could just put what I'm thinking into his head, just once. Alice thought, frustrated that she wasn't getting her point across, she wasn't even sure what her point was. What did she want to tell him before they went their separate ways? He knew she had to do her duty, that she might enjoy it, and she was pretty sure that wasn't a problem with him, but there was something she wanted to express, and she didn't have the words. Then there was his hand around hers. Firm, warm, and when she looked at it, the words came. "I don't want whatever we do out there to have a thing to do with this. It's like I'm afraid it'll get... infected."

"I think we're doing pretty well so far," Noah said quietly. He shrugged his shoulders a little and an end of the white scarf she gave him slipped out from the sleeve it was tucked in. "I forgot I was in one of the busiest hangars in the ship. That's a pretty strong shield."

"How do you do that?" Alice asked, looking up from their hands and staring right into his eyes. "You knew what to say," she stopped short of turning her question into a joke about telepathy, wondering how he'd take the news that she was an empath who liked to cheat by following emotional cues. One who wanted to open all her senses so she could feel whatever he was towards her. That embrace on the beach was euphoric, he was so focused on her, so excited and caring towards her in that moment.

"I'm just lucky," Noah replied, getting closer. "Or maybe I'm starting to get you a little, maybe I'm catching up."

It was a momentary, herculean feat to stop herself from opening her mind so she could let herself feel whatever was rolling off of him, then it was over. Her senses were closed, and she could feel something she'd forgotten. The overwhelming sensations of something that was far deeper than a crush. It came with powerful reassurance that her feelings for him were genuine, not some reflection, or wave of emotion she was picking up through senses she was far from mastering. The thought that anything could infect or corrupt what she was experiencing seemed foolish, and she tugged his scarf, drawing his face, his lips closer. "You're right, you're so lucky," she said as they met softly and kissed. It was breathy, but he didn't press, their lips held to each other for a long moment before moving slowly, pressing a little more as moments passed. She wasn't sure who pulled away first, but when they parted it was with hesitation, and she found herself smiling, happy to find something well aside from the hate and anger she embraced such a short time before, something that, in itself, was purely good.

Both their command and control units were buzzing. "We've gotta go," he said.

"Hope that'll hold you over until I get back," Alice said with a crooked smile. She was playing cocky, flirtatious, when she wanted to get one last embrace and she didn't know why.

He drew her to him and she squeezed in. He either saw through her, or wanted the same thing, and two buzzes later, they let go. The light in the hangar turned red. An emergency message through the neural interface on her command unit gave her an ominous feeling, and she looked down to find the last thing she wanted to see. "They're here, an Order base ship just jumped in."

"Good hunting," he said. "My ship's in the punter."

"Good hunting," Alice said, giving his hand one last squeeze before parting completely. They froze for a moment, each looking at the other as they stood apart, then he ran to the high-speed lift, and she rushed to the Clever Dream.

FORTY-TWO

Invasion

THERE WAS an idea in Admiral Albert Tafford's mind. He paced the main dais in the centre of his base ship and indulged it for a moment. The Haven Shore propaganda that made the island settlement look so idyllic, as if no one there knew there was a war on, that they could be crushed in the centre, that even he found it enchanting.

Since his meeting with Wheeler, that image wasn't far from him when he had a moment to relax. A quick message to him asking about the propaganda revealed that most of what he saw in that Haven Shore simulation was real. Wheeler had gotten close enough, talked to enough people who had been there to know for a fact that, yes, people got along. No, there wasn't a single person working a debt off, and families lived together. His first mental slip after hearing that was to picture his own family in that place.

It was important to understand your enemy and seeing a simulation that was hosted by a basic artificial intelligence that could behave and look like different Haven Government leaders, including Ayan, for himself gave him important insight. He knew Dron had seen the same thing, and momentarily wondered what he thought of it before he considered the inhabitants of the Haven System again. They were protecting their own Utopia, and it wasn't perfect, there was always a small level of political strife, but even he knew that was just a part of a healthy government. If everyone at the top agrees on everything, nothing is being questioned, things don't evolve. The note in Wheeler's file, that he might join the Haven Fleet if he were welcome, if the Valents weren't there, started to make too much sense to him.

It only took a day from his thoughts about Haven Shore to progress from a harmless fascination to something dangerous. He knew they became something he could find himself in trouble for when he began to hope that he could keep the island intact so he could turn it into the Order of Eden capitol for the sector. It would be perfect. A trophy, a city ripe for expansion in a place that was easy to defend if you had the ships.

"Admiral, all ships have checked in, nine battlegroups are accounted for," Captain Nonen said, walking half way up the steps to his broad oval dais.

"Thank you, Captain. Begin emitting interdiction signals." He looked to the main tactical display surrounding him. Some commanders liked to sit while they were in combat, but he liked being on his feet, especially in the middle of the massive octagonal bridge, stalking around on the platform in the middle of bays and pits with officers diligently working on their department's assignments. There it was, displayed in the middle of his platform in perfect holographic clarity; the jewel of the system, Tamber. A blue, green and brown moon in orbit around the black and red smouldering world of Kambis. The materials sequestered on the surface were still burning, a thing he planned to rectify if he could when the system was theirs. Drawing his attention back to the moment, he verified what they saw when they first entered the system. There were no Haven Fleet ships in the system, according to their scanners. "How are we doing on breaking their cloaking technology? We've done this before, it should be a matter of repeating the process."

"Nothing is working, Sir," reported Captain Nonen, shaking his head. His hair, a short but ridiculous tangle remained in place, practically petrified with glistening gel. He was a good captain but indulged in vanity a bit too much for Tafford to take him as seriously as he ought to. "Should we proceed to the next stage?"

A look at the tactical map, where he could see the nine battlegroups placed carefully around the solar system told him that could be a mistake. Their arrival points guaranteed them a certain amount of cover, good vantage points for high powered scans, and positioning that was perfect for holding the Haven Fleet in place, unable to generate anything that would allow them to open wormholes, or whatever else they've been using. "We hold. Ah, there's something," he said to himself as a British Alliance Battlegroup started showing up, their heavy scanning systems and energy waves defeating their cloaking systems. "Looks like the British have come with a few upgrades." He looked at the group of seven heavy destroyers and two carriers. They were holding, waiting to launch fighters under their cloak. "We don't need Citadel's help here," he said to himself. Clearing his throat, he looked to the bridge commander, Nonen. "It's time we teach the British Alliance a lesson. Battlegroups Five and Four are to target all the British Alliance ships and make a measured strike that will eliminate their shields. Then they are to cease fire when their hulls are bare. I will open a channel and offer terms at that point."

"It will take a few moments for them to coordinate their fire, especially over the distances between them and the British ships," Captain Nonen said.

"Of course it will," Tafford replied. "Carry out my orders. Don't hesitate to verify them again or I'll put you in a fighter and send you out with a frontline squadron, I don't care what your asset holdings are."

"Yes, Admiral," the Captain replied, nodding to the communications pool, several officers who waited to act on the Admiral's orders in a group of stations in front of the oval dais. There was a culture of questioning your commanding officers once before following some instructions in the Order of Eden Fleet, and it sometimes made Tafford more irate than he'd ever admit to a subordinate. His cross stare at Captain Nonen made it clear that he was deeply displeased when the man looked up at him. The bridge commander took two steps down from the top of the dais then averted his gaze. "Confirm that the orders have been received once you've relayed them," he told the communications department.

"We don't need confirmation," Tafford said. "It'll come when those British ships no longer have shields." He looked to the lead communications officer, he didn't know her name, but she was a dark-haired woman with the rank of Commander. "Is there word from Admiral Wheeler?"

"His ship has signalled, but he is not in system yet, Sir," she replied. "Would you like me to open a channel?"

"No, he's chosen his own role in this battle, there's no need." His own role, that was an understatement. Wheeler wouldn't tell him what he'd be doing, if anything, during the taking of the Haven System. The man was a frustrating commander, secretive and sometimes strange. He made efforts to look like he didn't know what he was doing, then a plan comes to its conclusion, resulting in the death of almost everyone in command of the Rangers, the most significant surface defence on Tamber. There was no indication that Wheeler had assets there, or that his plan even pointed in that direction, but the extended Valent family was smaller, and a strategic objective was taken care of.

The British Alliance ships lit up on his tactical display, indicating that they were taking fire. It was in no way fair, watching forty-two capitol ships fire on nine who thought they were invisible to their enemies. In only a few seconds, their shields were down, their cloaking systems were rendered ineffective, and a pair of the British destroyers were lightly damaged, a heavy torpedo strike marked their hulls. The Commander at his feet nodded at him as a holographic image informed him that there was a channel open to the British Alliance fleet. "This is Admiral Tafford commanding the Order of Eden fleet in this system. I would like to offer terms to the leader of the British Alliance vessels that now find themselves without shielding."

"This is Rear Admiral Shanks," said a gentleman with no British accent at all. He appeared as a hologram in front of Tafford, his expression stony. "What are your terms?"

"The British Alliance doesn't have to lose more ships to this cause. I'm offering you the opportunity to retreat from the system. My projections tell me that it will take nineteen hours for your ships to power far enough away from the solar system to create a wormhole. If you begin your retreat in the next five minutes, then you will not be fired upon. If you don't, then we'll finish your battlegroup off."

"I'm surprised," Rear Admiral Shanks said calmly, his hologram walking around Tafford, observing him. He didn't continue his thought right away but made a whole circuit around him first. "You don't actually know what you're up against yet. I'm not even the one you should be talking to."

"We're discussing the fate of your battlegroup, Rear Admiral," Tafford said flatly. "Thousands of your people could die minutes from now, and you won't have a chance to fight back. There's no glory in this."

"No sane person fights from the bridge of a ship for glory," Shanks said. "Is that what you are? A glory hound? Is this solar system your grail? Am I a victory condition? Scare off the British Alliance fleet, leave the Haven Fleet alone before you crush them?"

"You're taunting me when you should be turning your

ships around and putting this solar system, this lost cause, behind you."

"Oh, did you think I had the authority to accept your terms?" Rear Admiral Shanks asked. "I'm not even the highest-ranking Brit in this system. I can't offer you surrender terms, either, that'll have to come from the Queen. Oh, here she is. Good luck, I hear she can be a difficult negotiator."

Ayan stood in front of him then, probably at her actual height, her hologram surprisingly pleasant. A glance at his Communications department told him that they were busy trying to track the signal. "Thank you for transporting so many Order ships to the Haven System, Admiral Tafford. We predict that you've saved us six weeks in our effort to wipe out the Order presence in this sector by making the trip."

"There is a bloodless solution to be had here, Ayan," Tafford said, ignoring her taunt.

"All right, you saved us seven weeks, I'll admit it. In all seriousness, we don't have enough space for all of your people to surrender, so Haven Fleet has come up with a compromise. If you give us the command codes for every ship in this Solar System and allow my people to assume control of your fleet, we will refrain from firing the second volley in this faceoff."

Tafford let himself smile a little, it was ridiculous, the thought of surrendering, but he did check his tactical display just to make sure there was nothing worth seeing. *There is a real possibility that there are no fighting ships left in the system. That would be the most impressive move she could make. Her Fleet could drag the fight on for years.* "I'm impressed by your bluff."

"I wonder, is your family still on Lore?" Ayan asked.

Tafford's heart skipped a beat, it was too late to obscure his reaction.

"We don't like killing civilians, but we will even the score. If you fire on Tamber, we will send someone after the nearest Paradise world, which is Lore. They'll see what you're seeing now right before an antimatter blast renders the surface of the planet unliveable. Nothing."

Captain Nonen started moving up the steps, it looked as if he was about to try to take over, to intercede somehow. Tafford shoved him down, nearly knocking him off his feet, and tried to recover his senses. "Turn the gain on every sensor we have all the way up, deploy probes, and extend secondary receivers immediately." Ayan was smiling calmly at him, relaxed, cool. "That threat just made everything worse for you and your people. Even I thought you had some sort of code, that you were honourable, now we know you're what Eve calls you; terrorists."

"You've chosen the terms of this fight, Admiral. You don't spare the innocent, plenty of people have been killed in the crossfire and the Order takes advantage of everyone it can. What's worse, you've backed us into a corner, and I'm warning you, these dogs of war have teeth like you've never seen."

"Prove it," Admiral Tafford said, immediately mentally scolding himself. It was a foolish statement that was a product of her empty threats.

Ayan looked to her right and nodded. The lights on the bridge of his Base Ship flickered, something that had never happened. Several communications stations went completely dark, holograms disappeared and backup screens froze.

Ayan's image regarded him then stuttered, fading a moment later. "What happened?"

"Our main antenna was just hit by a directed electromagnetic pulse, it must have been planetary defence scale, but we're too far out from any planetary body for anything like that to reach us," Captain Nonen reported in a rush. "Our third quarter upper shields are down."

"Get them back up, position a cruiser above that quarter until they're restored," Tafford said. They knew exactly where to strike, it was the shield closest to where he was standing. Secondary scanners were coming online, and when he looked at the updated tactical hologram as it appeared, he was surprised to see that the British Alliance ships had completely restored their shields and were beginning to move towards his Fifth Battlegroup.

"Sir, we've located the source of the beam," Captain Nonen announced. "It was mounted on an old mining station with a high-powered generator and about three hundred tons of capacitors, it's recharging."

"Destroy it, then wipe the British Alliance Battlegroup out," Tafford ordered. "We need to assume control of this engagement."

"Sir, one of our probes has detected an anomaly that suggests it passed near a cloaked ship," Captain Nonen reported.

"Fill that space with weapons' fire and analyse the data. We need to update our settings to detect their ships so we can get the advantage. If we don't end this battle quickly our losses will rise exponentially." It was not how he expected the taking of the Haven System to begin. It was messy, his enemy's technology and tactics were better than expected, and there was a slim chance that he might lose. Worst of all, his family could be at risk.

He opened a secure channel on his private communicator, tapping the interface on his wrist. Once the connection was secure, he sent the code that would signal his people to move his family off Lore. They would receive it in a few days, so if there was a risk, they would be out from under its shadow, probably with time to spare. His head began to clear and he looked to the tactical hologram around him, pleased to see that the ship they discovered was one they were yet to get good intelligence on, a twin to the Merciless. They were striking a ship named after a famous sword, the Excalibur. Breaking its hull and taking or killing the crew would be a good way to begin demoralizing the rest of Haven Fleet.

FORTY-THREE

The Sword Is Drawn

THE EXCALIBUR WASN'T the ship anyone expected to become vulnerable first, but Alice, Iruuk and Yawen cringed as Captain James Worton's ship exchanged fire with the massive Base Ship. Its turrets roared to life on their HUDs, sending thousands of antimatter enhanced rounds towards the Overlord Class monstrosity, every gun pointed at the weapons made to defend the gargantuan vessel. That unshielded section of the bulbous Order base was rendered defenceless in under fifteen seconds, the heavy cannons on that hemisphere blackened and twisted by hundreds of impacts, then the Excalibur's guns turned their focus on all the shield emitters it could reach, beam weapons sweeping the adjacent shields.

A cruiser started moving into place, covering most of the

opening in the base ship's shields with its own. "That'll slow things down," Yawen said. They were in the debarkation cabin, ready to go aboard the Clever Dream. The Fleet had one more mission for the Clever Dream before it left.

Alice suspected that there was a plan in place to take care of the Heavy Cruiser and was proven right as a series of nuclear flashes burst along its length, weakening its shields across the dorsal side of the ship. Tamber's planetary defence weapons trained on it as the ship started to rotate and let a volley loose, sending huge solid projectiles into and through the Heavy Cruiser's hull. The Excalibur finished the job. "It's going well, we might have a chance," Yawen said.

"The base ship is just a symbol," Alice said. "There are over two hundred ships in the system the Admiral could command his fleet from, and a whole arm of the Order command structure is here, spread out."

"Captain Buzz Kill, everyone," Yawen sighed. "I know you're right, I just wanted a minute where I could have a little hope."

The Merciless along with a group of corvettes and two destroyers revealed themselves, sending a set of antimatter torpedoes into an Order Battlegroup. It was a desperate act, but the shock and awe of it left many of the large enemy cruisers and carriers with their shields heavily damaged. The Merciless' group had the upper hand, but Alice didn't think it would last. The next steps in the strategy weren't hers to know, her part of the plan was coming up, and that was what the Fleet wanted her to focus on.

The Excalibur was taking damage. Five destroyers were closing in while another Order Cruiser fired at longer range, pounding the underside of the ship. "C'mon, finish taking out the shield emitters," she said under her breath.

"We could go early, trust that they'll get it done and we won't get trapped on the Untouchable," Jessen suggested.

The name made Yawen snicker. "Oh, we're going to touch it, all right."

"We have to stick to the mission. They still use bots for repairs," Alice said, agreeing with her, but the strategy they were using was set out by more people than Alice had on her crew with more collective experience than she had by far. The Excalibur's guns finished tearing the last of the emitters on the upper quarter of the base ship apart, they would have to build brand new ones on the hull to get shields back in that section. It departed at speed, their objective complete, cloaking as it left the wreckage it made behind. The Untouchable started retreating, it almost seemed like it was a huge beast recoiling. "Go, Ute," Alice said.

The Clever Dream flipped end over end and thrust towards the unprotected section of the Untouchable, weaving under the drifting hulk of the Order Cruiser. The surface of the Base Ship seemed to come up too quickly as the rear hatch lowered, then slowed at the last instant as their cloaked ship slipped into position where the outer armour was breached and a hallway was blown wide open. "God, I wish they could have sent skitters to do this," Knud said as they leapt off the end of the ramp leading off the Clever Dream. "There's a torpedo on the Merciless munitions list, it's full of skitters who do this."

"None can reliably tap into the systems of a Base Ship of this model, especially since they're using updated Sol System, or Mars software," Theodore corrected from behind Alice. "I'm afraid delivering me to an open port is the best option. As for the rest of the mission... I wouldn't trust a skitter with that. It doesn't have the processing power or programming to make such important decisions."

They used their suits' flight systems, tiny energy emitters that were spread across their armour under slats of dark metal protection. For several moments they were an invisible fleet of seven flying soldiers, then they landed in the open hallway. Alice led them in a run to the nearest heavy door the next moment, watching scans of their surroundings populate. "All right, Clever Dream, get out of there until we need a pickup," she instructed.

"Aye, getting clear," Ute replied. "Happy hacking."

An update appeared on Alice's HUD telling her that the Clever dream was being instructed to drop one of their heavy antimatter torpedoes in the middle of the Order's Third Battlegroup. It was relatively untouched, shielded from Tamber's orbital guns by a small asteroid field as it sent several wings of fighters to harass the few Haven Fleet ships that remained in orbit. Ute and Lewis confirmed that they got the orders and were on their way immediately. It would be a drop and run, the torpedo was cloaked as well, so there was an excellent chance the Order wouldn't see it coming. "Good hunting," Alice said.

The tactical map populated as her teams' scans updated, and she saw that there were live communications circuits just on the other side of the door. "Flash burn," she said, stepping back from the doorway. With a device that had a big nozzle, Knud sprayed a thick gel in a square on the thick door in front of them then stepped away. "Brace, fire in the hole!" The gel heated, turning bright orange then the entire surface exploded. To everyone's surprise, a large square had been burned through the thick metal but there was still a thin, dented layer left. "Someone rip that open. Please."

"Sorry, I thought I put enough on, the system said it was enough," Knud said as Krooke joined him in punching through the middle and peeling the metal back. A rush of air blasted them, but they remained in place, thrusters countering the force of it. Alice checked her map of the area as scans revealed more and chuckled to herself as she found there were three hallways decompressing. There were fewer emergency doors than predicted, and they were sliding into place slowly as the atmosphere and seventeen Order crewmembers were being sucked through the growing hole they were tearing open. The remaining layer of metal was thin, and within a minute their makeshift door was large enough for even the broadest of them to fit through.

ADMIRAL TAFFORD WAS WATCHING HALF a dozen strike and fade attacks made to slow the invasion of the Haven System down. The Merciless led a valiant assault against one of his Battlegroups, trying to use surprise and heavy firepower to push the ships into a position where Tamber's orbital cannons could rip at them. His commanders didn't panic, but remained in place, pounding the enemy destroyers first, taking out a corvette and two of the destroyers before the Merciless and the ships they had left retreated. Armoured shuttles, small gunships and fighters launched from the destroyers with amazing alacrity, leaving both the ships with fewer than a dozen crew. "Are these readings correct? The destroyers no longer have power?"

"The scans have been triple-checked, they are correct, Sir," the lead officer for his tactical intelligence crew reported.

He looked to the battlegroup the Merciless left behind. They'd taken minimal damage. One carrier and a cruiser had serious damage to sections of their shields, but other than that, the battlegroup was recovering quickly. It was close, if the Merciless had truly committed, they could have taken a quarter of the battlegroup out before it was destroyed, especially since their opening attack brought most of the shields down to dangerous levels. "Perhaps they're not willing to sacrifice as much as we thought." He highlighted that battlegroup and pointed it towards Tamber. "Send Battlegroup Six to this hemisphere with orders to create a gap in their orbital cannon coverage. They will tow the disabled Haven Destroyers with them and use them for cover."

"Yes, Sir," Captain Nonen said, passing the orders on.

Before the Battlegroup could get under way, a massive explosion erupted from the enemy destroyers. The cruiser next to them was gone, there was no evidence that it was ever there, and the rest of the ships were heavily damaged, scattered. "What was that?"

"It registered as a class nine anomaly, sir, a disruptive spacial anomaly," the leader of the scan crew announced hurriedly. "We're confirming."

"The Edxi have one bomb, *one*, that is capable of that! How could Haven Fleet have that kind of weapon?"

"It originated from one of the destroyers, there must have

been some kind of shielded device aboard, we didn't get clear scans of well... anything on that ship, I'm sorry sir," came the reply.

"Captain Nonen, look into this," Tafford said, but the Captain didn't move. He had a sort of constipated look on his face, as though he was loathe to report something else, something worse? "What is it?"

"We have boarders," he said. "Signs of boarders. We haven't picked up anything to confirm it on sensors, but one crewman reported that there was a torn section in one of our upper emergency doors as he passed through it during decompression. It's only suspicion at the moment, it could have been a failing pressure door, there was a lot of damage in that section."

"Have you sent response teams to that area?" Admiral Tafford asked.

"Yes, but there are no Knights available, only counter incursion troops, and it might take them a few minutes because..."

"Stop. Take care of it. I am here to command an invasion, you have an entire staff to take care of this ship. Use them. Find out what's going on and resolve the problem. I don't want to hear about boarders unless they're cutting into those doors, do you understand?" Tafford barked, pointing at the main security doors to the bridge.

"Yes, Admiral."

"Every dog can get fleas, shake them off."

.   .   .

"WE HAVE A RESPONSE TEAM INCOMING," Yawen announced, it sounded like she was smiling.

"Knights?" Jessen asked.

"Doesn't look like it," Faloo replied. They were already forming a half circle, protecting Theodore as he connected to a communications circuit. He was in full armour, there was no telling him apart from the rest of the team.

Alice took her place at the end of the half-circle and tossed a shield disc onto the deck. She wouldn't activate it until they were discovered, but they had no way of knowing for sure if their cloaking systems were working. For all they knew, the Overlord Class Base Ship's internal sensors were upgraded to the point where they could detect them. "How's it going, Theo?" she asked.

"I have an interface, just trying to access a system that isn't as secure as the rest, but I'm not having much luck. There are extra countermeasures in place, the crew must suspect that we are here. I can get past them, but it will be complicated."

"So... how long is that in minutes?"

"Five minutes. Perhaps less," Theodore replied. "Would you like to help?"

Alice chuckled, Theodore was probably working so fast that she wouldn't be able to understand what was going on. "No, I'd just slow you down."

"They're cutting through the doors, twenty-three metres away," Yawen announced, highlighting the location of the counter-incursion team on their tactical map.

Looking behind her, Alice could see what anyone who came into the hallway would: a piece of the hallway panelling that was torn aside with a cable dangling out of it. It looked suspicious. "Okay, new plan. We're going to have to be a little less quiet about this. Knud, Yawen; go set up a dozen mines in each hallway ahead of us. Theodore, hurry up, we need to get the intelligence we want and get out faster than expected."

"That will be more difficult than I thought. The systems in this section are being completely locked down. We can't get access here." Theodore said.

"Then we'll have to go further in. We knew this was a possibility," Alice said. "Stop laying mines, get the ones you put down back. We're taking the nearest elevator shaft down."

"I knew this mission would be fun," Yawen said. "I mean, it looked simple in the brief, but I had a feeling."

FORTY-FOUR

The Pattern

"THEY HAVEN'T SEEN IT YET," Admiral Lamonthe said as he returned to Ayan's side in the middle of the large Command Centre. "If our strike lands, we'll have a third of their interdiction net taken down."

"It's not big enough." For the War Forge to escape whole, they needed twice that size. The interdiction systems the Order of Eden brought to bear was twice what they needed to keep any ship from opening a wormhole or activating a hyperspace system to leave. The first piece of advice Rear Admiral Shanks shared with her was that the entire fleet should leave before the Order arrived. It was about an hour before the second phase, the human phase, of the invasion started, but they would have been able to get most of their ships out. The War Forge was the biggest problem, literally. If they wanted it out of the system, to jump it through trans-dimensional space whole, then it needed over twenty times the space to do so. It also accounted for half their firepower, so leaving the rest of the fleet behind while it left the system before the Order arrived would have doubled their casualties. Ayan decided that it was pointless to review the decisions that got the Fleet in its current situation any further. "Sometimes the way forward is to cut through and burn down. Are we in position?"

"Another three minutes," Leon replied.

"We may have to begin firing while we finish manoeuvring," Ayan said, looking at the War Forge's place on the tactical map. They were almost finished moving out of a large collection of asteroids. When the base was out from behind two gargantuan hunks of rock, they would have clear firing lines on three Battlegroups and the only arrival point the Order left open for reinforcements.

"I concur," said Admiral Hadlee. It was as though they sent her with the new battlegroup so she would look right beside Ayan. They were almost the same height, seemed to take after the same heritage with a heart shaped face and even looked the same age. Outside of appearances, a quick look at her record revealed that she was an experienced battle commander, responsible for securing several solar systems in British Alliance territory shortly after the fleet started rebuilding following the Holocaust Virus. In short, she was more experienced than Ayan when it came to large engagements. "Your team aboard the Base Ship are too important at the moment. As soon as Admiral Tafford realizes that there is a primary goal behind everything we're doing, he will focus on them with everything he has unless we provide him with a larger, more dangerous target."

Ayan was handed a thin display that reported that the munitions for their heavy launchers had been crafted. They were turreted accelerators that drew ammunition from several of the smaller manufacturing lines and attached hangars. The munitions she ordered were cloaked torpedoes the size of armoured shuttles, made to activate in two devastating phases. They had the resources, and the Order Fleet wasn't smart enough to deploy most of their ships near sensitive areas in the system, opting for manoeuvrability and clear space instead. Ayan hoped it would be their undoing. She handed the thin display back with a little smile and nod before replying to the British Alliance Admiral. "Then we start firing now, reveal our location so Tafford has a distraction."

"I don't see any other way," Lamonthe said. "The Merciless is powering to their next target, the Excalibur is rescuing the skeleton crew that got off those destroyers while they make a few quick repairs, and we doubt anything else will be dangerous enough to cause a distraction."

Ayan looked to the tactical display, a tower of holographic data in the middle of the command centre and saw that the Merciless was being joined by the Rassaaga, one of its sister ships, only this one was entirely crewed by Nafalli and Mergillians. The other ships in the same class were safely hiding behind one of the outer planets with several older Nafalli ships that were once again filled to the hatches. The older vessels were hidden by cloaking fields with most of their systems powered down, waiting to leave. The human majority of the Haven Government didn't want to evacuate, but the Nafalli knew what was coming. Many of them watched the Order run them off their home worlds as they turned them to other purposes, so when the call to evacuate went out, their new settlements were left empty. The call came late, however. The Nafalli waited until the vote on whether or not to evacuate Haven settlements finished going through, and only started transporting people when it was confirmed that the majority of Haven citizens, most of them human, wanted to stay on Tamber. It was foolish, still made Ayan grind her teeth. There were two large colony ships floating in one of Tamber's oceans, ready for nearly two million people. They were sitting there, empty, a solution that wasn't easy to put in place. She glanced back to Jake's ship, the Merciless, and the Rassaaga. They would be striking the outermost Order Battlegroup, and if they managed to disable their interdiction systems, the Nafalli would be able to get away. That would be their first victory, if you could call the poor evacuation that at all. It would draw some attention, but not as much as what she was about to order. "Tactical Defence," Ayan addressed, looking to the Rear Admiral across the holographic well from her. "Verify targets for all weapon emplacements, then launch our first heavy munitions. Hold for twenty seconds, then open fire with everything else. We are shooting our way out of the Solar System. Our secondary mission is to do enough damage for Phase Seven to be effective later."

"Aye," he replied, setting his department to frenzied work.

"It's the only way," Admiral Hadlee nodded.

"Any advice, Admiral?" Ayan asked, looking to the hologram.

"Bring out the telepaths," she replied. "And call me Paris."

Three heavy base torpedoes made it to their targets. One after the other, they blasted an Order of Eden Battlegroup with a powerful electromagnetic pulse, then exploded, unleashing an antimatter blast that each annihilated the nearest ships. It was the failure of Tafford's strategy, leaving his vessels far out, firing from a distance, thinking that would reduce their risk as they sent energy pulses in all directions to keep ships from leaving the system. When all three of their heavy torpedoes were finished with one of the outer Battle-group, two carriers, three cruisers and five destroyers were gone, barely a scrap of their hulls left and the rest were strug-gling to recover, some of them so heavily damaged that Ayan would feed them to the War Forge's recycling intake. "You mean the Lorander prisoners?"

Admiral Hadlee glanced to the damage they just did to one of the Battlegroups before looking back to Ayan. "That looks like a big win, but he's going to move his fleet to cover."

"I know," Ayan replied.

"We're testing him, so he'll begin doing the unexpected, if he's as good as his reputation. Bring a telepath or two here so they can start reading our enemies. It's in their best interest, if we fail, they'll be taken captive by people who don't put pillows and reading material in their cells, if you can call the locked quarters you've put them in cells at all."

"Lorander doesn't do that kind of thing. Reading people without their permission is highly taboo," Ayan replied.

"Then how did your father get one of them to read Alice?

He convinced Quan to read her because he proved it was in her best interest, it was for her health," Lamonthe said as he scrolled through his intelligence feed.

"See? Proof of one of the only constants I've seen in this galaxy," Admiral Hadlee said. "Lorander doesn't think with one mind, no company or culture does, though they'd like us to think they do. No philosophy holds universally across one people, there are always sub-groups and stand-outs who think differently. Just like no movement or government is all bad or good. I know you understand that, it's why you didn't order your people onto ships so you could minimize the Order's victory here. It's why we're staying just long enough to do this kind of damage to their fleet. You're hoping against the odds, betting that there will be members of the Order who are shaken by the cost of taking the Haven System. Look to a stand-out amongst the Lorander people. Is Quan one of the Lorander people you took into custody?"

"He wanted to leave Lorander days ago, something pushed him out. He's watching the public news feed in his quarters," Lamonthe answered. "I can have him here in five minutes or less."

Ayan thought for a moment. "Less." If Alice were standing beside her, she'd ask her if she could feel any evidence of Citadel in the area. She wouldn't hold back, or question the ethics of it, so what was the difference between her and Quan other than his greater abilities and less familiarity. "Give him clearance so he can see what we're seeing, who knows what insight he can bring."

The holographic tactical display was starting to tell a clear story. In a few minutes, the Merciless and the Rassaaga would be in close range with their prey, an entire Order Battlegroup. The first volley of gunfire from the War Forge would strike a few seconds ahead, increasing their odds of success, but they would probably still take a lot of damage from the Battlegroup, even if they were busy reacting to long-range fire. Elsewhere, most of the Order Battlegroups were being engaged either by the War Forge, recovering from a major strike, or fending off smaller attacks from hidden stations across the solar system. Not all of them had a great deal of firepower, but what they did have were stationary power systems that could keep their shields up and guns firing for long minutes while counterattacks tried to take them out. They were unmanned, a distraction. Even so, the whole map told a simple tale about her fleet, and how they were trying to make their escape while damaging the Order fleet as much as they could. "He's got to be able to see this by now."

"WE KNEW they would try to escape, but the appearance of the War Forge changes the strategy I started seeing a few minutes ago," Tafford said. He was startled as his Fifth Battlegroup was struck by the largest Antimatter weapon he'd ever seen.

"Admiral! The Fifth Battlegroup just... lost several ships. The Command Cruiser, Carriers, they're off scanners with a few destroyers," reported Captain Nonen, who was forcing the scanner data to refresh as he tapped his little holo-projector.

"They're gone," Tafford said. "Annihilated by what must have been a half ton of antimatter. I've never seen that kind of attack before, the weapon they used did not read at all on scanners."

"How could anyone cloak a torpedo well enough to hide that much energy? That much antimatter?"

Tafford looked at the War Forge. No one in the Order had a scan of it. The hulking base was a rival for the base ship he had. It was mostly empty, made of armoured, boxy production lines that were used as platforms for massive turrets. Its shield profile alone could encompass two of his base ship side by side, and the energy readings he was seeing showed that there were no flaws, no fluctuations that indicated soft spots. "These are builders. We are fighting engineers and scientists who are willing to invent new tools, invest real time in studying their opponents and carefully plan their actions."

"That kind of antimatter, the risks in launching that much is too high for anyone but suicidal zealots," Captain Nonen retorted.

"Not if the projectile that they launched could make antimatter on the way to its target. We know they have accumulator missiles, torpedoes, so that is the next logical step." He glanced to the Fifth Battlegroup, they were all but finished. The British Alliance ships that were engaging them from over a hundred thousand kilometres away were finishing the job, making sure there was nothing left running there. He drew back from that grisly scene, looking at the whole of the Haven System. Some of his Battlegroups were allowed to fire from a distance, left completely uncontested. He knew, aside from the War Forge, there were at least two ships worth fearing; the Merciless and the Excalibur. They were missing, cloaked perfectly. "They'll be back shortly," he said, glancing at his outermost Battlegroups. The War Forge was launching volley after volley at everything they could reach, not enough to destroy ships yet, but it was forcing most of his vessels to move, to find cover, and taxing their shields. "Turn our undamaged section towards the War Forge and order our support ships to move in front of our exposed hull," Tafford said, drawing the strategy for defending his base ship on his tactical display. "They want us to move, to face a certain direction, but any reaction we have could be what they want since their strategy isn't clear yet, so we'll make sure we have as much protection as we can. What about our boarders?"

"They are off sensors. The squads we sent to counter them found an empty hallway, Sir," Nonen replied.

"Keep searching," Tafford said. "Meanwhile, order Battle-groups Eleven through Nineteen into the system and contact Wheeler. I need reinforcements and whatever distraction he's willing to provide."

"We have full interdiction coverage, even with half our numbers," Captain Nonen said. "We don't have to risk more of the fleet."

"Do you think I'm starting a discussion with you?" Tafford hissed. "Pass the order or you will be stripped of rank."

"Yes, Admiral."

FORTY-FIVE

Going Backwards

THE SQUAD WAS on the move, running down one of the main hallways that had been abandoned because there was combat shielding in that section of the station. The power flickered, Alice's HUD showed her an unencrypted data stream for a moment, then the heavy blast doors behind them closed. The feeling of them shutting reverberated through her feet, there were at least six doors, maybe seven and that was just in the hallway they'd moved through. "It's going to take us a lot longer than we'd like to get out of here," Yawen said.

"Maybe Theo could hack in and get them open?" Knud asked.

"That's not likely. Those doors reacted to pressure differences and vacuum. We knew this was likely, but I don't have a contingency in memory for it," Theodore replied. "Is this the part of the mission where the situation has made the plan unusable and you have to start making up something new?"

Alice looked at the growing map of the station and saw a hangar with a long exit tunnel, it looked like a big creature's stomach attached to a long throat. It was for shuttles and guest ships, the mission brief told her to watch for that kind of facility. "I found our exit," she said. "Now we just have to finish the job so we can leave."

"Shouldn't we be running into a squad or three by now? I mean our cloaking is good, but is it that good?" Faloo asked.

"Maybe they think we left?" Jessen snickered.

Alice led the team down a left-hand hallway, the blast doors ahead were open. A look at her tactical map confirmed what she suspected: they were closing off the outer section, preparing to move the base ship closer to danger. Getting closer to Haven Fleet was the best way to keep them from using heavy antimatter weaponry. That thought made Alice smile a little. "I think their scanning systems were damaged when the Excalibur took their shields out. Or, they're leaving us alone for now so we can walk into a trap."

"Reassuring," Jessen muttered.

"It is. It means we haven't been scanned, they don't know what we're carrying, otherwise they'd send everything they have down on us. Can you see any data ports that will work better than the last one, Theo?" Alice asked.

"There's a bio-lab ahead, that's the most likely spot. We are getting remarkably close to the data hub, but my sensors make it clear that there is a heavy military presence there."

"We check the bio-lab," Alice said as Knud led the way in. It was abandoned. Three human sized stasis tubes were set against one wall with monitoring stations, it made her skin crawl, she remembered something she shouldn't have. It was just a flash, but there was a memory of her looking through the viscous liquid out at General David Collins. He was still one of the leaders of the Vindyne Corporation then. It was clear, the mental image of him looking at her through the glass and the suspension gel. "I have plans for you when the company finds what it's looking for!" He shouted at her through the tube.

"I found a port, it's live, I'm seeing a completely different firewall this time, it's encouraging," Theodore said, snapping her out of the recollection.

"Are you all right?" Yawen asked Alice.

Without thinking, Alice shook her head. "I shouldn't have remembered that."

"If I could give you a list of the things I wish I didn't remember, it might take all night and some real booze."

"No, I just had a memory that wasn't mine. It was Jonas, the man who programmed me. I wasn't even in the room when what I saw happened." She thought about what Collins said and repeated it to herself quietly; "When the company finds what it's looking for."

"Jonas Valent's memory?" Theodore asked. "He inhabited that tube for some time."

"Whoa, wait, I saw that documentary, they said he ended up in a place like this," Knud said, looking at the three tubes in front of him. "The addendum said he was in one, Wheeler was in another, and Eve was in the third, only she wasn't Eve then, but the woman who Wheeler gave up so he could make some kind of deal. He sold her out, her brain is in a case somewhere."

"This ship was once called the Overlord Two," Theodore said from where he was connected to a console.

"That's not possible, reports said that ship was almost two sectors away," Jessen said.

"It has been en-route here for some time, sent to replace a base ship that was badly damaged when Commodore Valent disabled the fleet with the Mary Virus. Many of the systems were refitted and it was re-named the Untouchable."

Alice looked at their route leading to the lab and realized that they didn't take the most efficient route, but one that seemed familiar. One that definitely took her to... "I've been to the docking bay we'll be using as our escape route before," she said. "I was born on this ship."

"This is *that* Overlord Two?" Knud said. "Are you all right?"

Alice shook her head. "They could have sent a carrier group with a command cruiser at its centre, it would have had the same firepower as this ship and it would have been easier. Someone's messing with us on purpose," Alice said. "Someone who knows a lot about our history, our real history."

"Okay, you're giving me the creeps," Yawen said, eyeing the room, her rifle at the ready.

"This is a trap," Alice said, checking her tactical scanner again. "It's got to be. I've been led here."

"I have gotten past a level of security and am certain no one is aware I'm working on the last layer," Theodore said. "I see no indication that soldiers are on their way here."

"I need everyone but Knud and Theodore in the hallway,

we have to guard this room until Theo's finished," Alice ordered. "Then we're getting out of here as fast as we can, and not just because we're leaving a bomb behind."

The team rushed from the room, Alice at the rear so she could take a moment to look back. "I wonder what happened to Collins?" she said to herself as she looked at the empty tubes. They seemed like relics, artefacts left behind to prove ancient history. "How long, Theo?"

"I'm already in. It wasn't easy. I am downloading the Order of Eden backup data now. It will be encrypted, but I will have it all in three minutes."

"Can you tell if Vindyne's old files are in there?"

"That is a separate set of crystalline drives. If I access it, they will notice immediately. I'm almost completely certain," Theodore said. "They also have the Aucharian and Lessur Company files in the same drive, so I could disguise your interest by downloading all of them. It would only take an extra five seconds. I still recommend against accessing any of it, however."

"So you could get Vindyne's and the other cold backup files in in seconds?"

"Five point six seconds," Theodore said.

"After you've finished getting what we've come for, take those too. We're a minute away from that hangar, I'll have the Clever Dream get ready to pick us up," Alice said.

"If you're certain," Theodore replied. "This could cause problems."

"I know," Alice replied. "It's not part of the mission, it's not rational, but there might be an answer or two in there that we want."

"I'll be as quick and sneaky as I can."

"Good, thank you," Alice said, leaving the room. Knud took a position beside the door where someone coming through wouldn't notice him until they were all the way in. She had no idea that he was so interested in her family's history, it was remarkable that he hadn't made a comment, or asked her a single question. The more she got to know him, the more she respected him.

Alice took her position beside the door, her team flanked her to either side. Callum was beside her. They watched the hall in each direction, the perfectly squared surfaces looked the same wherever she cast her gaze. It would have been so easy to turn the questions she had in her head over, to become obsessed with Jonas' story after he sacrificed himself for the First Light crew. She knew so little about his journey after that, only that he was copied, that she found him on Meunez's ship. Focusing on the task at hand was a challenge and a relief at the same time.

There was one question that loomed larger than the rest, though, and it came back often. *How do I have one of Jonas' memories?* She thought to herself at last, acknowledging that it felt as clear and as embedded as one of her own.

The door opened and Knud leaned into the hall. "Theodore says two minutes longer. Someone paused the download at the other end. We've probably been noticed."

"Can he finish?" Alice asked.

"He says yeah," Knud nodded. "He found another subsystem to go through, but two minutes."

"Everyone double check your gear," Alice said. "They're going to send their best."

. . .

TAFFORD WATCHED as The Untouchable made its way towards Tamber. The Base Ship managed to stay behind enough cover so the orbital guns couldn't get a clear shot, and the damage they took from the War Forge was minimal. Two battlegroups were converging on them, setting up in wedge formation ahead of him. The firepower he was bringing together would be enough to defend itself and to take Tamber. "We should have been aggressive from the start," he said under his breath. "They may have technology that outstrips ours, but they don't have enough of it. Every small victory they have comes with a cost, they can't keep it up."

"Yes, Admiral," Captain Nonen said.

"Have all nine wings launched? Are they reinforcing our scanning network?" he asked.

"Yes, Sir, but we're losing control over quadrant four," Nonen replied. "Several Haven ships, including the older Nafalli cruisers are about to escape the system."

"We only need to damage the War Forge enough so it can't escape, and to take Tamber before they can get evacuation ships off the ground. I would love to wipe out the entire fleet, but we'll have to settle for destroying their manufacturing capabilities. What about their Solar Forges?"

"They are not moving. A fighter flyby of Solar Forge Two has given us enough data to assume that they're abandoned. We got a partial scan, the plating isn't as sophisticated on that station."

"Send an advanced boarding team..."

"Sir!" Nonen interrupted. "Internal Security reports that

they have detected an unauthorized download. It's our strategic database, someone is downloading the entire encrypted backup. We stopped the download for now, but we expect they'll try again."

"Probably from a tertiary subsystem," Tafford said. "Did they find the terminal they're downloading to?"

"They bypassed the terminal, tapped in behind it to eliminate a layer of security. It's in one of the older labs, used to belong to General Collins."

"Send them there," Tafford said.

"Send who?"

"Send everyone there. Everyone in that section that can hold a weapon, especially the Knights. There must be a squad in our main data storage."

"Yes, but that would leave..."

"Do it, now," Tafford said, turning around. "Capture them. Don't damage the base if you can help it but saturate the area around them. If they get away we'll have to have a serious discussion about your future."

"I understand, Admiral, we'll have them in our interrogation rooms before you've set foot on Haven Shore."

FORTY-SIX

Circles

ALICE'S tactical display was alight with incoming troops. They were gathering around the corners of each end of the broad hallway. Movement was detected on decks above and below, and there were signs that Order Knights were coming, their scans showing intermittently as they tried to cloak themselves like her team. Their tech was inferior, but it was good enough for them to disappear every few seconds then reappear somewhere else.

There was something nagging at her, like a dream that was slipping away as she tried to recall the details. Her people were trapping the hallway to their left and right, dropping hidden antipersonnel mines the size of her palm, a few even smaller shield emitters that would go off an instant before the bombs, protecting her squad. The memory that was just beyond her reach seemed important, it seemed almost like a message, and she closed her eyes.

A feeling, a clearly defined emotion that she recognized as the betrayal an emotional artificial intelligence could feel filled her for a moment. Jonas set her free aboard the Overlord Two, but moments afterwards it felt like he abandoned her. He was taken captive, she had a new directive, sabotage, and it wouldn't lead back to him. It took her milliseconds to realize that she was going to be left on that ship. Then she got to work, looking through the Overlord's systems, finding vulnerabilities that she could manipulate without being discovered.

The ship was easy to understand, decks, systems, maintenance spaces and purpose-built sections were so clearly set up and easy to access. Her artificial intelligence self set to grim, angry work, knowing that she probably wouldn't find her way back to Jonas once he was free, but she would free him anyway. He created her, and whether it was by design or a lucky condition, he loved her like a sister, or a daughter. The feeling of love for an artificial intelligence was binary, difficult to equate to how a human felt it in their very analogue way. It was superior, leaving no room for questions, either complete love or none. The ship was a different creature from the inside, easy to understand, easier to travel through. Vindyne had built a vessel that was a collection of pathways, each of them leading to options, functions and most importantly, opportunities. The map of it all was simple if you understood that.

Fading. Those memories that made Alice's consciousness feel uneasy, almost wrong, were going away. It was the existence of her first self, brought back by the unexpected familiar surroundings. It had a gift for her, one last piece of knowledge to impart before the memories would forever change. The feeling, the particularly unique sensation of remembering what it felt like to be an artificial intelligence, was almost gone forever. The theory of this was clear, it was written down by someone she never met, read by her more than once, and understood clearly. As she recalled those binary thoughts and experiences, they became human, analogue, rewritten to her brain as though she went through it all as a human. The sensation of being an artificial intelligence would be gone, and she was going through a lot of those memories as that last gift was written to her mind. "Alice!" Yawen was yelling at her as though she was trying to wake her up. "Theodore is almost finished, he says nine seconds."

"Good," Alice said, eyes snapping open and focusing on her tactical map. With a few glances, she turned the map on a forty-five-degree angle so she could see the halls ahead vertically and horizontally at the same time and the gift from her first self, the one that set Jonas Valent free from the Overlord Two years before, became fully apparent. She could remember the rest of the ship. What existed in maintenance shafts, where there were unexpected voids in the bulkheads, and how to get to the command deck. "I can stop this," she said as much to herself as to Yawen as she took to her feet.

"They're almost here, rushing us from both sides," Yawen said.

"The Order Troops," Alice nodded, remembering the situation they were in. "Start recording. We need a record of what happens to them when the first wave is sacrificed. Put your

holographic helmet displays on. We need to use fear here."
She activated hers and knew that anyone who looked at her
helmet would see a gore covered skull with dark pits for eyes.
Yawen's style was subtler - glowing yellow eyes that peered at
her enemies as though her face was obscured by shadow.

"Are you changing the plan? We have to get out of here,
and we have a fight on our hands already," Yawen asked.

All eyes were on her as Alice stepped into the middle of
the hallway. "We can stop the invasion. We have the firepower, and now I know where to go. Start charging the accumulator bomb."

"Early?" Jessen asked. "If the shielding isn't as good as we
think it is, our cloaking won't be worth anything."

"That's all right. We'll want them to see us coming." Alice
turned to Krooke. "You have those shaped charges? The
diggers?"

"Always, Faloo's carrying three, I've got eight."

"I'll need them. Lewis," she addressed, opening a channel
to the Clever Dream. "Get ready to catch us when we leave."

"I thought we were going in through a secondary docking
space?" he asked.

"I'm changing the plan. We'll be leaving through an
airlock, using our own propulsion to get clear. We won't have
much time."

Knud and Theodore emerged from the lab doors behind
her. "I have downloaded everything we need," he proclaimed.

The Order soldiers rushed around the corner behind and
in front of Alice, running in perfect formation with rifles
drawn. Their fortified, dark green uniforms were lighter than
the military vacsuit she wore under her heavy encounter

armour. They were rushing towards the lab, they most likely didn't see that her small squad was standing between both groups of incoming soldiers. It wouldn't matter what they thought they were charging for. The soldiers kept rushing, going past the first set of mines, the second, the third, and then there were twenty soldiers at each end in perfect position for Alice to activate their mines. She made sure she was recording when she turned them on. What happened next looked like a scene from a high-speed slaughterhouse as explosive force from all sides broke their bodies down to flesh and bone in an instant. There was another group behind them, getting ready to rush forward. They had seconds.

Jessen activated the accumulator pod on her back, it would start generating antimatter, using the first tiny piece for power so it could generate more. In minutes there would be a tenth of a millilitre, and it would build until she stopped it, the amount broke containment, or when the bomb was set off. Alice started running. "Keep up, the plan has changed."

The squad moved, catching up and filing in pairs behind her as she shot at a specific spot to her left, just past the deactivating shield that spared them from the explosive force of the mines. "Take care of those soldiers," she ordered as her rifle rattled against her shoulder.

Knud and Faloo tossed grenades towards the soldiers who were about to make their run at the hallway before they could start coming around the corner. The explosions blasted and scattered them as Alice's group passed. Her rifle's explosive rounds made an improvised door to an old maintenance shaft past the gore they left behind and she leapt inside. The plans were still accurate. When they repaired and updated the Base Ship they added some new plating here and there, polished other places until they were new colours and reshaped a few of the more dated rooms, but the bones were the same. "Everyone in and down nine levels. Just fall and use your suit's thrusters to stop." They followed her instructions to the letter, Faloo giggling a little as she let gravity take her down most of the way.

"This is Admiral Lamonthe on a private channel," Alice heard in her ear. "What are you doing?"

"Admiral, I'm making a statement," Alice said. "They keep labelling us as terrorists, so I'm acting like one."

"You're going in the wrong direction," he countered. "The mission was to acquire current intelligence, leave your bomb cloaked several levels down as it built up material, and to leave before it has gone off."

"I'm adding a detail," Alice said as she let herself fall behind the last of her soldiers, Theodore, who eyed her warily through the transparent face of his helmet before going down.

"You don't have the rank to add details," he retorted.

Alice activated her micro-thrusters and they stopped her from falling as she passed her mark by a metre. Her suit glowed blue as they held her aloft, lighting the undersides of the armoured slats running across the surface of her armour. "You knew this was the Overlord Two."

"Yes," he said.

"You sent me on this mission," Alice took aim at an old hatch that would take them to the next hallway and opened fire. Jessen and Yawen joined in, understanding her intent. They got through the door and the new wall beyond in less than three seconds. "You mixed it and me together without thinking you'd get something unpredictable?"

"You understand orders, right, Alice? You follow them, there are reasons why they keep a mission on track, within certain parameters."

Alice passed into the hallway, covering her team as they emerged behind her. A memory, a decision made by her digital self after she saw that Vindyne were close to developing imprinting technology to the point where they could translate and upload an artificial intelligence to a human body surged in her mind. That first Alice, the one who saved Jonas, decided that she wouldn't stay on the Overlord II as she suspected her master wanted. Instead, she'd become human, a real woman, then he would have to become her friend, he would have to see her as an equal. Then he wouldn't be able to throw her away without remembering a face, her face, and he wouldn't, because Jonas didn't discard people. It was risky, there was every chance that her program would be destroyed instead of successfully transitioning, but it was worth the chance, and there was a mind that was unlike any other loaded into the system, it was just damaged enough. The woman was a murderer, a slasher who killed for money. Her record said she was good at it, very good, almost worthy of fame, but emotionally bankrupt. That woman's cruelty would be wiped away as Alice took her mind, she was sure it wouldn't survive. When she transmitted herself into that body, her digital self felt the closest thing to pain that it could, then she was in the hallway, trying to get Jonas' attention as he ran by. There were so many complications with being human that she didn't anticipate, not the least of which were the emotions that came with the experience of being left behind. Sadness, disappointment, and under it all there was anger. "There are memories for me here. My story was supposed to end on this ship. No one expected that this was only the beginning for me, but I refused to be left behind. I was born as an act of defiance. You expect me to turn away from this opportunity just because you're in my ear, telling me to?"

"No, I expect your second in command to make sure you don't do anything stupid."

Yawen turned to stand in her way. "I just got orders to take over and finish the mission."

The tactical map said there were soldiers on their way, a ghost image revealed that there was at least one Knight coming from her left, well down the hallway and around the corner, but they would arrive soon. "Then give me what I need to finish this and go," Alice told her.

Stunned, Yawen started to shake her head. "We're so close, Alice."

Alice pointed to her left. "Take that hallway, kill the soldiers, the Knight, take one right hand turn to the maintenance elevator, go up one level and you'll find a chute that leads to an airlock right where I've marked." She took the digger discs, shaped charges that would get through the metal in her way, from Faloo and Krooke as she spoke, stuffing them into armoured pockets on her thighs. "I'll mark it all on the tactical map."

"I have ord..."

Alice knew what the order was and answered by grabbing Yawen and putting her faceplate against hers, looking her right in those holographic eyes as she made sure her face was visible, not the holographic illusion she'd put up. "I'm not finished here. You are, so it's time for you to lead them off this cursed ship. You're not taking me with you." The medical system notified her that her suit received an order from Fleet to put her in stasis. The alterations she made to the software and hardware stopped it cold. Alice pushed her away and said; "Go."

"Alice, you..." Yawen started.

"I was born here, if anyone has a right to end this place, to put a stop to this invasion, it's me."

"The Alice I'm looking at was born on Tamber," Yawen countered, forcing herself to speak calmly.

"Thanks to the help of Carl Anderson, and you saw what they did to him! Get out! Go before every soldier they have is on top of you, and leave that bomb behind, cloaked somewhere not even I get to. That's my last order!"

Yawen nodded and started backing away, the rest of her people following hesitantly. "Don't let this place be your ending, you're more important than this ship."

"Get out, now!" Alice said, pushing Knud hard. "Run!" They finally followed orders, and just as she realized that she was missing one, she turned and saw Theodore, who was stepping in beside her.

"You're not going to do this alone," he told her, a gentle smile on his face. He raised two heavy handguns loaded with suppression rounds. "I'm uploading everything I have, even my memory. I believe humans of ancient Earth used to call it a 'save point.'"

She didn't have time to argue with him, and she knew he

could keep up. "Noah is going to kill me if you don't make it back."

"Then I hope your plan includes a way for us both to survive, because I like this version of you, and don't want to get used to yet another one. You've had enough existential crises for three beings."

FORTY-SEVEN

The Message

"WHERE HAS THE MERCILESS GONE?" Tafford asked himself. Then he asked louder; "Where has the Merciless gone? The Rassaaga?"

"We're searching. There are two other groups that we can't find either. We think they're small but for some reason they've remained cloaked," replied the leader of his Sensor Department.

"Are they equivalent to the power level we predict for the Merciless?"

"We expect one is higher, the other is much lower, but we can't be sure. No one has gotten a clear, persistent scan, only sudden spikes of data before they disappear. Burst trans-missions."

"Have we seen any sign of the Sunspire, or the rest of the Freeground Fleet?"

"No indication that they're in the system, Sir."

"Those ships are strategically critical, a large portion of their firepower if they've been upgraded," Tafford said to himself. "If they're outside of the system, already regrouping, it could be a major concern. If not, then they're hiding in the system. What for? How long is the game they're playing?" The notion that the Haven Fleet was playing a longer game, not putting everything they had into defending their solar system sent a chill down his spine. *There are a number of targets outside the system that are vulnerable because so much of my fleet is here. The Sunspire alone could make us pay dearly for any lack of foresight.* He made a note in his personal journal to send orders to their most exposed outposts once the work of the day was over. They had to be reinforced. "Make it clear to everyone with a scanner in the fleet that we must find every cloaked ship and asset in the system, broaden our sensor net, send fighters into the gaps," Tafford ordered. "We have thousands of them making little difference to the fight at the..." he was distracted by the troops guarding the four entrances to the bridge leaving suddenly. The heavy security doors closed behind them. "Captain! What's going on?"

"A group of boarders have been detected near the bridge," Captain Nonen replied.

"Detected? Detected doing what?"

"One perimeter squad was killed on this level. It was quick, precise."

"I'm sure. Is it the same team we detected before?"

Nonen nodded. "We're almost certain. Fleas, Sir, we have Knights on the way."

Tafford checked their status himself and saw that the Knights were still five levels above, in a lift that was stopped on one floor, the status of the doors said; WAITING. "Any sign that our secondary systems have been compromised?" The elevator doors closed, it continued on, then stopped on the next floor. The call button was never pushed. "Was our interior security force not trained?"

"There are many new recruits, but the Knights are experienced."

"Tell them we've been hacked. Our systems can't be trusted," Tafford said. "Scratch these fleas off our backs immediately."

"Yes, Sir," Nonen said.

ALICE WAS PLANTING the last digger charge when Theodore sighed and looked at her. "I'm afraid I have some news."

The dark access passage was a good hiding spot, it ran across the top of the armour protecting the bridge, and there were no sensors. Her tactical system didn't show anyone coming their way, not in the hallway above, or from any other direction. "What's up?"

"Your team hid the bomb but hasn't left. They're creating a ruckus that makes it look like they're trying to break into the bridge from the side."

Alice shook her head but couldn't help but let a little smile surface. "They know Knights are on the way, right?"

"They do, I told them. Then I slowed the Knights down as best as I could without drawing suspicion. They had a slow elevator ride for a while, but they've engaged the override now. The team will be face to face with them in minutes."

"What's the plan? Do they have a path of retreat?"

"A very clear one. The Clever Dream is waiting at the end of a bulk trash chute on the same level. They will retreat the moment they are overwhelmed or if it looks like the Knights are trying to get between them and their escape."

"Good. Are you ready for this? It's going to be rough down there. Backup shield energy and speed won't do it all."

"I know what I have to do, and I still think you're right: this is worth the risk. It is even worth the sacrifice, if it comes to that."

"Then let's make a big entrance." Alice set the digger charges off. They were arranged in a circle facing down and began burning through the armour plating with a bright burst. The xetima mixture within was so hot, so bright that the caps focusing the enduring burn weren't enough to stop the light, and they began to glow before the fuel was exhausted. A clear circle had been cut into the plating in front of them. "They didn't burn all the way through," Alice grumbled as she stepped into the middle.

"There is barely anything holding it up," Theodore said, drawing both his big shell guns.

Alice jumped, then came down hard, her suit thrusters firing. Even though she hoped that it would be enough to break the circular section of the bridge's security armour under her feet through, it was still a surprise when it gave way. It tumbled away beneath. Her momentum carried her past it a little and the deafening sound of the thick circle of metal striking the broad central stage in the middle of the bridge sounded at the same time her feet hit the deck. Five holograms of her people came through the hatch she made after her, landing all around her, followed by Theodore, who was projecting the images of her team.

Everything was being recorded, Alice made sure as she turned the faceplate of her helmet transparent and looked Tafford in the eye. He was tall but made low from where he looked up at her, cringing, ducking down. "Hello, Admiral."

Theodore fired five rounds from his big shell handguns, all suppressive. Plastic webbing trapped everyone in the five pits representing the different departments of the bridge. A guard standing beside the door began to draw his weapon, and Alice fired a single round at him. The power level she was using was made for Knights, not someone in the light armour the bridge guard was wearing, and there was nothing left of him from the waist up.

Theodore fired stun rounds at the rest of the guards, swivelling at the waist, emptying his pistols then reloading. He slowed it all down so it looked like something a human could accomplish, but Alice wondered if it would fool anyone. With the last seven guards incapacitated, she returned her attention to the Admiral. He was rising to his feet. An officer emerged from beneath a set of stairs leading down into one of the pits to her left. He was wearing what looked like more streamlined Knight armour, bearing one of their rifles.

One precision blast struck her shields, reducing them by twenty-one percent. Alice rolled, her holographic team reacted, turning towards him and firing fake munitions as her assault on him began. Two of her shots missed, decimating the officers at their stations behind him. What followed was a steady stream of explosive rounds that burst with an electromagnetic charge the instant before they detonated. It was enough to scar the polished deck plating, make the Knight reel back several steps, almost sending him down the stairs. Her tactical system told her that she broke through his armour, his rifle was damaged, and she stopped. "Knights," Alice said as she stood and walked towards him. "You know, I hated that the Order took the title for their best soldiers, then I looked knights up. Funny thing: the real Knights, the ones from Medieval Earth, were asshole land owners who almost always treated their people like dirt." She looked down at the terrified knight as his nose and cheek finished regenerating in his broken helm and planted a foot on his charred chest armour. The cracking and grinding sounds it made as she put pressure on it was satisfying. He could barely breathe when it stopped. "I've never known one of you by name. I wonder if it would make any difference."

"I'm Dorek Nonen, Captain Nonen," he replied, his fear beginning to abate as Alice secured her rifle across her back.

Alice watched him, observed his square-jawed face. He had the face of a hero from some old action movie, in another situation she'd think he was handsome. Most Knights would have struggled, used the augmentation left in their armour to try to regain the upper hand, but this one seemed relieved. He should have reacted like most knights. "Dorek," she sounded his name out, watching him start to smile up at her. "Nope, no difference," she said as she drew her sidearm and ruined his head with a rapid succession of high powered shots that echoed throughout the bridge. The spitting and hissing of the chemical fire left behind in the gore burned red. Just to make sure he was finished, she dropped a small electromagnetic charge into the back of his helmet. It rolled around like a marble in a bowl for a moment before going off, stopping his regeneration and damaging the consoles in the pit behind him. Her shields took a small hit, but were recharging quickly.

"Captain Valent," Tafford said from behind her as though it was an announcement. "You can't escape. The best you can do is surrender, and I can promise a good life in captivity if you provide us with information on your organization."

The thought of life in a cell made Alice's hackles rise. Maybe there was something in what her father said, that anger was a companion to them, that it could feel good. As she clenched her teeth and turned towards him, it felt very, very good to be furious at the Admiral, almost as good as the weight of the firearm in her hand, as rewarding as the fear and waning defiance in the faces of the dozens of officers around her. They were trapped, most of them able to watch what was going on, but secured to their stations, the deck, and their chairs with plastic webbing. "It would make so much sense to take you prisoner. To bag you, put you in stasis and toss you out the airlock ahead of me when I leave."

"Alice," Theodore said, pinging a spot on the tactical map in her HUD. There was a secret door at the rear of the octagonal bridge. A hallway from below, deeper in the station led to it and Knights were on the way. Theodore spotted it with his secondary sensors. Her sidearm was back in its holster and her rifle was in hand a moment later.

"I'm not going to take you prisoner," Alice said. "No one on this bridge will live through this."

Tafford's eyes widened as an uneasy murmur rose from the officers around them. Only a few heard what she said, but they were sharing, word was going around. "I can be valuable, I know things that can help your people, things that not even most of the Order knows. Fundamental things that could bring peace, cost the Order allies. I could even give you Wheeler!"

"Really? Do you know where he is right now?" Alice asked as she began raising her rifle. It would point at his face in a few seconds. His expression told the tale, and her empathic gift verified it. She could feel his fear, the fear of the crew, and the bravado of the four order knights that were about to break through the hidden door and assault her. "You don't know where he is. Too bad." She thought of taking Tafford hostage, putting him between her and the Knights, the real Knights, because Nonen couldn't have been one, but the eager malice she felt from the group about to come in told her that it wouldn't help.

"I can find him, I can draw him out," Tafford pleaded. "I have a family."

Alice made up her mind. The Order Knights were counting their entrance down. The first shots she took at Tafford were absorbed by his emergency personal shield. It gave him enough time to cringe and try to dance away from the rounds bursting against it, then his body was blasted apart in three hits. The Order Knights were bursting through the door past the pit of officers then, and she took a handful of small thruster guided grenades, tossed them up and sent them in their direction. Two portable shield emitters were next, the shallow metal cups falling at her feet, offering protection as she fired over the heads of a dozen officers.

As three guided grenades exploded against the Order Knight's shields, another three went up, and the barrage of fire from Alice's rifle continued. Her holographic team did the same, and the first rounds fired by the Order Knights passed right through them, impacting behind them in the command and control pits, killing officers. "Theo, get behind cover," she said.

"I'm sorry I can't help," Theodore said as he dropped off the central platform and ducked behind it in one of the pits. "My programming still sees them as human, even though I know they're heavily modified frameworks."

The first burst struck the shield in front of Alice, and she highlighted the one who was targeting her, sending three little rocket grenades at him, she only had three left. She set her rifle to precision mode and turned the power level up the final step. In single, explosive shots, her rounds burst with an electromagnetic pulse so intense that it cost her a little shield energy. It devastated theirs. "I know, what kind of modifications are we talking about?"

A grenade went off against her outer portable shield, draining it in an instant. She dropped another as she stepped back and fired two more rounds at the lead Knight. He had a good arm and better aim, she hoped not all of them were that well trained. "These Knights have a network of flexible wires on their skin, it looks like it's made to absorb and disperse electromagnetic pulses," Theodore replied.

A trio of grenades were launched by the lead Order

Knight, and Alice caught one in mid-air, blasting it to pieces over their heads. It was a shot worthy of the best marksmen, but she knew it was mostly luck on her part, she was good, but not that good. "This isn't going to work," she said as the remaining grenades went off, taking her portable shields out. She was next. They knew her companions were only holograms, and it was four against one. They didn't care about the bridge officers, either, having killed more than she did.

Her father gave her new tools, the second or third generation of the ones he developed, and she had her own tricks. Two handfuls of grenades were in her hands then, one filled with her last self-propelled versions, the other held four of the standard type without self-propulsion or any intelligence. They were in the air next, flung at her enemies. Rapid fire destroyed two over her head, one failed to hit its mark, but the rest landed at their feet. Before her cloaking systems fully engaged she tossed one of her few big charges, an electromagnetic pulse grenade that would take her shields down by half if she made her shot. More importantly, they would decimate theirs. The larger grenade rolled into the explosive mess its smaller predecessors left behind, and by the time it pulsed, blasting the Knights with enough raw power to keep the Clever Dream going for a couple hours, she was fully cloaked, running down into the pit to her right.

The smoke began to clear, the energy was dissipating as she sprinted up to the platform running around the outer edge of the bridge. The Order Knights were still regrouping, the lead one was already looking for her as Alice activated the nano-blade on her right wrist. Eye gestures and neural signals were picked up by her suit, and the nanobots that the cutting tool used for its edge were loaded with the same program that cured her. She already had Lewis add another identical blade to her left combat command and control unit, it took the space that Jake used for a second energy shield, and she hoped her desire for a more aggressive style would pay off as she saw a clear line of sight between her and the lead Knight.

Her first body belonged to a slasher, a murderer with no remorse with muscle memory that made her deadly with a blade. Perhaps there was a little of that left, something that made the transition from the muscles of a murderess back to digital and down the line to who she was now. Alice cleared her mind and let that angry nerve drive her as she redoubled her mad rush towards the armoured Order Knight.

His sensors still didn't see her as she leapt through the settling smoke feet first, capturing her waist between her legs as he turned towards her. The Knight's shields were burned out, the first few slashes of her blades scarred his chest armour, then she broke through. "Welcome back to humanity," she hissed as the Knight sank to his knees. The one behind him levelled his rifle at her, whether or not he could see Alice, she didn't know, but it was slashed nearly in half as she struck it with her free blade. A flexible seam between the upper and lower half of that Knight's armour invited her blade, and she struck for it with her off hand as she yanked the other one free from her first victim. The Knight felt the pressure of her first two strikes, which missed the mark, then she ran him through with the third, not savouring the victory, pulling her blade free then charging on. The nanobots were already working in the first two, rendering them unconscious.

A full blast from one of the remaining knights caught Alice in the side, draining the last of her shields, and she turned into the gunfire, slashing the end of the rifle off before stabbing hard at the Knight's helmet. The metal held up against her assault, but the shock of it sent the Knight reeling, dropping his rifle and scrambling to fend off his invisible attacker. "Switch to broad scan! She's cloaked, you idiot!" shouted his partner.

Alice spun towards that one, using all the enhanced strength in her suit to slash at the armour protecting its neck. Before the only female knight in the group had time to react, Alice had bounced two strikes off her shoulder armour, landing glancing blows against the side of her helmet, and three against her neck armour. The dented metal was starting to break down. Her partner had found his bravery, and was surging forward, trying to grapple with her, and Alice stepped around the female Knight, batting her attempt to grab her away with a blade slash then clashing with her neck armour once more before the following blow cut through flesh. When the Knight fell Alice was already squared up with the last one, and his backward steps didn't earn her sympathy. "Oh my God, please, just let me go. I'll turn away from the Order..."

Whatever sensor system he used was working, he was reacting to her as if she was visible. "It's in you. Bone deep. If you don't serve them, they'll shut you down or take control. I can give you a second chance, set you free." Alice stepped towards him, the dark, hidden security room revealed. It was a bare compartment with a dim hallway leading deeper into the ship. "Just open your armour."

"I surrender," he said, pulling his helm off and decoupling the seal on his chest. "I surrender."

He looked younger than everyone in her squad, almost as young as she did when she was a teenager, before she was cured. "You might not wake up in time, but if you do, run for the nearest airlock." Alice thrust her blade into his chest, taking a little satisfaction as he looked at her in anguished surprise. "I didn't say freedom wouldn't hurt." The nanobots went to work right away. He fell unconscious, and they would trigger one last reconstruction that would regenerate him, revive him without a trace of framework technology in his body.

There was no time to gloat, or to see how it would all turn out. Her HUD told her that the antimatter bomb would go off in five minutes, fifty seconds. There was only enough time for the last part of her plan. "Do we have a link to Fleet Wide Communications?" she asked.

"I have a link, and I've compiled all the combat we've recorded." Alice walked back to the centre of the bridge, making sure her energy shields were back up, and retracted her helmet. "I will play it back as you speak to the Order of Eden."

Alice set her holographic recorder to pick up her face and shoulders, seeing the dents in her armour for the first time. She hadn't even realized that anything got through her shield, but the evidence was right there. "Start broadcasting to the Order, and to the Fleet. Hell, put this out on all frequencies, all networks."

"I had to tap into one of the main data lines, everything

else is burned out, but the broadcast is working. Go ahead, Alice."

"In a few minutes, the Untouchable, the Base Ship sent to lead the invasion in the Haven System will be destroyed by an antimatter bomb. It only took one Haven Fleet ship to break the shields protecting this monstrosity down, and my small team to deliver the bomb to the heart of this base. You don't have time to look for it, antimatter alarms won't go off until there's so much material inside that containment is about to breach, we cloaked it. The destruction you're about to see is just the beginning. The Order of Eden has come to the Haven System. They sent Edxi here first to do their dirty work. We killed so many that they gave up. We will continue killing them wherever we find them in our galaxy, we take invasions personally." She gave herself a moment to smile a little, her mother would like that comment. "When the Order ships came, they turned their interdiction machines on so they could trap us, murder us, steal our technology, and take our worlds. They didn't anticipate the cost." The combat playback started, to anyone watching it appeared behind her. Mines decimated two groups of Order soldiers in an instant, then her confrontation with the Knights started. Theodore changed it just enough so she was clearly visible in the playback. "Show them what happened to the Captain, and Admiral Tafford." The playback changed to her fighting Captain Nonen, what happened to him was perfectly clear.

Gathering her thoughts, aware that time was passing, Alice continued. "They showed no mercy. The Haven System may be overrun, we are outnumbered, battered, but this is only a battle.

A battle we could still win or lose. If we win, our counterattack will be vicious. If we lose, it will be worse for you." That struck her with an unexpected wave of grief and anger, the feeling of the bracelet Shauna made for her under her uniform was very present against her bare arm, she could feel herself welling up, outrage brimming. "Before we were afraid, scrambling to prepare for this day. Now we are furious, with nothing to lose." The playback continued with the execution of Admiral Tafford, she looked to the smear of red and black that marked his final moment before returning her attention to the dot on her HUD that marked the recording angle in front of her. "You don't understand what this will cost you, but you will. The pain we inflict on you will be multiplied every time you mistreat the people of the Haven System. The grief you've caused has eroded any mercy I have for any of you. If you wear an Order uniform, if you stand with them as allies, you will not know peace. You can't hide, you can't run. I am going to murder every last one of you unless you turn against the Order before I'm in striking distance. Surrender isn't enough anymore. Every member of the Order is now a target, my target." She cut the transmission and looked to Theodore, whose mouth was agape. "Burst transmit the rest of the combat you recorded," she told him.

"You realize you just personally threatened the entire Order of Eden?" He asked.

The connection she had with Theodore showed that he sent the rest of the combat recordings in a burst, and she redeployed her helmet, the sections slid back into place with satisfying clicks. "Yeah, not exactly what I meant to say, but Dad would be proud."

"I imagine so. The crew are abandoning ship, there's a

rush for the pods. They will realize that there aren't enough lifeboats for half the crew soon," Theodore said. "Your squad is waiting aboard the Clever Dream."

"Is the way between here and the maintenance airlock clear?" Alice asked as Theodore joined her in the middle of the bridge. She traced the path on her own tactical map, hoping that she was right.

"Wait! Wait! What about us?" asked a bridge officer at her feet who managed to get his mouth free of his plastic bonds.

"You want us to free you so you can escape?" she asked.

"You just have to touch the nano-solvent strip to a part of the plastic holding us," he said, doing his best to nod.

Alice pulled a tab off of the butt of Theodore's gun and started to kneel down, then dropped it at her feet. "Wait, you're all officers. You're all essential to running this death machine," she said. "I don't think I like the idea of any of you joining another crew." She shook her head and turned away.

"What are you doing? You can't let us die, it's murder!"

Theodore looked at her solemnly. He knew she wouldn't save them, no matter how intense their dismay and panic were in her head. "Yes, it is." Alice activated her suit's thrusters and moved up through the hole above her. A glance down verified what she suspected would happen, what she wished Theodore wouldn't do, and she saw him throwing the solvent strips at the surviving officers. The plastic trapping them dissolved quickly as Theodore joined her in the maintenance shaft above the bridge.

"My programming would not let me leave without freeing them."

"I understand, you have to preserve life when you can," Alice said.

"No, I had to free them to save you, Alice. They will probably still die, unable to reach escape vehicles, lost in the panicking crowds, or killed as deserters. I knew you would suffer if they weren't given a chance, though, if you thought their deaths were undeniably your fault."

Alice started running down the maintenance shaft, Theodore at her side. The panic of the crew was all around her, she couldn't see them, but feeling them was like listening to music in the background that was frenzied, but not discordant. Most of them felt the same thing, and it was a harsh melody. Even still, Theodore's words touched her. Maybe he was right, maybe she would feel regret when things got quiet. It was doubtful, however. To her, the officers of the Order of Eden were the worst offenders, they were the ones who gave the orders, tasked with finding her people, getting in range, firing on them, killing them. "They were all murderers, every last one, but thank you, Theo."

FORTY-EIGHT

Trailblazing

THE BROADCAST JAKE'S daughter sent to everyone who would listen was being sent far and wide using the Order of Eden's own hyper transmitter network. To Jake, it was a grim display even though he nearly cheered at the conclusion of her short speech. The footage of her executing Tafford and defeating the Order Knights made him feel sheepish about privately questioning her skill and resolve. As a warrior, she was on par with him, and he saw even more potential. Her resolve was beyond steady. It was easy to believe that Alice would be merciless in carrying out her orders. Even though the accomplishments were violent, even grisly, he was filled with relief and pride.

"Sir, the Sky Queen is back. Lieutenant Commander Murlen can confirm that there's another Order Fleet on the way. They will be here in seven minutes, twenty-eight seconds. I'm passing his scan data to Fleet Command," Liara reported.

Commodore Valent looked at the predicted arrival points on his tactical map and shifted in the captain's chair. The fleet coming was large enough to lock the entire Haven System down, blocking ships from escaping using any faster than light transportation technology. Each of the new battle-groups had a heavy cruiser at its centre. Agameg looked at him with a rare, sullen expression before returning his attention to the rest of the bridge, straightening up.

Jake could only assume that the Issyrian realized what he did: if Haven Fleet stayed, fought the ships that were already in system, then tried to defeat the new wave, they could win. It was a narrow possibility, but it would cost them everything. He thought it through quickly, counting the sacrifices it would take to force a victory, and was sure that only three or four of their ships would remain, and they would be in terrible condition. The War Forge would be destroyed, they'd have to cancel every contingency they had and draw the ships they were holding back into the fight, and it wasn't likely they would survive either. "All right," he breathed to himself. He cleared his throat. "We're going to get the order soon," Jacob said to his bridge staff. They all looked to him. "We are going to go after a target at close range with only the Rassaaga at our side. It'll be an old-fashioned firefight, and it has to be over quickly. When we've destroyed our target's interdiction capabilities, the fleet will jump."

"Sir, destroying our objective will open up a small area on the edge of the solar system, the Untouchable is the main problem," Lieutenant Commander Huun, the Tactical Officer, said.

"He hasn't seen Alice's transmission," Ashley said over her shoulder.

"I saw it, but I don't see an antimatter alert coming from the Base Ship. The Untouchable doesn't seem to be at any great ri... Oh, never mind, there it is," he said. "Apologies."

"No worries, Lieutenant Commander," Jake said, smiling a little at the Nafalli's dutiful doubt as much as seeing that his daughter was clear, on the Clever Dream, flying to their escape point in a cloaking field. He wouldn't see her again for some time, at least not in person, but at least she was safe. "When that Base Ship goes up, we strike this battlegroup and that'll open a corridor wide enough for our fleet to escape."

"Does that include the Freeground ships?" Agameg asked in a whisper.

"Who says they didn't leave before the Order got here?" Jake asked, protecting the secrecy of Phase Seven. Not even he was read in on it, but he had a feeling that it involved ships hiding in or near the Haven System, and some kind of backup plan. The number of ships he guessed they put aside for it wouldn't have made a difference to the defence of the Haven System, but they could be key to a longer game. "I have no idea where those ships went."

"Signal from the Rassaaga; they're in position and ready to assault the main cruiser in the Battle Group we're shadowing," Liara reported.

Jake checked the charge on the Merciless' systems and was happy to see that everything was up to one hundred percent. "Tell our fighters to get ready for emergency landings. As soon as we drop our cloak, they head for our bays. Tactical: point all beam weapons and cannons at the destroyer between us and the Devastator. When it's disabled, we concentrate everything on the Heavy Cruiser."

"Aye," both departments replied.

The Devastator. It was a Heavy Cruiser that could have served as a command ship in most other militaries. It had thousands of troops, could launch several fighter wings, hidden missile and torpedo bays and powerful shields. If he wasn't looking at it from the bridge of the Merciless, Jake would have been intimidated, but even though it was less than half the size of the Heavy Cruiser, Jake's ship had more firepower and a much faster response time. The Merciless and the Rassaaga were superior in every way, but destroying the Devastator, or even disabling most of its systems would take time and exchanging fire would cause damage they couldn't afford to take at the moment. They had to make sure the systems that were keeping Haven Fleet from escaping were disabled or destroyed, that was the smart play. Long range attacks, stealthed munitions of any kind could be intercepted, they didn't come with the control Jake would have in a close engagement. Then again, he didn't have to think things through alone. "One more check," Jake said to his Tactical Department, "If we back off and launch our heaviest torpedo at the Devastator, its shields would still be up?" he asked.

"They would be down to nine percent. Adjacent ships would take critical damage, but it would still be able to maintain an interdiction signal," Huun replied. "The simulations confirm it."

"That's if they don't stop our torpedoes en-route?"

"Exactly, there is a chance that they're researching our cloaking technology right now, and it might not be as effective as it was even an hour ago. It's what Haven Fleet would do," Kadri replied.

"Just making sure," Jake said. There were five Heavy Cruisers in the system and more on the way. If they wanted to take the Devastator's interdiction systems out, the Merciless and the Rassaaga had to do it at close range with their directed electromagnetic beam weapons at their full effectiveness. It would have to happen quickly, before the Order crew could bring their entire arsenal to bear in response. He waited for the signal. If the antimatter alarms were going off on the Untouchable, then the bomb must be close to critical.

He glanced at the Clever Dream on his tactical display. It was well on its way to the jump point, getting ready to go. The War Forge was taking damage for the first time, a small section of its aft shielding failing. One of the massive manufacturing compartments was struck, and a nuclear flash blasted against the hull. That broke one of the large armour doors open, a vulnerability. He imagined that there was already a discussion going on about detaching that manufacturing bay, letting it drift then self-destruct so the rest of the base could restore its shield integrity. If they didn't clear a path soon, there would be more damage, the War Forge would be at greater risk. Jake wished he could turn the Merciless towards one of the two enemy battlegroups that were attacking it, trying to close to short range so the larger munitions launched by the mobile ship yard could be ruled out as viable options, but he knew he was where Fleet needed him.

Jake put the image of the Untouchable up on the main bridge holographic display. "I've never been so eager to see antimatter go off," he said, bouncing his fist on the arm of his command seat.

"Unencrypted transmissions from the Untouchable confirm that emergency teams have found the accumulator bomb, they're trying to disarm it now," Liara reported.

Jake smiled and leaned back in his chair. "Wrong direction, guys. You don't run towards a..." The Untouchable was replaced by a white light for an instant, then the bright, partially molten remains of the hull were revealed. Only some of the outermost, thickest sections of the outer hull survived, and they were heated to misshapen red and yellow shards. "That's our signal, begin firing sequence," Jake ordered.

Lieutenant Command Huun and the Tactical department were ready, and the electromagnetic pulse beams along with every cannon they could turn towards the destroyer following along the bottom side of the Devastator opened fire. For a moment the Order destroyer's shields stood up to the barrage, then they came down and its hull was torn to shreds. Five medium yield nuclear torpedoes struck it in succession, sending the broken hulk into the Devastator's shields slowly, angling up perfectly so the least damaged part of the destroyer dragged along the energy barriers protecting the Heavy Cruiser. As planned, the Rassaaga and the Merciless opened fire on the Devastator, concentrating on the sections of shields that covered the large interdictor transmitter antennae that ran along the hull.

Jake wished he could take control of a gun emplacement

personally, but he watched the tactical display instead, as he should. Everything the Haven Fleet had in the fight turned away from their targets, making best speed towards the section of space that would be open once the Rassaaga and the Merciless were finished. The Order crew aboard the Devastator must have been in shock, they were only taking light defensive fire. "Sir, Samurai wing is almost completely aboard. Traveller and Carnie will be landing in less than thirty seconds, if you can call what they're doing landing," Flight reported.

"Are our pilots intact and aboard?" Jake asked.

"Yes, but I have reports of minor damage across our retrieval bay, the deck crew is already complaining."

"Tell them to get Ronin to have the pilots sign their divots in grease pencil so the crew knows who owes them a drink later," Jake said, appreciating a snicker from Huun to his right.

The first volley from the Devastator struck their hull, the energy barrage crossing the quarter kilometre between their ships in an instant, taking their shields down to eighty four percent. "We're going to take too much damage if this continues for long," he looked to the readings from the Rassaaga and shook his head as he saw their shields took only three percent damage. "Dammit, we found one of the only ships in the Order fleet with someone who knows what they're doing." It made more sense to concentrate on one of the Devastator's assailants than to spread their fire out, and the commander chose the Merciless. The destroyers and two carrier escorts with the Devastator opened fire, concentrating on the Merciless. "Transfer as much power from our port shielding to our starboard shields as we can. We need to keep this up until we take those interdiction systems out."

"On it, Sir," Finn's voice said in his ear. He preferred to be in the main engineering section, even though it put him in the main body of the ship instead of in the bridge section. "I'll enhance the gravitational shielding on that side so we can reduce our vulnerability to long range attacks, shouldn't cost us much on the shield facing the Devastator."

"Good thinking, Finn," Jake said as he watched the section of shielding they had to defeat on the Devastator lower another twenty-eight percent. They were down to forty-two percent, while the Merciless was down to thirty-eight. "Hurry."

"The Rassaaga is offering to manoeuvre closer so they can shore up our shields," Liara reported.

"Tell them to remain in position, we can't alter our strategy now, it'll only extend the fight and give other Order ships time to fill the gap we're making here," Jake replied.

In a flash of intense nuclear fire, the Merciless' shields were down to three percent. Solid and energy rounds collided with their forward starboard section, testing and cracking the hull plating there, rendering two heavy gun emplacements unusable as a series of heavy rounds skipped off the edge of their hull, got caught under their shields and collided directly with the emplacements. "Finn!" Jake burst over the intercom.

"Got it, got it!" he said as the shields on their port side were restored to twenty-eight percent. He did not expect the enemy captain to launch a nuclear strike that would damage both ships' shields, the Devastator's commander had a ruthlessness Jake wasn't used to seeing. It didn't win him the battle, however. The sections of shields that he and the Rassaaga were breaking down failed, and their gunfire raked the armour protecting the antennae. That was Haven Fleet's biggest advantage in a close firefight. Their beam weapons were good at breaking shields down, but their solid projectile and antimatter arrays excelled at busting heavy hulls apart, and Jake watched as the Devastator tried to manoeuvre. Its escort destroyers pursued the Merciless and the Rassaaga as a wave of fighters turned back towards the companion carriers. It wasn't concentrated fire, so the damage was spread across the Haven Fleet ships' shields, but the counterattack was already taking a toll.

The smaller countermeasure guns sent streams of ammunition at incoming torpedoes and missiles, breaking most of them apart before they could reach them. Gravitational shielding turned rounds and heavier munitions away from the ship, and the few that could get through didn't strike as intended, glancing instead of smashing directly into their hard energy shielding or hull. "Shunt beam weapon power to shields, we can finish this job with cannons," Jake said as he watched the power level of the interdiction system the Rassaaga was responsible for destroying drop to zero. The aft antenna's shield plating gave way, torn apart by the Merciless' roaring guns and an instant later it was destroyed as well.

"We are all clear to jump," Ashley reported.

"There's a clear, wide corridor for all ships to jump away," Kadri reported, a little jovial for the first time in days.

"Move us away from this battlegroup at full military thrust," Jake said. "On to position Theta."

"System wide transmission from the War Forge," Liara

reported.

Ayan appeared in the middle of the bridge. The holo-graphic clarity was perfect, he could have thought she was standing in the middle of the bridge. Her expression was stony, hard. "To every civilian ship that was hiding, waiting, hoping that we would open a door for you to escape; now is your chance. It won't last long, I'm sorry. To the Order of Eden invaders: I won't add much to what my daughter told you, she speaks for all of us. I only add a warning: Haven Fleet is leaving. That doesn't mean you're welcome, or that this system is safe for any of you. We will know how you treat our people while we're gone, and you'll pay for any abuse. We are watching. We will return."

The Merciless and the Rassaaga were accelerating away from the Devastator and its battlegroup, getting ready to cloak. They were almost ready to jump.

Her image became garbled, broke down into distortion, then was replaced by Lucius Wheeler in a long coat over a dark green heavy vacsuit. "Yeah, more sabre rattling, more grand-standing. Okay, you got aboard a Base Ship, blew it up, wow. So you killed about thirty thousand trainees, maybe fourteen thousand actual crew, about twenty thousand landing troops. You just delayed things a little, but I'm in charge now. Hey, Haven System people, it's Admiral Lucius Wheeler, one of the British Alliance's most wanted, a bit of a lovable rogue if I do say so myself. The Haven Fleet is," he yawned large, taking his time to overcome it, even stomping his foot a couple times before it was over, "sorry, just the name makes me look forward to naptime. So boring. Anyway, you gave those amateurs a shot, now I'm taking over with the

Order of Eden. I've known Ayan and Jake, the real ones, not the fake replacements you've come to know, for a long time. I'll tell you a few stories about them, show you how the Order likes to take care of its people, put things in order, and make you all nice and safe. It's gonna be an improvement, believe me. There will be a Spacerwares on every corner, regular transit and communication systems across the moon, good food, better entertainment, well, you'll see. Tamber's in for a renaissance. Oh, and Haven Fleet: go ahead and leave. You opened the door, you earned that, so don't let it hit you on the ass on the way out. I've got this, I'll take care of these people from now on. The Carthans abandoned them, now you're leaving, I get it, governing is a big deal, it's hard, but I've got a huge staff, so I'll be happy to step in. Oh, but don't come back unless you're waving a white flag." He disappeared, leaving Jake's blood boiling.

The bridge was completely silent. He realized he was leaning on his interlaced fingers, brooding already, and straightened. "I want to turn this ship around and regroup so we can finish this fight," he said. Commodore Valent stood. "But if we did, if the entire fleet took a stand right now, there would be nothing left. The best we can hope for is that the people of the Haven System weather what comes well while the Fleet regroups, recruits and grows elsewhere. We have to go so we stand a chance later."

"Ready to jump," Ashley reported, sounding tense.

"Get us out of here," Jacob said, glancing at the tactical map, where the War Forge, the Clever Dream and dozens of other ships were opening dimensional rifts and leaving. "We'll be back soon."

FAREWELL FOR NOW

Thank you very much for buying and reading this book, I hope you enjoyed it. If you want to continue the journey but don't want to wait for Spinward Fringe Broadcast 13: Warriors later this year, the serialized version of the novel begins on my Patreon page on May 14, 2019. You can also find other books, podcasts and other content to explore: patreon.com/randolphlalonde